M .

2

1

FOX ON THE RUN

FOX ON THE RUN

David Pascoe

ORION

Copyright © David Pascoe 1999
All rights reserved

The right of David Pascoe to be identified
as the author of this work has been asserted by him in
accordance with the Copyright, Designs and Patents Act
1988.

First published in Great Britain in 1999 by Orion
An imprint of Orion Books Ltd
Orion House, 5 Upper St Martin's Lane
London WC2H 9EA

A CIP catalogue record for this book is
available from the British Library

ISBN 1 85797 763 7

Typeset by Deltatype Ltd, Birkenhead

Printed in Great Britain by
Clays Ltd, St Ives plc

1 041518 01

To Prue and Stuart, of course.

Prologue

It was dark in the cave, darker than the night outside, and worse than that she was not alone. The creatures in there with her might have been rats she thought, though the rustling sound was more like wings. There was a little light at the mouth of the cave: the reflection of a three-quarter moon on the sea. The sound of waves had grown louder over the past half-hour, and she realised that the tide had gone from ebb to flow.

The rustling of wings and the slap of sea water on rocks at the cave's edge . . .

She edged towards the deep vee of granite, the cave's dead end, the roughness of stone grazing her hands. She was feeling her way as a blind person might, arms stretched out in front, feet flat and moving slowly over granite and sand.

I'm going to die, she thought. Soon I shall die.

That flap and slap in the roof space again. She looked up, but saw only darkness. If she screwed her eyes tightly shut for a few moments, then opened them suddenly, looking towards the cave mouth, she could see lines of moonlight on the water; she could also see that the waves were building – white caps pale and glistening against the jet undersides of the rollers. A wave broke through the narrow entrance and hissed across the sand-and-pebble floor. Things in the roof moved and squabbled.

Backed up to the quartzy, angled rock-face where the cave ended, she sat, elbows on knees, making herself small, as if small would make a difference; as if small wouldn't be noticed; as if small might be less likely to perish. She was tired and hungry and thirsty and scared. Most of all, scared. She felt out of control, loose and trembly, in the same way that your heart lurches and bangs when a mad person gets onto your train, when the car in front warps into a skid at ninety, when the person you love starts to say, 'There's something I have to tell you . . .'

Fear ran in her bloodstream, a zippy line of chemicals. She lowered her head and tried to breathe evenly to calm herself, but the sound of her heart whacking against the membrane of her ear, a deep, bass-drum boom, was the rhythm of panic.

I'm in a cave somewhere in Cornwall.

I'm a fugitive from justice.

I'm wanted for the murder of Michael Lester, a man I used to love, a man I didn't kill.

I'm the cello player in the Hebden string quartet.

I'm waiting to drown.

The wave-break at the cave mouth threw up a fan of spray. Kate couldn't see the lip of water as it moved in on her, but she could feel the growing chill in the air, the growing dampness. She knew that if she tried to swim out, even now, she would die. No way of swimming to landfall: her best distance ever was one-length-and-sink. She had sought shelter in the cave, and fallen asleep there, exhausted by fear. Now it was her cage; soon her tomb.

She waited for every third wave, always the strongest, and judged things by that. A hard, flat slap of water, the run-and-hiss up towards her in the dark. A finger of cold swamped her feet, soaking her boots and the bottoms of her jeans. The chill spread through her: fear and cold running together.

She heard a fidget, a whisper of wings, and something flew out towards the pale outline of light that traced the cave's open arch: one, two, three . . . then a thin line of them, going while the going was good. Kate saw them for a fragment of a moment, shadows on shadows, lifting from the upper arch of the entrance like smoke.

Another rush of wet, a wavelet this time, lapped at her and rose, soaking her to the knee. She was as far back and as high as she could get. She thought of boats on the ocean. She thought of houses, where fires burned in the hearth. She thought of music in summer gardens.

I didn't kill him.

But no one believes that.

PART ONE

One

The Whole World conference had been in session for three days and Kate Randall was feeling guilty about not feeling as guilty as she should. Next to her, Michael was shifting and muttering. His scowl had deepened as the morning's meeting wore on. Kate was feeling bad because the posters of starving children, the films showing refugees murdered in their tracks, the lectures that revealed first world skulduggery in the face of third world desperation, had finally brought her to saturation point. And she knew that famine-fatigue was the worst sin of all: when you cared, but genocide became a headcount; when you *cared*, but hunger and disease provided only images that you'd seen before and would see again. And again.

Michael Lester's discomfort had nothing to do with compassion overkill, but everything to do with a fierce and self-fuelling commitment. Kate knew these murmurings, this restlessness, and she gave him ten minutes before he lost patience. The speaker was offering a laundry list of calamities in a voice that could barely have stirred dust. Michael had tabled a topic for discussion and knew that time was limited. He lasted a few minutes longer than Kate had anticipated, then stood up and bellowed his impatience and resentment.

An usher asked him to leave. Michael suggested to the usher that he marry his mother: that was more or less what he said. Kate had been through moments like this a couple of times before. She gathered her bag and her scarf from the back of her chair. She and Michael had been together for a little over two years. He worked as an environmental journalist. His speciality was lighting fires under the feet of people who he thought could use the heat. Two newspapers had been successfully sued by business corporations.

In each case, the editor had been obliged to tell Michael that, much as he liked a man with the courage of his convictions, and though his admiration for outspokenness was great, well ... Michael was now freelance. He had found that editors were more accommodating when they could spread the risk.

A second usher joined the first. Michael was still shouting. The man at the podium had bowed his head and stepped back slightly; a smile of mildness and tolerance played about his lips. His benign pose and the wispy smile were a perfect example of liberal spite. He waited for Michael to burn out or be turned out.

One of the ushers laid a hand on Michael's arm. Michael shoved him off. A second hand appeared. Michael flung it away. The audience were slow-handclapping in that smug, self-regarding way audiences have. Kate thought the next move would be for Michael to slug one of the ushers, then be kicked out of the hall. Instead, he stopped in mid-shout and barged up the row to the aisle, banging knees and ankles. Kate followed, beginning to feel angry now that they were on their way out and the shouting done. Angry with Michael for making a fool of himself; angry with herself for not being sufficiently angry about things that mattered.

She caught the door of the lecture hall on the rebound from Michael's angry shove. He was already halfway across the lobby and heading for the street. She emerged into the afternoon traffic-mist of a seaside town – the conference hall, then four lanes of vehicles that might have been soldered head to tail, then a grimy promenade, then a grey sea of slops and scum and limp, greasy breakers barely a hand's breadth high. A light, oily rain was falling. It was the perfect place for a conference on the environment. Every view was propaganda; every breath was a vote gained.

'Let's go to Greece,' Michael said. 'If I don't catch a glimpse of the sun pretty soon, I'll become hysterical.'

'You are hysterical – aren't you?' Kate was shifting things around the room in the hope of making patterns she could live with. It seemed to her that the furniture and artefacts in hotel rooms were arranged according to some dark and brutal system of feng shui that guaranteed bad sleep, bad moods, bad karma and bad room service.

'Am I? No, I don't think so.'

'Was that you getting thrown out of a conference hall a few minutes ago, or was that your long-lost twin, Badass Lester, who also happens to be a journalist and first-class pain in the neck?'

'I can't listen to those people. Whine-whine, sorry-sorry, I'll trade you my sweet reason for your anti-personnel mine.'

'But you do listen. You listen until you can't bear it another moment. You listen until you want to kill them.'

'I listen so that I can later write articles demonstrating what a bunch of inept and gutless weasels they are.'

'You need the evidence . . .' she suggested.

'I need the evidence, yes.' Michael smiled and came across the room to help her move a small chair back to the place where she'd first found it. 'Sorry. I pissed you off.'

'No. Yes. No, I shouldn't have come. I care about things . . . but I care in the same way that anyone does – civilians, not people like you.'

'You don't have to attend the conference itself. I thought it might be a sort of . . . little holiday.' Kate threw her head back and laughed. 'Yes,' he continued, 'well, I did just offer you Greece. Were you listening?'

'I was. I can't come.'

'Sun, olive groves, retsina, the Med sloshing back and forth like a tepid sewer.'

'I'm in Poland next week, Belguim the week after that.'

'No, *after* the tour. Belgium and Poland first, bit of Bartók, bit of Beethoven, then Greece, lots of Zorba and zither. Bring the cello, it can have its own seat belt. Practise on our balcony in the cool of the evening. Greeks will gather with candles and garlands. The cries of seabirds will echo the singing of the strings.'

'Fuck off,' Kate advised him. She was laughing gently. 'What balcony? Who says there'll be a balcony?'

'I can get balcony.' His Greek accent came with a flexed bicep. 'I can get sunwashed villa lapped in bougainvillea where balcony is attached.'

'Can you get darkly handsome, muscle-bound, music-loving millionaire with low-down sex drive and own recording company?'

'I'm hurt.' He put his arms loosely round her waist and delivered a kiss, keeping his mouth in place in the hope of getting one back.

She took a small step sideways and he held her more firmly. 'I can't, Michael.'

'Which? Greece, or make love to me before dinner?'

'After Belgium and Poland, there's a recording date. Then concerts here. Not here, I mean London. London and Glasgow.'

'Do cellists never go on holiday?'

'It's rare.'

'And what about the pre-prandial shag?'

'I was thinking of having a bath.'

'Perfect timing, then.' He kissed her again, and when she turned from him slightly, kissed her neck, as if he hadn't noticed.

I'll tell him soon, Kate thought, but I won't tell him tonight. Can't tell him tonight. Wrong time, wrong place.

She reflected on how odd it was to think such a thing while she was doing what she was doing. Michael gave a little gasp of approval and arched his back towards her, encouraging, his hand stroking her hair.

I'll tell him soon, I'll tell him when there's an 'r' in the month, tell him when there's a full moon, tell him the next time I ladder a pair of tights, tell him if it rains on Friday.

The room had white, translucent window blinds. When Michael turned her onto her back, she could see the shapes of gulls, angling and gliding down the wind.

I'll tell him when I get back from the tour.

He grazed her breasts with his late-afternoon stubble. A chill ran through her, and she discovered it to be pleasure. She was enjoying it; enjoying him; and that was only possible because, suddenly, her mind was made up. He was becoming the past, and sexual excitement was a form of nostalgia.

It hadn't always been that way. Kate could still remember their first meeting, first date, first time in bed together, though now the memory seemed weighted towards happiness, over-bright, like a recollection from childhood. Sex had been easy for them, as if they had known one another in some previous life. They knew what to do, what to avoid. They found time for each other, as if the world wasn't pressing; as if they knew nothing would dare interrupt. They exchanged ideas, like people who have just discovered language.

That business of being so caught up in someone, Kate thought, it's tremendous. It's what *living off your nerves* really means. But it was so fast, she reflected, so intense, that there was always a high risk of an accident. All too often, someone had to become a casualty.

She sat at dinner while he talked, and counted out the days. It wasn't a spiteful thing; she wasn't gloating; and it didn't please her to possess the secret of his future. But the addition and subtraction of it was oddly comforting. A decision had been made, a time set, and now things were no longer quite in her hands. Michael was talking about the use of pesticides on crops, and eating his food with undisguised pleasure. Kate laughed, and he saw the joke. The ability to laugh at himself was one of the things that made him lovable.

He was lovable. His commitment to a cause, his honesty, his selflessness. Even as she worked out the mathematics of separation, she knew exactly how lovable he was. The only indulgence she allowed herself was that he would be sure to find someone else very soon.

Poland next week, she thought, then Belgium: five days there. Then home. And she knew she wasn't planning to tell him before she went because she needed to concentrate, to practise, to shut herself away with the score and with the other members of the quartet, free of any distractions.

'Get married,' Annie Forrester had once told her. Annie was their viola player. 'Get married – then all that emotion-and-sex stuff doesn't matter any more.' She was laughing when she spoke, and tuning up, but the smile faded quite quickly from her lips.

Michael got up and walked out of the restaurant. It happened
with such suddenness that he seemed to leave in mid-sentence.
Their table was by a window, and Kate was facing the street. She
looked over her shoulder, expecting to see him on his way to the
door, but he must have been moving at a half-run. When she
turned back he reappeared, as if he were starring in some sort of
bizarre optical illusion. He went down the front steps of the hotel
and crossed the road, hopping and weaving between cars, waving
a hand at them to say, *Sorry, in a hurry, sorry . . .*

As Kate watched, he came up behind a man walking on the far
pavement, alongside the promenade rails. Michael's hand went
out to the other's arm, but he must have spoken first, because the
man turned, startled, then backed off a few paces as Michael
reached out. His quarry was fiftyish, bald, and carrying the sort of
excess weight that makes a coat tug and wrinkle at the buttonholes. He shook his head, as if to say, 'Not now,' or 'Nothing to
say,' and pulled his arm free, but Michael boxed him in against
the rail.

Kate watched as the man listened, his head turned away, in
boredom or denial. Michael spoke for about three or four minutes,
then the man looked up, and directly at him, as if to say, *Okay?
Finished now?* Michael's face creased in anger, but he let go and
the man hurried away. Michael had taken his jacket off in the
restaurant. Now his shirtsleeves billowed and wagged in the sea
wind, as he watched the man down the street.

'His name's Stephen Cawdrey,' Michael said. 'He works for an
outfit called Green Globe. He edits their news-sheet, which is how
I know him.'

He didn't offer more, so Kate asked, 'And what were you telling
him?'

'I was telling him that he's the mutant son of Jabba The Hut,
and a gobshite besides.'

'Yes. I meant why.'

'I know you did. Have you thought any more about Greece?'

'In the best of all possible worlds . . .'

'Ah,' Michael said, raising his glass as if offering a toast. 'Not a world we're ever likely to enjoy.'

The sodium light in the streets meant that the gulls never slept, squawking over stranded starfish and the emptied bait cans of night fishers, or letting go those long, plaintive cries, *weep-weep*, that overlapped and fell away in the wind.

Or maybe, thought Kate, they sleep in shifts.

Musicians hear rhythm in everything: the hotel heating system, a generator, a motorbike whining into the distance, someone running the shower in the next room. Kate listened to all this while Michael slept. Mostly, she heard the gulls, *weep-weep-weep*; the gulls and the sound of the sea.

It was like being in Greece.

Two

'When I get back,' Kate said. 'Ten days from tomorrow. I'll tell him then.'

Her sister pulled some dresses out of her wardrobe and laid them on the bed. She smiled. 'Any of these would fit you,' she said.

'I know what that smile means,' Kate observed. 'It means you're full of shit.'

'No,' Joanna said, 'it means *you're* full of shit.'

'I like the green,' Kate said.

'Of course you do. It's Issey Miyake.'

'So can I have it?'

'Borrow it.'

'Yes, borrow it.'

'It's the only . . .' Joanna broke off. 'Yes, okay. I bought it when Nick and I got divorced. Same day. Same hour, practically. Walked out of court and got a taxi to Chelsea. I was in the shop forty minutes after agreeing joint custody.'

'How is Nick?'

'Fine. In America making money, which is good for everyone, except the inhabitants of the Niger delta. Michael would hate him.'

'They'll never meet.'

'You're sure? . . . about ending things, I mean.'

'We've run out of relationship. Isn't that what counsellors say? Sounds like all those bottom of the barrel remarks, doesn't it? Bin end, end stock, end of line.' Kate was standing in her underwear and shrugging into the green dress. Her voice was muffled. 'Well, it's the end of line all right.'

'For you.'

Kate's head emerged. 'In all honesty . . . yes. Just me.'

'He doesn't have any idea?'

'Not sure. I don't think I can stop to think about that. I mean, if I stop to think about how he feels, I write him a reprieve. It's wrong.'

'Run out of relationship,' Joanna said. Her smile meant: *Easy. That's an easy thing to say.*

'He's obsessed. I get worn down by his anger, by his bleak view of the world.'

'Accurate view of the world, perhaps.'

'Oh, sure, yes, I've no doubt. But it's one thing to be concerned, quite another to eat, sleep and breathe concern. I admire him: I mean, his fierceness and his dedication. He takes all sorts of risks, you know? He makes things difficult for himself when others would take the easy route. It's one of the things that first attracted me to him. Now . . . he seems so difficult to be with,' she smiled, 'apart from in bed, where there isn't space for us and the third world.'

'You're talking to a divorced single parent with no prospect of men, or even man,' Joanna told her, 'so please don't whine. I've come to associate the term "fun in bed" with a video and ice cream straight from the tub.'

'How often is it,' Kate wondered, 'that the things you first like about someone turn out to be the very qualities that sink the relationship?'

'Often.'

As if it were an afterthought, Kate said, 'I admire him.'

'Ah – that *does* sound terminal.'

Kate turned this way and that in front of the mirror. 'What do you think?'

'Looks better on you. Perfect for an embassy reception.'

'It'll be a collection of old farts and old farts' wives,' Kate observed gloomily, 'none of whom will have heard any music for years apart from the national anthem.'

Joanna found a bag for the dress. 'I thought it was different this time,' she said, meaning Michael. 'It looked different anyway.'

'It felt different,' Kate said. 'But then it always does, doesn't it? At the start.'

Back at her flat, she packed the dress and then practised for a couple of hours. Practice was all work, as usual. Performance was work with rewards – the only difference. Sometimes, she felt as far from music as it was possible to get. At other times, it was the only, the absorbing, the limitless passion. Quite often, those moments stood next to one another, all but indivisible.

She had propped the cello against the wall and poured her first glass of wine when Michael rang. He said, 'I love you.'

'Where are you?' Kate could hear a background of hum and thrum.

'In the car. I said, "I love you".'

'I was practising,' she said. 'You didn't call earlier, did you? I switched the phone off.'

'I didn't call you earlier, but I am calling you now. I'm calling to say good luck for the tour. And to tell you I love you – that was the other reason.'

'Good,' she said, 'thanks. I'm exhausted already. A day of rehearsal, two hours of practice, packing . . . I'll probably doze off over Beethoven. Where are you going?'

'Do you want me to drive you to the airport? Easily done.'

'I'll get a cab. Really. I might share with Annie.'

'Okay, right.' Michael was on the point of hanging up. He felt much further away than the end of a telephone. And Kate was further still. He hadn't got a hands-off rig for the phone, and when a black cab cut him up on rising ground by the Embankment, he dropped the phone into his lap.

Kate said, 'Michael? Michael . . .' and paused a moment, then assumed he'd hit a reception black spot. By the time he'd got the phone back to his ear, she had rung off.

He redialled to say goodbye. Goodbye and have a great trip. And play well. And I love you. Then he tossed the phone over his shoulder onto the back seat and said, 'Bitch!'

He found the black cab and took its lane space with a quick

14

swerve, getting a horn-blast in response. 'I hope your fucking strings break, your bridge collapses, your bow unravels.'

He baulked a BMW at an intersection, waved a cheery hand at the driver and ran the red light.

'I hope your plane crashes into the sea.'

He drove quickly and without much skill, approaching Parliament Square. 'It'll be fine.' He was still speaking out loud. 'It'll be fine. Everything will be fine.'

Tim Farnol's office was about the size of a walk-in closet and less tastefully furnished. He said, 'There's to be a division. I haven't got all that long.'

Michael offered him what could have been mistaken for an amiable grin. 'I haven't got long . . . There's a metaphor in that.'

'What will you do with the material?'

'I love that kind of talk,' Michael said. 'Material. What will I do with the *material*. Run up a pair of curtains, I expect.'

Farnol sighed and looked away. He was wearing MPs' uniform: striped suit, blue shirt, dark tie. His hair was cut boyishly, as if he still believed photographs of himself taken in the seventies, and it looked foolish sitting atop the jowly face and fat neck. 'Just tell me,' he said.

'Publish it. I'll publish it, of course.'

'I can't have that.'

'You can't have it? Think again. You've got to have it.'

'It's too much of a risk.'

Michael pretended to work out a quick sum on his fingers. 'Yes? Let's see. The material could have come from a number of sources, couldn't it –?'

'And I'm one of them.'

'But there are others. Here's something else: I'm an investigative journalist. I investigate. That's what we investigative journalists do. What we *never* do is reveal our sources. So several fingers might be pointing at you, but others will be pointing in different directions, and no one's ever going to know the truth of it anyway. That's how much risk attaches to the *material*. Now let's look at the other risk you face. That's where instead of publishing and protecting my sources, I publish and accuse you, specifically, of corruption. Same material, different approach. Here's the difference: in the first scenario, you hand me the material, everything that's material to the material, if you see what I mean, which makes my life easier, gives me an exclusive, and allows me time to pick off some of the bastards who are bigger bastards than bastards like you. In the second scenario, I start with the sketchy but very, very interesting information that I've already got, and get to the full story – as I surely will – a lot later, and a lot more pissed off. You can see the difference, can't you? One way, I'm happy and you're anonymous. The other way, I'm angry and you're hung out to dry.'

Farnol didn't speak. He was looking at the reflection of light on the polished surface of his desk. After a moment, he started to rub the wood with a finger like a craftsman, following the grain. Michael gazed at him relentlessly; behind his eyes, he was counting. When he reached a hundred, he thought: I've lost him. Damn! He's going hardball, or else he's going to fess up. In the same moment, as if overlapping Michael's thought to contradict it, Farnol said, 'What guarantees do I have?'

'None at all. I could be lying in my teeth. But look at it this way. If you make me dig for this stuff, if I'm into archaeology here, then when I do publish, your name's going to be all over it. *There's* a guarantee. I'll certainly guarantee that much. The other way: same story, no names. Or, at least, not yours. If I'm being straight with you. And I am. Help me out, and there's every chance that I'm telling you the truth. Hold out, and I'll definitely fuck you. In fact there's a bit of tittle-tattle, a bit of *material*, that I could throw in for good measure.'

Farnol found a whorl in the grain and sent his fingertip round it again and again. He said, 'Everyone knows about Vanessa.'

Michael shook his head. 'Not quite true. Your colleagues know about Vanessa, your friends know about Vanessa, your wife couldn't care less about Vanessa, and your children know *Auntie* Vanessa. But your constituents don't know. And the tabloids don't know.'

'Are you having fun?' Farnol asked. 'Is this fun?'

16

'No,' Michael shook his head, 'it's not. Not at all. But I want that material, Farnol. The *material*. I want it because it's something important and it's something dangerous and, worst of all, it's something secret. It shouldn't be, but it is. When I said, a moment ago, that I'd publish it, you said, "I can't have that". Well, let me tell you something I can't have. I can't have gobshites like you putting people at risk for money, and lying about it for money, and keeping it secret for money, and using privilege and power to cement the whole thing over, like Chernobyl, cemented over, all the things that hurt people, and put people at risk, and disadvantage people, cemented over, and bastards like you sitting on top of the pile counting your fucking money. I can't have that.'

'Oh, dear,' Farnol said, 'I'm up against an idealist.'

Michael smiled, then the smile became a laugh. He was laughing because Farnol was struggling to seem cool, to seem as if he still held a vestige of control, and instead he sounded like a man on a mountain road who has just felt the brake pedal collapse under his foot.

Farnol had the floppy disk in his pocket: of course he did. Michael took it. He said, 'You're as safe as I can make you. No one will hear your name from me.'

Farnol shrugged. 'I don't accept I did anything wrong.' He went back to tracing patterns in wood. 'Anything *that* wrong.'

'Of course you don't,' Michael agreed. 'It's like being tone deaf.' He went to the door and opened it. A bell was sounding and people were scurrying up and down the corridor. 'You're not to blame. In a decent society, all people like you would be kept together in some institution or another where you could play games, and shout a lot, and generally make fools of yourselves. Except –' he paused, looking down the corridor, then back at Farnol, '– here you are already.'

Michael lived in a cottage that backed on to Ham Common. It was London but not London, which was why he liked it. Also, it was quiet. He poured himself a drink, switched on the desk lamp by his laptop computer, and brought up onto the screen the information that had been on Tim Farnol's floppy disk. He smiled. The *material*.

He had looked at it the previous evening, of course, as soon as he'd got home. It was what he wanted. It was everything he'd hoped it would be. His first move had been to copy everything to his hard disk; then he printed it out; then he started to make notes.

There was nothing much there that he didn't already know or hadn't guessed at; the difference was that it came with Tim Farnol's inside knowledge; his authority. It was publishable because it was authentic, not guesswork or surmise. And there were one or two things, one or two *crucial* things, that Michael hadn't known.

He worked for half an hour, then glanced at his watch. An hour to take-off. He imagined Kate at the airport: pictured her. It was something he liked to do, and hated doing. Liked it, because it brought her up on the screen in his mind, where she moved and spoke and thought according to his direction. Hated it, because he knew that this was a Kate of his inventing; a Kate Kate didn't know; a Kate she would deny.

Kate sat in the airport bar with the other members of the quartet, and thought about Michael. She and the other three women talked about the tour, about audiences, about promoters, about this tricky passage and that. Kate had her cello with her: she never checked it in. Cabin crews were used to making exceptions and let her have space in the storage compartments. She thought about Michael, and they were good thoughts.

This was Michael's imagining.

He conjured her up in his mind's eye: a little above average height, perhaps, maybe five-nine; hair that was just-blond: tawny was about the right word; a straight nose, a perfect nose, her best feature; a wide mouth, a broad brow, hazel eyes that would have been nicer if they were a touch bigger; flat planes to her cheeks because she was slim, and her face was narrow across the points of the jaw. He held the picture as whole as he could, though as he constructed one part, another would start to slip. Long neck;

round breasts, soft breasts, quite full but not out of proportion; no, *terrific* breasts; a little too much on the hips, perhaps, a little heavy there, though he loved to watch when she parted her knees for the cello and would shift her hips, just wriggle slightly, to find position. She laughed at something one of the others had said: was it Annie, the viola player? Laughed and said something that made the others laugh in turn, then picked up her drink, and fell into her thoughts – thinking good things about Michael.

Michael's imagining. Thinking good things about me, he decided.

Kate sat in the airport bar with the other members of the quartet, and thought about Michael. When he had called her from the car, the previous night, to say, 'I love you,' she had felt a lick of panic; for the first time, a genuine touch of fear. For a moment, she hadn't been able to quite pin the feeling down, then she'd known what it was: stage fright.

'I love you,' he'd said. And again, 'I love you,' and something in her had frozen. 'I love you . . .' And what he wanted was clear in the way he spoke, clear in the repetition. A week before, she would have been able to trade him a kind remark for that declaration; a month before, and he would have heard the same from her and might not have noticed the blank pause, like a bad connection, that came between his voice and hers; a month before that, she wouldn't have been able to identify that pause herself. Now the feeling that lay in her was something she had only experienced once before: on the evening of her first solo concert, when she had walked out to applause and lights and sat down to play, and her fingers locked. She had simply sat still, head bowed, for two minutes. Two aeons. Two lifetimes. Then she had started to play. But the feeling about Michael wasn't going to unlock, and she knew it.

She heard something one of the others said – was it Annie? – and she turned towards her, vaguely aware of a note of alarm. Annie's drink was on the floor, ice cubes in a puddle of vodka, the glass broken at the stem. Annie was bent over her folded arms, clearly in pain. The others had stood up, concerned looks on their faces, one with an arm round Annie's shoulders, another stroking her hair.

Kate said, 'Annie . . . Are you okay?' The other woman was breathing deeply, trying to control the pain; there were tears on her cheek. She looked up and said that no, she didn't think she was okay, and could someone please fucking do something, like now, because she definitely wasn't okay, and really, listen, now would be a good time to do something, okay? – *now*!

Joanna made scrambled eggs and a pot of coffee. They ate in the kitchen. She asked, 'When do you get her back?'

'Appendix out tonight – emergency job – a couple of days in hospital, three perhaps; then take it easy for a week.'

'They can restage the tour . . .?'

'I don't think so.'

'Lousy luck. What will you do?'

'God knows. I'm unemployed.' Kate bit into a piece of toast. 'Maybe I ought to go and see Michael.'

'Ought to? I thought you'd already decided that when you got back from –'

'Yes. Sure. I had. I mean tonight.'

'Oh.' Joanna shrugged. 'You don't have to. Stick to your original schedule. Take some time off. Go down to Penarven.'

'I thought Penarven had been sold.'

'Meant to. Couldn't. Nathan loves it and I love it.'

'You haven't been there in a year.'

'No, we haven't. But we still love it – the house, that bit of coastline, the woods. It's rare in Cornwall to get both sea and trees.'

'Nick pays for it,' Kate guessed.

'And uses it. We have a rota. He's away until after Christmas. Michael thinks you're in Poland. Go. Clean air, long walks. Bit like Randall family holidays.'

Kate laughed. 'You swimming from bay to bay, me climbing cliffs with a ten per cent overhang, father yelling, "Go on, go on, a five-year-old could do it".'

'I liked those holidays.'

20

'I didn't mind being under canvas. It was sometimes being under snow that bothered me.'

'You loved it,' Joanna said. 'You were a brilliant rock-climber.'

'Head for heights and a desire to live: great combination. Not a great hobby for a cellist, though. My adventure holidays are over.'

'So get up at lunchtime and drive straight to the pub. Maybe you'll find some brawny type mending nets on the beach – become a fisherman's friend for a week.'

Kate smiled, her mind elsewhere. 'Fisherman's Friend is a lozenge, not a doxy.'

'They're hot and they get licked; it'll do for me.'

'I might go away. A week's skiing would be great. Or I'll spend a week in the gym and relocate my stomach.'

Joanna waved a dismissive hand. Kate's gym routine was a source of amusement to her; amusement heavily tinged with envy. Kate looked at her watch. It was ten-thirty. She said: 'It's only Ham Common. I could be there in under half an hour. Get it over with.'

Joanna said, 'You make it sound like a root canal.'

'If I were in Poland,' Kate said, 'I could take the time. But I'm not.'

Joanna's six-year-old son, Nathan, appeared at the kitchen door. He was rubbing both eyes, like someone who has just seen something startling. 'What are you talking about?' he wanted to know.

'Virtue,' Joanna said. 'Probity. Emotional rectitude, fair dealing, straight talking, honest injun.'

'Can I have some ice cream,' Nathan wondered, 'and watch television for a couple of hours?'

It was mid-October, and the air seemed to carry grains of frost. Kate gave Joanna back the Issey Miyake dress and borrowed, instead, a quilted jacket with twelve pockets and a fur collar. It was a coat she'd always wanted.

'It's Canadian,' Joanna told her, 'and that's real fur. Watch out for sabs.'

'Is that why you never wear it?'

'I wear it,' Joanna said firmly, 'in the winter. Which is

approaching. That coat's strictly on loan. Anything found in any of the pockets is mine.'

'Treasure trove,' Kate told her.

Kate drove a small jeep, and though she knew it was nothing but style and foolishness to steer a four-track called Rio Bravo round urban streets, that was exactly what she liked about the vehicle. Aquamarine bodywork, black leather seats, cross-country tyres.

She stopped short of Michael's door – about halfway down the street. His cottage was at the bottom, last but one in a cul-de-sac, a quiet road backed by the park. She pulled on the handbrake, but left the engine running. It was eleven-fifteen, and Michael was still working. From where she sat, Kate could see the shape of his window, where four lighted rectangles fell into the street. She let the engine run for ten minutes. Nothing changed. She drove the last few yards and switched the engine off.

Three

While they were talking, the phone rang, and when Michael picked up there was no one there.

'Except,' he said, 'there *is* someone there, of course. Some bastard or another. Some pig's ass.'

They weren't talking about anything much: how Annie had caved-in at the airport, whether the tour was insured, why Poland was a better gig than Belgium. Kate hadn't got round to the rest. She wondered whether what she intended to say was written in her face. It was. Michael had already seen it there. He opened a bottle of wine and told her that he was working on a piece of dynamite.

'Let me see it.'

'You'll see it before anyone else does. Not yet, though.'

'Which pig's ass?'

'I don't know. Well, I could make a guess. I don't mind the funny calls: the harassment. What bothers me is that they know who to harass.'

'You mean, they know you know something you shouldn't know . . . and they shouldn't know that.'

'You've got it.'

He smiled, because he knew something he shouldn't know . . . and she knew that. He wondered whether it was too late, now, to chase her back from the brink. Not too late, he decided. Never too late. He opened some wine and poured two large glasses. She hated to drive when she'd been drinking.

She said, 'Look, Michael —' and the phone rang.

'Could be a worried man,' Michael said, 'an MP. Or it could be some people the worried man has spoken to. That's a less happy notion.'

'Why harass you? What's the motive?'

'To unnerve me? To make me think twice?' They were genuine questions: Michael wasn't sure either.

He poured more wine. They talked about this and that, then were silent a moment. When Kate looked away, and started to speak, Michael got up and went out of the room. She said a couple of things that were hard to say, then turned to find him gone. He came back two minutes later, wearing a smile and carrying a CD.

'Who is this guy?' he asked. 'I saw something about him in one of the supplements and I bought it on impulse. Do you know his stuff?' He took the disc out and handed Kate the case. An orchestral piece by a fashionable fake who wore a kaftan and a seraphic smile. Kate hadn't heard the music, but knew it would be bells and strings and weeping woodwind, helped into the ether by distant choirs. Michael put the disc on to play, then sat beside her on the sofa, letting his hand stray to the back of her neck, his fingers pinching the nape, then stroking, as if to ease out the tension of a bad day. It had always been a sign between them that meant 'sex next'.

Kate got up and turned off the CD player. She backed away from him a little, as if trying to get him in focus, and found herself standing close to the window. She could feel a slight draught.

She said, 'I don't love you, it's over, I'm sorry, I used to love you but the feeling's gone, there's no point, is there, in keeping on when one of us feels like this, you must have noticed something, it's been like this for me for a while now, I'm sorry I didn't tell you earlier, but I didn't have the guts. I'm sorry.'

In any case, that's what she thought she'd said. It certainly sounded like that to her: jagged rhythms, everything in a rush, nothing considered, no attempt to soften the blow. In truth, when she'd finished, she couldn't really remember a word of it. She only knew that she'd said what she intended to say by the stricken look on Michael's face.

What happened next came as a complete surprise. Michael got

up off the sofa, walked across to her, and slapped her, back-handed, across the face. She took a step back and he slapped her again, not connecting properly this time, but she jerked back to dodge the blow and her head rapped the window. He grabbed the front of her shirt, close to the neck, and shook her to and fro until the buttons tore from the buttonholes. Her head wagged like a doll's. He twisted the material into a garrotte, tightening it at her throat. All she could do was hold his forearms, as if she might absorb some of that wild energy; as if some of the shock and loathing and fear might earth through her.

He kept pulling a hand free, as if to hit her again, and each time Kate managed to get a hold on his wrist. She thought that if he caught her with a third slap, she'd pretend to pass out, because one was anger, and two was pain, but the third would be vengeance and that came from a darker, deeper place. The third slap might really be the first: the start of something else, something dangerous and addictive.

Michael released her, suddenly, making her stagger. He started yelling, standing flatfooted, bending towards her, the colour in his face mounting. She noticed everything: the jots of spittle on his chin, the way his mouth was trembling, that the tip of his nose moved when he yelled, that he never blinked or looked away, his eyes holding her eyes. He said everything it was possible to say that might hurt. Then he said everything it was possible to say that might persuade. She watched as the energy drained away from him, ounce by ounce, seeming to make him deflate piece-meal, until he had to take a grip on the window sill and his gaze swivelled away from her, and he started to pant like a frightened animal.

It terrified her that she had never understood how much he loved her. Two years; more – two years last July; and she had never seen the depth of feeling in him, the depth of need. And now, all that had converted to depth of loss. Although Michael had half-turned from her, head slumped, shoulders slumped, his misery, his energy, still ran in the room like a black flood. He was recovering, not spent. She stood stock still and waited to see what would happen next.

* * *

Frieda Metcalf waited too. Her dog sat at her side, nosing scents that flowed from the common, anxious for bushes and grass, but leashed up and resigned to patience. The couple in the window held their tableau: the man turned away from the woman, head down, seeming exhausted by his anger; the woman, backed up to the window, watching him, looking to be on the brink of movement, but lacking the nerve.

It had been a hell of a row. At one point, Frieda had thought she'd have to call the police. The man was blind with anger and free with his hands. He might have gone on hitting her; he might have choked her. Then he was screaming at her; screaming and boxing her in against the glass. Now they'd reached some sort of plateau. Frieda stood in the shadow of roadside trees, thrilled to look in at these other lives that were dangerous for being so unhappy.

The man turned and stretched out a hand, touching the woman's face where he'd slapped her, and she suffered him to do that. His hand dropped to her breast, and she suffered him to do that too. For a moment, they faced one another, his arm outstretched, his palm covering her breast, as if this might be some ritual of greeting. Then his hand went to the back of her neck and he drew her in and kissed her. She stood like a statue as his face moved against hers, his head rocking as if to drive the kiss home. As if to nail it to her lips.

Like a statue, Frieda thought. He broke the kiss and they stayed nose to nose, or else he was holding her there, his fingers still at her nape. Frieda wasn't sure; but she could see he was talking to her. Not yelling, talking. The dog whined, got up, sat down again.

'All right,' Frieda said. She waited a little longer, but the couple in the window weren't going to offer her any more excitement. It was talking now; all talk.

She moved out of the shadows and into the light of the street lamp, then across the road that led to the common.

Kate looked round the room as if she were checking for an escape route. She noted their reflection in a mirror over the fireplace: her own face, expressionless; the back of Michael's head; his raised arm. She half turned, hoping to gain release, and found both her face and his face in the window pane. She concentrated on small things, small events, as if their ordinariness might rub off: the music, still playing; the screen-saver pattern on Michael's computer; his paintings, his books; her jeep parked outside; a woman taking her dog for a last-thing walk across towards the common.

Michael said, 'You don't mean it.' He walked away from her and collected his drink from the coffee table, then fell onto the sofa with a laugh and a shake of the head, like a man who has just arrived home, tired and a bit fed up, wanting nothing so much as a quick drink and an early night. Then he said, 'I'm sorry. I ran off the rails.'

'A bit.' She wanted to mollify, not challenge.

'I just . . . Maybe I just ask, sometimes, for more than you can give. More than I have a right to expect.'

'It isn't that. It's not your fault. It's not even your problem.' Jesus God, she thought, the old ones are the best ones. Next thing, I'll be telling him I just need some space.

'Sit down.' Michael spoke as if he had something to say, but when she sat, on a small armchair across from the sofa, he just looked at her, like an interviewer expecting a question or comment.

They sat in silence for more than five minutes, until Kate said, 'Maybe I should go. We could talk later. I know we need to talk.'

'No,' he said. 'Stay. Don't go anywhere. I don't want you to go. It doesn't help if you go.'

'What helps?' she asked. A balm, a bandage, a splint.

Michael shook his head again: he seemed to be making a choice. What would help? Maybe this; maybe that. He said, 'Come to bed. We'll talk in the morning.'

'I wasn't planning to stay over, Michael. Surely you can see that.'

'I can see that you're upset. We're both upset. Come on . . .'

'It's not . . . Upset isn't it. Isn't the point. I can't just . . .'

'Look, I feel — I'm tired, aren't you? There'll be a time to talk about this. Something's wrong, I can see that.' He laughed. 'I think

I've understood that much. All I'm saying . . . Let's just . . . Let's go to bed, and tomorrow . . . if not tomorrow, some other time . . . we can talk to each other about what happened this evening. What was said. How we feel.'

'I know how I feel. I can't . . . We can't go to bed, as if . . .'

But she knew they could; and that she probably would, because it was what he wanted. He thought it might make a difference. Earlier, she had fixed on those small items, small moments, because they were ordinary, and ordinary things survived; they bore the brunt of everything, and simply remained, like wallpaper on the exposed staircase of a bombed house. In the same way, Michael was looking for something that might join the torn ends of their relationship – being close, being together, sex, sleep, waking the next day and deciding to forget.

He walked over to where she was sitting and crouched in front of her. He put the back of his hand against the place where his slap had landed: an infinitely gentle parody of the blow.

'Come on, Kate . . .'

And she felt a little surge of heat, a pulse of excitement; it stemmed from power; from the knowledge that it would be the last time she would make love with him; and that his yearning, his eagerness, was something she could take without having to return.

She stayed a while in the bathroom: a space for herself; a little stolen time. She decided to take a shower. She looked at the one or two possessions of hers that she'd installed in his bathroom: cleanser, a small bottle of Ysatis, basic make-up, loose tampons, a razor. It pleased her to think of abandoning them: simply walking away. She put a mental check on the clothes she kept there; nothing crucial, she decided. She realised these moments of selfishness were part of her defence, like making love out of power and pity. But they didn't disguise the fact that she was sad and hurt herself. No one gets away free; not really free.

She looked at her face in the mirror and saw the swelling alongside her eye, already darkening at the centre. There was a graze and a thin line of dried blood where his fingernail had nicked her. It stung.

Michael heard the shower running. He was trembling, trying to do the things he would normally do. He backed up his work on the computer then, on impulse, copied Farnol's file to a new floppy disk and made out a label that read 'Dynamite: remember?'

He looked round for Kate's coat and saw it in the little hallway, draped over the banister. Of the twelve pockets, four were on the inside. Michael found a small zippered pocket in the tail of the coat, just below the waistline: a secure place for a passport, maybe, or a wallet; he slipped the disk in and pulled the zip. He had been intending to give Kate a back-up disk anyway, but now his motive was more to do with their continuing involvement than with security. He had always been secretive when working on a story, especially if it contained sensitive documents, or people in the public eye. You protect your friends, just as you protect your sources. Now he wanted Kate to have a stake in things; a stake in him. Something that might bring her back.

The shower stopped. After a moment, he heard her pad through to the bedroom. Just the way it always was. He closed down his computer and switched off the lights. *Hey*, what a row. What a fight. He gave a little laugh. What a *blinder*. But all couples had them. It was over now. And there she was, Kate, upstairs, no longer angry, just as he was no longer angry, and waiting for him in bed.

Just the way it always was, Kate thought. All couples had them — little habits in bed, things they always did. Now she was doing them with Michael, just as she had before, as if she'd never told him, as if he'd never slapped her, as if she'd never seen his naked desperation. The feeling of power she'd had earlier, the flicker of lust, had given way to a kind of sorrow, but also to relief. She had told him; it was done; the rest didn't seem to matter much. When he entered her, she gasped and closed her eyes, letting him think what he would. They fell asleep in each other's arms because there was no reason not to.

*   *   *

Kate woke, thinking at first that it was morning, then realising that things were too still and dark for that. Michael had gone. She rolled into his space and looked at the clock: three-fifteen. She lay there for a while, listening for a noise that would tell her where he was, but the house was silent. She began to wonder whether 'gone' might mean 'out of the house', and that worried her. On the other hand, she didn't want to go downstairs and find him there, insomniac, drinking whisky, growing sadder and angrier as the gloom and depression of three a.m. set in.

Finally, she got out of bed and put on her white towelling robe. There was a light burning at the top of the stairs that hadn't been on when they'd gone to bed. She said, 'Michael?' in a half-whisper, and listened for a reply. Something scraped — didn't it? — a chair or stool, maybe in the kitchen. She wasn't sure. Outside, a thrush, fooled by the sodium street lights, started to sing.

'Michael?'

She went down to the hallway, feeling suddenly cold; the birdsong seemed louder. The light was on in the living room, but the room was empty. The computer was on, its fan humming slightly; the screen-saver was 'flying through space'. Her face in the mirror looked curious: eyes wide, lips parted.

'Michael?'

She found him in the kitchen. He was naked, turned half-away from her, standing with one arm braced against a chair back, the other across his midriff. That was what she'd heard: the chair leg scraping the floor. His pose reminded her of Annie and the spilled drink and the ambulance at the entrance to Terminal 2, its lights dancing reflections off the glass doors. The coincidence struck her as ludicrous. She laughed, and said: 'You too? What is it?'

He turned as if he were noticing her for the first time, and she took a step towards him. As she stepped forward, he stepped back. He seemed about to speak, but all he could do was utter a strange sibilant whisper, as if he were urging her to silence. *Shhh . . . shhh . . . shhh . . .* The movement staggered him. The whisper became a hiss of pain, and she saw that his face was creased with fear.

30

'Michael,' she said. Then, because there was nothing of recognition in his eyes, 'It's me.'

He stepped back again, bringing himself more fully into the light, and then she saw the blood that had run from under his clamped forearm, down over his belly, his groin, his thighs. Was still running. For a moment, she couldn't see what in hell was causing it: some accident with glass, was it? She assumed the cut was on his forearm, deep, obviously, and in need of attention. Then he took a step towards the door, and she saw the handle of the kitchen knife, just the handle, because the blade was all the way in.

There was a delay, and then something swarmed up to her head and exploded there. She lost her balance, and flung out a hand to the same chair back that, a moment ago, he had been using as a support. She couldn't see; then that passed and she could see but couldn't breathe. Michael took three more steps, which brought him to the kitchen door, then he went through and out of her vision.

Each of Kate's indrawn breaths was a word – his name – as if speaking were the only reliable way of taking air into her lungs: *Michael, Michael, Michael, Michael,* the two syllables broken-backed and carrying such a weight of horror that they lost their meaning entirely. Not a man's name, but a code for fear and guilt and terror. Kate knew she must follow him, but couldn't: not at once; her legs wouldn't work. Her mind, though, was working like a clock.

Two thoughts came to her: I told him we were through; now he's killed himself. The second was: *But what in hell happened here?* She was looking round the kitchen at the mess: strewn implements, broken plates, a blind almost torn off one side of the window, blood on the work surface, blood on the table, blood on the floor and the chair and the draining board.

All this took five seconds, maybe ten, then she was through the kitchen door and into the living room. Michael was walking round the room, his eyes wide, his mouth open and soundless, his hands clenched round the knife. She went to him, her arms out, and he tried, again, to speak. A long spit of blood left his mouth

31

and splashed the front of her robe. For a moment she had hold of his arm, then he wrenched himself free, terror and shock lending him energy, and he half stumbled, half ran into the hall, making for the stairs, Kate going after him, crying, now, and calling his name over and over because she couldn't think of what she ought to be doing or saying.

He fell onto the stairs and she tried to keep him there, holding his shoulders, talking to him. There was a moment's pause. She could still hear the bird, still feel the coldness in the hall. Then she saw why: the door was open. Michael was taking long, shuddering breaths, his body still, his hands and feet moving to gain purchase. He levered himself up and ran back into the living room, moving in a falling, listing, fumbling sort of a gallop, and leaving blood-gouts like little bombs.

It was a mad pursuit: bizarre, grotesque, following the rhythms of pain and panic. Michael slipped and fell, got up, fell again, pushed her off when she tried to steady him. She was trying to make him stay still, stay in one place, conserve whatever life he had left in him.

Hiss ... hiss ... hiss. Michael spat at her like a snake, blood freckling his chin, his lips and teeth swamped. He was always ahead, falling and rising, one hand clapped to the seat of the pain. It was terror that was driving him: as if there were a place he might get to where none of it was true – not the knife, not the blood, not the unspeakable feeling of weakness that loosened his muscles and sinews even as he hobbled from room to room, limbs jerking and flailing, like an animal that has been pole-axed but won't lie down.

Blood everywhere, shipping out of him as he floundered. Their voices clashing: hers calling his name, or howling in anguish, or saying the meaningless things people say: *No, God, no, please, please, please*; his the awful, formless *hiss ... hiss ... hiss ...* that spilled from his mouth along with strings of blood, webs of blood.

They came back to the kitchen, and Michael's feet went from under him, slipping and slithering on his own gore. The impact when he hit the floor brought from him a great belch, and he jackknifed against the pain. Kate knelt beside him, cradling his head. The fall had jerked the blade, his hands round it, tight, the cutting edge slicing his fingers.

He said, 'Take it out,' the words shockingly distinct. 'Take it out.' Although the effort of speech was costing him more than he had to give, he kept saying it. It was all he could say. His heels drummed on the tiled floor. Kate looked towards the telephone in its bracket on the wall. 'Take it out,' he said.

She gripped the haft, holding his hand too, because he couldn't have borne to let go, and drew back the blade. A gusher of blood hit her, and she put her hand to his wound, instinctively, just as he did.

'Michael,' she said. 'Michael, I have to phone.'

As she watched, his eyes were losing their light. He was staring at her and shivering furiously, his mouth open, but clenched: lips tight round the awful O-gape of fear.

'Michael,' she said, and left him and went to the phone. When she returned, he was staring at the place where her eyes had been. Breath like a feather moved a dribble of pink froth at the corner of his mouth. He lifted an arm to her, and she caught him under the shoulders and pulled him up into an embrace, holding him without having to look at him.

The hiss was deeper in his throat, now, and softer. Tiny movements transferred themselves from him to her: a shiver, a hand-clench, a tremor like the shadow of a leap.

She felt him die as she held him, but held him just the same, as if nothing could change while they stayed just as they were, exactly as they were. She was still holding him when the paramedics arrived. While they were busy with him – trying him, testing him – she went upstairs and into the bathroom.

She was blood from neck to knee. Her white robe was soppy with blood. When she stripped it off and looked at herself in the wall mirror, she saw blood on her throat and on her breasts, a fan of blood over her belly, in her pubic hair, across her thighs. Her hands and wrists and forearms were thick with it.

She got into the shower and stayed there until the police started beating at the bathroom door.

Four

Everyone knew what to do.

The scene of crime officer had constructed an uncontaminated path to the body, so far as that was possible. The photographer and the video operator were in. A police doctor had pronounced Michael Lester dead and given a probable cause. Evidence had been bagged and removed, including the knife. Detectives were carrying out a careful, methodical search. A house-to-house enquiry was in progress. Other lines of enquiry had to do with who Michael's friends were, whether his parents were alive and, if not, who was the next of kin. The AMIP squad occupied the house as soldiers occupy gained ground. They were still waiting for someone from forensic.

The only person who didn't know what to do was Kate, but she was being helped by DI George Webb, who had organised WDC Carol Tanner to be with her while she had her fingerprints recorded for elimination purposes; now Tanner sat by the door in the interview room making notes while Webb and Kate talked.

'You could see a doctor,' Webb said. 'Perhaps you ought to.'

'I'm fine,' Kate said. 'I'll be okay.'

'The shock of something like that . . .'

'I'll see someone later. My GP.'

'Or I could call a relative, a friend. Is there someone you'd like?'

'Will I be here long?'

'No, I don't think so.' Webb appeared to think more carefully about the question, then came up with the same answer. 'No, there's no reason. I'll need to talk with you again.'

'Yes.'

Webb looked down at the three sheets of paper that lay on the table. 'I expect you'll think of other things: things you haven't mentioned here.'

'Perhaps. Yes, I shouldn't be surprised. I'm tired, mostly. I just feel exhausted.'

'Sure, of course. It's shock. You will see someone?'

'Yes.'

Webb looked at Kate's statement again, and rubbed his finger under his nose, chasing an itch. He was in his early forties, and starting to accumulate forties flab. He'd been good-looking in his youth, and you could still see that in him: the even features getting rounder, the cheekbones going under.

He read for a couple of minutes, switching the sheets back and forth. 'You went upstairs and removed the robe you were wearing. Then you took a shower.'

'That's right.'

'After the paramedics arrived.'

'Yes.'

'Okay.' He read for a little longer. 'And why . . . What made you do that? Take a shower.'

'I was covered in blood.'

'Okay.'

Kate shifted in her chair and straightened her back. She felt heavy, as if she had eaten a large meal. The room was overheated. She put her palms to her cheeks, then wiped her mouth with a finger.

'I don't want to upset you.'

'No . . . I see.'

'The fact is, taking the knife out wasn't really the best thing to do.'

'Yes. The paramedics said that. I didn't know. I mean, at the time . . .'

'No, of course.' Webb lifted a hand as if making a polite refusal. 'Look, he would have died. He was dying. There's no way round that.'

Kate felt herself start to cry, without any warning, without any chance of holding it back. Webb waited, head bowed, reading the

35

pages. 'It hadn't occurred to me,' she said. 'He wouldn't . . . It didn't make a difference?'

Webb pursed his lips and shook his head, but then said, yes. 'Yes, it made a difference. I mean, it wasn't the right thing to do. What I'm telling you is he wouldn't have lived. I'm sure of it. The post-mortem will tell us more, but I've seen a lot of this.'

'He might have lived.'

'No,' Webb said, 'that's the point. He wouldn't have. Not in my opinion.'

A silence fell between them. Webb continued to read, but seemed to have nothing else to say. Finally, Kate asked, 'Maybe I could go now.'

Webb looked up as if startled to find her still there. 'Yes, of course. You're sure we can't make a call for you?'

'Stuart Donnelly,' Kate said. The name had come into her head for no reason that she could think of. Donnelly was a friend of Michael's: a lawyer who had a reputation for being radical. He and Michael had worked together sometimes, Donnelly covering the legal angles, letting Michael know just how far he could go in the face of criminal libel or the Official Secrets Act. She and Donnelly had met half a dozen times or more.

Michael was dead, she was in a police interview room, Donnelly was somewhere at the end of a logical train of thought.

He was a big man, heavy, and he wore his hair long – to mark himself out, perhaps, from clipped and proper colleagues who liked the whole business of striped pants and black jackets and horsehair wigs. He had a reputation for defending difficult cases and, still in his late thirties, was a big earner. He asked Kate a number of questions: how had she been treated, had she given a statement, what had been said to her? And where did she want to go?

'Just take me home, Stuart.'

'To your sister's perhaps? Would that be better?' There was a hint of Scottish in the voice, a faint music.

'I'll call her later. I want to get home.' It was an instinct: to be among your own things, behind your own door; safe.

Donnelly spent some time with George Webb, then took Kate to his car. As they were driving, he said, 'They'll want to see you again, of course.'

'They told me that.'

'And they've kept your jeep. I'm not sure why. You didn't drive Michael home in it last evening, anything like that?'

'He's been in the car, yes, but not for a week or so. I went to Michael's place from the airport. I was supposed to be on my way to Poland. It's ...' She stopped, unable to tell the story again, because it had to end in fear and death.

'Don't worry,' Donnelly said. 'I'll hear it another time.'

Neither spoke for the rest of the journey, except when Kate had to give directions. When they pulled up in front of her flat, Donnelly said, 'There must be someone I can call.'

'I'll do it,' Kate said.

'Shall I come up?'

'No. Thanks. It was very kind ... to come.' Kate smiled apologetically, as if there were a formula for situations such as this, and she'd forgotten the protocol. She opened the car door. 'I thought he'd killed himself. I told him I couldn't go on seeing him. I thought he'd done it because of that.'

'No,' Donnelly said, 'no one thinks that. No one thinks he killed himself.'

She took her clothes off, the clothes that had been draped over a chair in Michael's bedroom, and left them on the floor of the bathroom. She took another shower; *her* shower in *her* flat ... as if she were starting again from a certain point.

She dried herself, and found a nightdress, though she rarely wore anything in bed; she had to unearth it from the bottom of a drawer.

She stood in the middle of her own living room and looked round at the small objects, just as she had in Michael's house, earlier. Little enduring things. Things she owned.

Nothing had changed. The bowl of pot-pourri, a blue vase, books on a shelf, a photograph of Kate herself halfway up a difficult rock-face in the days before a fall had broken her nerve. A pot of pens and pencils on her desk. A miniature bronze of a cellist, set on a low table. Her diary, a stone from a beach somewhere, unopened mail. Nothing had changed.

She turned, slowly, as if making sure of everything, accounting for it. She did the same in each room, getting to the bedroom last. There, she lay down, listening to the build-up of morning traffic in the street.

The ordinariness of that, and the fact that it was light, allowed her to sleep.

She dreamed the photograph: the one of her on a tricky climb. It was just as it had been – as if she were remembering the ascent in every detail, the technical problems, the moments when she went fingertip by fingertip, the moments when the holds were good and the rock firm, so that she was able to walk her way up, arms and legs cranking in alternate rhythm. Michael was already at the summit. He and Stuart Donnelly were chatting together, legs dangling over the drop and looking down at her as she moved towards them; she could hear Stuart's fluting accent. She wanted to say, 'Be careful; it's a hell of a drop. Move back a bit,' but then realised how silly it was to issue instructions to a couple of old hands like Michael and Stuart.

It started to rain, and the rock grew slick. The handholds were narrower. She couldn't work out why in hell she was carrying the equipment pack. It was heavy, and now, to make matters worse, she was going to have to peg on to the wet rock.

She looked up towards them and saw that Michael was holding a CD. He showed it to Stuart, and asked, 'Do you know this guy's stuff?' and the first notes of the Elgar, that first thrilling attack, cascaded down towards her.

She woke immediately and reached for the telephone. When Joanna answered, she said: 'They've got my cello, Jo. It's in the jeep. They've got my bloody cello.'

Five

'Stay here,' Joanna said, 'don't go back there. Don't be alone.'

'Alone's okay,' Kate told her. 'Alone's preferable. No offence, Jo.'

'Then get out of London. Go down to Penarven as I suggested.'

'I think I've got to see them again. This man Webb.'

'What for?'

'Because I was there when it happened. Because I was upstairs when Michael was being murdered downstairs. He thinks I'll remember things I haven't said yet.'

'Will you? I mean, have you?'

'The thing is, I was asleep. I don't know how, but I was. And, in some ways, it's the worst thing. You know, someone in the house, that happening to Michael. He's dead and I'm alive, untouched, you know – *unscathed*. But I was in a shop on the way here, I stopped to get a paper, to see if it was in there, and I thought about being in the house when it was happening, and I started crying. I stood in the middle of this bloody newsagent's and started to sob.'

Joanna was pouring coffee and making Nathan a sandwich and being busy. Busy, busy, busy. She felt cold, as if there had been a sudden temperature drop; she'd been feeling that way since Kate telephoned.

'Me,' Kate said. 'I was crying for me. The thought of me upstairs and a man downstairs killing Michael. Me upstairs in bed, asleep. Me at risk. Me threatened. It's ridiculous. It's shameful.'

'There isn't a proper way to feel,' Joanna said. 'I can't imagine that there are good and bad reactions to something like this. Proper and improper.'

'There was stuff all over the place, Jo. In the kitchen: things thrown around. There must have been a fight. There must have been noise. How in hell did I manage to sleep?'

'You always could.' Joanna opened a drawer and removed a small bunch of keys. She held them out to Kate. 'Take them. If you feel like getting away, just go. Get there early, so you can put the heating on, then shove off to the pub. It only takes a couple of hours to warm up.'

'I might. Okay.' Kate took the keys.

'There are tins of things, there's pasta, and tea and coffee.' Nathan drifted in and collected his sandwich. 'Or stay here with me,' Joanna said. 'Reconsider.'

'Cornwall, perhaps.'

'They must have some sort of a theory, haven't they?' Joanna asked. It had been her second question when Kate had phoned. The first: Are you all right? The second: Why?

'I told them he was working on some project or another. He called it dynamite. And there were a couple of funny phone calls while I was there. They didn't seem that interested.'

'What then?'

'I don't know. They didn't say. Webb — he didn't really say.'

Nathan was watching cartoons in a room down the hall. Each time a silence developed between the sisters, it was filled by crashes and bangs and loony-toon voices. Rat-a-tat music.

Kate spread out the lunchtime paper she'd bought. The story was across pages two and three. Her name was there along with Michael's. 'A break-in, I suppose,' Kate said. 'Someone after drug money. He heard something and went downstairs.' She let Joanna read the paper for a few minutes, then said, 'I told him. The last thing that happened was I told him. We had a row. He hit me.'

'Is that what happened?' Joanna was looking at the bruise on Kate's face. 'Jesus.'

'I shouldn't have stayed. I mean, I wasn't going to.' She shook her head in a puzzled way, as if trying to find reasons. 'It seemed the best thing to do.'

Joanna put her arms round her sister. It wasn't something they did often, and they didn't have a method for it. They looked over one another's shoulder.

40

'I just want it to be gone,' Kate said. 'I want to go back to where it hadn't happened and stay there.'

'You stayed,' George Webb said. He had come to talk to Kate at her flat. WDC Tanner was there. She sat on a chair, knees primly together. Webb was looking round the room, like a browser at a sale. 'He attacked you, but you stayed there with him. Stayed the night.'

'You've got my cello,' Kate said. 'It was in my jeep. I never would have left it in there normally. My mind was on other things. I forgot about it.'

'It's there,' Webb assured her. 'It's in our car park. Perfectly safe. You can have it back any time you like.' He was waiting for an answer.

'I didn't know what else to do. He was upset. It seemed okay.'

'But you hadn't changed your mind?'

'No.'

Webb looked at the rock-face photo. 'Is that you?'

'Yes. I used to —'

'You made love with him. You had sex.'

'It was complicated.'

'Why stay there, if you'd gone to end things between you? Why have sex?'

Kate looked towards Carol Tanner. She was examining her hands. When Kate turned back to Webb, she felt Tanner's gaze lift. 'Things get complicated sometimes,' Kate said, 'don't you find that?'

'You went there to end it. He attacked you. You then had sex with him. I'm just trying to get this straight. A sort of order of play.'

'It's all I can tell you. I went to sleep. When I woke up —'

'— just after three —'

'— Michael wasn't in bed. I went down to find him. You know all this.'

'Just in case,' Webb told her. 'Just in case something comes to mind.'

*　*　*

Kate lay awake, listening and watching: night noises; the glow of her clock; the pie-slice shadow from the half-closed door. After an hour or so, she got up. It was just after three a.m. She packed quickly: sweaters, jeans, T-shirts, walking boots. She went down to the jeep carrying her bag and the Canadian jacket.

At that time of night, it was easy to get out of London. The roads were never empty, but the serious nose-to-tail traffic was still parked in suburban streets and driveways. The late-night streets, as always, had an air of faint hysteria about them, an element of risk. She drove quickly, getting through intersections on amber, or when the lights had just snapped to red, and came onto the motorway with a sense of elation. The traffic there was mostly coaches and trucks. Five hours later, she was driving up the narrow track that led to Joanna's cottage. It stood on its own, on rising ground with a small oak wood at its back. It was a mile or so from the village: Penarven. If you looked down from the sloping front garden, you got a view of three fields falling away to the sea.

Kate bumped across the rough ground alongside the cottage and parked the jeep at the back, alongside a row of shabby timber outbuildings. The jeep was right for the terrain, Kate thought. Suddenly it looked at home; apart, perhaps, from the aquamarine panels. She unlocked the place, dumped her bag, then got back into the jeep and drove another nine miles to the nearest town and found a café where she could get scrambled eggs and coffee. After she had eaten, she walked down to the quay and out along one arm of the crab-shaped harbour, so that nothing was before her but the sea, running green and grey against the blunt stone wall. The wind was warm but blowing strongly, and piling white caps along the wave-tops.

It's a dream, she thought. None of it happened. I told him I couldn't see him again, and here I am, recovering in Cornwall while he recovers in London.

The town was busy when she walked back towards the jeep.

She bought some fresh fish, vegetables, bread, fruit, a bottle of whisky. She couldn't connect with anything. She felt ill; or if not ill, crazy. All that made her glad was that no one there knew who she was, and no one cared.

Six

George Webb ran a good team. They all worked towards a common end, and there were few mistakes. No one was allowed an ego, not even Webb. The information they collected, the guesses they made, the evidence they gathered, was part of a common wealth. A commonwealth. It was one of Webb's pep talks.

He toured the room, looking at pin-boards displaying photographs, abstracts of reports, keynotes from statements, diagrams. There was a colour close-up of Michael Lester's wound. There was an exploded view of the house, with blood-splashes highlighted and analysed. DS John Adams was working at a VDU, checking the house-to-house.

Webb peered at the screen. 'What?'

'Nothing,' Adams told him. 'The important people down there don't have a lager and a tandoori in front of the telly. They're out mixing with other important people. Or else the other important people are round their place for dinner, and they're all drinking and talking and cracking quails' eggs and failing to notice the murder that's going on down the road.'

Webb laughed. He said, 'I just talked to Mrs Metcalf again.'

'The woman with the dog.'

'That's her.'

'Same story . . .?'

'Same story with a bit of embellishment. He gave her a smack, all right. Mrs Metcalf was going to call the police.'

'Why didn't she?'

'He stopped smacking and started yelling. She thought that was better. And her dog needed a dump. She's a good witness; rock-solid.'

Adams brought up a new screen: the file content of Michael Lester's computer. Webb got closer. 'Nothing that matters,' Adams observed. 'Old stuff. Nothing before the fifteenth . . . What's that: a week since, isn't it?'

'We've checked his disks?' Webb asked.

'Yes . . .' Adams said; meaning: there's a strange thing. 'Disks. We couldn't find any.'

Webb straightened up. 'Well, who knows?' he said. 'Who knows about that? It's odd, but . . . who knows? Maybe they're at his office.'

'Does he have an office?'

'Whatever. Wherever.' He pulled a chair over from a nearby desk, and sat alongside Adams. 'It's late,' he said, and Adams knew that meant time for a drink. He took a bottle of Scotch from his desk drawer, and he and Webb lit new cigarettes. Farmers eat beef. Policemen smoke. Adams was tall and skinny, all elbows and angles. His stubble was very dark, like a tattoo, and made his lips seem unnaturally pink.

'Tell me what I'm thinking,' Webb instructed.

Adams nodded. 'He was nuts about her. She called round to give him the bad news. He gave her a smacking. She's not the sort of woman to take kindly to that.'

'So she killed him.' Webb was smiling.

'No, that's not it. He smacked her, he went crazy, he yelled a lot, he calmed down. Everything looked okay. Soon she'd be able to go home. Mission accomplished. But he hadn't calmed down. Not really. She went to go: he wasn't having it. Once she's out of the house, that's it – gone forever; never see her again. He imprisoned her. Made her a captive.'

'Locked the door –'

'– the door was open –'

'She unlocked it, that's later, trying to escape, the door was as far as she got.'

'Okay.'

'Or else she unlocked it after he was dead. An open door supports the intruder theory. Some druggie after the video.'

'Okay.'

'He made her a prisoner. She tried to get away. Another fight, maybe more wrestling this time, more body contact, he's angry, he's thinking about losing her, thinking that her mind is already somewhere else, maybe *with* someone else . . .'

'And he fucks her.'

'Rapes her, right. He rapes her.'

'Which is why she owns up to it. Says they made love.'

'But it's something else – he rapes her. And it's . . . what would you say?'

'Self-defence. She might want to say self-defence.'

'She didn't mean to do it.'

'It started as a threat, okay: "Keep away from me". He's raped her. That's over. Well, it's over for now . . . And she wants to get away, of course she does.'

'But he doesn't want to let her go.'

'She's still his prisoner. He's obliged to keep things that way. At least, until he's worked out what to do. He's still fired up. If he lets her go, who knows what she'll do?'

'She's going towards the kitchen door. He says, "No", maybe stands in front of the door, grabs her arm, pushes her back.'

'There's the knife on the table. Just a threat. "Get out of my way, I mean it" sort of thing.'

'And he comes at her.'

'Absolutely.'

'To get it off her.'

'Right.'

'Yes . . . It's interesting that you should see it that way,' Webb said, 'because I've been doing some thinking along those lines, too.'

Adams closed down the computer and poured two more drinks. 'What have we got?' he asked. 'In reality.'

'Not much. Everything, but not much. However, there's forensic yet to come.' Webb looked round the room, as if more and better evidence might flag itself in some way. 'Think of something else. Think of alternatives.'

'Some druggie after the video.'

Webb laughed. 'Sure. Of course. What else? So, we'll have to wait for forensic. See if you can push them along.' He got up and stretched and downed his drink. 'We'll keep everything else up and running: lines of enquiry.'

'Do you want anyone else to talk to her?' Adams asked.

Webb shook his head and yawned. 'She'll be fine. She'll be no trouble.'

Kate was having dreams. She would fall asleep, and dream, and wake, and fall asleep again, and the dream would come back. Or a different dream. None of them was about Michael, but they were all about death.

After the fourth dream, she got out of bed and went downstairs to the kitchen. She put lights on so that the whole house threw a glow into the night: the little gardens back and front, the pastureland beyond. She unlocked, found a torch, put on the Canadian coat, and went out. She started down the track that led to the fields that led to the sea. Images from the dreams were still with her, colouring the night.

There was a three-quarter moon and a stiff wind blowing. Kate sat on the cliff top, head bowed because the wind was stealing her breath. Michael's eyes lay behind her own eyes when she closed them – his stare, the pupils clouding. She saw the zero his lips made, the freckles of blood. Something in his face was fading, withdrawing, as if a lifeline were slowly unravelling in his grip.

She walked a mile along the coastal path, using the faint glow of moonlight off the sea to guide her. Blackthorn bushes whipped and flurried round her head. She thought it was good to be out there, alone, a long way from people, a long way from London.

Sometimes she heard noises: animals moving in the verges; or heard their cries. She came out of the tunnel of blackthorn to some pasture, and two horses swerved and turned in the darkness, galloping away from her approach, a racket of thudding hooves.

All this was happening at the edge of her attention, so deep was she inside her own imaginings.

The knife, when she withdrew it, made a strange squeak. A creak. A slithering squeak. The lips of the wound puckered.

Michael's eyes, Michael's face, seemed covered with dark gauze. Moment by moment, a new layer was laid, darkening his features, making his expression more and more difficult to read. The light going out.

She came to a coastguard observation point, a flat-topped cubicle with, for some reason, a picket fence round it, and used that as an excuse to head back. It would have been just as easy to keep going.

The cottage was a little beacon, all lights burning. She hung the Canadian coat on a peg on the back door, kicked off her boots, and lay down on the sofa. She was asleep in seconds.

The dreams returned as if she had never left them.

Seven

Stuart Donnelly said, 'Listen, wait a moment, I'm not sure you quite understand. I'm not sure I understand. But Kate Randall isn't my client.'

'No?' Webb asked. 'I thought . . . when you collected her from –'

'No. I'm a friend of Michael Lester's. Was a friend. We'd worked together a few times, and there was a bit of a social life. I met Kate as Michael's partner.'

'You're not her brief?'

'I'm not.'

Donnelly had asked for coffee to be sent in. Webb was stirring his without drinking it. 'Can you tell me where she is, though?'

'You've got her address . . . phone number . . .?'

'Oh, yes.'

'Not there?'

'No.'

'Her sister's.'

'Okay,' Webb said. He put down his coffee spoon and took out a pen, but Donnelly was already writing the information down for him. He handed a slip of paper across his desk.

'I did tell her that you'd probably want to talk to her again.'

'We have,' Webb assured him. 'A few times.'

'Are you getting anywhere?'

Webb shrugged. 'Yes, I think so. I think we are.'

'Can you tell me?'

'We're charging her with murder. When we find her, that is.'

Donnelly looked at Webb for a moment, as if he'd missed some vital link in what the man was saying. 'Kate Randall?' he laughed. 'Good God.'

'Why? Why "Good God"? It hadn't occurred to you?'

'My mind hadn't gone in that direction, no.' Donnelly looked out of the window, as if he might see Kate hurrying by, looking guilty. 'You're sure?'

'Yes.'

'Why are you telling me?'

'Well, she's going to need representation, you know each other, you've some knowledge of the case . . . More than that, she might get in touch with you. You can let me know where she is; or tell her that I'd like to talk to her.'

'But not that you intend to charge her with murder.'

'No. Not that.'

'What have you got?' Donnelly was acting like a brief, now.

'Lots. Forensic, mostly. Witnesses. Pretty good guess at motive.' And Webb was acting like a copper. 'More than anything, the fact that it's far and away the most likely solution, as you know.'

'Do I?'

'Lovers fight. Passions run high. Heat of the moment.'

'Intruders intrude,' Donnelly observed.

'Look out of your window,' Webb said. 'I'll bet you that the next bird to fly by is a pigeon. There's always a chance that it'll be an albatross, I grant you. But I think it'll be a pigeon.' He smiled and drank his coffee. 'How many times have you seen it? A domestic. Some go further than others.'

'She told you about the job he was working on,' Donnelly supposed. 'He made enemies, there's little doubt of that.'

'No, she didn't.'

'No?'

'She told me there *was* a job, but she didn't tell me about it, because she didn't know what there was to tell. If indeed there was a job. She's the only person to have mentioned it.' Webb shook his head. 'Of course journalists make enemies. They've sometimes made an enemy of me. A knife in the gut for an unkind word — I've never heard of anything like that. Have you?'

'He must have made notes . . . there must be material relating to —'

'You'd certainly think so. Nothing on his computer. In fact, he hadn't used the machine for a while. No floppy disk. No written notes. To all intents and purposes, he was having something of a fallow period.'

'Murder? Or manslaughter?'

'That's for the DPP.' Webb finished his coffee in one go. 'So, if she calls . . .'

'Yes,' Donnelly said. Then, 'Listen, I don't think so. I don't think you've got this right at all.'

'There you go,' Webb observed. 'A denial already. I expect to see you in court.'

Joanna sat down, then stood up again. She put a hand to her mouth. She said, 'Leave. Would you leave, please?' It was as much as she could say without choking.

'Yes, sure, of course.' Webb backed off towards the living-room door; WDC Tanner backed off. Through the window, Joanna could see a black van parked in the road. A man in a helmet and bulky, sleeveless jacket walked across her lawn and went towards the back of the house. Three others followed him.

'We'll leave. It would help us if you'd let us have a look round the house.'

'No. I just want you to go.'

'Or we could come back and do that in an hour or so. That would be without your consent, of course.'

'My son is upstairs. He's six. He's away from school with a heavy cold. He's up there in bed.'

'I'll be the meter man,' Webb said. 'I'm good with kids.' He waved his hand towards the street. 'Or I can send this lot in on their own just a bit later. They make a lot of noise, I'm afraid.' He laughed. 'They scare *me*.'

Joanna went with them. Webb and Tanner and one other officer took the upper floor. Nathan was sleeping when they went in. Webb opened Nathan's closet. Next, he pulled out the little camp the boy had made under his bed: an old duvet, some cardboard boxes, soft toys, stolen biscuits. Joanna wanted to kill him. She wanted him to die of leprosy. Nathan woke as they were leaving and gave Webb a wide-eyed look. Webb looked straight through him.

Downstairs, other AMIP men were at the front door ready to leave. Webb smiled and said, 'If your sister gets in touch with you, you are legally obliged to tell us everything you can. It's an offence not to. You understand that?'

Joanna stared him out. She said, 'You're crazy to think what you're thinking. You're out of your fucking mind.'

'Where's that?' Webb asked. He was looking past Joanna at a snap-frame crowded with photographs, one of several pictures in the hallway. He went closer, brushing past Joanna to do so. Nathan appeared at the top of the stairs and looked down at the uniforms and helmets. Several of the men were wearing holstered guns.

'This is a holiday place, is it?' Photos of Joanna and Nathan and Nick, when being a family was still possible; of Joanna and Nathan on their own; of friends; all taken at Penarven: the cottage, the garden, the oak wood; of Kate in a straw hat, sunbathing, Kate setting out for a winter walk, Kate standing in the smoke of the barbecue. 'Somewhere by the sea?'

'Cornwall. Penarven. Near there.'

'So,' Webb reminded her. 'If she calls, or turns up here, or you think you know where she might be . . .' He handed Joanna a business card.

'I don't,' Joanna said. 'I would have expected her to be at home: at her flat.'

Webb waved up the stairs to Nathan, a jolly smile, and the boy waved back.

Donnelly phoned ten minutes after the police had left. He said, 'If you know where Kate is, the best thing is to tell them.'

'I don't know. But would you expect me to do that? Without letting Kate know? Who is this man Webb? I can't –' Joanna broke off and put the phone down. She could hear Donnelly talking. She said, 'Wait! Wait a bit!' loudly enough to be heard. She was in the kitchen, making something for Nathan's lunch. She leaned against the work surface, breathing hard; she felt dizzy; her heart was knocking in her throat. She stayed still for a minute or more. When she picked up, Donnelly was still there.

'It's ludicrous,' she said. 'Anyone who knows her would know that.'

'I'd better tell you,' Donnelly said, 'that almost every relative of every accused person says that. They all say it. They all feel it. Except for the professional criminals, of course. Criminals are a class apart.'

'It's . . . Now that they've gone, it's as if nothing's happening. None of it's happening.'

'I know what you mean,' Donnelly said.

Joanna stayed silent. She was trying to think what best to say. She was suffering a weird sense of separation from what was happening; as if a second Kate was wanted by the police, and a second Joanna was on the phone to Stuart Donnelly. Ordinary lives aren't built to cope with such events. She said, 'What should I do?'

'Okay. Well. Do you know where she is?'

'Yes. I mean, I might. I didn't lie to them.'

'Didn't tell them either – didn't tell them your guess.'

'No.'

'Christ . . .' It was a sigh of irritation.

'But I think they know. He saw a frame of photos of our place in Cornwall, and asked a lot of questions about it.'

'You think she's there?'

'Look, she could have gone to France. Or Poland: she was supposed to be touring there and she talked about wanting to see the country. She was also talking about skiing. Maybe she found a resort somewhere.'

'Or she could be in Cornwall.'

'It's possible.'

'Tell them.'

'Does that mean: If you don't, I will?'

'No, it doesn't. I don't know where she is any more than you do. And in any case, I haven't been asked.'

'What would you do, then, if you were me? If you had been asked?'

'Tell them.'

'Would you tell your sister first?' A pause. Joanna said, 'Hello . . .?'

'We haven't had this conversation, Joanna. We haven't spoken.'

There was no answering machine at the cottage. Kate had walked into the village and picked up some food. She hadn't bought a paper. When she was almost home, it had started to rain, a cold, heavy fall that came out of nowhere, blowing up across the cliff and slanting inland. The phone was ringing when she walked in, and stopped before she could get to it. She stowed the food in the fridge and put some coffee on. She was feeling for her wallet – so many pockets in that coat; the simplest thing to do was to scrunch it with your fist until you met resistance. That was when she felt the shape of the floppy disk. She hunted it down to the tail pocket and took it out. The label said, 'Dynamite: remember?' She was drinking coffee and deciding what the disk might mean, when the phone rang again.

After she had listened for a minute, a little more than a minute, perhaps, she put the phone down and walked through to the living room and the front window. The lane below the rising ground was empty. A dozen gulls were floating in on the wind, backed by a sky of fast-moving white-grey cloud.

She went back to the phone. What amazed her, what made her feel stranger than anything, was the fact that she felt calm.

'Why do they think that?' she asked Joanna. 'What makes them think it?'

'They didn't say. Stuart Donnelly says they believe they've got a case.'

'They'll show up here soon enough, won't they?'

'I'm pretty certain he knew. He looked at the photos.'

'They didn't ask you where the cottage is? How to find it?'

'No.'

'The local people will know. Their Cornish colleagues.'

'It was about midday,' Joanna said. 'It would take them a good four –' She broke off. 'No, of course. The police down there.' Neither sister spoke for a moment; then Joanna said, 'You sound okay.'

'I am okay. It's ludicrous. What they're saying is ludicrous.'

'I told them that. What will you do?'

'Wait. What else?'

She put the coat on as if about to go out, but sat at the kitchen table, watching the rain falling in strong, oblique lines across the back pasture. As she watched, it lifted suddenly, then stopped. The ground was sodden.

She wrapped the floppy disk in a polythene food bag and put it on a ledge inside the chimney, to the right of the ingle.

She went through to the living room, and sat at the window there, so she could watch the lane. A line of drips from the guttering creased the glass, coming like clockwork, hypnotic and compelling.

She invented their theories for them. She made up the dialogue. She set the scene.

The row. Michael hitting her. Tears, pleas, refusals . . . things quietening down, only to flare up again in the kitchen. Michael really violent, now. And she really scared.

He comes towards her, fist raised. She takes up the knife.

The row. Things quietening down. Michael and Kate in bed. Her revulsion, realising it was a mistake, Michael seeing the disgust on her face. Her flight to the kitchen.

He comes after her. She takes up the knife.

She hadn't meant to. *I didn't mean to.*

It's just one movement, one attempt to get free, one gesture. Without the knife, it's a shove; a punch at worst.

I didn't mean to.

It made sense. She could see it all. From their point of view, she could see it all.

More than anything, she needed time to think. At present, she had too much time, and too little. Less time would have left her no option. More time would have allowed her to work out what best to do.

She thought of the first step, then the second, then . . . First: herself on the drive back to London. Then in a cell. *I can't do that.* Being charged. Then the courtroom. How long did all that take? Months. *I can't* . . . Then the prosecution putting their case. And they had a case. Stuart Donnelly had told Joanna that they thought they had a case. *No, I can't do that.*

Too long to think; not enough time to think.

And, in the end, all her thinking came to nothing, because when she looked down and saw them in the lane, two cars nose to nose, a van a little way off, when she saw the men moving up towards the house, their uniforms, their guns, when she saw all this activity, she acted on instinct.

Without thinking, she put on the Canadian jacket. Without thinking, she left by the back door and ran across to the jeep parked alongside the outhouses. She started the engine and drove directly up the hill towards the oak wood. The boundary to Joanna's property was marked with a shaky wire-and-post fence and a wicker-weave gate. The jeep's bull-bars took out the gate. Then she was jouncing over mud ridges and thin turf and scree, driving the edge of the wood, looking for a way through.

I can't do that. I'm not ready for that.

The cars came past the house and into the back pasture, revving furiously, the drivers looking for a purchase on the slope. They needed to be in low gear, not cutting the turf too badly, and turning aside from the ruts if they could. It wasn't easy. The lead car caught the edge of a sudden dip in the ground and came down hard on the offside wheel, catching the axle. The impact made the driver bite his tongue, and he howled, putting one hand to his mouth while the other yanked at the steering wheel. When he accelerated, the car slewed. He slammed from first into reverse, then back again, then again, trying to rock the vehicle free. The second car went round him, crabbing and climbing, kicking up showers of turf. It caught the gate under its wheels and ploughed a furrow with it, before the angle of the frame came round and lodged under the chassis. The car stopped and a man got out. He ran to the front of the car and started to wrestle the gate free. The driver backed off to give him a better chance, and the car slithered twenty feet down the slope.

The uniformed man in charge of the operation was an inspector called Jim Sorley. He was calling in: 'Suspect absconded, in pursuit'. Except they weren't, not really. He watched the first car rock free, and the second begin to snake up towards the trees, but he knew that 'pursuit' didn't really describe what was going on. He was asking for area coverage, roadblocks and helicopter support.

One car skirting woodland, the other making a slow, careful turn that brought it back to the house. Sorley climbed in and they drove back to the lane. He made radio contact with the car on the crest. They had sight of the jeep and gave location and direction.

'Fuck it,' Sorley said. The driver was taking the lane heart-stoppingly fast, siren and lights going. 'Fuck-fuck-fuck it.'

The rain had come back. Up on the high ground, the driver of the second car nudged the downward slope, like a swimmer testing the water. The jeep was crossing a field and heading for a minor road about a mile and a half away, twin plumes of water rising from the cross-country tyres. The police car edged down the hill, lost traction, skidded, corrected, then travelled sideways for fifty feet before turning round completely and rear-ending a tree. In the same moment, the jeep hit the road, fishtailed, and drove out of sight.

Sorley was in the back of the first car, holding a map. There was another officer in the passenger seat. 'It's likely that she doesn't know where she's going. It's also likely that she's not stupid, which means she'll assume that we'll be coming at her from several directions. Sooner rather than later, she's going to have to abandon the jeep. Where would you go?'

The non-driver was watching the road with a fierce intensity: watching the bends, watching the concealed intersections. Fence-posts blended to a blur. Without turning round, he said, 'Two possibilities. Try to get a lift. Maybe a truck. Or else hole up and think things through.' His voice seemed a little high, and a little shaky.

'If she keeps to the route she's chosen, she'll reach a major road in fifteen minutes. But will she make it?'

The radio told them that a helicopter was in the sky and searching.

'She's caught,' the non-driver said. 'There's nowhere for her to go.'

'You're right,' said Sorley, 'she's caught.'

The road was wide enough for one large car, but not wide enough for two small ones. They were travelling between tall hedgerows. They met a dip in the road and were airborne for what seemed a long time. The driver clipped the verge, corrected, clipped the opposite verge, and found his line again. He was having a good time; smiling a secret and invisible smile.

Kate stayed on the road for a mile, then found a gate entrance to a broad field. She pulled off the road and up to the gate, opened it, drove through, closed the gate again. The field sloped downwards which, in that landscape, usually meant seawards. She thought it was a footpath route to the town, but wasn't sure of that, any more than she knew why she was going cross-country. Something to do with avoiding other vehicles. She wasn't reasoning well, but she knew they would be looking to cut her off. Buying time was the only plan she had in mind. She saw herself finding a call box, speaking to George Webb, dictating terms of some sort. Letting him know that whatever he thought, she hadn't killed Michael. Asking to hear something of his evidence . . . this *evidence* they said they had.

The jeep dug in across the terrain, slewing a little, but never losing traction. Kate thought she would find a place to ditch the vehicle, somewhere close to town, then walk in and try to find a ride. Then she topped a little rise, and felt the ground go from under her.

It was a terrace of some sort, or else the trench left when a hedge had been grubbed up. The jeep came off the rise and nose-dived. It was like driving into a dry moat. The seatbelt held her, but drove the breath from her body. The engine stalled and the vehicle tipped, but didn't go over: at least, not at first. That happened when Kate started the engine, and tried to get traction from the front wheels: her only hope, since the back wheels were airborne. The tyres churned and spat mud up under the chassis, then the jeep lurched and turned turtle, slowly, coming down on its roof with a crackle of denting metal. It rocked back and forth a couple of times, then settled. Kate stayed still for two or maybe three minutes. She was trying to regulate her breathing; she was also waiting for the strong feeling of nausea to pass.

Eventually, she released the seat belt, at the same time grabbing the headrest of the passenger seat. This allowed her to lower herself into the roof space and get to the door catch. She levered it back and the door part-opened, then stuck. She kicked hard, using the heel of her boot; there was a grinding sound, then the door flew back.

As she stepped out, she heard at once the *whup-whup-whup* of rotor blades. The chopper was further away than it sounded, maybe half a mile back and headed in the wrong direction, but she knew that unless her luck was phenomenal, they must see her soon. It was a bug-copter, the shape of a dragonfly, the pod big enough for two men. At the far end of the field was a small wood of scrub oak and beech, stunted by the inshore, salt winds. Without looking back at the chopper, Kate started to run towards the wood, a direct line across open ground.

She hit the trees and found cover. Then she looked back. The helicopter was circling: banking so that the rotors caught the light of the sun as it pushed through clouds. The pilot seemed to be about to head out to sea — going round to search the next cove, perhaps — and Kate thought, *Christ, they're going to miss me.* But even as she thought it, the craft tilted, and banked, and came back fast, making a direct line for the field and the jeep. It made two passes over the ditched vehicle, rocking to and fro, then circled again to pass over the wood.

Kate had already moved back into cover among the trees. The pod was overhead and low, and she felt its presence as a shrew feels a hawk. She found an eyeline through to the field, and saw that the pilot was quartering the pasture, looking for level ground. There was none, but he sidled in sideways close to the jeep and held the undercarriage a couple of feet off the turf, just above the deep rut where the vehicle had foundered. A second man opened his door, climbed out onto the landing bars and dropped into the field.

The wood was all wind-noise and pea-green light. The trees were widely spaced, a little undergrowth and some saplings between, but enough room for Kate to keep up a steady jog. Her rhythm was that of the gym treadmill: the rhythm of three times a week except for touring dates; she knew her pace and she knew how to be economical with movement.

Her thoughts were clearer now; running helped. She realised there was little chance of making it to the town. The men in the helicopter hadn't seen her, but it wouldn't take a genius to calculate her likely distance from the crash based on the last sighting they'd had of her. The answer would be: not far. They'd saturate the area: likely routes out, and likely places to hole up. Roads would be monitored, especially close to town. Barns and outbuildings, cafés and truckers' stops. And woodland.

Instinct had already made the decision for her: most of the time, she was running downhill, not climbing towards farmland, not jogging along one of the paths emerging in sight of farms and the first few houses. She didn't have sight of the sea, but knew it couldn't be more than a mile distant. And the same instinct that had turned her in that direction was also at work in telling her what to do next. Not providing an answer: there was no answer. Not guaranteeing her safety: she was about as unsafe as she could be. It simply had to do with certain images of self-preservation that every creature has at the back of its brain: find a small place, find a dark place, get as far in as you can go, stay quiet, stay still, wait for the hunter to give up and go away.

She came out of the wood on a high field above the sea. The sun was threading between clouds and throwing flashes of brilliance on the water: a vast signal-mirror in a clumsy hand. Before her was the field, a fence, then the coastal path, then a high, steep cliff above a tight horseshoe bay. Since she had started to run, she'd covered four miles or more over rough ground. It wasn't the limit of her capability, but she felt it was close. She took a breather, standing in the grey-green shadow of the trees at the fringe. Important to save something for that last run down to the cliff path; important to make sure that she was alone when she broke cover.

The harder she looked, the more things seemed to stir at the edges of her vision. As if figures had risen – heads and shoulders – just above that far dip where the field fell away, only to back off quickly when she looked. As if a line of men had emerged from the blackthorn that separated the field from the path, then melted back among the branches when her head turned towards them. She looked until her eyes ached. All she could guarantee was sheep and gulls.

She covered the two hundred yards between trees and path at a dead run, looking neither right nor left, and broke through the hedge at a point where a farm vehicle had already done some damage. The path seemed a more dangerous place than any other, and she ran it as fast as she dared, the desire to find a route down to the sea fighting with a fear of rounding the next bend and seeing her pursuers coming straight at her. The cliff was too steep to descend: a near-vertical tangle of thorn bush and briar. She felt exposed, as if a spotlight were on her and tracking her as she ran. She didn't want to meet anyone. Even a pensioner with a poodle was dangerous: capable of remembering, capable of lifting a telephone.

After ten minutes, she came out onto a bald spit of headland, where a path had been worn into the cliff face. It was slight and very steep, but people had been down there before her. Kate followed it, shuffling against the vertical and leaning backwards. The path followed a long diagonal and she walked with the sea always before her, long slicks of sunlight running across the swell. Gulls were riding the thermals above her head, holding position just light of the cliff edge.

She went down, listening all the time for the blunt chug of rotor blades. The sunlight dazzled her. She heard nothing but the wind and the cries of gulls.

Find a small place, find a dark place.

The cave had a leaf-shaped entrance, narrow and tapering, and Kate had to squat down to get in. She shuffled over fine sand, packed hard, and a shingle of granite and quartz pebbles. After a few yards, the space opened up, and she could stand – just – inside the tiny, dark vault. She waited for her eyes to adjust, then walked from side to side; at its widest, the cave took five paces. For all she could see, it could have stretched back forever: there was enough light to make out the point where the cave seemed to end, but then there was a fold in the rock, which might have been a turning, might have been a dead end. She felt her way back, fingers tickling the walls, feet tapping the small boulders and outcrops on the cave floor. She went on level ground for ten paces, then came to a rockpile that led up to a little plateau. What had seemed a dogleg was the back of the cave: cul-de-sac.

Get in as far as you can go.

Kate found a place to sit. The cave mouth seemed a mile away; it also seemed close enough to touch. She felt secure, or she felt trapped, she couldn't decide which. All she could hear was the sound of the sea. All she could see was the swell, sometimes green, sometimes gold-and-green when the clouds moved away from the sun. She was waiting for the sound of voices. Waiting for a silhouette as someone ducked down into the leaf-shaped cut of light.

Stay quiet, stay still, wait for the hunter to give up and go away.

Dark fell at seven. She had slept on and off, hit by the exhaustion fear brings, and coddled in the cave's deepening darkness.

The tide had turned without her noticing it. Now it was too late to try for the beach. There was no beach. She could hear the rustling of wings in the roof, five feet, no more, above her head; she could hear the slap and patter of waves against the cave mouth. She waited for every third wave, always the strongest, and judged things by that. She thought the cave would fill; she thought there was no doubt of it.

I didn't kill him.

Take it out, he'd said, his voice shrill and high. She'd grasped the handle of the knife. The blade as it withdrew made a squeak. A creak. There was a geyser of blood.

A third wave broke into the cave, soaking her boots and the bottoms of her jeans.

I didn't kill him.

But no one believes that.

Eight

Webb felt like an eavesdropper. He felt like a tourist. One copper on another copper's patch. There are handshakes and warm smiles and very little trust. He stood at the back of the briefing room, waiting for Jim Sorley to call him forward. This area of operations was a hunt for a fugitive, nothing complicated, nothing tricky, and Webb leaned on a door jamb, eyes half closed, as he listened to Sorley giving an update. He was pointing at a greatly enlarged section of an OS map.

'We lost her here: this cottage, about a mile from Penarven. She was seen driving this road –' he slapped the map '– and seemed to be heading for the motorway. The helicopter found her jeep here: in the middle of farmland. It was inverted and the bull bars had shoved through to the engine. A mess. No sign of any blood in the cabin or on the surrounding grass, so we assume she came out of it okay. However, even though there's no evidence of harm, she might have broken a limb, or be concussed. We've put as many men on the ground as possible.' His audience numbered ten, all ranking officers. 'You, and the men assigned to you, are their replacements. I'm working a shift. You each have a copy of the rota.

'Our starting point is the jeep. From there we're radiating out: farms, farm buildings, woodland. Woodland is bloody difficult. It's not as if we can use beaters to flush her out. Our best guess is that she'll try to get out of the area by cadging a lift, so we're checking approach roads, petrol stations, roadside pull-ins. On the outside chance that she got further than we think, we're also looking at motorway service stations on the eastern and western carriageways, but that's very unlikely. We're looking at harbours and marinas, too, but that's a long shot; we're not wasting much time over it. Basically, she's boxed-in and we're going to find her. She needs food and liquid and eventually she'll need shelter. Our only problem is that it's a big area and inevitably we're spread thin.' Sorley paused and looked to the back of the room. 'DI Webb,' he said.

Webb stayed where he was, letting the audience turn to him. All he said was, 'She's wanted for questioning in relation to the murder of Michael Alan Lester. You've had a description: she's thirty-four, slight build, fair hair worn shoulder length. We're working on getting a photograph of her, but I hope that by the time it's ready for distribution the woman herself will be with us. Officially, we're saying she's not to be approached, but that's for the punters. She's a middle-class girl and she'll be no bother.' He shrugged. 'I had her and I lost her, that's about it. And I want her back.'

One of the audience half lifted a hand. 'Did she kill him, boss?'

'Definitely,' Webb told him.

Kate had been in retreat — first the floor of the cave, then the muddle of rock, then the dark vee, the false turning, the escape that was no escape. Now she was standing on the highest part of the granite lip in the deepest part of the cave, and the water was round her waist. She thought that she would wait another ten minutes. Another five. After that, if the level rose, she would try to swim out. There was no hope of her making it to land — she knew her capabilities — but it was better than standing still and waiting to drown in the dark.

She was cold. That was the other factor, the other problem. She was so cold that she wasn't sure whether her limbs would obey her. She tried to imagine what it would be like: that first plunge. The mouth of the cave was gone, engulfed by the sea. She would have to swim down to find it. To be that mobile she would have to take off her clothes. She tried to remember how long people could survive in such conditions, though it probably didn't matter that much. Joanna had been the swimmer during those long outdoor summer holidays. Kate could always make a ten-mile walk in driving rain, or go at a dizzying rock-face, or use a map and compass to get back from the middle of nowhere. Swimming had always bored her: plough up, plough down, lousy view. She could manage the equivalent of four lengths, maybe, and that in good conditions.

She waited the five minutes, and couldn't detect any difference. Another five, and she still couldn't make up her mind. She put her hand on her belt buckle; the water was about at that level: a little lower when the wave-pulse retreated, a little higher as it flowed in. Ten minutes after that, she was still in the cave. The water had neither risen, she thought, nor fallen. Fifteen minutes later, she saw a tiny fragment of light, a crescent, and realised it was the uppermost curve of the cave mouth coming clear of the waterline.

Kate leaned back against the granite and closed her eyes. She fell asleep in that position, and slept on as the water inched down her legs, as the wedge of light grew thicker and brighter, as the echo of waves on the cave walls grew fainter. She woke again after thirty minutes, giving a leap of shock because she didn't know how long she'd been asleep. The entrance to the cave was filled with light from the three-quarter moon and the sea water was falling back with every wave. She couldn't get any wetter, so she waded calf-deep through the surf and came out onto the shingle. More than anything, she was cold. More than anything, she wanted shelter and something hot to drink.

The sky was clear: which for Kate meant no searchlights, no sound of helicopters. She sloshed through water that came knee-deep, then almost thigh-deep, then just ankle-deep as she got back to the cliff path. She waited in the lee of the cliff, listening, but heard nothing apart from the sea and the wind. The climb seemed long, and made her breathless. She looked up at every step of the way, watching for torchlight. When she finally made the summit, she sat down and put her head in her hands. It was fear that had weakened her, she knew that. She walked for a hundred yards or more, continuing in the direction she'd originally taken, and found a place where she could get off the path and onto the farmland that bordered it. The field that she came into had been sown with beet. She crossed the furrows, climbing at an angle to take a more commanding view of the cliff path.

No lights. No voices.

There was a windbreak hedge on the far side. Kate found a gap and hunkered down on the leeward side. After a minute, she stood up and stripped off her boots, socks, jeans and briefs: all sodden. The Canadian coat was wet below the waistline, but otherwise dry. She spread her clothes on the hedge, anchoring them by weaving them between the branches. Her jeans, she fixed further, using her belt. The inshore wind was strong and Kate was shivering; the sea water had been very cold. She stood, half naked, and bent to chafe her thighs. She slapped at her buttocks and lower legs. The climb up from the beach had done some good; now she worked at taking the numbness out completely.

After a while, her legs tingling and sore, she tied the sleeves of the coat about her waist, wrapped the quilted material round her legs, and sat behind the hedge, knees to chin.

Moonlight travelled across the pasture in swathes, chased by cloudshadow. A pair of hunting owls called back and forth. There was a hint of frost in the air.

I'm not going to make it, she thought.

Webb sat at the window of his hotel room, the light off, a glass of whisky in his hand. He'd brought his own bottle in. He could smell the sea, but a row of houses prevented him from seeing it.

He had slept for a couple of hours, then woken, disturbed by the fugginess of the air conditioning and the noise of people getting back late to the room next to his. Now they had switched on the TV and were raiding the minibar. They'd had a great night so far, and it wasn't over yet.

Just past three a.m. Three-fifteen, in fact, when he looked at the clock-radio built into the bedhead.

He thought, I had a doubt or two, then you ran. Now I know. Why else would you run? Domestics: they're simple. It looks like what it is. The problem is, no one knows how easy it is. How *easy* it is to kill another person.

He was talking himself into it. He'd been talking himself into it all along.

How *easy* it is. Without the knife, it's a punch, a defensive gesture. With the knife in your hand – hey, the man's dead. Suddenly he's dead.

You didn't mean it.

He sat for ten minutes or so, listening to the *wash-wash* of waves two streets away. The people in the next room were sharing the shower. Webb was a married man, and shower-sharing was a faded ambition. He sighed and tilted the bottle. We'll catch her tomorrow, he told himself.

In the west country – Kate had heard it a number of times – a clothes-horse was the *win'er-'edge*. The place where you spread your clothes to dry when the weather wasn't good enough to put them out on the garden blackthorn. The winter hedge.

She took down her briefs and tested them against her cheek. They were dry. Her socks were almost dry. Her jeans were still wet, but no longer sodden. She had decided to lay up for another day, if she could; maybe they would decide she'd managed to get clear of the county; maybe the search would move further afield. She wanted to wait, but she also wanted food and drink. The next move was to get close to habitation before first light, and she knew that the cliff path would bring her to the upper outskirts of the village. She crossed the field to the break in the hedge and, as much because she was still cold as to make time, broke into a loose jog.

It took an hour of running and walking. The scattered houses in new roads above the village lay under a grey light. They were brick built with glass front doors under pole-and-slab porches, and they had a view of the harbour. Villagers moved up to them, if they could, from the whitewashed fishermen's cottages with postage-stamp windows and six-in-one gardens. Kate chose a cul-de-sac that ended in a garage block, with a sports ground beyond that. She got in between the breeze-block of the last garage and the sports ground fence, and settled down to wait. Among the debris, wind-trapped by the fence, Kate found two plastic store bags, and a five-day-old newspaper. There was just enough light from the street lamps to read by. Kate turned the stained pages: NHS crisis, unemployment, overcrowded schools – the strictures of a poor country.

It proved a long wait. She watched the lights coming on in upstairs windows; then came the low hum of radios; then more lights ticking on down each house: stairs, hallway, kitchen, as the early risers came down to breakfast.

Ordinary lives, she thought. People with ordinary lives, and ordinary days ahead of them. Just the kind of life she hated; just the kind of life that, now, she wanted more than anything.

So go back. Go back, hire a good lawyer, make a fight of it.

I don't think so.

Why not, for Christ's sake?

It's not a fight I can win. Not yet, anyway. I need more ammunition.

You're innocent; doesn't that make a difference?

Not necessarily. In fact, not at all.

Come on . . .

Remember that guy went to prison for twenty-three years and there hadn't even *been* a murder?

This is different.

You're right, it is. They've got much more evidence against me than they had against him. Anyway, he wasn't the only one. It scares me. Cells scare me. Evidence scares me. Prisoners scare me. *Cons.* Know what happens in prison? To people like me? Ever hear about that?

Yes.

The thought scares me, all right? All of it. Scares me to fucking death.

Tell them what happened. They'll believe you.

I already told them; and they don't.

They'll investigate. They'll find things . . .

Things? *Things?* You don't get it, do you? Listen, they think I did it. They think I killed Michael. Their job is to prove that I did, not that I didn't. And they're a good way down the track. Look at the evidence. No one else was there. No sign of forced entry. I tell him we're through. He hits me. We have sex. Or – this would be their version – he has sex with me. Later, someone stabs him. My fingerprints are on the knife. I'm covered in blood, so I get in the shower, leaving him where he lies. My version of events is that I know nothing; I was asleep. You be the jury.

Okay, you've heard my suggestion; now let's hear yours.

Find out what *did* happen, and why.

How?

Christ, I don't know. Look for evidence.

How?

I don't *know*. Get lucky, perhaps.

Do you feel lucky – hiding in caves, crouching here like a scavenger, like a little hunted animal?

Shut up, okay? Just shut the fuck *up*!

Scavenger. Little hunted animal. The image strayed onto her inner eye. A fox under cover, breathing hard, ears pricked to the baying of the hounds.

A couple of men left their houses, and shouted good morning to one another. The milk van chugged down towards the end of the road and turned. While the first few deliveries were being made, Kate offloaded milk, bread, eggs, water, yoghurt and some processed cheese into the store bags, and went back to her hiding place. When the van had rattled down the road, she went over the fence and into the sports ground. She could cross it, going uphill, then drop down across arable land to the place where the cliff path came in above the harbour. It was still early, before six a.m., and it was unlikely that she'd meet anyone on the beach. Even so, she trekked back a mile or so along the path, to avoid dog-walkers and fishermen, then found a path down the cliff. The tide was out, clearing all the points and headlands along that stretch of coast. Kate walked along dense, wet, packed sand. Granite boulders reared up, jagged edged – wrecking rocks at high tide if you didn't know the waters.

She reached a deep fold in the cliff where she could tuck in against the wind, and drank some of the milk, before eating a couple of raw eggs and some cheese. After that, she went all the way back to the cliff face, found the most sheltered spot, lowered her jeans and briefs, and squatted.

Full daylight, when it came, was a high, bright blue with fast running cumulus and a swell on the sea. Gulls were chalk-white against the sky, slipping and sliding on the wind. From the cliff, anyone could have seen her as she walked the tideline; but who would have cared? Someone out early to glory in such a day. Someone out early, and now heading for home.

Home was the cave. Despite everything, Kate felt safe there. She stowed her food at the far end, then ducked back out into sunlight to do some beachcombing. She looked among the rocks and boulders: places where timber might get trapped. It took her further from home than she wanted to go, and left her in the open longer than she wanted to be there, but in the end she found what she was looking for: planks and some blue hawser-rope wedged in between two outcrops of serpentine, along with cans, plastic bottles and some gutted fish. There were four planks, and it was impossible for her to tell which she needed, so she tied them at intervals along a length of the rope and looped the ends over her shoulders as if she were pulling a sled.

By the time she got back to the cave, her hands were chafed and red from the rope, and she could feel a clutter of little aches where splinters had gone under the skin. My hands . . . my *hands*. She flexed the fingers of the left as if fingering her cello. It felt stiff and painful. She took a few more splinters as she tried the first plank across the end of the cave.

It made a perfect fit: she didn't even need the rope to tie off to the spurs of rock on either side. She stood as she had stood the previous night, making herself as tall as possible, and judged the position of her belt buckle against the rock. That was where the water would come to. She positioned the plank two feet higher, gave it a shove to wedge it, and used another plank as a mallet to beat the ends into place. It was firm. She pressed down on it with her palms, and heaved herself up, legs outstretched. She could half lie on the plank, her shoulders and head propped against the rock. When the time came, she would fold up the coat to make a pillow.

It had taken her until noon, and she felt tired. The sun had moved round, so that the cave was flooded with light to about a third of its depth. Kate went to the cave mouth and sat there cross-legged, soaking up the sun like an old squaw at the door of a tepee. The tide was on the turn.

She thought about the floppy disk, wrapped in its food bag on the chimney shelf at Penarven. *Dynamite: remember?*

She had a conversation with herself, in which one Kate (startled, irritated, frightened) challenged the other (resolute, determined . . . and also frightened).

You could have stayed put. You didn't kill Michael. Why run? Now everyone thinks you did it.

Webb thought so from the start. Remember the questions he asked? He had you guilty there and then.

Necessary to prove it, though.

Oh, yes? I could name four – no, five – cases of wrongful imprisonment off the top of my head. Evidence lost, ha-ha. Evidence withheld. Evidence squirrelled away, only to appear years later. Evidence altered. Witnesses changing their minds. Those are the cases I know about: the famous ones.

Why should it happen to you?

Are you concentrating? It was about to. They were going to charge me.

So what's the plan? Swim to France, hitch-hike to Argentina, ask for asylum?

Let me paint you a picture. You're not sitting here, scared, hunted, but nonetheless swamped in sunlight, listening to the gulls and the sea. You're in a cell. Just prior to that, they watched while you had a bath, then stuck fingers up you just about everywhere you've got a cavity, to make sure you're not carrying drugs. But now you're in a cell, surrounded by people who, just for fun, would like to rape you, hurt you, show you who runs the

place. Yes, they're women. And no, it doesn't make any difference. It's going to be months before you come to trial. In the
meantime, you're going to be trying to prove your innocence. You
had a fight with Michael. You were going to leave him. He beat
you up. Someone gutted him with a kitchen knife. Nothing stolen.
No sign of forced entry. His blood all over you, which you washed
off pretty fast. And that's not all.

Isn't it?

No.

What else is there?

I don't know. But they know. They say they have a case. You
want to know what made me run? When I saw them coming up
from the lane – what made me run? *They have a case.* It means,
they've made up their minds.

I don't feel safe.

I don't feel safe. But I feel as if there's something I can do.

What?

Get that disk. Find out what's on it. Find out what Michael was
working on. Dynamite: remember?

That's not going to happen by staying here with a couple of
pints of milk, some Evian and a raw egg.

A day. Here for another day. Give them the chance to move on.
Find a small place, dark place, stay still, wait for the hunter to go
away.

Okay. Then . . .?

Time to take a risk.

Big risk?

Pretty big. We'll need enough for a drink.

As in pub drink?

That's right.

Root round in the pockets of the coat. There'll be loose change.

Okay . . . Six pounds. And a few pence.

Enough for a drink, then.

Enough for two or three.

Joanna had met Stuart Donnelly at his office. It was late, after
seven, so Joanna had asked a neighbour to sit with Nathan. The

boy was still asking questions about Webb's visit and she was determined to keep anything to do with Kate at a distance from him. Donnelly poured them both a drink. He said, 'I can't really act for her if she's not here. I mean, she's a fugitive from justice. You're nothing like her.' It was a smiling afterthought as he handed Joanna her drink. Until now, she had been a voice on the telephone to Donnelly.

'She has rights.'

'At present, that's debatable. If she comes in . . . if they catch her . . . if she then wants me to act on her behalf, I will.'

'Even though you were Michael's friend.'

'I was Michael's colleague and I liked him; we weren't really friends. In any case, as you point out, she has rights.'

'What do the police mean?'

'Mean?'

'About having a case against her. They want to charge her with murder. What is it that makes them think she's guilty?' Joanna sipped her drink. 'Because she's not.'

'You're sure?'

'Of course I'm sure. And don't tell me that all relatives of guilty people say that. I know. You told me before.'

Donnelly shrugged. 'All I know is that there's some forensic evidence, and there's a witness. Bad enough as separate events. Even worse as a combination. There's also the fact – as DI Webb pointed out to me – that most things are what they seem to be. Especially domestics.'

He sat on the edge of the desk, and smiled at her again. Are you flirting with me? Joanna wondered. Because if so, you're a bastard. A bastard I might need.

Donnelly said, 'Look, as soon as they bring her in. I'll act for her. In fact, I'll call Webb and tell him that. Okay?'

'Okay,' Joanna said. Then, 'As soon as they bring her in . . .?'

'It's a matter of time,' Donnelly said. 'Got to be.'

'How much time?'

He shook his head. 'Not much.'

Kate lay on her plank, above the water level, and watched

patterns of light play on the walls. The day was fading and the reflections were pale, like the evening sky.

The two Kates hadn't spoken to one another for a while. Now the risk-taker said, 'Tonight and tomorrow. That's all.'

'Okay.'

'Can you make it? Another night, another day?'

'There's water, bread, cheese, eggs.'

'That's not what I mean.'

'Okay. Yes. I can make it. Listen: what can happen? I get caught.'

'Very philosophical.'

'Let's not get caught.'

'No. I'm for that.'

'I'm cold. I need this coat round me, not under my head.'

'Something happened earlier today. While I was sitting by the cave mouth, sitting in the sunlight.'

'What was that?'

'I missed Michael.'

'That always happens when you end something.'

'I know. It was more than that. I felt guilty.'

'That's crazy. There's nothing to feel guilty about.'

'I know. It just shows . . .'

'What?'

'How easy it is. How easy it is to think the way they think.'

'Is that what happened back at Penarven?'

'They have a case. That's all that was in my head. I was running before I could think another thought.'

A third wave kicked in through the entrance and sent a surge up to the plank, slopping against Kate's legs. Wings stirred and fussed in the roof.

'I'm glad not to be in that cell.'

'Yes. I'm pretty scared, to tell you the truth.'

'Yes. But I'm glad not to be in that cell.'

Nine

Enough for a drink. Enough for two or three.

It was a village pub and to get there Kate had walked more than twelve miles. It would have been better, she thought, to go to a pub in town, because she was looking for a pick-up, preferably someone passing through: a late tourist, a salesman, a nature lover. But the town was simply too risky. The village she had walked to lay in a fold of hills, a little inland, and was famous for its food. Kate had eaten there a few times with Joanna, and knew of its reputation.

The bars were divided along old-fashioned class lines, and the division was plain to see: a public bar with flagstones and boots and a dartboard, with loud voices, and a ceiling of smoke; then a saloon bar with carpet, tables laid for supper, horse brasses on dark, wooden pillars, chatter and discreet laughter. As Kate went through to the saloon, a roar went up from the public bar: someone called Jeff was winning a drinking contest.

There were a couple of men sitting at the bar who could have been waiting for someone, could have been alone. Kate ordered a drink and took it to a table. It was ten-fifteen: late enough that she wouldn't become conspicuous by sitting there all evening; also late enough for the place to be pretty crowded. All she needed was a lift out of the county. London would be terrific, but out of the county would do.

After ten minutes or so, she went back to the bar. The barman was watching TV between serving drinks, the screen mounted high among the bottles and optics, the sound switched low. She said, 'I hope you don't mind. I gave the name of the pub to the AA. I've broken down a mile or so back. I told them I'd be here.' She gave a grin and spread her arms as if to say, *Look at me.*

'I slipped and fell getting out of the car. On the verge. Found a patch of nettles.' She thought it would help to explain the way she looked: the Canadian coat bearing water stains, sweater ripped, hair awry.

The barman looked her up and down; his eyes slid away from her breasts. 'Okay,' he said. 'What name?'

'Mitchell.' She didn't know where she'd got it from. It sounded neutral; a nothing sort of name.

'Mitchell. Okay.'

'I don't want them to take the car and not me. I have to get back to London.'

'Don't worry. I'll let you know if they call.'

'They might turn up here, I suppose.'

'I'll let them know. They'll ask for you. I'll let them know.'

'Right,' she said, and went back to her table.

She thought she'd been just emphatic enough – just loud enough – to be heard by those people closest to her in the bar. Her best hope, she knew, was a single man. One of the guys had been joined by a woman and two friends. The other was still drinking alone, reading a paper. The idea was that she'd become increasingly anxious as closing-time drew near; increasingly loud; increasingly in need of someone to offer her a ride to London. Or halfway there.

At ten-forty, she went back to the bar and asked the barman a few redundant questions. At ten-fifty-five she gave a repeat performance. The bars were beginning to empty, now, but the lone man was still there. Kate thought he was showing some interest.

The barman shook his head, and said sorry – no call, no yellow uniforms. Kate became agitated; now she was in trouble: maybe they'd towed the car and forgotten about her. The barman showed her where the payphone was and she made a call with her elbow braced against the wall to hide the thumb that was cutting the connection. The fictitious call registered anger and distress: someone had fouled up; now she was stranded as she'd feared. She went back to report her problem to the barman, who was polishing glasses and replacing them under the bar while watching the late-night news summary. If the 'give me a lift' ploy failed, her next move was 'call me a cab'. It wasn't an idea she liked. She'd already assumed that cab companies would have been circulated with a description and a warning to look carefully at lone women asking to be taken long distances.

As Kate crossed to the bar . . . as the barman turned and stooped to place a glass on a shelf . . . as she was composing the final episode in her maiden in distress speech, which would be aimed more at the single man still sitting at the bar than the barman himself . . . there came up on the television screen the face of someone she knew but couldn't quite place.

It took two beats. Two heartbeats. Then Kate walked straight through the bar and out of the door. She hadn't been able to see whether the barman had turned back in time to catch her image on the screen. Maybe, maybe not. Or whether the guy at the bar had registered it. The only sensible reaction was to assume that they had. Maybe they wouldn't make the connection at once. Or make it at all. Maybe they would think as she had first thought: *Don't I know her?* And the second thought would be: No. Must look like someone else. Someone I used to see from time to time.

But maybe they'd have recognised her at once: It was her. *Her.* Just gone out the door!

Kate ran down the B-road that led away from the pub and towards open country. There were high banks on either side, ditched and hedged, with the topmost branches going a good fifteen feet above road level. She was looking for a gate. She was still looking when she heard the sound of an engine behind her. The road had narrowed, and the side ditches had become a strip of verge. There was nowhere to go. Her best bet, she decided, was to get as far in to the hedge as possible. The wind was still up, just as it had been all week, and clouds were spilling across the moon. If she got lucky, the hedge, and Kate along with it, would be in shadow when the vehicle passed.

She left it until the last moment: there were headlights on the road behind, just falling short, when she threw herself at the hedge and stood still. It was a bad bet. The moon didn't betray her

– a long skein of cloud was pushing over its face – but the headlights of the vehicle caught her four-square.

It was an old flat-bed pick-up, dented and mud-plastered. At first, it seemed as though the driver hadn't noticed. Then he hit the brake, and the truck stood up slightly on its front wheels as the back slewed round. There was a sound like tearing canvas, and the cab slewed sideways across the road. Kate gave a cry of terror, and ran out towards the centre of the road. Everything was movement and noise, the truck cannoning forward on locked wheels, the grinding sound as its tailgate tore into the bank and the lower branches of the hedge. The side of the cab clipped her, bundling her up the road like a bale of hay. For a second or so, she was all right, up on her feet, staring back at the lights of the truck, and turning to run. Then she took a couple of steps, and sat down. And then she lay down, head full of dizziness and dark, in her ears the terrifying racket of her own breathing.

Ten

The Canadian coat had gone, her socks and boots had gone, and she was warm. The room was small. It seemed foggy and there was a strong smell of fried food. She was in an armchair next to a small coal fire, and she felt sick, and a man was sitting opposite to her smoking a cigarette, and nodding in a companionable sort of way, as if they were husband and wife across the hearth.

After a while, he mashed the end of his roll-up with his fingers and lobbed it into the fire. He said, 'I was drunk. Still a bit drunk. I see you, but I couldn't miss you.'

Kate put him at forty-seven or eight. Or he could have been ten years younger. He was small and thin and bald: just a fringe of dark, greasy hair around the crown, a tuft where a widow's peak would be. He was wearing a canvas jerkin over a roll-neck sweater and a pair of army surplus camouflage trousers.

'Are you all right, now?'

'I might be sick. I think I'll be okay if I sit still.'

'I'd been to the pub. I'm sorry. I see you but I couldn't miss you.'

'I have to . . .' Kate made a move to rise.

'Come on,' he said, 'I'll take you.'

He stood outside the bathroom while Kate threw up, then led her back to her chair.

'It was who could drink the most inside a minute. I won five times. Free drinks, see.'

Someone called Jeff was winning a drinking competition.

'Is your name Jeff?'

He looked at her as if she had brought a rabbit from a hat. 'How did you know?'

'I heard you. I was in the pub too.'

80

'I'm still a bit drunk,' he said. 'Are you all right?' It was the kind of circular conversation drunks can't avoid.

She said, 'How long was I unconscious?'

'No, I'm just down the road from where it was. I brought you straight here. Not long.'

'Why didn't you take me to hospital?' Though she was glad he hadn't.

'I was drunk,' he said. 'Still am a bit,' and she let her annoyance flood up at the repetition before she saw the logic in what he'd said.

'The police . . .'

'That's it. Bit drunk, see. You all right?' And for the first time, she heard the worry in his voice.

'I think so. I've got a headache.'

He went through to a ramshackle kitchen and came back with some aspirin and a tumbler of water. She swallowed the pills and finished the water, suddenly thirsty. A little black cloud crossed her vision, making her blink, and she put her head down, slowly, onto her lap.

'Have you got somewhere I can sleep? Just for a while.'

Upstairs, his bed stood plumb in the centre of a room that was otherwise completely unfurnished. A bed; just a bed.

He said, 'Be careful round the other side. Don't go on the far side by the window. There's a touch of rot in him. Touch of worm.'

The sheets were several weeks old, piled on the sagging mattress. Everything smelled: and that was the only virtue: that it was *everything*, so Kate wasn't able to tell whether the sheets were foul, or the mattress, or whether it was the smell of rot in the room.

He brought her a pail, in case she needed to be sick again, but by the time he returned, she was asleep amid the foul nest of bedding.

Jeff looked down at her fondly. 'Oh,' he said, 'I'm glad I've got you. I'm glad you come along for company. It's nice; I like it. I'm glad you come along,' and he leaned over and placed his hand carefully on her breast.

First, there was a grey light at the window, and slanting rain. Then she could hear cello music. After that, no more than a couple of seconds after, she registered the rank sheets and the stench of decaying wood. She got up and went to the window. Through the rain, she could see fields, sheep, a line of trees that thickened into a wood where a hill rose into the mist. As she backed off, a floorboard shifted under her feet, and she danced away from it to the edge of the room where the joists were stronger, then sidled round to the door. She realised that she was wearing her T-shirt, but not her sweater. She felt exposed: those dreams where you appear naked in a public place.

The Canadian coat was hanging on the end of the bed. She slung it round her shoulders, then went to the top of the staircase. There was no sound except for the music. When she went down, she found Jeff standing at the stove and smiling like someone with a secret to share.

'Eat something,' he said.

'Okay.'

Kate sat in the chair where she'd found herself the previous evening. There was a heaviness about her, as if she'd slept too long and too deeply, but otherwise she felt fine. Jeff was frying eggs and bacon and bread.

She said, 'Don't you have to go somewhere? I mean . . . sorry . . . it's afternoon, isn't it?'

'Bit past three.'

'But you don't . . .'

'I ain't got no job. Bit on the social, bit on the side, that's me.'

'You like this?' she asked, nodding towards the radio.

'All I can get. That and some local thing that's all talk.'

'But do you like it?'

'I prefer a nice bit of singing.'

'It's Brahms,' she said, as if he might care. 'Second cello sonata.'

'It's better when someone's singing.' He put her plate on the table and took a loaf of bread and a pat of butter from a cupboard. The food was fried in lard and the plate had a ketchup stain round the rim. Kate was hungry, so she ate. Her sweater was drying in front of the fire. Jeff saw her eyes go to it.

'That was all muddy, where you went over in the lane. I give him a wash.'

'That's very nice of you.'

'The rest's muddy and all.'

Kate looked down at the jeans she'd slept in. Dried mud had patterned them with streaks and whorls. 'It'll brush off.'

'I could give him a wash.'

'It's fine. I ought to go. I live in London. My car broke down. I went to the pub to phone the AA –'

Jeff was laughing a little wheezy laugh and nodding his head as if to encourage her in her story. 'That's right,' he said, 'that's right . . .'

'Listen . . . you haven't got anything else to do. Why don't you drive me to London? I'll pay you whatever you think's right. Ten pounds an hour? And pay for the return journey too. What do you think?'

'That's right.' Jeff nodded, coughing slightly through his laughter. 'Your car broke down, didn't 'e?'

'About a mile from –'

'No,' he said. 'No. You're that girl they're looking for.'

In the silence that followed, Jeff rolled himself a cigarette and got it going, brushing strands of glowing tobacco off his camouflage fatigues with a hand that seemed too large for the wrist.

'Here,' he said, 'there's something I want to show you.'

He went to a cupboard by the door, and brought out a bayonet in its scabbard. Kate felt dazed, as though someone had slapped her for no reason. She felt dizzy. As Jeff walked over to her, he unsheathed the bayonet. The steel sang as it came clear, and Kate stood up, as if that might make any kind of a difference. Jeff reversed the weapon and laid it across his arm, hilt foremost, a commoner offering his sword to a monarch.

'Take him.'

'Why?'

'There's a history.'

Kate lifted the bayonet and held it awkwardly, outward, as if defending herself. Jeff took a step backwards and nodded. The dramatic urgency of the music coming from the radio made her want to laugh; laugh and cry.

'That was mine.' He pointed at the weapon. 'Mine in the Falklands. Goose Green. He were a good friend. Squaddies' friend, the bayonet. Close-up work.' Suddenly, he fell into a stance, giving a little leap and coming down, feet planted like a boxer's, arms holding an imaginary rifle. He made a lunge towards her, then withdrew. 'In and twist,' he said. 'That's it. Right in and give him a twist, then out and look for the next.'

Kate said, 'What are you going to do?'

Jeff came close to her and took the bayonet away, holding it vertically between them like a sword of virtue. 'You wait,' he said. 'You wait.' He went to the cupboard and replaced the bayonet. In its place he held a small tin cash box. 'Sit down, then,' he said, and opened the box. Inside, wrapped in scraps of velvet, were medals arranged on a long clip. 'Falklands,' he said, 'Bosnia, Northern Ireland, out there ... you know –' he tapped his forehead with his knuckles because the name had escaped him '– the Gulf.'

Kate looked at the medals, their striped ribbons, their gleaming faces. The Africa Star; the Italy Star; the War Medal; the Defence Medal. Any junk shop; any market stall. Jeff went back to the cupboard again and took some videos down from a shelf. 'Come on,' he said, 'come on,' but waited for her to go first into the dark little parlour with its smell of stale tobacco and mice. Jeff had a TV-video system the size of a small cinema.

'There you are,' he said, pulling an armchair along for her. 'Just there is where you are,' and he put the first video tape into the player by touch, never taking his eyes off Kate until he was able to sit down in his own chair, a little back of hers and closer to the door.

Soldiers streamed across a barren landscape, radio aerials whipping, automatic weapons held at the ready.

84

'That's me,' said Jeff. 'There I am, look. There's me. See that? See that? Me.'

Kate nodded. 'Yes,' she agreed, 'you're right . . . right . . .' The figures were just silhouettes.

'Fixed bayonets, see,' Jeff told her. 'Squaddies' friend, him is.'

There were three videos, and they watched them all. Jeff pointed to himself, to someone, and crowed with delight. Sometimes the figures he pointed to were too far and too indistinct to be much more than a blur; at other times, you could see their faces. The fact that they bore him not the slightest resemblance didn't seem to occur to Jeff. He simply said, 'That's me, there I am,' of a man fifteen years younger and wearing a moustache, and, 'See that? See that? There's me,' of a senior officer a head taller. Kate looked round the room when she could. The door was out of the question. The single window was latched and, for all she knew, the latch was painted into the frame.

When the final video ended, the TV reverted to a game show. They sat on for ten minutes, then Jeff said, 'We could have a beer.' Kate was about to reply, when he said, 'What do you usually do?'

'Do? I don't understand.'

'Do you usually watch him?' He meant the game show.

'No. Not usually.'

'You watch the other side, then?' He changed channels.

'The thing is . . . I have to get back now.'

'Let's have a beer,' Jeff said.

'Then I have to go.'

'No,' he said, a note of surprise in his voice: as if she hadn't quite understood the situation. 'No . . . You're that girl they're looking for.' There was a pause, then he added, 'That's the point.'

Twice that evening, Kate needed to go to the bathroom. He stood outside the door, while she gazed at the latchless window – just a pane of frosted glass – and wondered if she could break it and get through before he came in. He had the key, and she knew that, in truth, there wasn't a chance.

Jeff was drinking beer, and needed the bathroom more often

than Kate. He took her in with him and held her wrist, his other hand fumbling into the fly of his combat fatigues. Kate looked at the floor, at the window, at the door, at the stained bathtub, while his stream clattered into the water trap.

They watched TV until midnight. Jeff said, 'I'll take you to London in the morning if you let me see what you look like.'

Kate was confused. She said, 'You know what I look like. You know who I am.'

Then she understood, in the same moment that Jeff stood up and placed one hand on his skinny chest, the other by his belt buckle, a grotesque version of one of the Muses, demonstrating modesty; one of the Fates.

'I had your titties in my hands while you was sleeping, but I didn't see him at all.'

Oh, Jesus, Kate said to herself. Jesus, Jesus, Jesus. She thought of the bayonet in the kitchen cupboard.

'Just to see what you look like. Touch him a bit.'

Kate closed her eyes. When she opened them, Jeff had shuffled nearer. He put a hand on her shoulder, though he was looking directly at her lap. 'Then back to London in the morning. Don't say nothing. Don't tell no one, not me.'

Kate said, 'Can I have a beer?'

'You said you didn't –'

'I know. But I'd like one now.'

He took her into the kitchen and flipped the cap off a bottle, then set it down on the table.

'Show first.'

Kate reached out, grabbed the bottle and took a sip, putting it down again. Then she stripped her clothes off fast, before he could choose a place or tell her how: boots and socks; jeans and briefs in one go; then sweater and T-shirt and bra in a single quick action.

Jeff said, 'No, not –' then broke off. He stayed put. He was staring. The only movement was a faint twitching in his hands as they hung at his sides. Ten seconds passed; maybe fifteen.

Kate smiled. 'All right?'

'Turn about,' he said.

She lifted the bottle and took a swig, still smiling, then turned, feeling her neck prickle as she presented her back to him.

She heard him say, 'Just touch him a bit. Hurt a bit. Touch and hurt a bit would be all right.'

When she faced him again, it seemed he hadn't moved a muscle, but he looked serious, like a man who has just received important, or bad, news. He said, 'We'll go up now, then; better go up,' and moved towards her, his hand reaching for her wrist.

He hadn't seen it: it seemed that he hadn't even thought of it. Kate brought the bottle round in a sharp arc, catching him low on the head, just below the level of the ear. The glass shattered. Jeff's reach enabled him to grasp Kate's wrist, as he'd intended, but he went down onto one knee, then toppled sideways, sitting with his legs tucked under him. His head was bowed: a man severely disappointed.

Kate yanked her hand free and looked wildly round the room. Alongside the fire was a group of irons and a hand shovel. She skipped round Jeff and grabbed the shovel. When she turned, he'd put a hand up on the table and was in a crouch. As he half straightened, Kate swung two-handed. There was a comic *clang* as the shovel hit the back of Jeff's skull. He pitched forward onto his face. Kate picked her clothes up off the floor. The muddle of jeans and briefs was under Jeff's leg. She rolled him with her foot and tugged them out. One leg of the jeans carried a bright red splash of blood, narrow, like a horse's blaze. Jeff was still lying flat, but he was muttering to himself, a slurred and seamless ramble.

She dressed fast, then ransacked the room. She took a torch, kitchen matches, and all the food she could stuff into the Canadian coat. She found a family-sized bottle of Coke in the cupboard. She took the keys to the truck. She took the bayonet.

Jeff was on his knees, but his forehead was still touching the floor. Whatever he was saying, whatever it was he wanted her to know, was coming, now, in a fluting rant – a furious, sad ululation – first loud, then falling away, then loud again. He managed to turn his head to look at her, still mouthing. The words were broken and disconnected, scrambled fragments, and his eyes were unfocused.

Kate went out into the night. It was wild: the wind up to a half-gale or more, airborne twigs slapping at her as she crossed the yard. The truck was unlocked. She opened the door and stepped up, but caught her ankle on something down by the wheel – a hank of rope, perhaps, or some old engine-part. She tried to shake herself free, but couldn't. When she looked down, it was Jeff – holding her ankle. His free hand clawed at the back of her coat, going for a purchase on the quilted material. Kate screamed and swung the bayonet. The scabbard connected with Jeff's shoulder; he felt the blow and made a grab for the weapon, slipping, fighting to keep his balance.

Kate held the bayonet high, out of his reach as he went down to his knees again. His eyes were looking inward. 'Off!' she screamed. '*Off, off, off, off, off!*' Each word came with a blow. She caught him on the shoulders, on the upper arms, on the chest. '*Off! Off! Off!*' She caught him on the crown of the head and he slid away from her, his face striking her boot.

She started the truck and drove through the yard. She was shaking so much that it was impossible to keep her foot steady on the accelerator, and the vehicle covered the ground in lurches and skids. The yard gate was open and she drove through, having no notion of which way to go.

After she'd covered ten miles, she pulled over and opened the door and threw up onto the ground without getting out of the cab.

Eleven

Checking signposts on the back lanes, Kate drove as straight a line as she could, heading away from Jeff's place and towards a main road. The risk of being stopped was no less now than if she'd been able to steal a vehicle three days before, but she thought the truck was probably better camouflage than most.

The wind beat at the hedges and the roadside trees, shoving the truck across to the wrong side. Kate heard again the clang as she landed the blow with the shovel. She felt the dead weight in him as his face hit her boot. The wind seemed to carry his voice, high-pitched and meaningless and mad.

She came to a main road after half an hour and swung east. Almost the first thing she saw was a police car heading west. She smothered an instinct to speed up, or to take the next junction back to minor roads. The rear lights of the police car faded in her mirror.

How long? she wondered. It would be crazy, she knew, to try to take the truck all the way to London. In that heap of tin it would be a seven- or eight-hour drive: even when she flattened the accelerator, she was only getting fifty-five. So how long, before she found somewhere to pull off, ditch the truck, and find another way home?

Another patrol car went by. Just traffic cops, she knew that. Just traffic cops, but her nerve was failing her even as she thought it. Jeff, she said to herself, Jeff: why in hell couldn't you have been a Mercedes driver? The thought made her laugh. She laughed so hard that tears came to her eyes and made driving difficult.

Why couldn't you have been a BMW man?

That clang of the shovel as the blow landed. His confused, addled, damaged thought-stream.

*   *   *

It was easy to keep going, and she had to fight with herself to stop.

They won't find him till the morning. Seven o'clock at the earliest. In fact why should it be seven? The milkman? I don't think so. Daft Jeff. Unemployed Jeff. Jeff the butt of jokes at the pub. It'll probably take three days before anyone bothers to wonder where he is.

He's lying in full view.

In full view a long way from anywhere.

Even so . . . It's not really to do with when they find Jeff, is it? Jeff or no Jeff, you're being hunted. There must be roadblocks, don't they do that? Random checks at the very least. They want you. They're looking.

For this truck? Really?

This truck is a pile of crap. You assume it's safe because of that. Think though: you haven't checked, but it's probably lacking tail lights, brake lights, number-plate light and insurance. Get this on the motorway and see how far you travel.

So it's a risk.

Yes; and look where the last risk got you. And there's another thing.

There is?

Everything you've said about Jeff so far means you think he's dead. *When they'll find him. How long he'll lie there.* You're talking as if he's dead.

The other Kate was silent for a long time.

Now if that's true, it's bad enough, God knows. But suppose he's not. Not dead. Where is he now? I'll tell you: giving the cops a description of this truck. *This* truck.

Kate pulled off into a lay-by and cut the lights.

It was a rutted, scimitar-shaped pull-in, littered with trash. There were no street lights, but a dim sodium glow from the A-road settled like a dew, bringing a lurid orange tinge to discarded store bags and newspapers. A tall, spindly hawthorn hedge screened the road from farmland beyond.

Kate found a metal five-bar gate at the far end. She opened it and pegged it back with a rock. The wind made the upper branches of the hedge turn and swirl; it rattled the poles of the gate. At the corner of the field, where the ground was lowest, she ran the truck close to the brambled tangle of the hedge, right under its shoulder, and left it there. She took the Coke and the food, and trudged back. The bayonet she left in the truck.

She sat in the lee of the hedge next to the gate and drank some of the Coke. The food she'd taken from Jeff's cupboard was bread and cheese and some ham in a cellophane packet. She made a crude sandwich and munched on it in the dark. Before she finished, images came to her of Jeff with his box of medals, Jeff on the floor after she'd hit him with the bottle, Jeff falling away as she clubbed him with the bayonet.

Off! Off! Off!

She spat out the sandwich. After a moment, she started to cry.

Owls were hunting over the pasture and along the fringes of the trees; they were close; their cries seemed to put them almost within reach. The wind was like a vast fist. Branches sawed and clashed in darkness above her head.

Kate dozed and dreamed a series of broken images, then woke with a start, a name on the tip of her tongue. The man Michael had been shouting at in the street that evening at the environment conference: she'd watched them through the restaurant window.

Why think of him?

Images from her dream came back to her: Michael bloody and dying, Jeff falling after the bottle exploded against his face, Webb questioning her, his smile the false grin of a serpent, herself playing the Brahms, Michael standing in the street yelling at . . .

Cawdrey, she thought it was. Or Cowley. What had made Michael so angry? Something to do with his project. The *dynamite.*

Yes, Cawdrey. Stephen Cawdrey. She had met the man before, and in Michael's company. He was a journalist, like Michael, who wrote on green issues. Talk to Cawdrey, she thought. Find out what caused that row. Then it occurred to her that talking to anyone who knew her was pretty much out of the question. Or making contact with anyone who knew her. Suddenly she felt a sense of isolation so extreme, so bleak, that it was like a physical shock. She hunkered down again in the lee of the hedge, out on her own, cast off from friends and home, hunted, utterly lost.

She waited for three hours. No one saw her. Not the family whose car limped in to the lay-by. Not the AA patrol man who came forty minutes later and fitted a new alternator. Not the couple who pulled in for furtive, five-minute sex, white rumps and breasts bobbing in the misty orange light. Not the half-dozen drivers who stood backed up to the wind, letting their pee furl away into the dark. Not the trucker, who sat high up in his eight-wheeler, having a coffee break, then a nap in a curtained-off area at the back of the cab. He woke after thirty minutes and clambered back into the driver's seat. Kate hopped up on the steel footplate on the driver's side and rapped at his window. He looked curious rather than alarmed: as if stranded hitchhikers were part of the job.

He was carrying slate to London, having already made a delivery in Penzance, and was glad of the company. His name was Colin; married, three children, small dog, large mortgage – he listed them as if they were double-entry assets and debits. They stopped once, at a motorway pull-in, and Kate claimed to be too tired to join him, so he offered to bring back coffee and a sandwich. While he was away, she slipped into the space behind the cab and lay on the truckle-bed.

There's a system of averages that dictates the spin of a coin or the turn of a card. Sometimes it works for you; sometimes you think luck has turned her face from you forever.

Colin went into the men's room, then the cafeteria. He read a paperback while he ate. Later, he bought a chocolate bar from the shop before going back to the truck. In doing all that, he four times passed a poster with Kate's face on it, asking travellers to report any sighting of her. Colin didn't notice the posters. He climbed back into the cab, and drove Kate to London, dropping her close to Hammersmith Bridge at six a.m.

Kate had no knowledge of that turn of luck. She didn't think she was lucky at all.

Joanna was lying awake when the phone rang. Nathan had come in to her halfway through the night, telling of bad dreams. She had taken him back to bed and settled him, saying she would stay with him till he slept. She slept herself, waking an hour later when Nathan turned over and kicked her in the small of the back. Since then, she had fallen in and out of sleep, troubled by nightmare scenes that continually woke her, as if Nathan had passed on to her his black menagerie of monsters and ghouls. She lifted the phone, and looked at the clock at the same time, fearful that she might have overslept.

'Jo, it's me.'

Joanna sat up fast, like an animal suddenly alerted to danger. She said, 'Don't say where you are. Don't say anything important. Are you okay?'

'I'm fine.' A pause. 'Not really. I didn't kill him, Jo. I didn't kill Michael.'

'I know that, for Christ's sake.'

'Listen, I just wanted to make contact. Let you know I'm all right.'

'What can I do? There's nothing I can do, is there?'

'No. Don't worry.'

Joanna laughed. 'Are you serious?'

As she spoke, a voice crossed hers, tangled with hers. There was a pause. Then a second voice said, 'It's up and running. Few seconds.'

'Okay. Tell them to make it fast.' This was Webb's voice.

Joanna sensed an absence on the line as Kate hung up. She heard the first voice, distant but clear, say, 'She's gone.'

There followed a pause like a chasm. Joanna waited; all the time Webb's breathing was loud in her ear. He said, 'Stupid bitch.'

'Stupid,' Webb said. He was standing in Joanna's kitchen. 'That was a stupid thing to do. I could charge you with obstruction.'

'I had no chance to talk to her. You came on the line.' Joanna smiled at Webb. 'Is that supposed to happen?'

'You warned her off.' He consulted a transcript. ' "Don't say where you are. Don't say anything important".'

'I didn't want to know. Don't want to know. I can't help her, so I'd sooner stay ignorant. I have a child to think of, you know? I didn't say it for her benefit, I said it for mine.'

'You expect me to believe that?'

'Believe what you like. I was about to tell her to give herself up. Then you suffered your odd little electronic blooper. Sorry. Your fault, not mine.' Despite what she was saying, Joanna's tone was tight. A tic had developed under her eye.

Webb coloured up, red around the jowls, but it wasn't embarrassment. He said, 'If she phones again —'

'Do you think that's likely?' Joanna asked.

You learn fast about life on the street. About how to live on the street. You learn about places you can go, and how long you can stay there. Kate didn't look great, but she didn't look down and out, either. The Canadian coat almost covered the blood-splash on her jeans; she had brushed most of the mud off, simply using the flat of her hand. She was almost out of money: just a pound or two left. She wanted to go across town, away from the west side of the city, but the bus fare would have used up all her cash. Instead, she walked a couple of miles to a neighbourhood she didn't know well. Her feeling was that since she was a relative stranger there, no one would know her, or expect to see her. No one would look for her. There was no logic in it, except that she felt safer. She bought a newspaper and went to a café for a coffee. That left her enough for a couple of phone calls.

She spent as long as she could over the coffee. There was nothing about her in the paper: Michael was old news; a dead issue. She thought it wouldn't take the police long to link her to Jeff, but that hadn't happened yet: Jeff was news in waiting.

She left the café and walked a circular route, staying away from main roads. It was still early, but the gates were open in a small cemetery. She sat on a bench among the broken pillars and weeping angels, as mothers wheeled children through in buggies, or commuters took a short cut. When that traffic ended, there came, one at a time, walking slowly, old people wanting a breath of air and somewhere to rest. They dotted the benches through the breadth of the cemetery, each making a nodding acquaintance with the place, their next long rest, as if each short visit made them better prepared for the last.

There was sunshine, now, where earlier there had been high cloud cover; a dew lay on the grass. Kate walked through to the far gate, leaving the old folk to their contemplation, one to a bench, as if they already understood the awesome isolation of death.

She went to a library and took the telephone directory to a table. There were four entries for S. Cawdrey, and two for Stephen. She borrowed a pen and a scrap of paper from the main desk and wrote them down.

It seemed logical to try the Stephens first. Stephen-one was the wrong man. Stephen-two didn't answer, but his wife did. She said that, yes, he was Stephen Cawdrey the journalist, and no, he wasn't at home. In fact, she didn't expect him to be at home ever again, and who the hell was this?

'A friend,' Kate said.

'Yes? And just how many fucking friends has my husband got, I wonder? Fucking friends. Friends for fucking.' She laughed like someone who has just discovered that the worst thing can be just around the corner. *Funny meeting you like this . . .*

'No,' Kate said. 'I don't know him well. I met him a couple of times. I'm working on a story. He might be able to help me out.'

'If you're tall and blonde and under thirty, he'll help, no problem.'

'Is there a way I can get in touch with him?'

There was a pause, then a clatter as the phone was put down. The line wasn't broken, though. Kate thumbed in the last of her money.

Cawdrey's wife came back to the phone and gave Kate a

number. She said, 'Tell him I remember him in my prayers. I pray he gets a terminal illness.'

Kate tried to make a collect call to the number, but the operator reported an answerphone.

And the next move is . . . Kate thought, knowing that there was no next move. At least, nothing obvious. She needed to buy some time: to think, to plan, to come up with an idea. Cawdrey was one way to go. That aside, there was nothing much open to her except the streets: and they were wide open.

It's an environment. If you're out there, you have to adapt.

Kate walked to the Strand, then cut through backstreets towards Covent Garden. There were people shopping, people walking, people late for meetings, people collecting sights and views; but all Kate could see were people dossing, people begging, people lying up in doorways. From time to time, she would see a nest, a spot-camp, whose owner had left for a while on some mission or other. The nest would consist of a sleeping bag, sometimes a blanket as well, a bundle of newspapers, a tin or small box for the loose change that was asked for in a rhythmic monotone. Clearly, the dosser expected these things to be there when he or she got back. Who would take them?

She spent all day on the streets. She had no money, no food, nothing to drink, no hope of help. When she looked for a chance to steal, she found the city was locked tight against her and her kind: store detectives, alarms, tagged items, watchful shopkeepers who expected thieves, looked for them, wanted to find them. She went to libraries, to small parks, to department stores. In one of them, she used the bathroom and washed her face and hands. In the store café, she pretended to be looking for someone, weaving between tables and scavenging an empty mineral water bottle, which she took back to the women's room and filled from the tap. She wanted nothing so much as to take a bath and wash her hair.

It seemed to her that she barely stopped moving, though she had no destination and no purpose. Being homeless didn't just mean no home; it meant no life. She thought of the figures she had so often seen huddled in doorways, sleeping at ten in the morning, at midday, at five in the afternoon, at midnight. Boredom and purposelessness, the great narcotics. Along, of course, with the Great Narcotics, each with its pet name, its perfect sobriquet: *smack, crack, dope, shit, stuff*, which provided a purpose, which provided a destination.

Much later, she found her way to dossers' Mecca. Piccadilly Circus in the small hours: a colony, a foreign land. The all-night chemists are like a private practice.

Kate walked to Shaftesbury Avenue and down into Soho. She found a nest built onto the stage door step of one of the theatres, the upper flap of the sleeping bag thrown back as if the sleeper had got up to switch off the lights. She stole the bag and walked quickly through small streets: neon, strip joints, peepshows, porno-stores, drunks, beggars, doors that led to whores, doors that led to darkness.

The route took her back past the Circus and, finally, down to the river. She descended a flight of stone steps and settled with her back to the pillar of a bridge. It was colder there, but at least she wasn't sharing the space, and being near the water helped in some way: the stretch and scamper of reflected light, the pulse of the water, the insomniac gulls. Just downriver was the concert hall where she'd last played the Elgar – three months before. Three lifetimes.

The sleeping bag smelled bad, but she couldn't say of what. Booze, sweat, cigarette smoke . . . other things. It smelled of *stain*. The cold seeped through, a stain of its own. She lay awake for a long time, then slept and dreamed Jeff's death. If it was a death. She could feel the jar in her arm as she hit down with the bayonet. It seemed more real to her than the event itself. She woke with a cry, chilled to the bone, and with a low cramp: her period had started She picked out a seam of the bag, pulled a handful of kapok and stuffed it into her briefs.

Another day, she thought. I can do another day of this. That's definitely all. That's all.

Some time close to morning, it started to rain. Kate woke with an idea.

Twelve

Hunkered down against the Embankment wall, still inside her stolen bag, hand out, the litany constantly on her lips of '*Can you spare any change, please, can you spare any change, please, can you spare any –*' Kate made a little over twelve pounds in the course of the morning. She bought some tampons, water, a slice of pizza, chocolate and a hairbrush.

She made two phone calls, spent time in a library, wandered the streets, walked upriver until she came to trees and scrub opposite grey wharves, and sat for an hour watching the river traffic going to and fro. A heron was fishing the shallows, watchful and still. Later, she went to an afternoon performance of a movie.

The second phone call had gone according to plan.

'This is the Queen Elizabeth Hall. I'm calling to advise you that your ticket for this evening's concert is at the box office and must be collected at least half an hour before the performance.'

The lady calling from the box office had a slight but attractive Scottish accent.

Joanna had opened her mouth to tell the woman that she'd made a mistake; then she realised that she'd heard that accent before. 'Thanks for letting me know,' she said.

'You can pay at the time of collection, or you could leave a cheque in lieu.'

'Sorry,' Joanna said, 'I didn't catch that.'

'Pay this evening. Or leave a cheque in lieu. It doesn't matter which.'

'Okay,' Joanna said, 'thanks. I'll pay this evening.'

The first phone call had been to book a ticket in Joanna's name.

It was the sort of mish-mash concert that Joanna would dislike: Brahms, Strauss, Mahler, Stravinsky.

The film was a Hollywood thriller: the usual mixture of extreme violence and sentimentality. Kate couldn't decide which seemed the most dangerous. She flinched from the gunshots, from sweaty male faces, from screams of hatred, and flinched as much from the saccharine moment when honour and kinship were invoked as a means to slaughter.

Crouched in the dark, watching gunflashes and clenched fists, she wondered for the first time who had put her here. Someone had. Someone had murdered Michael. Someone with a face and name.

At six-forty-five, she went to the concert hall, bought an orange juice and sat in the lobby for a brief while. Then she went to the women's room and locked herself into the end cubicle.

She had no idea what would happen next.

Joanna left home after kissing Nathan goodnight and telling the babysitter where to find coffee and a snack. She was leaving early so that she could make the journey by bus; she thought she'd stand a better chance, that way, of knowing whether she was being followed. In any event, she had decided to assume that it was inevitable.

At the stop, she waited with three other people, none of whom looked like a policeman, unless policemen were sometimes pensioners, or were overweight, middle-aged black ladies, or had tattoos, lip-studs and violet eyeliner.

Joanna's shadow waited until the bus was approaching, then said a word or two into a mobile phone. A car came alongside as Joanna stepped onto the bus.

'Do we think she's at it?' the driver asked.

The shadow grimaced. 'I fucking hope she is. If I sit through a fucking evening of this stuff for no result, I'll be well hacked off.'

'No,' the driver said. 'She's off to have a good time.'

'Her sister's wanted for murder.'

'Doesn't mean she has to stay indoors, does it? Something to take her mind off things.'

The shadow was bored. It was a crap job. That day he'd journeyed with Joanna on little jaunts to the local Eight Till Late, the bank, a couple of food shops, the newsagent's . . . He'd been with her to take the kid to school, and he'd been with her to collect him. Crap. A crap job. He closed his eyes. 'I was on a sure thing tonight.'

'Woman or a dog?' the driver asked.

The shadow laughed. 'I could hardly tell the difference.'

If they had understood, Joanna thought, anyone following her would be female: if they'd seen through the silly pun: *in lieu*. Anything she did, anything she tried, would have to be done at just the right time.

She collected the ticket from the box office, got a drink at the bar, then bought a programme and sat at a table to read and drink. As they were gonging the performance and the foyer began to empty, she went into the women's room. There was a short queue – three women. Everyone was in a hurry; annoyed with whoever was in the far cubicle and taking her time. Someone entered and stood behind Joanna, so she moved to wash her hands, letting her place in the queue slip. Finally, she went into the first cubicle and waited there until she could hear no more sounds of taps, or the roller towel being pulled, or the air dryer whirring. She emerged and looked towards the far cubicle.

She said, 'Kate?' in a voice almost too low to be heard.

'Jo.'

'Oh, Jesus. Jesus Christ.'

'You have to go.'

'There's a moment . . .'

'No! Joanna, you have to go. Go now. Please! Please go!'

Joanna opened her handbag and removed a much smaller bag: an evening bag, silk and jet. She lobbed it over the top of the cubicle.

'Now go.'

'Kate, for God's sake.' She wanted to see her sister, hold her for a moment.

'No! Joanna – no!' A pause then: 'Is there anything I ought to know?'

'They say they have a witness. They say there's forensic evidence.'

'What?'

'Kate, I don't know.' Joanna was choking back tears. 'Stuart Donnelly told me. I don't know what they mean.'

'Go into the concert, Jo. Please!'

Joanna turned as the door opened and an usher came in and hurried towards a cubicle. There was nothing to do but leave. In order to send Kate a signal – *there's someone else in here* – she asked the usher a question: 'Are people going in?'

'You'd better hurry,' she was told.

Joanna walked out into the foyer and through to the concert hall. She didn't want to listen to music, or be in the hall where Kate had played so often, or be among people, but she sat it out, and in the interval bought herself a large Scotch, followed by a second, and went to the women's room, where she waited until the far cubicle fell free. She sat on the seat and looked round for a sign. Too risky to leave a note, of course, but something . . . something . . .

In the paint on the door, at about eye level, someone had scratched three Xs, three kisses, and a basic sad face: a circle, two dash eyes, and a turned-down curve for a mouth. It could have been done with the zipper tag on an evening bag. It could have been done by anyone.

Joanna touched it with a fingertip, funny little, tragic little graffito.

Kate felt a presence behind her for half an hour or more, until she had lost herself in the streets of Soho. No one had been following her, but the possibility had been enough to make her back itch, make her head prickle. In Soho, the crowds were thick. She felt as if they were a door closing behind her. Finally, she summoned the courage to stop. She went into a pub, bought a drink with the last of her begged money, and sat within sight of the door to drink it. No one came for her. No one noticed her.

She went to the women's room and locked herself in, as if she kept these little bolt-holes all over London, and opened the evening bag. There was a credit card, a letter, and a thick wedge of new bank notes. Kate counted the money: five thousand pounds.

Dearest Kate,

Five thousand is the most I can raise without having to beg at the bank: and there's no time for that. Use the credit card, but give me a few days to get an overdraft facility. The PIN is 1695. I don't know what to say. Stuart Donnelly says they've got a witness and forensic evidence but I don't know what it is, and neither does he. It's all so dreadful. I know you didn't kill Michael, but I don't properly understand why you ran away. Well, I do. If I think about it, I know I do. They've made their minds up, haven't they – the police?

They're listening on the phone – it's tapped, I mean – but then you've worked that out for yourself. I liked your imitation of Aunt Gemma: that Edinburgh lilt, so genteel. I miss her, don't you?

Oh, God, I'm writing as if this were a normal letter. I'm chatting. I don't know what to say to help you, or what to do either. The only thing I can think of is to establish a point of contact. A dead letter box, I suppose I mean. The Polish Café in Queensway has a message board where fading émigrés leave notes for each other: revolutionary handbills, or the next chess move, or something. I occasionally go there for a coffee on my way to college. I'll go every Tuesday and Thursday in the morning. I don't give my first tutorial until about ten. Leave a message there, if you need to, under the name Z. Cybulski. Remember that film dad loved – 'Ashes and Diamonds'? Don't write anything that lets anyone know where you are unless it's crucial – I don't know whether I'm being followed. I think so. It's all so bloody farcical. I'll leave messages for you under the same name. If you go in any time after ten o'clock and there's a message for Cybulski, it's for you.

It's the best I can do. If it doesn't help, I'm sorry. I'm sorry about everything. I can't think of anything else to say, except I'm sorry, I'm sorry, as if I could have done something because I'm your big sister. I love you.

Jo

Kate was beginning to look like a dosser; she certainly smelled like a dosser; but there were some small hotels that catered specifically for the almost down, the almost out. She went to a late-night chemist, then bought a room for the night. There was no bathroom, but there was a sink. She stripped and washed, then stood naked over the basin and washed her hair several times. After that, she washed her underclothes and her T-shirt and her socks and hung them on the radiator.

The bed was narrow and sagging, but the bedsheets were clean. When she pulled the curtain, the room was still in half-light: the hotel was on a main road and a haze of neon hung in the air all night. Traffic went by all night. There were voices on the street all night.

Kate slept as if she were in hibernation.

Next day, she bought clothes and make-up and a small rucksack to carry them in. She changed in the women's room at the store, put her foul-smelling jeans and sweater in the store bag, carried them out with her and stuffed them into the nearest garbage bin.

She was beginning to feel better. She was beginning to feel that the city was too big for one person to be sought and found.

She went to a busy hairdresser's in the West End and had her hair cut short: from shoulder length to a three-inch crop; she would dye it herself, she decided. Webb might guess that she'd have a haircut, might even find the place, but he wouldn't be able to ask whether he was chasing a blonde, a brunette or a redhead.

She went back to her flophouse and dyed her hair black. Since she had paid cash in advance for a two-night stay, she cleaned the sink and walked out. After that, she booked in to a small but likeable hotel up in Hampstead. It was a part of the city where she'd never lived and, in trying to think as her pursuers might think, decided to stay away from her own patch. She took a shower, and after the shower she took a foam bath.

While she lay in the suds, she re-read Joanna's letter five times, like a refugee with some token, some dream, of home.

She wished Jo had thought to put her mobile phone in the jet-and-silk evening bag.

Kate's fingerprints were on the door of the truck, on the steering wheel and the gear shift, on the dash and the driver's mirror. They were on the cupboard door, the chair, the door handles, the headboard of Jeff's bed. They were on the neck of the bottle and the haft of the bayonet.

They were also on just about everything she might be expected to touch in her apartment, but to make identification easier — since other people touch household items — they dusted Kate's cello. No one else touched that.

'This is embargoed,' Webb said. 'Get the co-operation of the press. I don't want her to feel less safe than she does already. One issue: Michael Lester. One issue is all.'

Sorley looked at him, an eyebrow raised. 'What's the trade?' he asked. 'Any red-blooded editor would love this. Blood-crazed woman. First her lover, now this gormless bastard. Is she a man hater? Is she mad? Women killers always tickle the public's fancy. They'll run her picture alongside Myra and Rosemary West.'

'Make promises you can't keep,' Webb said. 'I don't know. But I don't want her to think she's beyond a reasonable chance. Apart from which, he's not dead.'

'All a matter of time, isn't it?' asked Sorley.

Jeff lay hooked up to tubes that ran fluids in and tubes that took fluids out. A policeman sat with him. They'd been waiting for two days for him to wake up. The consultant had laughed and shaken his head. 'First he gets bottled, then he's belted with a blunt instrument, then he lies in the rain all night and half the next day, he's got multiple fractures of the skull, though none of them serious, I agree, and he's got pleurisy. It's only by God's good grace that he didn't drown: he was found lying face down in a puddle. I don't know when he'll come round. I don't know *whether* he'll come round. He's mending. Somewhere in his brain, there's a delay switch that'll turn him back on when the time's right.'

'He could die before that time comes?' Webb wanted to know.

'He could. He might.'

'Will he?'

'As I said: he's mending. That's all we know at the moment.'

Jeff slept on, his face purple and yellow and green with bruising, the white pillow under him, the white sheet drawn up, so that he resembled nothing so much as a livid and furious eye, wide open and staring, between pale, unblinking lids.

Kate lay on her hotel bed and looked at the ceiling.

Maybe I could have done something else, she thought. Talked to him? Talked him out of it? Not hit him so hard? Not hit him so many times? But how do you make those decisions? To hit this hard, not that hard; this many times, not that many times? What's hard? What's hard enough? How many times is enough? Just enough?

Just touch him a bit. Hurt a bit. Touch and hurt a bit would be all right.

She slept for a while, and sleep brought up a clutter of images that made her cry out, and work her legs like a runner. She woke with the dusk, feeling weary, but got up off the bed and went out to a call box and dialled Stephen Cawdrey's number.

A young woman answered, and said, 'Wait a moment,' almost before Kate had asked if Cawdrey was there. She heard the woman say, 'It's her,' as the phone was handed over.

Cawdrey came on the line already angry. 'Lynn, I don't know what you want. What do you want? Your cheque's in the mail and I'm planning to disembowel myself in public. That suit?'

'I'm not Lynn,' Kate said. 'I'm not your wife.'

She had a picture of Cawdrey looking over his shoulder at the young woman and grimacing angrily, because his *'Jesus Christ!'* was directed at someone other than her. He said, 'I'm sorry, it was . . . You know Lynn?'

'No. She gave me your number, that's all.'

'Okay. Well, I'm . . .' He paused. 'So how can I help?'

'I'm a friend of Michael Lester's,' she said. 'I was working on a story with him before he died. I didn't know what to do, at first. Now I've decided to pick the story up. I've got Michael's notes. No one else would make much of them. They're cryptic: I mean, literally. Sort of encoded. SC – that's you. There's a lot of SC. I thought you might like to explain a few things. I mean, it seems you were doing something along the same lines.'

'I dropped that story. There's nothing in it,' Cawdrey said. 'Who are you?'

'Gemma MacIntyre.'

'Do I know you?'

'No, I don't think so.'

'You're a journalist?'

'Researcher.'

'Trying to make a name for yourself.'

'Trying to finish Michael's story.'

'There's nothing there, my dear. Let it go.'

'Well, there is. There's lots here. Lots here in Michael's notes. You're here.' Kate had started to busk, now.

'I am? Well, that's not so surprising. I think I was one step ahead of Michael. Two or three steps, perhaps. Which is why I knew that it was a dead end. I told him that.'

'The police had these notes,' Kate said, 'as you might guess. But they didn't have the key. Michael's sort-of shorthand. They didn't pay them any mind so far as I know. They didn't see anything in them. On the other hand – I've got the key, so I know what they mean, and I'm pretty sure that if they'd had the key, if the cops had had the key, you know, I'm *pretty* sure they would have wanted to talk to you.'

There followed a long pause, that only ended when Kate said, 'Hello?'

'You want a meeting?' Cawdrey asked. 'Is that it?'

Kate was inching forward like someone clearing mines on a moonless night. She said, 'No, I don't think so. I just need some help. I've reached a wall.'

'What kind of a wall?'

She took a step in the dark. 'Michael was angry with you. Very angry. You let him down. He kept an account of it.'

'He was taking risks I didn't want to take.'

'Taking them in a good cause.'

'There are a million new good causes every day.'

'I know about the risks,' Kate said, 'and I know why he was angry with you.'

Another pause. Then: 'How do I know –'

Kate cut across him. 'I know why you dropped the story.' No I don't, she thought, but I'm counting on you to tell me.

'Nothing illegal about it,' Cawdrey said.

'Nothing illegal, maybe.' Kate injected her tone with contempt.

Cawdrey rose to the implied insult. 'It was a retainer. I'm freelance. I work for who the hell I like.'

Kate smiled a slow smile. *Money*: he'd taken a bribe. She let the silence carry. *Who?* Whose hand in whose pocket?

'There's nothing there,' Cawdrey said. 'I'm hanging up. It's a dead issue.'

'Not now,' Kate told him. 'It's live again. And the money puts you right in the middle. A payoff. A bung.'

'What is it you want?'

'I told you – there's a wall. I can't get over it. Michael's notes don't tell me everything. Or, if they do, I'm not clever enough to see it.'

'If I can help . . . If I decide to help . . . What do I get?'

'Anonymity.'

'How can I be sure?'

'Trust me.'

Cawdrey laughed. 'Are you kidding? I'm a *journalist*.'

'Which means when you've said, "Trust me", you were always lying.'

'Not always.'

'Same with me. I'm not lying now. I'm not lying when I say: Help me, and I'll guarantee your name is never mentioned. I'm not lying when I say: Don't help me and it gets mentioned all the time to everyone. These notes give me lots. Lots and lots to talk about.'

'What's the wall?'

'A name, of course.'

Almost across the minefield, almost home, the wind kicking dust into her eyes, the little steel tread-triggers on the mines quivering in the wind like spikes of grass.

'Tim Farnol,' Cawdrey said, and put down the phone.

Kate went back to the hotel and used the headed notepaper in her room to make some notes of her own.

Michael's story: dynamite: remember?
Michael collars Cawdrey at conference: furious.
Cawdrey has taken bung to drop story.
Key name: Tim Farnol (MP for somewhere – Midlands?).
Floppy disk – still at Penarven?

It didn't look like much to save a life with. She had slept so much during the day that she wasn't at all tired. She watched TV for as long as she could bear to, then went out. Being on the streets was foolhardy and she knew it, but she felt as if she had stepped out of a cage, and the feeling was worth the risk. Her new short black hair made her feel secure.

She went to the Polish Café and left a message for Z. Cybulski: *Mobile phone works brilliantly, thanks. Love, Gemma.*

She drank coffee and watched old men playing chess with infinite slowness, infinite care, infinite love, each move sketched in the mind before the piece was raised, then sketched in the air before the piece was set down, then recollected with a troubled eye and a quizzical frown after the event. There was a radio playing music: a Beethoven piano sonata.

She thought, I should stay here forever: the old men and their slow-moving chess, Beethoven, this yellow light from the lamps, people smoking and talking as if it were a café in Warsaw . . .

Which is where I should have been that night, that awful night of Michael's death, where I should have played with the quartet, where I'd like to be right now – far from here.

She left late and walked back through the streets between

Queensway and Westbourne Grove. People were bedding down in doorways. She gave them money whether they asked for it or not: the city's feral children, ravenous, long-suffering, barely visible.

I could always go back to them, she thought, if people get too close. If I start to think too much about the cell, the courtroom, the eyes of the jury. If I'm almost within reach.

I could always go back. Barely visible.

PART TWO

Thirteen

You might think that two such men would have met at some discreet restaurant, or in a park, or on neutral ground of some sort. In fact, they met in the boardroom at Wideworld Industries as if there were no reason not to.

Larry Packer was head of security for the group of companies; he spent half the year in the UK, the other half in the USA, but he travelled, too. His air miles would have bought Uruguay. He dressed like a banker: dark suit, striped shirt, close-patterned tie. He was a tall man who had been good-looking the other side of forty; but hours on planes and in meetings had sagged his jawline and filled out his gut. He wore his dark hair short and slicked back. His broken nose was a legacy from college football days; he liked it; women had liked it once.

He poured coffee into two cups and handed one over. He said, 'We've got a situation here, as you can tell.'

The other man's name was Robert Corso. The men were about the same height, a little under six feet, but where Packer was bulky Corso was slim, though no one would have called him spindly. His dark hair was heavy and he wore it to the collar. His features were even, apart from a slight turn to the mouth, a twist, that lent a sour note to his smile.

Corso took the coffee and set it to one side. He had spent the previous hour reading a report compiled by Packer, and seen by no one but him. And now Corso. The report was stored in the wall safe in Packer's office; it had never left the building. Corso dropped the pages onto the table.

'A situation,' he said. 'You have – that's right.' He looked away from Packer, settling his gaze on the window, and the view beyond of neat lawns and car parks and twelve tennis courts that

113

any WWI employee could use. He appeared to be thinking about what he'd just read: making patterns, devising solutions.

Three of the courts were occupied. Corso watched a couple of points being played and lost. He said, 'Who killed Lester?'

'Well . . .' Packer toyed with his coffee cup, turning it in the saucer with one blunt finger. 'This was a guy . . . This was someone we hired to . . . you know, like the report says . . . like I said in the report . . . The idea was that he'd hassle Lester. Make life difficult for him. Dirty tricks, etcetera. First thing was to get in and find any material he might have. I mean, we knew he had *some.*'

'Thanks to Tim Farnol,' Corso said.

'Right, yeah, Farnol.' Packer shook his head wearily. 'Son of a bitch. He just handed it over without so much as a kiss my ass. Next thing, this Lester is on the fucking telephone. He telephones here, this building, right here. Any warning from Farnol that this might happen? My ass there is.' He grimaced, and scoured his lips with thumb and forefinger, as if Farnol were a taste gummed up at the corners of his mouth.

'So . . . well . . . get that material and anything else, any research, whatever, disks and whatever, wipe the hard disk on his computer, shit like that.'

'But he showed up –' Corso observed. 'Lester.'

'Stupid bastard showed up in the middle, right in the fucking middle. Well, our guy had done some of the stuff, you know, got his floppy disks, and fucked his hardware and etcetera. We think. We're not sure. He wasn't sure, because he hadn't finished looking when he shows up, yeah, you're right – Lester. Shows up and starts to . . . you know, our guy is, Hey, I'm outta here, but this Lester, he's a fucking hero, standing there buck-naked, swinging his goddam fists. *Jesus!*' Packer started to laugh. '*Jesus!* Bare-assed, his dick hanging out like a bell-pull and he's, like, Who am I? Who am I? – Evander Holyfield.' Packer's laughter grew, then faded. 'Our guy's trying to get out, but Lester's not taking it. They get to the kitchen. There's the knife block. They both reach for it. *Both* reach for it. You can see it, can't you?

Fucking mess.' Packer raised his hands like a preacher. 'Our guy won the bet.'

'But what's his –' Corso started to speak, but Packer cut across him.

'He shouldn't have done it, he didn't intend to do it, but he did it. Etcetera.' He poured more coffee. 'No, listen, I can't tell you his name.'

'I don't want to run across him. Or if I do, I want to know it's him. He's a problem.'

'No he's not. He's not in the country. He's not even in any *known* country. He's in never-never land, whatever.'

'Where exactly? No name, okay, but where exactly?'

'He's in small-town Australia. There's a deal he doesn't come back for five years. If he likes it there, not at all. He's living a nice life. His family is living a nice life.'

'Who knows about him?'

'Me.'

'Who knows about me?'

'Same guy.'

'Your board.'

'No.'

'Your MD.'

'No.'

'Someone who runs you; someone you report to.'

'No. It doesn't work that way. My job's my job. They don't want to know. It's always worked that way. I write a report each month. Well . . . It's true where it can be true. Mostly, nothing bad to report, etcetera. Mostly, things go along just fine. We're just a business like any business. You know how it is with multi-nationals. Stuff behind the fan all the time. Working with governments, working with asshole dictators, working with the CIA and those brand of guys, working with each other. Looking in each other's windows, too. You want to guess our annual budget for surveillance work? Covert work? Anti-espionage? Let me tell you. Millions.'

Corso didn't comment. After a moment, he said, 'It's not an easy problem.'

'No kidding. Listen, there was no idea of kill the guy. No one said kill the guy. I mean, that would have been . . . That's not how we operate.'

'No?' Corso asked. 'What about Niger? What about Ecuador? What about Uzbek –?'

Packer waved a hand. 'No, no, no, no, listen, that's . . . Where are you from?'

'Utah, then San Francisco, then New York. Mostly New York.'

'*Utah*,' Packer said. You mean, like, *Utah*?'

'Born there.'

'No shit.' Packer remembered the purpose of his question. 'Local stuff is local stuff. Local. It's not England or France or Italy or *Utah*. It's not the civilised world. We do business like anyone else. Disney, Exxon, Coca-Cola, Toyota, whoever it is, etcetera. Do what needs to be done if it can be done. Find a way. There's always a way. People are reasonable. People listen. Out where it's *local*, you know – anything's possible. Shit happens.'

'You want me to find the girl. Kate Randall.'

'That looked fine. That looked terrific. They decided she killed him. Lovers' tiff. Jesus!' Packer grimaced. 'I guess it's the obvious answer. Definition of a smart cop? – Cop with the obvious answer. Whatever. It was good for us. Good decision, good mistake. They catch her, they convict her, everything's forgotten.'

'Except they didn't.'

'That's right.'

'What do I do?'

'Find her; turn her in.'

'Anything else?'

Packer shrugged. 'It would be good to find out if she knows anything. She was seeing the guy. She might know stuff. No reason why she should put it all together. My thinking on her thinking? – Some guy comes in to rob the place, shivs Lester, the cops get the wrong idea. I'm getting information that they've got a good case against her: witness, forensic, motive. I guess she had lousy luck. You can see how it goes for some people – she's innocent, but suddenly she's looking guilty as hell.'

'Where's it come from? The information you're getting?'

'I have a petty cash facility, you know? People talk to people who talk to me.'

'Find her and turn her in isn't the same as find her and check what she knows. Because *check what she knows* might mean *turn her in* isn't a good idea.'

'No,' Packer said, 'I just want to know what kind of covering we might have to do. What kind of disinformation. She knows nothing? Fine. Turn her in and forget the rest. She knows something of what Lester knew? Turn her in, etcetera, but tell me and I'll make the necessary adjustments. It makes no big difference. There's no reason for her to put Lester's death in the same frame as WWI, whatever she knows. Two different stories. Burglar kills Lester; she goes down for it. Story one. WWI spends a million bucks covering ass. Story two.'

'If she makes a connection? If she's already made a connection?'

'Not going to happen.'

'Picture it.'

'I'll think about it when you tell me it's true.'

'Pretend to be thinking about it. Pretend I've just told you.'

'Why?'

'I need to know where the bottom line is.'

Packer made rings on a paper napkin with his coffee cup. He got up and went to the window, so that he could look at Corso's reflection without looking at Corso. The lawns were an even green, the cars were parked in neat lines, their bodywork throwing back long slicks of light from the afternoon sun. The sky was a high, hard blue. The tennis courts were a rich red and the players wore white sneakers and socks, white shorts, white shirts, white headbands. You couldn't better it.

'She could have an accident, I guess. How would you feel about that?'

'Bad accident?' Corso asked.

'Bad, yeah.'

'What do you think of my fee?' Corso asked.

'Professional,' Packer said. 'It's a professional fee. We can handle it.'

'Handle it twice,' Corso said.

Kate could see two possibilities for action: to talk to Tim Farnol and to look at the contents of Michael Lester's laptop. There had to be something, though; action of some sort. Something to *do*. Unless she felt like spending the rest of her days living in a small hotel above Hampstead Heath. Or maybe catching a boat to Alaska.

It occurred to her that whatever she might find on the laptop could be useful when she spoke to Farnol. So laptop first. She took a walk on the heath and checked the odds with herself.

They're poor.

I think I know that.

They're very poor.

If Michael's house is still being watched, then, of course, it can't be done. If it's not, then it can. Does that sound right?

If it's not being watched . . .

They'll have finished there, won't they? Done whatever they have to do. Why would they hang around?

For you.

Really? Would I plan to go back there?

Jesus Christ, you *are* planning to go back there.

Sure, right. But would they think that?

Do I know how they think?

It's a risk, I know that.

We've been taking risks. We wound up in a cave full of water. We wound up with Jeff.

I don't think they'll be there. I think they might still be at Penarven, but I don't think they'll be at Michael's place. It was *Michael's* place: that's the point. Not mine; his. Why would I go back? Revisiting the scene of the crime? Come on . . .

We can go through the park.

Kate laughed at herself. Okay. Through the park.

She placed a foot between the railing spikes and hoisted herself up, then cocked her free leg over and jumped clear. The line of houses stood about half a mile from where she climbed in. She wanted to be a long way back, and have a long, long look. She followed the line of the railings down towards Michael's road and the backs of the houses, stopping every twenty yards or so and watching. There was nothing to see.

The park had closed at dusk: that was two hours ago. She thought it best to arrive while people were still up and awake and making noise: playing music, watching TV, entertaining friends to dinner. Being busy. She reached the corner where the road began and stood in the angle of the railings, close by the first house. There were lights, but the blinds were drawn. She waited ten minutes. A dog-fox coughed down at the river end of the park, where the house lights petered out. A dog-fox, then an owl, testing the air with its rising call. The hidden life of London: wild.

House by house, she moved towards Michael's back gate. Then reached it. Then went inside and stood in the garden, waiting for lights to come up and voices to tell her not to move.

It didn't happen.

The garden was both familiar and utterly strange. She remembered summer evenings with a glass of wine and friends . . . But it was empty now in a way that had to do with loss; with things that were irrecoverable. She moved to the kitchen window and looked in. All dark, all still. She counted to the third paving of a little stone patio and reached underneath it for the spare key. It was there for when they came back from a walk in the park; for when Michael locked himself out, as he often had; for friends who somehow beat the traffic and arrived early for the weekend.

As soon as she set foot in the place, Kate started to shake. She sat down on a chair and put her head in her hands. She thought: *It won't be here. The laptop won't be here. Why didn't I think of that? They'll have taken it.* She wasn't sure that this was true, but if she managed to convince herself, then it wouldn't be necessary to go into the living room. She didn't want to go in there – further in, deeper in. She didn't want to be in the kitchen, or in the house, or in the street, or the entire fucking neighbourhood.

The laptop was exactly where it had been: on the desk, close to the lamp. She picked it up and put it under her arm, but she couldn't move.

Michael was circling the room, bent over his arm, blood flowing down his naked abdomen and thighs. And there was Kate, trying to hold him, trying to keep him still. He hissed at her. He hobbled round the room, like a stricken animal.

Michael, she said, *Michael, Michael, Michael . . .*

Hiss . . . hiss . . . hiss . . .

She went through to the kitchen and he was there on the floor; she was cradling his head. The knife emerged with a thin squeak; with a terrible *creak* of steel withdrawing, and the blood welled up.

She locked the door and replaced the key. She would never need it again. The park seemed darker and quieter than it had before; cars slipped noiselessly down the far road, each with a sense of urgency: each with its destination already in mind.

Kate put the computer into her rucksack and swung over the railings, then walked two hundred yards to a bus stop and waited with four other people. A bus came almost immediately: she got on and found a seat near the front. She stared out at the park as they passed it: the park and her own reflection.

Corso had been last onto the bus. He sat immediately behind Kate, watching her watch her own image in the glass. Watching his own image watching hers.

Her new black hair curled in the nape of her neck, a perfect image of vulnerability. He wanted to lift the strands with his finger, wanted to stroke the little cleft of the nape.

So close that he could breathe on her. He puckered his lips and blew very softly, moving filaments of her hair, raising an itch, so that she put her hand there and gently scratched the place.

They got off the bus together, but went in opposite directions. He turned, after a moment, as if he were intending to cross the street and had looked back to check the road. He saw her go into the hotel.

He'd been to Penarven that day, though the house itself was still under police surveillance and he'd been obliged to keep his distance. Then he had spent some time close to Joanna's house; he had even watched, for a little while, near Kate's apartment.

Who knows? People do strange things. You can count on them for it.

He had visited the streets where the other members of the quartet lived; he had sat in the quiet square opposite Stuart Donnelly's office; he had driven back and forth along the streets of the leafy suburb where Kate and Joanna's parents had ended their days.

He had gone to Michael Lester's house, crossing the park in the first hour after darkness, and walked those silent rooms, the beam of his torch cruising round like a spotlight, pointing out this scene and that, as if rooms could become famous, as if floorboards and walls and curtains could be the stars of the show.

Cries came off the walls, up between the floorboards, out from the folds of the curtains. Dark stains were everywhere. He could smell the panic and pain.

In the living room, he switched on Lester's computer and ran the files onto floppy disks. He checked the e-mail, and made a note of the e-mail address.

In the bedroom, he stooped and sniffed the pillows: his side, her side. He found her clothes in the closet. Like a hound taking the scent. He found a pile of tiny cards in a drawer: florists' cards bearing messages from Kate. He found a folder full of dates and names and places, together with a genealogical chart, a family tree, its branches heavy with the dead. He found some holiday photographs and took a couple from a developer's pouch with last year's date on it. He found a stack of CDs, among them Kate playing Elgar's Cello Concerto. He put it in his pocket.

In the kitchen he stood still next to the spot where Lester had died. He imagined Kate there, Lester's head in her lap. He imagined the fear, the shock to the roots of a life suddenly changed forever.

He waited in the park, on the river side, close to Michael Lester's house, sitting on his coat, back to a tree, night glasses resting on his knee. Every few minutes, he would sweep the area leading down to Lester's back gate. He had been there an hour, and had already decided to give it another two, when Kate had arrived in the wide, crisp, green O of the glasses, like an actor stepping onto a stage. He hadn't recognised her, but he'd known who she was.

The spin of a coin, the turn of a card. Sometimes it works for you; sometimes you're out of luck.

He had watched her go in, then emerge with the laptop under her arm. Between the two events, he amused himself by scouting the park for wildlife: foxes trotting and stopping, their narrow, rufous faces turned towards him; an owl roosting.

In her hotel room, Kate plugged in the computer and booted up. On the little desktop that ran under the mirror in her room was a box of floppy disks she had bought in order to download the contents of Michael Lester's hard disk. She was beginning to feel secure, now, with her new hair, with no news of Jeff, being just one person in a big city; secure in the way she'd retrieved the laptop by simply walking in and fetching it.

Nothing more than a spin of a coin . . . the right place at the right time. Kate would never have guessed the way fortune had turned for her, the coin spinning: good fortune, ill fortune, good fortune, ill –'

She was feeling lucky.

Fourteen

The computer had been cleaned: she could see that. Not wiped – there were files and folders still there, but nothing of any significance. Certainly nothing that could be described as dynamite. She checked the backup file and the waste-bin and found the same disappointing cleanliness. She checked the e-mail and a flood of colour suddenly swamped her cheek, as if she had wandered in front of a window, naked, and found a crowd staring in at her.

Kate, hullo –

In case you get this, somehow . . . I'll try other methods of getting in touch as well, but I'm not sure what they could be just yet. Perhaps I'll try your music colleagues . . . something along those lines. God, this is really a long shot. Michael's e-mail address is the only thing I can come up with at present.

I don't want to put my name down here; and I'm sending this e-mail from an electronic poste restante: a cyber-café. I came to the UK to talk to Michael, found he was dead, and have been here ever since, wondering what the fuck to do next. I'm a colleague of Michael's, though we hadn't ever met. I work mostly in the USA. But we had communicated for some time, and traded information on the environment, multinational corporations, stuff behind the fan. I'm an investigative journalist. Specialist subject? – the way the world is being sytematically fucked up by vested interests: work much the same as Michael's.

I talked with him by e-mail over the last couple of weeks before his death. Did you kill him? They say you did, but I don't think so.

Where are you, I wonder? You must be scared and angry. You can

talk to me. I'm not a cop, I'm not a trap. You don't have to get close.
Just surf across cyberspace to find me.

I'm not a trap, but I like to set them for some people. I've set a few for
oil companies and pharmaceuticals; for a few senators with more
bucks in the bank than they should have; for a few rednecks in Brooks
Brothers suits. So I'll call myself . . .

. . . The Trapper

Kate read it a dozen times or more. Finally she mailed a response:

Trapper: Why should I believe you?

Corso said, 'I've made contact. Just letting you know that.'
'You know where she is?' Packer sounded eager. He said, 'Hold
it, wait a minute, someone just came in . . .' Then there came his
distant voice: *Okay . . . okay . . . I'll get on to it . . .* An
unconvincing fake, as he fitted the microphone-sucker, or activated the perma-surveillance device.
Corso smiled. He thought, I've been done by experts, pal, and
waited for Packer to come back to the phone. 'I know where she
is. She's at Mikeless@mcmail.com. Don't worry. She's out of
reach, but not lost. Soon she'll be close enough to touch.'
He thought of the way her hair had stirred in the nape of her
neck; her hand coming round to smudge the tickle.
'This is between us, Corso. I don't want any loose information
flying about like leaves, you know? Like, stuff between modems,
etcetera.' This was Packer letting the tape know that he was doing
his job. 'And when I say between us, I mean, you and me
exclusive. Not my boss, not my boss's boss . . . and etcetera, you
know?'
'Don't worry – I'll know if anyone's eavesdropping.'
'What does she say?'
'She wants to know: why should she trust me?'
Packer laughed. 'You should've told her you're from Utah.'
'You were embarking on a programme of disruption with
Michael Lester. Harassment. Have I got that right?'

124

'That was the idea . . . before our guy pulled the knife from the knife block.'

Packer wasn't being careful about what he said. It was clear that he felt confident about the integrity of the phone line. Part of the million-dollar security package, Corso thought.

'What sort of thing was planned?'

'Anyone we had in our pocket who could make life tough for him . . . then putting stories his way that we later discredited . . . misinformation, etcetera. Then we'd go for personal stuff, sex life, see if we could get him picked up and then hidden camera work at the hooker's apartment and Lester getting his bone wet . . . well, anything. The usual.'

'Wiping his computer. Taking the disks.'

'Yeah. That was . . . well, that was our guy's job before he left for the outback.'

'He find what you hoped?'

'Yeah. We got the stuff back.'

'No. You got a copy of the stuff.'

'What –?'

Corso left a pause so that it could sink in.

'You saying,' Packer asked, 'that he made copies – this is a copy – there are other copies?'

'What would you do?'

'Yeah . . .' Packer was thinking ahead. 'She's got a copy.'

'Who knows?'

'She's got a copy, right?'

'I don't know, Packer. But it's not a long bet.'

'How long before you find out about that?'

'How long before she trusts me?'

Kate sat with a mid-morning coffee and watched the old men playing chess. The same old men, the same old gambits. Why should they change? The game they had played in Kraków was the game they played in London; the game each would play to his dying day. Kate found comfort in the careful rhythm of thought overlapping thought, the toying with this move or that, the slow raising of a head, of an eye, of a smile, as the victor looked across at his opponent, his oldest friend, his best friend, as if to say, '. . . and next time, it will be you to win. So goes the world.'

No one in there could possibly have been a policeman, unless someone had dragged out the Sherlock Holmes disguise kit. She couldn't be certain about people in the street, but she had been there for half an hour and why would they wait? She went to the counter and asked a middle-aged bottle-blonde with perfect cheekbones if there might be a package for Cybulski. There was.

As she handed it over, the woman said, 'He was a friend of my mother's cousin. Are you related to him?'

'I don't think so.'

'He was beautiful. You have seen the film?'

'Yes.'

'So beautiful. His dark glasses, his haunted face. You remember how he seemed to see ghosts wherever he looked?'

'Yes.' And she did remember. Her father had taken her to see a scratchy print of the movie at the NFT.

'You remember how he lit the glasses of vodka for friends dead by the Germans?'

'I remember.'

'He became fat,' the woman said. 'He was run down in the street. He became a drunk.'

She turned away to make coffee for someone, leaving Kate clutching her package.

It was a digital mobile, tougher to tap. Kate went back to her hotel room to make the call. She phoned the House of Commons and asked for Farnol's office. A secretary asked her who she was, and she said she was speaking from the office of Michael Lester's solicitor.

Farnol came on the line sounding wary. No, not wary, she decided. Worried. He asked what he could do to help.

'I'm a friend of Michael Lester's,' she began.

'My secretary said you were a solicitor.'

'No.'

'Then what is it you want?'

'Some information.'

'About what?'

'About why Michael Lester died.'

There was a pause long enough for a ship to sink. Finally, Farnol said, 'Who are you?'

'You know a man named Stephen Cawdrey.'

'Never heard of –'

'A journalist. Yes you do.'

'I'm going to put the phone down now.'

'No, don't do that. It wouldn't be wise. Because my next call would be to the police; the call after that to the press.' Kate raised her voice for the bluff, as if volume might seem to mean determination.

Farnol laughed; it wasn't very convincing. 'To tell them what?' He wanted to know; he *seriously* wanted to know.

'You expect me to give you a list? Over the phone? You want me to?' Kate, on the other hand, was very convincing. She wondered for a moment where the ability to make a lie so resemble the truth had come from. She decided it was desperation. She felt oddly nerveless, an actor long past first night, with the audience hanging on every word.

'No,' Farnol said, 'I don't want you to say another word. I want you to hang up and go away and stop bothering me.'

Kate delivered her best line. She'd never tried it before and didn't know whether it would have an effect. She was winging it.

'Michael Lester made copies of everything . . . You know what I'm talking about?' She waited, listening for a moment to Farnol's breathing. 'He gave me a computer disk. Cawdrey hasn't got the guts to use it. I have. But not just use it. Not just publish it. No. Say where it comes from. Link it to you. Understand?'

Silence: sometimes the best audience reaction of all.

'I know who you are,' Farnol said.

Kate flinched, then recovered herself. 'Good. I'd hoped you would.'

'We could meet.'

'Okay.'

'Bring the disk with you.'

Kate's turn to laugh. 'I don't think so. I'll bring hard copy.'

'Very well.'

'*Hard* copy,' Kate said, 'if you take my meaning. Hard for you. As in hard luck.'

'I'm here all evening,' Farnol told her.

Kate shook her head in pure wonder. 'You think I'm coming there? *Please.*'

'Where, then?'

Kate put herself at the other end of the city from where she was living, and in open space. She said, 'Richmond Park; by the ponds, tomorrow morning,' and nominated a time.

Farnol said, 'All right.' They arranged that Kate would call and confirm: half an hour before the meeting. Then Farnol asked, 'But what do you want from me?'

'The answers to some questions,' Kate said.

'Doesn't the computer disk give you those?'

The disk. He keeps mentioning the disk. As if he knows what I'd have found there.

'Some . . . not all,' she said. Then: 'As you know.' A shot in the dark.

It went home. 'What makes you think I'll give you the missing answers?'

He knows. He knows what's on the disk.

'Because things have changed. Because Michael was murdered. Because the answers I've already got are you. *Farnol*. The answers are Tim Farnol.'

George Webb had three meetings that day. The first was in the AMIP squad room. He and the team looked at what they'd got and decided it was thin. There were two detective sergeants on the team: one was still in Cornwall; the other, DS John Adams, was currently giving Webb some unpleasant news.

'We've seen everyone twice. The sister's tapped as you know. She goes to and fro between her house and the college where she teaches. We're keeping a presence at Penarven: DS Richardson and the locals, although we think the telephone call to her sister four days ago might have been made in London. Whether she's still here, what she plans to do, where she might go . . .' Adams shrugged. 'We're doing airports, and railway stations as far as we're able.'

'They're going to downgrade us,' Webb said.

There were seven people in the room: Webb, Adams, Carol Tanner, four DCs. At the mention of money – or the lack of it – a little growl went up: pack anger.

Webb continued, 'Less money, fewer officers. It can't be justified. She's gone – to all intents and purposes, she's gone. If we had fifty times the number of coppers and ten times the money and resources, there's no guarantee we'd find her. She's on the verge of becoming a statistic.'

On the wall were versions of a photograph of Kate Randall. In each, a police artist had taken a guess at how she might have changed her appearance: same length hair, but dark; same length hair, but blonde; short dark hair; short blonde hair; use of cosmetics to make the face seem thinner; use of cosmetics to make the face seem plumper; thin face, dark hair; fat face, dark hair . . . and so on through the likely permutations. One of them looked pretty much the way Kate looked now. Webb gazed at them. 'She's getting away from us,' he said. 'I reckon we've got a week or so to make a difference. Then down comes the financial guillotine.' He made a slicing gesture with his hand. '*Zip!*'

The team was allocating itself tasks for the rest of the day, when a call came in. Carol Tanner lifted the phone and spoke for a moment, then passed it to Webb, her eyebrow raised.

It was Tim Farnol rolling the dice. Farnol doing the only thing he could, reasonably, do. He said, 'I've had a telephone call from a woman whom I believe to be Kate Henderson.'

'Who?'

'The woman accused of the murder of –'

'Randall,' Webb told him. 'Kate Randall.'

'Sorry, yes. Right. Randall.'

'Why would Kate Randall call you, Mr Farnol?'

'Can we meet?'

'Oh, yes,' Webb assured him. 'We can meet.'

When he put down the phone, Carol Tanner and John Adams were looking at him expectantly.

'Tim Farnol?' he asked. 'Member of Parliament?'

'Member of Parliament and all-round rich bastard,' Carol noted.

'Member of Parliament, all-round rich bastard, and worried man.' Adams was guessing, the guess framing a question.

'Certainly sounded worried,' Webb said. Then he let them in: 'Kate Randall phoned him.'

'*Randall* phoned him?' Adams had been lifting his phone to make a routine call. Now he put it back. 'Our Randall?'

Webb shrugged. 'That's what he said.'

'She a friend of his?'

'He didn't even get her name right first time round.'

'Go on . . .' Carol Tanner prompted.

'Nothing. I mean, no explanation. He wants a meet.'

'Need company?' Adams wanted to know.

'You're curious.'

'You're right.'

'I'll see him first. Just me. He sounded jumpy. There's something hidden here. He's an MP – if there's something sleazy about this, he won't want an audience.'

'You're seeing him . . .?'

'Tonight. He's got an all-day meeting he can't dodge.'

'In no hurry, then . . .'

Webb shook his head. 'It wasn't that. He sounded . . . when he talked about meeting, he said "Tonight will be early enough".'

'You think he's got a line on her?' Carol asked.

'Something . . . I'm not sure what.'

Adams asked, 'But we might be able to get to her through him: is that how it seems?'

'That's what he was holding out,' Webb said. 'That seemed to be what he was offering.'

'Where there's an offer,' Adams observed, 'there's a deal.'

'You're right,' Webb said. He was thinking: *What deal? How close am I? Am I close?* Suddenly he was like a man who draws the second ace on the last flop. Not a sure-thing hand, but a better bet than most.

The AMIP meeting had been the first. Between it and the third came a meeting that was, in effect, three-in-one. Webb sat in a dressing room at the Royal Festival Hall, where he was about as welcome as a sick-slick on a bathing beach.

Annie Forrester took her viola out of its case. It was difficult for her to keep the hostility out of her voice when she said, 'You've got ten minutes.'

'I've got as long as I want,' Webb told her.

The other members of the original quartet were there: Victoria Pedrales and Nuala Phillips, both violin players; Kate's replacement was a cellist called Sally Nelms: they'd played with her before. Webb had agreed it wasn't necessary for her to be present.

'No,' Annie said. 'You haven't got as long as you want. You've got ten minutes. After that our preparation time starts and you're out of here.'

When Webb rubbed a hand across his mouth, Nuala could see it was a way of holding back anger. She said, 'It's a waste of time, Mr Webb. None of us has heard from Kate. We've already told your people that.'

'People on the run – people who need help – such people usually turn to friends.'

'If we heard from her and neglected to tell you,' Annie asked, 'wouldn't that be against the law?'

'It would, yes.'

'So are you assuming one or all of us has broken the law?'

'I'm asking you whether Kate Randall has contacted any of you in any way.'

'Same thing,' Annie said. 'You're assuming we've heard from her and kept quiet about it. You're assuming guilt.'

Webb's hand went across his mouth again. 'Or maybe you've heard from her since you last spoke to my officers.'

Annie leaned forward and spoke slowly, as if to someone with only a rudimentary grasp of the language. 'It's the same thing. You're asking us to say we're guilty of withholding information. We're not.'

Webb looked at his shoes, then he looked up. Victoria had

picked up her fiddle and was starting to tune it idly. She ran a little jig off the strings. A toe-tapper.

Nuala said, 'Are you staying for the concert, Mr Webb? We could wangle you a house seat, I expect.'

The jig became a reel, viola and violin together, now, playing softly. Both women had turned their backs.

Webb went to the door. 'Chas and Dave,' he said, 'that's me. None of this egghead stuff. Like all policemen, I'm very conservative and not all that bright.'

After he'd gone, Annie said: 'Anyone?'

The other two shook their heads.

'Where is she, though?' Nuala asked. 'Where the fuck would she be?'

'Out on a limb,' Annie said.

'Do you think she's okay?' Victoria was checking her bow. 'She's pretty fit, isn't she? – the gym and skiing, and she used to go rock-climbing in Scotland when her family went up. I mean, if she had to cope . . . I bet she's okay, don't you?'

'God knows,' Annie said.

Farnol was Webb's third meeting. He was sitting at a large table at the back of an Italian restaurant when Webb joined him, and reading parliamentary papers. Webb wondered whether the documentation with its portcullis crest was there to impress him. To remind him . . . Farnol poured Webb a glass of Chianti from a half-empty bottle and beckoned for a menu. When Webb had ordered, he shuffled the papers into a pile and stowed them in his briefcase. The meticulousness with which he did this, the tilting of the wine bottle, the careful recommendations from the menu – these were all delays. Farnol was like a man chatting brightly, while the dentist stands there, smiling patiently, mirror in one hand, drill in the other.

Finally, Farnol coughed, and started to rearrange the table furniture – toothpicks, ashtray, a miniature bottle of olive oil crowded with herbs and peppercorns. They followed a triangular pattern of strict rotation. He kept his eyes on these items while he spoke.

'Michael Lester was a journalist, as you know. Journalists like to play a game called Holier Than Thou. They booze, whore, rig their expenses, doorstep bereaved mothers . . . but that's okay because they're the whistle-blowers. No one blows the whistle on them. Different for people in what is laughingly referred to as the public domain. Meaningless term, except insofar as it refers to the open season journalists keep on all such people round the clock, week in, week out.'

Farnol opened his mouth to continue, but Webb moved the toothpicks slightly to the right, disturbing the pattern Farnol had created, and the man glanced up.

'Money,' Webb asked, 'or sex?'

'Sex,' Farnol said.

'Girls or boys?'

Farnol stared at Webb a moment, then restored the toothpicks to their rôle. 'Girls, of course. Women.'

'Lots, or one in particular?'

'Do I have to –'

'It's best if you tell me.'

'If I tell you in confidence,' Farnol assumed.

'In confidence,' Webb agreed, 'yes.' And when Farnol looked up from his triangular game, one eyebrow raised, he said again, 'In confidence.'

'Lots,' Farnol said.

'Well, that's much easier than one in particular. Were they prostitutes?'

'Some were. Not all.'

'And nobody's pregnant, or anything like –?'

'No.'

'Or got anything incurable?'

Farnol shook his head. He was eager to keep his own lie as simple as possible. He said, 'However, if my wife found out, she would act immediately. None of this brave face stuff.'

'Stand by your man . . .' Webb offered.

'Stand *on*, yes. *By*, no. I'd lose her, kids, house, career, the lot. My constituency party would be happy to stab me in the back, I should think. Have to resign, anyway.'

'When it comes to unofficial legovers,' Webb observed, 'we're a strangely puritanical country. What was Lester doing?'

'Nothing,' said Farnol, which made Webb look at him sharply. 'Nothing . . .'

'No, nothing. He had the information, I knew that. He let me know that. But he hadn't said what he wanted for it.'

'Any ideas?'

'Again, nothing. At least – nothing for the time being. It was in the bank – that was the impression I got. In a long-term deposit account, gathering interest, and waiting for a time when Lester might want to make a withdrawal. You know – wanted to know something, wanted some inside track, wanted what only I could supply. Information. Who knows – maybe he wouldn't ever have used it. He certainly wasn't gloating when he told me what he knew: wasn't taking pleasure. He could have offloaded it onto a tabloid for a fair sum. I wasn't sure. I know journos, though. I decided to think the worst. Some time, some day . . .'

The table furniture continued on its triangular journey. Webb wondered whether the triangle had real psychological significance, as in 'emotional triangle', or whether the constant movement had a looser connotation: 'shift the blame', or 'keep moving', or 'confuse the issue'.

'Kate Randall has got this information,' he said. 'Whatever Lester had, she's got it.'

'Yes.'

'She's been in touch with you.'

'Yes.'

'You know where she might be.'

'No, I don't.'

'Not where she is now. Where she might be at some other time.'

Farnol kept his eyes down. The angle of his head meant: *that depends . . .*

'What do you want from me?'

'Immunity.'

'Sorry?' Webb looked confused.

'I want things kept quiet. I want the information she's got suppressed.'

134

'There are people I have to talk to about that.'

'No,' Farnol said. 'No, you don't. It isn't going to be like that.' He paused. 'It's going to be like Norman Leary.'

Webb lifted his glass, but didn't drink from it. He twirled it so that the wine took the light, glowing, deep red. Finally he took a rapid sip, as if taste were the least important thing. He said, 'Norman Leary was guilty as charged.'

'Well, no,' Farnol said, 'no, I don't believe he was. In fact that's why his conviction was overturned as unsafe and unsound. Ten years late, though. Especially too late for Leary.'

'Guilty. It's why he killed himself.'

'He killed himself because of what was done to him in prison. And, before that, because of what was done to him by the judicial system. And, before that, what was done by you.' Webb shook his head and smiled. 'As certain people know,' Farnol offered.

'The unreliability of a prosecution witness; a judge's ruling.'

'They were the official reasons,' Farnol agreed. 'But mention could have been made of evidence withheld; evidence falsified.'

'But it wasn't.'

'No, that's right. As yet.'

'Leary was guilty. He killed her. I know that. Dead cert.'

'It's tedious to argue,' Farnol observed, 'so let's not. You can see how I want things done.'

'I *can* see. And perhaps *you* can see that I'm getting ever so slightly fucking angry.'

Farnol nodded, as if in sympathy. His hands moved continually: toothpicks, ashtray, bottle; march, march, march. 'We haven't ever met. This meeting didn't occur. That's the first thing. The second is this: I can haul her in, or I can cut the line.'

Webb stared. 'You hadn't better try.'

'Try?' Farnol asked. 'No, it won't be a question of trying. I can do either. And I will do one or the other.'

'Well,' Webb observed, 'you can keep talking. That can't do any harm.' Deals, he thought; it's all deals. Life's one long fucking negotiation. No such thing as a free Chianti.

'She has a computer disk. I want it returned to me unread.'

Webb seemed to ponder this, trying it for practicability. 'If another officer finds it? If the same officer slips it into his A-drive? I mean . . .'

'None of this will happen,' Farnol said, 'because you'll make sure it doesn't.'

A little spurt of anger slipped over Webb's lip: a little hiccough of bile. 'Farnol, you can't expect to order me —'

'You're not dealing with a snout here,' Farnol said. 'You're not bargaining with some lowlife. This is how it'll work, no other way: I get the disk; you never know what was on it; you get Kate Randall.'

'If I say yes and I'm lying?' Webb suggested.

'I'll implicate you.'

'How?'

'It doesn't matter. I could make some educated guesses about what weight of hard drugs goes into your nick and what weight is actually accounted for. I'm sure that would produce results. Or there's Norman Leary. I think I know where the notebook's buried, if you take my meaning. Or I could make it both stories on a controlled leak. As soon as the heat goes out of one, here comes another.' Farnol was smiling. 'Where the police are concerned, it's easy to dig some dirt, isn't it? The public expects it.'

Farnol put the toothpicks down with tremendous care. He said, 'Listen. Are you listening? Get me the disk and I'll get you Kate Randall. Tell me we never met, and I'll go away and try to work out my future. That's up to you. But lie to me — take her and refuse me my side of the bargain — and I promise I'll bury you.'

Webb sat still while the waiter put lamb cutlets and a salad in front of him, and topped up both their glasses. Finally, he said: 'It's not girls, is it?'

'It's girls,' Farnol said.

'It's a lot tastier than that.'

'It's girls.'

'You've got more than pussy in the kitty.' Webb laughed into Farnol's straight face.

'I'm telling you it's girls.'

'I know what you're telling me.' Webb ate in silence for a couple of minutes. 'Let's play a game. There's only one thing I'll hang you for, and that's security of the realm. Why? Because for that, anybody hangs: me included. So – is it security of the realm?'

'It's girls.'

Webb thought, Can he sink me? If I go even part-way with this, he probably can. Do I want to get out of this clean? Okay, then it's *we never met and you're on your own.* Try to force him, try to play copper, and he pulls the same stunt as if I lie to him. Only one choice: walk away, or take the deal.

Farnol called the waiter over and asked for another bottle.

'Not for me,' Webb said.

'No, it's not for you.'

One thing's for sure, Webb thought. It's not girls. Girls is what we're saying. *Girls* stands for whatever Lester had on this bastard. He asked, 'What does she want – Kate Randall? What's her angle?'

'She wants me to get her a passport.' Farnol's lies came easily: part of the job.

'Can you do that?'

'I expect I could, yes.'

'Have you told her you will?'

'Yes.' The triangle widened as the lies piled up. An analyst would have seen it.

The second bottle arrived. Farnol flapped a hand at the waiter, who set the wine down and left. Farnol waited for Webb to pour himself a glass, but Webb was looking away to the side, as if he could see things working out in his mind's eye.

Here's what to do, Webb thought. Take the deal and worry later. I expect this bastard can fuck my life up some way or another if he wants to. I'll stay clear of that. He can have his disk. Do I care what it is? Do I care what he's done? Politicians . . . It's money and the improper use of influence, or it's money and arms sales, or it's money and oil. The worst possible thing it could be is money and drugs. It's always money and some fucking thing. Who cares?

He asked again, 'Is it security of the realm?'

'It's girls,' Farnol said. 'Girls, girls, girls.'

'I'll get you the disk,' Webb said, 'and I don't want to know.'

Farnol gave him the time and place.

'You'll have to be there,' Webb told him.

'Yes, of course.'

Webb got up and walked out of the restaurant without looking back. Farnol poured his first glass of wine from the second bottle and ordered some cheese. He thought it might work. It was the only damn thing that would work. The only thing other than meeting Kate Randall and killing her for the disk. Not that he had contemplated that. Not that he had the balls for that.

This way was the only possibility: the semi-official route. The powerful enlisting the powerful. He'd seen the look of recognition in Webb's eye.

Webb drove home through a misty drizzle, the wipers flip-flapping across the windscreen. He hated the smear on the glass that fine rain seemed to leave; he liked things pin-clear.

If I read the disk, he thought, I might see something that will change my mind.

So I won't.

Might change my mind about Michael Lester and why he died.

So I won't.

About Michael Lester and why he died and who –

So I won't. And, in any case, I can't. Catch Randall, bury Farnol's disk, and I get the result I want. Get tricky, and Farnol can make everything go wrong; bring everything down; pull the lot to pieces.

So I won't.

But the very thought of it made his fingers itch.

Fifteen

A low ceiling of endless cloud was moving across Richmond Park, dragging with it a sweep of grey rain. The cloud went beyond the horizon, then a little further back even than that. It looked like it would never lift. You couldn't imagine the park in sunlight, or the park grazed by a brisk wind. It was grey rain until doomsday.

The walkers and wildlife watchers had gone to ground. A few stolid types with dogs were doing the round of the ponds. A string of riders went by camouflaged by rain, grey slickers, grey faces, grey horses: they had paid for the privilege. George Webb stood back from the trees above the ponds and blew slightly through his lips to clear the rainwater from his mouth: it was driving directly towards him and the seven other officers standing at neat distances from each other along the fringe of woodland. Tim Farnol was standing next to Webb wearing a waxed jacket, boots and a cap, and looking as if he lacked only the Purdey and the black labrador. Two of the dog walkers were coppers; so were the two horsemen going at the walk along the bridlepath that ran above the ponds.

It was a little past ten a.m. Webb said, 'Fucking weather. This fucking weather.' He could see the dog walkers, but the horsemen were nothing more than shapes in a mist.

Farnol checked his watch. He asked, 'Do you want me to wait until we see her, or go out there now?'

'How much longer?' Webb asked.

'Ten minutes.'

'Give it five. Better if she sees you.'

'How will she know it's me?'

'Apart from the fact that you look like the squire of the sodding manor, you mean? Well, maybe she won't. Not immediately. Maybe she'll have to come down and take a closer look. Good.'

A herd of roe deer were cropping grass up on the far slope. The riders returned at a controlled trot, and the stud buck lowered his head a moment, before moving away, taking his wives with him.

'Do they have to go up and down like that?' Webb muttered. 'They look like they're on fucking patrol.' The rain had soured his language, and a chill was stealing into the small bones of his feet.

Farnol stepped out of cover and started to walk down to the ponds. He thought, Maybe killing her was an idea. Maybe that would have been possible. Could I have done that?

He flexed his fingers, as if testing them for strength, or tractability. What was it like to kill someone? he wondered. Like cancelling a debt. Like retrieving a mistake. Like turning back the clock.

To entertain himself further, he let the thought flow: What was it like to kill a woman?

The rain couldn't chill or depress him. He felt eager, short of breath, and on the verge of irrepressible laughter.

Kate was walking a long diagonal down the slope towards the ponds. She and her companion were about fifty feet above the deer, which kept the dog out of their way. Not that the dog would harry the beasts, its owner assured her, but the stags could be unpredictable.

She had found Pete Lemon a couple of minutes after entering the park. He was taking his dog down to the ponds, and she had fallen into conversation with him by the simple expedient of losing her footing and grabbing his arm for support. The dog, a German Shepherd, had barked at her and run in with its ears back. Pete Lemon had called its name and reassured it, then had reassured Kate. The dog's name was Shep – for shepherd – which was perfect because, although he was no more than thirty-five, Pete Lemon wore a Kangol cap, a neatly belted mac, waterproof overshoes and glasses with a pale frame and a little chain to allow them to rest just below the knot of his tie. A soft moustache sat on his lip like soiled moss. The stigma of the unkissable. Pete Lemon referred to himself in the third person and by his full name: 'Don't worry about her. Shep and Pete Lemon went to obedience classes. She's just doing her job of protecting. But Pete Lemon's in charge.'

Pete Lemon was glad of the company on his walk. Kate asked him questions to keep him engaged. She was wearing a dark green hiker's anorak, the hood up and the drawstring pulled. In that, and jeans, and boots, she could have been anyone. From a distance, she could have been a man. As she walked, listening to Pete Lemon, she watched the ponds. Two other dog walkers, three singletons, one couple. She peered through the rain at the singletons and found Farnol almost at once. He was circumnavigating the nearest pond, and looking like a man who possessed no sense of purpose, neither hurrying, nor standing still to watch the wildfowl. A man deep in thought, it seemed. On a fine day, he might have looked almost plausible.

George Webb saw two men walking above the herd, their dog running forward, then circling back, then running forward again. One of them picked up a stick and threw it. The dog loped off in pursuit. He saw his own dog walkers, his dog *handlers*, and the horsemen reappearing through the hanging rain.

It would work like this: Farnol would take her on a couple of circuits to listen to what she had to say: what she wanted. No one knew what that would be. Whatever it was, Farnol would accede to it. Once Kate had joined Farnol, she was, effectively, lost. The dog handlers were close by, and the horsemen. Webb and the other officers would walk down from the trees once someone had made the pinch. Easy. But first, they wanted to find out what Kate had; or thought she had.

Farnol had suggested that they follow her: see where she lived. He was anxious about where the disk might be. Kate wouldn't have it with her, he knew that.

Webb had pointed out the folly in this: 'It could be anywhere. You want the disk? Get Randall. Once we've got her, we'll get the disk. It's all she has to bargain with.'

'Bargain?'

'Manslaughter . . . Which in any case,' Webb said, 'it might well have been.'

'You don't mind that? You'd be happy with that?'

Webb shrugged. 'I don't much mind what happens to them afterwards,' he said. 'I'm not a vindictive man.'

Shep brought the stick back and Kate threw it again.

'He'll do that for ever,' Pete Lemon told her. 'Until your arm gets tired.'

They were about eighty yards light of the ponds. Kate could see Farnol loitering in the downpour. Shep turned up with the stick and slapped it against Kate's thigh.

'Let Pete Lemon do it.'

'No,' Kate said, 'it's fine,' and she lobbed the stick further down the slope.

Corso said, 'See that?' He was pointing.

For a moment, Farnol thought this was a policeman identifying their quarry, but realised at once that no one would be that stupid. His next thought was that it was a policeman making contact with a warning: something had gone wrong, there was some change of plan. Then he saw that it was neither of these things. It was what he needed least: common man.

'What?' Farnol asked. Corso kept pace with him, but was nudging his arm. In one hand he held a pair of field glasses.

'Baikal teal,' Corso said. 'Amazing.'

Farnol walked on. 'I don't really take much of an interest,' he said. 'But thanks.'

Corso shoved the glasses at him so that he had to take them or drop them. 'Great view through these.'

One of the dog walkers passed by, pausing a moment to adjust his dog's collar. Farnol made a pass with the glasses. 'Great,' he said, 'very interesting.'

'No, you're looking in the wrong direction.' Corso raised the glasses to his own eyes and pointed them straight towards Kate as she lifted her arm to throw the stick for Shep. She stayed frozen in that pose, almost as if the backwards swing might topple her. 'Rare visitor,' Corso said, 'there you go: Baikal teal.'

Farnol looked again and saw grass, rain, deer, two men with a dog, a distant spinney.

'You're looking up,' Corso said. 'You want to look down. At the water.'

Farnol jerked the glasses to and fro while Corso stood behind him, pointing eagerly.

'Jesus Christ of Nazareth!' Webb leaned against a tree trunk. A fine spray of rainwater came off his lower lip. 'What? What is it?'

John Adams was getting a message from the dog handler. 'Some guy wanting to point out some rare species of duck. Shall we warn him off?'

'Leave it,' Webb ordered. 'Leave it alone.' He watched as Corso pointed up towards the far pond, up towards the slope, then took the glasses back from Farnol to have another look himself. 'Leave it. He'll go away in a minute.' He scanned the rain-sodden park in all directions.

He thought, Come on, you awkward bitch. I want you. You're the one that got away. The only one. Only one ever. You're making me look like a stupid bastard. I've seen my name in the papers and I don't like the stories that go with it. I get memos I don't want to read. I hear things from superior officers that I definitely don't want to hear.

I've done a deal for your bones, and I want them.

'Just there!' Corso said. He might have been instructing a child. 'Just there, straight ahead. Can't you see it?'

Farnol handed the glasses back. 'I really have to get on,' he said. 'I'm sorry, but I have to get on.'

As Farnol strode off, Corso brought the field glasses back to bear on Kate. She was staring at him, her face in the bright circle almost close enough to touch.

Kate watched the glasses swing back towards her and stay steady. She turned her back and started up the slope.

'Sorry,' she said, 'I think I'll head for home now. I'm soaked.'

'Okay,' Pete Lemon said, 'sure. We'll come too,' and he whistled up the dog. He was enjoying the chat. Mostly he had only Shep for company. He liked the sound of Kate's voice, and the way she was happy to throw sticks, and to talk about anything that came into Pete Lemon's mind. He wondered if he might meet her again in the park, if he came at just the same time, and entered by just the same gate. He even thought that he might suggest it. He drummed up a picture of what she was like under the anorak, and it made him catch his breath.

They walked back, taking a long half-circle to avoid the deer, and soon dropped down on the other side of the hill.

Webb watched. The bird fancier had wandered away. The men with the dog had gone too. That left Farnol, the dog handlers, the horsemen, and Webb himself together with seven officers just inside the tree cover. They walked round the ponds, or rode up and down, or stood and waited.

Come on, you bitch.

Back among the trees, the low monotone of the rain picked up, rising in pitch, rising in volume, beating against the leaf canopy. The sky seemed to fall just beyond the brow of the hill.

Come on, you *bitch*.

Farnol trudged in a circle. He pulled back the elastic inner sleeve of his waxed coat and glanced at his watch, then looked back towards the trees, asking Webb an unspoken question.

Come *on* . . .

Webb let Farnol make another five circuits, but knew that it was pointless. He dipped into his pocket and brought out a hip flask. John Adams came over; he knew the signs. 'Call it a day, boss?'

Webb nodded. He took a swig from the flask and handed it over. Adams said, 'At least we know she's in London.'

'Do we? She might've been winding this pillock up for all I know. Putting him through his paces. Seeing if he'll do as he's told.'

'You reckon she's that clever?'

'It doesn't take cleverness. Just forethought.'

Farnol joined them. 'What do you think?' he asked.

Webb pocketed the flask. 'I think you'll get another phone call.'

'I was there,' Farnol said. 'I went there. You didn't come.'

'Yes I did. I saw you.'

'Then why –'

'It didn't feel safe.'

'For Christ's sake.' Neither wanted to speak next. Finally, Farnol asked, 'So what do we do? Try again?'

'I'll need to think of something. A safe way.'

'You don't trust me. Ridiculous.'

'Is this a politician speaking?'

'I have as much to gain as you. As much to lose.'

'Wait for a call,' Kate said.

Carol Tanner put the phone down and shook her head. 'She's using a mobile. No dice.'

Webb had the whole team there. He said, 'She's got some stuff on Farnol – stuff that Lester had.'

'Stuff,' said Adams.

'Sex. Girls. Enough to mess his life up. She wants a passport in return.'

'He sells passports?'

'He told her he can help.' It was an easy lie, Webb thought – politician, scandal, career at stake. All the easiest lies possess large elements of truth.

'Could he?'

'If I could, he could.'

'Why doesn't he –' Adams asked, '– why didn't he?'

'Maybe he's more afraid of us than he is of her.' Webb turned away and gazed at the pictures of Kate up on the wall. Kate in her various guises. The possible Kates.

Kate: I've got a proper e-mail address: see the tag on this message.

Listen, how the hell are you? Stay in touch, for Christ's sake. As for how do you know you can trust me – think of a test and give it to me. I

145

don't know what. Something you need I can get to you somehow?
Money? A message I can carry? Whatever . . .

I could e-mail some of the stuff that Michael and I were working on,
but I don't want to put too much out into cyberspace. Too many alpha
geeks out there; too many mouse potatoes. But do the initials WWI
strike a chord?

Just mail me back and say what you want to do. What you want me
to do. In the meantime: Not all trappers wear fur hats, okay?

Your friend

Corso was looking at a photograph. He said, 'Yes. That's the guy.'

'Farnol,' Larry Packer said. 'Bastard!' Then: 'How did you know
it was a set-up?'

Corso shrugged. 'I followed her. She went to a park. There were
men walking dogs in straight lines. Other men were examining
trees.' Suddenly he laughed, loudly, as if someone had told a
terrific joke. 'Why do they *do* it?'

'It was like that? Straight lines, examining trees, etcetera?'

'No,' Corso conceded. 'It's the way it looked to me. They might
as well have been flying flags.'

Packer drummed the table top, his wedding ring making a
clunk to punctuate the tapping of his fingertips. 'Farnol,' he said.
'This is deeper stuff, you know? Well . . . this is stuff of a different
order. I don't know what to say to you about this stuff.'

'Say whatever you like.'

'Farnol . . .'

'Is ready to jump ship.'

'He was there and she was there.'

'That's right,' Corso agreed.

'They've talked. She's got the material.'

'And he set her up.'

'Asshole,' Packer said. He shook his head in mild wonder.
'Asshole, involving the cops.'

'If it makes you feel any better, nothing changed hands. I mean,
they didn't get close. Farnol didn't even know she was there.'

'There's a question here of how far we go with things. How
wide the net goes.' Packer was digging for euphemisms. 'How

much you're prepared to take on.' He swivelled his chair and continued to speak while looking out of the window – as if he were trying out ideas on his own reflection. 'Now he's a loose cannon also. Farnol: wouldn't you say? Used to be she was a problem and he was part of it. Now he's a whole problem of his own. Separate problem, that seem right to you?'

'I can see what you mean.'

'You think I've got that right?'

'Yes.'

'I've got that pretty much right, don't I?'

'Yes.'

'Well . . . If that's so – if I'm right about that – then it's just a matter of time before he pisses on my toe, wouldn't you say?' Corso nodded. Packer also nodded, and his reflection nodded back. Everyone in agreement.

'Well, you've got a line on her,' Packer said, 'you're the man to fetch her home, and the last fucking thing I need, the last *fucking* thing I need, is this jerkoff with his mouth and the cops and etcetera. The *last*.' He took a large, long breath and held onto it, then let it go. 'Randall. When will you know what she knows?'

'Tough to say.'

'Ball park.'

'Can't say, Larry. Really. If I knew, I'd tell you.'

'No,' Packer said, 'he's too fucking . . . I mean, he's a real . . . He could go off in any direction, pointing at her, pointing at us.' By *us*, he meant *me*.

'Okay,' Corso said. He nodded at Packer's reflection. Packer's reflection nodded back, then gave a small, reflected smile.

Trapper: You're interesting, but are you safe? I know those initials, yes. ML knew them too, didn't he?

Nothing I need, thanks.

Tell me something about ML that I might expect a friend to know.

A note came in to Farnol at five that afternoon. It was a request for a meeting later that day and was signed by Larry Packer. Well, not quite a request. Something a little firmer than that. The note said eight p.m. at Farnol's weekday flat. He had a place in the country where he kept his dogs, his horse, his children and his wife. The flat was for business and fun.

Because the note had said eight, Farnol got back at seven-thirty. He closed the front door and went into the bedroom. He wanted a shower and a drink. In fact, he wanted a drink in the shower. He stripped off his MP's uniform and walked into the drawing room wearing only his socks. He looked ridiculous like that, but so what? Who was there to see him?

He was pouring his whisky when he realised that he was one of two people in the room.

Corso said, 'No, have the drink. What do you take with it? A little water, maybe?'

Farnol added the water. He said, 'You're not Packer.'

'I'm not a burglar, either, despite –' and he held up his hands to show Farnol the surgeon's gloves.

'So?'

'Robert Corso. Larry Packer asked me to call in. Things to talk about.'

'You mind if I put something on?'

'Sit down,' Corso said.

'If we're going to talk, I'd sooner not do it bollock naked. Okay?' Farnol reached for a smile, but couldn't get hold.

'Sure,' Corso told him, 'I understand. In a minute. But now that we've started to talk, now that we have some sort of a dialogue in process, I'd just as soon keep going. I wonder if you know that we know that you passed a computer disk to Michael Lester.'

Farnol sat down as he'd been asked to do. The armchair was deep and tipped him slightly backwards, which made him feel even more exposed. His cock flopped loosely against his thigh. He said, 'Disk?'

Corso laughed. He said, 'I'd be happier if you didn't do that. You know – *disk*? Like that. All that happens is I say, "That's right, a disk", and you say, "I don't know what you're talking about", and, Jesus, I get so bored.'

'No,' Farnol said, 'I didn't give him a disk. You mean a

computer disk?' He shook his head. 'No. Who told you this? Can I talk to Packer? I'd better talk to Packer about this.'

'Okay,' Corso said, smiling, 'skip it. Instead, you can tell me about Kate Randall.' He held up a hand. 'Now, please don't do any, "Kate who? I'm sorry, I don't think I know anyone of that name". And please don't do any, "This is preposterous, who do you think you're talking to, get out of my flat". Because I've just done it, and you can see how boring and unconvincing it sounded.'

Farnol said, 'Why don't you tell me what it is you want me to say. That way things might move along faster. And I still want to talk to Packer.'

Corso strolled over to Farnol and said, 'Drink your drink. I'll get you another.' Farnol drank. He needed the whisky more than ever now that the disk had been mentioned; now that Kate Randall had been mentioned. He handed the glass to Corso, who replenished it and set it down on the arm of the chair, then said, 'Give me your hand.'

'What?' Farnol laughed: a stutter, high in the chest.

Corso took Farnol's arm and laced a plastic handcuff round the wrist. 'Lift up,' he said.

Farnol tried to stand, but he wasn't obeying Corso's instruction. He pushed Corso's shoulder and made to take a step forward. Corso hit him, hard, just below the sternum. Just before the man sat down again, Corso passed the strip of plastic under him and fastened the other wrist, so that Farnol was sitting on his bindings. He was breathing in long, rasping gasps. Corso went behind him and slipped a thin noose round his neck. It was cord, closely woven. He made it snug, then ran the long end down to the bottom of the chair and tied it off to a leg. Farnol's head was pulled back; he stared up at the ceiling, arms at his sides like a man sitting to attention. He was still seeking enough breath to live by.

'Now,' Corso said, 'I'd be glad if you would tell me your name and your wife's name and your children's names.'

There was a long pause. Corso crossed the room, not bothering to look at Farnol, and got himself a drink from the whisky decanter.

'In your own time.'

'Tim Farnol,' Farnol said. 'Matty, that's Matilda, that's my wife, and Tom and Jemima and Katherine.'

'Okay. Well . . . listen . . . I want to reassure you. I didn't ask that question out of any unpleasant motive. They're not in any trouble. I just wanted to be sure that you were able to speak. You, however, *are* in trouble. How much depends on how often you lie to me. Best thing to do? Don't lie at all.'

Farnol told Corso what he wanted to know. It was a trouble-free interview for the most part. On a couple of occasions, Corso had to go and stand behind Farnol and repeat a question. He took up the slack on the cord that ran down the back of the chair, and turned his hand over, taking a tuck, bringing the man's head back, and back a little more, until, through enveloping darkness, Farnol saw the light. That was all there was to it. Farnol had urinated into the chair, but they didn't mention that.

Corso left half an hour later. He looked the flat over to make sure everything was as it should be. It was.

Sixteen

Webb went from room to room. He said, 'Jesus Christ.' He looked at the blad of photos taken by the first team in. The SOC officer was there, a DS called Martin Fletcher. The forensic officer was there, too. His name was Nigel Rivers. His colleagues liked to call him Rivers of Blood. Rivers had a sense of humour, so he quite liked that; he also liked his work; he was known to be a fast man with a saw.

He said, 'Asphyxiation, no doubt of it. Don't quote me.'

Webb turned to Martin Fletcher and pointed to a photograph. 'Did you have a good look at him before they cut him down?'

'Didn't cut him down, boss. Not until the doctor and Mr Rivers got here.'

'Okay,' Webb said. He pointed to the bed – the bed in the photo – where some capsules lay on the coverlet like pupae on a cabbage leaf. 'Where are these?'

'Bagged and labelled, boss.'

Webb turned to Rivers, his finger still on the photo.

'Amyl nitrate,' Rivers said. 'Guess what . . .'

Fletcher guffawed. 'No guesses needed.'

'What will you say?' Webb was asking Rivers.

'You put a garrotte round your neck,' Rivers said, 'and you tie it off to the wall light fitting. You stand on the bed. You've given yourself a little slack in the cord, so that you can control how choked you are. Slide down a little and let the cord take the weight . . . you like that, of course you do. It gets too much? Stand up and ease off, and give yourself another thrill in a minute. Meanwhile, just in case that's not big enough for you, just in case you've been there before, you can break a couple of ampoules of amyl under your nose. That'll get the pleasure centres going in the cerebral cortex. Fizz-fizz. And while you're sliding and choking – while you're choking and sniffing – how about working a dildo up your ass with your free hand, because, listen, why should pleasures come singly, or just in pairs?'

'That's what you'll say?'

'Yep. Sorry if it dents his reputation or upsets his loved ones, but what we have here is a classic case. They were doing this in ancient Rome. Of course, it'll all be in officialese. No mention of pleasure. He overdid it with the amyl, his synapses closed down for a bit, he slumped . . .' Rivers made an expressive whole-body motion: someone going down like a log. 'Click! He switched himself off like a light.'

'Why keep your socks on?' Webb asked.

'Who is there to impress?' Rivers asked.

Webb had taken the blad home with him. He sat in an armchair, looking at the photos, but mantling the book as a raptor mantles its prey: his arms spread, his back slightly bent, the open display sheets held close in. He was keeping them from the eyes of his wife, Janice, who was sitting opposite to him at the table. They were eating a late supper of calves' liver and bacon.

She said, 'Is it that bad?'

'Not really,' he said. 'You wouldn't want to see.'

Janice was slender and well-dressed. Webb's colleagues thought of her as a classy woman. Even in the house, she looked good. Webb used to like that; now he thought that she always looked as if she were ready to leave; ready to go somewhere.

Later, when she took her clothes off and walked towards the bed, Webb watched her catching sight of herself in their mirror-faced closets. She saw that Webb had seen, and said, 'What d'you think?'

She was still wearing her scent. No make-up, now, but the scent, made muskier by a day's wearing. They made love just as they always did. It was Janice who put out the light and composed herself to sleep.

Webb thought, I'm glad. Now things are the way they were. No complications. Sure, I haven't got Farnol as bait. But who knows whether that would've worked? Who knows whether she was serious?

No deals, now. I catch her, she goes down. Forget the disk. What disk? I'm glad he's dead and out of the way. Out of my light.

And bringing the disk to mind, he thought: Not girls, of course. Not security of the realm. No – this other stuff: the garrotte, the ampoules, a plastic man deep in your asshole.

And bringing that to mind – clandestine pleasures, the secrets people keep – Webb found his imaginings growing richer and stranger.

Who does she dress up for? he wondered. Who does she make herself special for?

He meant his wife.

Kate: Things about ML . . . Okay. We didn't talk all that much about matters outside of work. Still, I think you went on holiday together last year, and it was France or Italy. Wasn't it Italy?

I know he liked to trace his ancestry: he mentioned to me that he found a John Lister who fought at Agincourt; it came into the conversation once because we were joking about the fact that my family liked to say – my dad really – that our ancestors came from Ireland: whoever they might have been.

The only other thing that comes to mind is I called him once close to his birthday and you had sent him flowers. He told me he liked to get flowers from women. He liked flowers.

That's the best I can do. I can't help you with any novelty birthmarks and the like. I guess that's your department, right?

The Trapper

Corso clicked 'send' and sat back, taking a sip of whisky. The enlargement still hadn't given him enough information to be sure whether the holiday had been France or Italy. In fact, it could just as well have been Greece. The cypresses, though – he made it Italy by the cypresses.

The whisky was Irish – in honour of his fake relatives.

Behind him, Kate was playing the third movement of the Elgar: adagio; slow, mournful notes curling out into the room.

Ian Grant was the last person Webb had wanted to see that morning, but the fact that Grant was his superior officer hadn't left him a hell of a lot of choice. Grant sat with his heels up on his desk and his head slightly bowed to read a sheaf of notes in his lap. He looked like a cowpoke whittling at the hitching-rail.

He said, 'You had her and you lost her, that's where it starts.'

'No arguments there,' Webb agreed.

'What was this operation in the park? Who mounted that?'

'Me. Information received.'

'Received from whom?'

'We thought . . .' Webb had this ready. 'We thought we'd picked up something during a fast phone call she had with her sister. Face it – she's out there with no resources that we know of. It looked like a meet.'

'Not so?'

'Not so.'

'She's not the only one short on resources, George.'

'I know that.'

'Policing has to be cost-effective these days. There are budgets. Your forensic bill alone –'

'I know.'

Grant nodded. He was shuffling the notes like an after-dinner speaker. 'You got called in to this Tim Farnol thing. You went to the scene.'

'The West One team thought I could help.'

'They did?'

'Farnol had some contact with Michael Lester, it seems. There was correspondence.'

'Anything there?'

'No. Lester bitching on about the environment. Farnol used to be a junior minister, remember.'

'No, I don't.'

'It was old stuff. Nothing there for us.'

154

Grant looked up. He was smiling. 'Says here he'd got a foreign body in his body.'

'Vibrator. Full cock and balls job. He'd roped himself up to a light fitting.'

'Will it come out?' Grant asked.

'Depends on the tabloids, I expect. When I spoke to the team DI over there, he said the family are trying to keep it to a heart attack due to overwork.'

'No,' Grant laughed. 'The dildo. Will it come out? I saw a case once – rigor mortis set in, only thing to do was shove it all the way in and bury the poor bastard.'

Webb laughed because his boss was laughing. 'Let's hope they don't tell his wife.'

Grant laughed some more, but he was looking at his notes again and shaking his head. 'I reckon you're in trouble here, George. I'm considering a significant cut in resources for this investigation. A serious downgrade. You're no nearer catching her than you were last week. Could be anywhere, couldn't she?'

'I'll find her,' Webb assured him.

'Anywhere. And look like anyone, couldn't she?'

'For Christ's sake leave me a full-strength team: at least for another week.'

'You don't know, do you?' Grant stroked his chin: a parody of the thoughtful man. 'Tell me something, George, just how *is* she managing to survive?'

'We're checking street people: beggars, dossers, people in squats. Only other possibility – she's getting help.'

'From . . .?'

'That's why we went to the park: the sister would be the best bet.'

'No evidence of that, though?'

Webb shook his head. 'No.'

'She has to have money, George. No one can last out there without money. What's she doing? Turning a trick?'

Webb laughed. 'She's a cello player. Beethoven and suchlike.'

Grant looked at him. 'So what? Don't cellists fuck?' Webb could see that it was a joke. He was annoyed with himself for taking the bait. 'So,' Grant continued. 'You don't know. She could be starting a new life somewhere, couldn't she?'

'I don't think so. I'll get to her. All I need is time.'

'Which is money, George.'

Grant went back to his reading. After a while Webb got up and left.

Packer said, 'One thing I'm not happy about here – well . . . you had her and you let her go. You followed her to Lester's place. Let her go. Followed her to the park. Let her go. You don't think this was chancy? Like, chancy is definitely the word I'd use to describe that course of action.'

'It's fine,' Corso told him.

'Not so fine, not really. Not now.'

Kate had checked out of the hotel in Hampstead: the hotel Corso had followed her to. The hotel where he had expected to be able to find her.

'She's going to want to know me,' Corso said, 'don't worry.'

'No? Don't? I *am* worried. You're depending on this e-mail link. It's not the same as having the girl, is it? Having the girl in view.'

'What should I have done? Kidnapped her? You want me to find out what she knows – how? – beat it out of her? And where she's put the disk? Beat that out of her too?'

'It's been known to work. I've seen it work.'

'I've seen it fail. I've seen people die. I've seen people hold out to buy time to kill themselves.'

'Is that her? She like that?'

'I don't know what she's like – *exactly* what she's like – but I know she's laughing at the cops and staying alive somehow, so I know she's tough and resourceful and clever, and I think I know best how to deal with that.'

'You hope.'

Corso watched cars driving in and out of the parking lot like components in some vast, interlocking puzzle.

'No,' he said, 'I don't hope. I'm using my judgement: it's what you're paying for. But any time you want me off the job, that's fine, just settle my contract and I'll be out of your hair. What's more, you'll be out of mine.'

Packer shook his head, slowly, without taking his eyes off Corso. 'I didn't say that. You have to make the decisions, etcetera. That's your skill, right?'

'Right,' Corso said.

'Farnol,' Packer's face brightened, 'that was terrific.'

'He didn't think so.'

Corso wasn't a crude man, but he made the joke to break the atmosphere that had suddenly invaded the office. Packer threw his head back and laughed. 'Heart attack is what the papers said. How'd you bring that on?'

'It wasn't a heart attack.'

'That right? Why do they say it was?'

Corso took a polaroid photograph out of his pocket and slid it across the desk. Packer took a look. After a moment, he got up and went to the window, angling the snap to get more light.

'Jesus Christ.'

Corso held out his hand for the photo and Packer flicked it back like a playing card. 'What?' he asked. 'You got an album of these?'

Corso said, 'Now you've seen it, I'll destroy it.'

'Yeah. Do that.'

'Listen,' Corso said, 'she'll come in. Don't worry.'

The Linden Tree, W11, 9p.m. Wear red and black.

She'll come in ... Corso had smiled when the brief e-mail came up on the screen. She'll come in and she'll be glad of a friend.

He sat in the Linden Tree, reading a paper, a glass of beer on the table in front of him, and let the noise and smoke swirl round him. He hated pubs because he hated crowds and, most of all, he hated crowds when they were drinking and yelling and braying with laughter, but he sat there, all sweet equanimity with his paper and beer, because it was part of the job.

He was wearing a black jacket and a black roll-neck. There was a red rose in his buttonhole. She walked past him and he pretended not to notice.

Kate had stood just inside the door, where the crowd was thick, and watched as he read. Then she had gone out of the pub and walked down the road to the tube station and bought a ticket.

Too much of a risk, she thought. Who is this guy? Michael never mentioned him to me.

Michael mentioned everything to you?

Most things.

How do you know?

Okay. I don't. But he still looks like a risk to me.

Look like a policeman?

What does a policeman look like, for Christ's sake? Looks like a *risk*.

In what way?

I don't fucking *know* in what way. Okay? I expect you're right. He's fine. He's for real. He doesn't mind harbouring a fugitive.

What do you do, otherwise?

Sorry?

I'm asking: what's your alternative? You need help. Someone to help you. As things stand, you're out on a limb. Especially now that —'

Now that Farnol's dead.

Heart attack. That was bad luck.

Especially for him. But it closes down the only lead we had.

There's the disk. If I knew what's on the disk.

Go to Penarven and get it.

I don't think so.

Exactly. You need help. You need someone to talk to about this. You need advice. You need contact with the real world. You need a plan. You need . . . what is it? . . . you need a co-conspirator.

This guy?

He's a journo. He's a colleague of Michael's.

You sure?

Okay, let me put it to you another way. He's all there is.

Kate had gone back and found him still there. She walked past him as if she were pushing through, looking for a friend. Had he seen her? She didn't think so. There was a door on the far side of the bar that let into a side street. Her nerve broke and she went out.

I'll think it through.

Think what through?

There's the e-mail. I can get to him any time I want to. He's there. In fact, he's *always* there. A little eager, perhaps?

Meaning what? You expect to sit down at his table and say hello and then the SWAT team storms into the pub?

Possible.

Im-possible. You've walked to the pub twice now. Do you imagine they've let you walk away for the second time?

Kate went into a small French restaurant four doors from the Linden Tree and ordered a cheese omelette and a glass of red wine.

He'll be gone soon.

I know that.

You gave him a time. Nine o'clock. It's a quarter to ten. He won't stay.

There's the e-mail.

Go back and see if he's still there. You need someone. You need help. You can't do it alone.

Maybe he just wants a story. Have you thought of that?

Find out. Who knows what he wants? Find out.

The waiter brought her half a baguette and a glass of burgundy. She tore the bread open and took a good mouthful of the wine. Corso sat down opposite to her and smiled. The waiter returned.

'What are you having?' Corso asked.

'Cheese omelette.'

'I'll have that,' Corso said. 'Green salad, *pomme frites*, and bring a bottle of . . . what is it?'

'House,' Kate told him.

'The house red.'

Neither of them spoke for a full minute. Finally, Corso said, 'Is that your hair?'

'No.' She laughed. 'Is it obvious?'

'Well . . . no, I wouldn't think so. I just figured you might have made some changes. Your colouring makes you more of a blonde.'

159

His voice was soft, languorous almost, with long vowel sounds; an attractive accent, though Kate couldn't tell the region of America he came from. She knew it wasn't that New York twang.

Kate said, 'It was France. The holiday was in France.'

'Yes? I couldn't remember. Why would I? I knew you went somewhere and it was south. I called Michael a few days before you left.'

'Look,' Kate said, 'I don't know whether there's any point in my saying this, I mean, I don't even know whether you care, or what it is you want from me, or how honest you are . . . I didn't kill Michael.'

'No. Fine. I didn't think you did.'

'Then who was it? Do you know?'

'Nope.'

'You said you were talking to him – same story, same research . . . was that it?'

'No, not really. Same area. We traded information. I know he was a tiger: you know – once he'd gotten hold he wasn't inclined to let go.'

'Then how can you help me?'

'Okay, well . . . I was hoping you'd tell me.'

'You just want the story.' There was ice in Kate's voice.

'Hey, hold it, you don't know that. What in hell makes you say that?'

'You're asking *me* for things. I thought you'd be offering things.'

'Things?'

'Help.'

'Sure, right, I am. That's what I'm doing. You want help? Here it is. But I guess I have to know how best to do that, right? I need you to tell me what that might be.'

Kate got up and went to the women's room. She locked herself into a stall, pushed her jeans and briefs down, then sat and put her head in her hands. She felt suddenly shivery and it hurt to pee.

I don't know about this guy.

160

Okay. Climb out of that little window: you'll squeeze through. Stick him with the bill. Apologise by e-mail.

He thought it was Italy.

That's what makes him credible. A mistake. It's human. And he knew about the flowers and about Michael's boring bloody family tree. He knew Michael.

Think so?

It's obvious. And look – where's the SWAT team?

No, but –

Are you going through the window?

No.

Corso thought, She's good. She doesn't have knowledge, but she has technique. She staked me out in a busy pub, people, smoke, noise . . . Maybe she even had a look at me before that moment when she came in and walked past me.

The idea came to him as a surprise, but once it had occurred to him he thought, Yes, I'll bet she did. It felt right. She'd looked in on him and he'd been reading his paper and some instinct, the instinct that had saved his life a couple of times before, hadn't worked. She hadn't triggered it. She'd looked in, and gone away, and come back later to walk past him, heading for the far side of the bar and that other door. And he'd lost her again. Not for long, but he'd lost her. While she was making up her mind, going to and fro with how far she could trust him, he'd lost touch.

So she's good. But she doesn't know that.

And, in any case, she hadn't gone far. Wouldn't go far. She had already made up her mind, though maybe she didn't know that yet. What else had brought her back after that first look? What else had stalled her in a restaurant just four doors from the pub?

Kate buckled her belt, then splashed water on her face. It's either the heating in here, she thought, or I'm starting to run a temperature.

When she got back, the waiter was putting the omelettes on the table. She was hungry: as if she hadn't eaten for days. Corso watched her as she ate, head down, eyes down, until she had half finished, and she felt herself flush, but didn't know whether it was his gaze or the onset of a fever.

'Who killed Michael?' he asked.

'I don't know. I came down, he had a knife in him . . . sticking out of him. He panicked and ran round the house. I couldn't catch him. I couldn't even keep up with him. He was running and bleeding and making this dreadful hissing noise. Then he died.'

'That sounds terrible. That must have been so –'

'A burglar?' Kate's mind switched back to his original question: *Who?* 'I don't know.'

'Why do they think it's you?'

Kate laughed. 'Yes, well, I wish I had the answer. My sister tells me that they've got some forensic evidence, whatever that might mean. And a witness.'

'Whatever that might mean.'

'It can't be someone who saw me kill him, because I didn't. So what this person did see – I don't know. I've got no idea. A witness.' She paused. 'Well, we had a row. Michael hit me. Someone might have seen that.'

'Hit you?'

'He'd never done it before.'

'Row about what?'

'Me leaving. I was leaving him. I should have been in Warsaw, but the trip was cancelled. I went to see him – to tell him. I'd never . . . I'd broken up with people before . . . you know. But it was never like this. I'd never seen anyone so upset about anything.'

'He was in love with you,' Corso said, and Kate wondered if Michael had told him that, because it sounded so convincing, so profound, when he said it.

'I didn't know it could go that deep,' she said.

'No?'

'No,' she shook her head in wonder, 'not really.'

'Never been that way for you?'

'Not like that. So deep.'

Corso poured more wine. He said, 'Are you okay?'

'Fine. It's hot in here: do you find that?'

'It's warm, yes. Why did you run away when they came for you?'

'There's a man called George Webb. A policeman. I mean, he's the guy in charge of the case. He thinks I did it. He *knows* I did it. He *wants* me to have done it.'

'You sure?'

'When I knew they planned to arrest me . . . I thought back to my conversations with him. Yes – he's got me down for it. That's as far as his thinking goes. I could see a cage: a cell. I couldn't see getting out once I was in. It was a feeling, not any kind of a certainty.'

'Feelings are the best thing,' Corso assured her. 'Feelings tell you what you need to know.'

'That's all,' Kate said. 'That's about it.'

'Nothing else that helps you? Nothing else that prompts your feelings?'

Kate ate in silence for a while, which was as good as an answer. Corso smiled inwardly. She'll come in, he thought. She'll be glad of a friend.

'There's a disk. A computer disk. I was down in Cornwall – when they decided to arrest me.'

'Yes.'

'I found the disk in my coat pocket. There was a label on it. Just said: "Dynamite: remember?" That was something that Michael had said about the story he was working on.'

Corso lifted his glass. As if it didn't matter a damn, he said: 'Where's the disk? Could be useful to you, couldn't it?'

'I can't tell you that.'

Corso affected puzzlement. 'You don't know where –'

'Until I trust you.'

'Oh, sure, right, of course. No, that's . . . I'd do that. Good thinking.'

'Would you?'

'Well . . . I'm not . . . I mean, how do I really know what I'd do in your position? It's lousy. A lousy position to be in. But, yes, I guess so. I'd need to trust you before I'd tell you stuff like that.'

'I can't get at it. I don't even know if it's where I left it.'

'In Cornwall?'

As soon as he spoke, Corso could see that he'd taken a step too far. Kate put down her fork. She said, 'All in all, I feel like shit.'

Corso called for the bill. He said, 'I'll take you home.'

'Just find me a cab,' she said.

'Wherever home is. I had wondered about that. About how you were making out.'

He pushed an envelope across the table. Money. Kate took it. If she let him know that she didn't need his help, he'd start to wonder why. Joanna was taking too many risks already. There had been a regular letter at the Polish Café: not that there was much to say, but Joanna knew that the mere fact of being in contact would give Kate strength. She just wrote fond things, memories, family jokes, and sent love; always love . . .

'A cab would be fine.'

Kate was shivering slightly and her colour was high. Her hand, when Corso took it to steer her round the table, was hot.

They walked to a main street, Corso leading the way. A couple of times, Kate said, 'Quicker this way . . .?' Or, 'There's one . . .' But he held her arm in his, guiding her to a junction where the yellow lights of cabs were coming in from all directions. It was also the section where his car was parked. He handed her into a cab, and said, 'We'll talk, okay? E-mail. Let me know how you are.'

Kate nodded. She had wrapped her coat round tight, and was shuddering every few seconds, like an engine about to fail. Her eyes were bright.

He had memorised the licence plate of the cab as it had drawn in to the kerb. Now he ran past eight cars to get to his own and pulled out in front of a line of traffic, raising a chorus of klaxons. He cheated a red light at the next roundabout and made an educated guess about which exit to take. The traffic was heavy, as always. London traffic. When he was confronted with another choice – north or south – he chose north, and picked the cab up after a hundred yards. He could see Kate in the back: the shape of her head, her collar pulled up. He settled in a couple of vehicles back, keeping an eye on traffic-light sequences in case he needed to get closer.

The first hotel had been in Hampstead; the new one was in Primrose Hill. Corso watched Kate in, then sat in his car to watch the place. He might see her drawing the curtain, or looking out, and be able to pinpoint the room.

That didn't happen. After a while he drove back to the place that WWI had rented for him: a mews house in Notting Hill. He poured a Scotch, then fell into an armchair and lifted the phone.

Packer was being a horse for his kids: on hands and knees while they rode him and yelled and pummelled at his ribs with their toddlers' feet. His wife watched Packer playing the lovable father and thought he was good at it. He played the lovable husband, too, and was good at that. He liked to play.

He said, 'Beth, will you get that and say I can't come to the phone?'

She handed him the cordless phone, still ringing. 'You know you'll want to take it, Larry. Here it is.'

Packer went onto one elbow to answer and the kids tilted to one side. They screamed in a good-natured way, as if that's what their father might have hoped they'd do.

'Yeah,' he said. Then, 'Enough, okay?' in the same breath.

'What's that?' Corso said.

'I'm a horse. Don't ask. Kids, etcetera.'

'We had cheese omelette and house wine at a little bistro. She has a computer disk. I don't know what's on it, but it sounds risky. She's hidden it somewhere. I put her in a cab, then followed her home. I've tagged the hotel she's now in. I'm pretty certain she's got the 'flu or some such.'

'And she trusts you.'

'We'll get there. This is just the start of something. We met. We talked. Now she's home and safe. "Trust" is a word slowly forming in her mind. It's like an idea she hasn't had yet.'

'Sounds like a slow process.'

'There's a time scale on this?'

'No time scale. Just . . . I'd like to get it off my desk, you know?'

'Some things can't be hurried, Packer.'
'Yeah? Not in my experience.'
Corso laughed. 'You must be a lot of fun in bed.'

*Kate: You didn't look too great. My opinion? – You're coming down
with something. If I can help, just call. In the meantime . . . here I am.*

*I bought your recording of the Elgar cello concerto. I love it. I mean, I
love the piece, and I love the way you play it. That third movement:
heartbreaking.*

Okay? Here I am . . .

The Trapper

He looked it over for tone and style. This was the part he liked
best: the fabrication, the being someone else. Getting just the right
pitch, somewhere between the casual and the earnest. And now
this faint flirtation; this personal-but-at-one-remove stuff.

He liked the feel of the tug on the line; the notion that
somewhere, out of sight, in deep water, the real Kate was on the
hook. The Kate he didn't know yet. The Kate he would draw in,
gently, coaxing her towards the shallows.

He liked the pretence, the acting, the mask. He liked the dark
deceit. It would bring him the real Kate. Naked Kate. His Kate.

He clicked 'send'.

Kate got into bed. The sheets seemed to graze her; they might
have been hemp and horsehair. She tucked both hands between
her thighs and drew her knees up. Her teeth were chattering.

She thought, I didn't ask his name. He's still the Trapper.

That's right, you didn't ask his name – and he didn't give it.

Maybe he doesn't trust me. There's a thought.

Soon, her own heat began to fill the bed, and she wanted to
throw the sheets off, take a cold bath, stand by the open window.

I'm ill, for God's sake. People in my predicament don't get ill.

It's the 'flu.

No kidding?

Take something.

Haven't got anything.

Call room service.

Too ill.

Go to sleep, then.

Too ill to sleep.

But she did, and dreamed of Pete Lemon. They sat on either side of a hearth, Shep lying between them, and he smiled at her in a way that seemed to bring her great comfort. He was shelling peas, using the same technique her mother had always used: a colander on his lap, his thumbnail sliding down the seam of the pod, his thumb running inside to loosen the peas.

She thought, Home. I'm home. This is the place to be.

She could see the garden through the window, and imagined that her father must be there, just out of sight, pulling weeds or raking the leaves shed by the silver birch.

Pete Lemon got up and took the peas to the stove where he poured them from the colander into a saucepan of water. Then he reached down and opened the oven and took out a box of medals and a bayonet, and suddenly the dream was Jeff, and Michael with the bayonet deep in him, and Jeff wearing his medals, and standing aside to point at a second Jeff who was pursuing Michael round the room, using his stab-and-twist technique.

He grabbed Kate's arm to get her attention, and said, 'That's me, look, there, there I am, that's me.'

> Kate: I'm worried about you. It's been four days, and I thought you looked lousy when we parted.
>
> I'm giving you an address: 17, Calley Mews, W11. It's your choice, okay? Your call.
>
> I'm also dropping this Trapper stuff. If you need me, here I am.
>
> Robert Corso

She was taking every 'flu remedy known to man, but couldn't seem to break the fever. Also, it hurt to cough . . . no, it hurt to *breathe*; and breathing was difficult enough anyway. She hadn't eaten, although room service had sent up bottle after bottle of mineral water. It was just a small hotel, and the manager was kind enough to ask if she was all right. Kate told him it was the 'flu.

She'd be better in a day or so. If not, she would cancel the rest of her business arrangements and get the train home to Norwich.

She told him Norwich because the area had been a childhood holiday once: rain at Southwold, winds cutting in on Dunwich beach. The whole family had hated it.

Each time she got up to go to the bathroom, her legs threatened to tangle under her and she felt light as chaff. She hacked up sputum that was dark and thick and flecked with blood. The world beyond the window was as close and as distant as a movie screen.

Next day, the manager called her a cab, and told her he'd hold the room if she liked: the hotel wasn't full. Kate thought that whatever happened, she would move on. The room smelled to her of her own sickness and the bathroom was a white-tile torture chamber.

She asked the cab to stop a couple of streets from Corso's house. Her rucksack held almost nothing, but it felt as though she were hauling bricks. When she arrived at Corso's door, she was light-headed and nauseous – a breath or two, a pace or two, from fainting.

He opened the door to her ring. It hadn't occurred to her that he might have been out.

Corso put in a call to Packer. He said, 'I need backup.'

'Like what?'

'Do we own a doctor?'

'No. Don't have anyone like that. Name the problem.'

'Kate Randall has 'flu. More than that, she has either bronchitis or pneumonia.'

'She's where?'

'With me.'

'There's always a silver lining,' Packer observed. 'But we don't have any medical people.'

'Can you get me some drugs?'

'That's a lot easier. What is it – penicillin, etcetera?'

'That's right.'

'Okay, I'll get them to you.' A pause, then: 'Listen, how bad is she?'

'I've seen healthier women.'

'She's not going to die on us – anything like that?'

'If she dies, Larry, I'll let you know.'

'Because if she looks like . . . I mean, if that's a possible, if that's a maybe, we better sweat her first. I mean, she could've laid tank traps all over. "If I die, this; if I die, that" . . .'

'It occurred to me.'

'You agree?'

'Sure. If necessary.'

'Who decides?'

'I decide.'

'I'd better come round there.'

'If you come round, we *have* to sweat her. If she sees you. If you complicate things. No, Larry. You can't come round here. This is a sensitive balance; things are on the tip, and it's going our way. Keep your distance.'

'But if she –'

'I make the decisions. Or I walk. We've done this dance already.'

'I'll bike the stuff to you,' Packer said. 'I'm praying for her speedy recovery.'

'Good,' Corso said. 'Ever had any luck with that in the past?'

Seventeen

The fever deepened, and for a whole day she didn't really know where she was or what was going on. Corso gave her liquids and food supplements. The liquids she soaked up; the Complan and packet soups she vomited back, over him and over the bed. He changed the sheets. He responded to her wild, wide-eyed, meaningless questions with meaningless answers. He stripped her naked and swabbed her body with lukewarm water, leaving her wet so that evaporation would lower her skin temperature. He did this every hour on the hour. He propped her against a bank of pillows to give her a four-hourly cocktail of penicillin, vitamins and paracetamol.

Kate roamed in her own mind: dark territory. Jeff sliding into the mud of the yard, her blows falling like the rain; Michael hobbling, falling, shedding blood. In one imagining, they sat in an otherwise empty concert hall while she played, their bloodied heads bobbing in time with the music. Corso stood at the back, a late arrival.

After that day, things changed. The fever broke early the second morning, and she began to worry. Corso brought her food, and talked to her, and went out of the house on various errands, so that she could have left if she had wanted to. She didn't want to. She was worried, but the inertia of illness was enough to help her to find reasons for trusting him.

The principal reason, of course, was that she was still free.

Two days later, she was weak, but walking. It felt inexpressibly strange to be in his house, in his bed.

'Where have you been sleeping?' she asked him, and he

indicated the armchair she was sitting in, and the armchair he was sitting in.

'I put them in alongside your bed. You didn't notice.'

'You're a good nurse.' It was all she could manage of 'thank you', as if gratitude would bring a greater intimacy than she could afford. She noticed the T-shirt she was wearing: a plain workout-grey gym shirt with the legend 'NYC Forty-second Street Sweats' on the front.

'Did you undress me?' she asked.

'No, I hired an undressing nurse for that.'

She gave a half-laugh, then said: 'Sorry. It's weird. The whole thing's weird.'

'You were burning up. I had to cool you. I rolled you onto a towel and sponged you down, and left the windows open to the night air.'

Kate didn't speak for a while, then she asked, 'What did I do?'

He shrugged. 'Nothing. You lifted your arms and legs for me like a child . . . you know, when a child's half asleep. You turned onto one side and then the other. You liked it best when I dampened the back of your neck. You put your hand up to keep the sponge there. And you talked, but I don't know what you were saying.'

He told her all this as if she were slowly recovering from memory loss.

'Have you got children?' She was thinking of his remark about the half-asleep child.

'I used to.' It was a lie.

'Robert Corso,' she said.

'That's me.'

'I don't remember Michael ever mentioning you.'

He shrugged. 'No? Okay . . .' Then: 'You need to take a couple more days.'

She laughed. 'Before doing what?'

'Whatever you had planned.'

'Oh, right. And what would that be?'

He had made her some scrambled eggs, and she was eating out of need rather than pleasure, lifting and lowering the fork mechanically. Then she stopped, the fork stalled in mid-air, and stared at the wall as if she could see her future there. Suddenly the entire hopelessness of her situation fell in on her, like a tunnel collapsing. The deaths, her flight from the police, the nights spent sleeping rough, anonymous hotel rooms, this strange room, this strange man, this mess of egg that fell off her fork and back onto the plate. She started to cry. A black depression moved on her like bad weather flowing in from the horizon.

Corso sat quietly while she wept. He calculated whether it would be an advantage or not to put an arm round her, and decided it wouldn't. That arm would carry ten times the intimacy that stripping and bathing her had brought.

That night, he slept on the sofa in the living room. Kate came in to him at about three a.m. A little after three, he noticed. He sat up and said, 'Okay?'

She was standing just inside the doorway, the grey of the T-shirt making her legs seem long and very white. She said, 'The disk is in my sister's cottage. Where I was staying. It's hidden.'

'How well hidden?'

'I don't know. No one knew about it: the police, I mean. So why would they look for it?'

'Do you want me to go and get it?'

'No. But I want to get it. I can't think of anything else . . . You know: anything else that might help.'

'How strong do you feel?'

She laughed. 'A feather in the wind.'

'Very pretty.' He laughed too, then they fell silent, as if something else had been said: something more important. After a moment, he said, 'You need a couple of days to recover; I told you that.'

'What do we do?'

'I'll hire in some videos. What do you like?'

They watched 'Philadelphia Story' and 'How the West was Won' and 'The African Queen' and a fistful of Hitchcock movies. She asked him to get 'Ashes and Diamonds' because she remembered watching it with her father. She wanted to see Cybulski in his dark glasses, lighting tots of liquor in memory of his dead comrades.

She slept on and off, sometimes for three or four hours at a time.

She wanted to hear some music, and he came back with Brahms and Beethoven and Mozart, which was fine, and didn't surprise her. He also brought Sibelius 4, which did.

She said, 'You don't live here, do you?'

'Of course not.'

'Because there's nothing here that seems permanent or old.'

'I told you – no, I don't. I live in America. I'm renting this.'

'Where in America?'

'Utah.'

'Where's that?' she asked, and her head nodded towards sleep as if Utah could do that to anyone.

She listened to the dark melancholy of the Sibelius, low notes that reached the pit of the soul. It seemed to her that whole piece was a monument to despair. She thought that Corso had either chosen it from ignorance, or as a sort of bleak joke: *How much worse can things get?*

She heard it through, then started it again. The music overwhelmed her; she focused on it until her concentration went beyond mere listening: there was just the music, and she heard every note, as if nothing lay beyond music, nothing beyond *this* music, nothing beyond the idea of music.

When he came into the room, she was lifting the CD from the player. She said, 'What was this? Kill or cure?'

'Bad choice?' he asked; and she had no idea whether he was genuinely confused or not.

'We could go tomorrow.'

'You're feeling okay . . .'

'Well enough.' And when he looked at her, questioningly, she added, 'I have to do something. *Do* something . . .'

'Sure,' he said. 'Well . . . I'll drive.'

* * *

'I'm just touching base,' he told Packer.

'And things are going good, right?'

'We're fetching the disk.'

'Where from?'

'Cornwall.'

'Stay clear of trouble.'

'You'd prefer that? Me too.'

'The disk,' Packer said. 'That's good. That's great. That's almost home and dry.'

'Listen,' Corso said, 'if it's all there is . . . If there's no danger of other leaks – from her, I mean, what was it? – "If I die, this; if I die that" – you want me to turn her in, or should she have this accident we spoke about?'

'The accident . . .' Packer was thinking it through. 'The accident's beginning to look . . . you know . . . a good bet. But I have to know. Absolutely *have* to know that there's nothing else to worry about. You have to give me assurances, there. That has to be a, like, guarantee. I can't let her go until I know that. I don't want this bitch coming back to haunt me.'

'Okay.'

'A guarantee.'

'Okay.'

'What?' Packer asked. 'You want to whack her? She beginning to annoy you? What?'

'No,' Corso said. He sighed. 'I'm bored, I guess. But no, nothing like that. I'm just asking you. If I'm sure –'

Packer made his mind up. 'If you're sure, right, whack her, that's fine. I've got your money in the bank.' He laughed. 'And your ticket back to Utah.'

She slept in the car, as if sleep would make her invisible. To help with invisibility, though, she was wearing a beret and a leather jacket with a fur collar that she'd bought with some of Joanna's five grand. She turned the collar up and leaned against the side window and closed her eyes.

Corso drove with a deft touch, tolerant of London's sharky drivers, the suits in Mercs, the boys with spoilers. He pulled out to overtake a truck as they hit the motorway and got a horn-blast and a flash of headlights from a father of three in an assembly-line saloon; a moment later, the guy came past on the inside, mouthing a stream of fuck-yous and beating his fist. Corso smiled and gave him a little wave of encouragement.

Kate dozed, then woke after an hour. She said, 'This is dangerous, isn't it? How dangerous is this?'

'They could be watching the place.'

'In which case – what?'

'In which case, we'll have to be clever.'

'Why would they still be watching?'

'They don't have too many points of reference. My guess is that they'll be there but not permanently. We might have to pick our time.'

She said, 'There was a guy called Tim Farnol. Member of Parliament. He's involved in some way.'

'How's that?'

'I think he knows what's on the disk.'

'Yeah? How did he come up?'

Kate mentioned Michael's row with Stephen Cawdrey; and that Cawdrey had given up Farnol.

'You're a sleuth,' Corso said. 'Any sleuthing blood in your family?'

'Not a drop.'

'Amazing. Where's Cawdrey?'

'Skulking. He's taken a payoff of some sort: I'm sure of it. He didn't want to talk about anything.'

'He knew it was you?'

Kate gave him Aunt Gemma's voice: 'No, it was Gemma MacIntyre, a researcher who once worked for Michael Lester.'

'A sleuth and an actress. You don't think Cawdrey's a danger?'

'I think he's crawled in somewhere and pulled down the lid.'

They rode in silence for ten miles. Then Kate said, 'But Farnol's dead.'

'Sorry?' Corso mixed confusion and surprise in equal measures.

'He died of a heart attack . . . I can't remember how many days. Before I got ill.'

'But you talked to him – am I right?'

'On the phone. He was scared.' She paused. 'Jesus, maybe that brought on the heart attack.'

Corso shook his head. 'More likely to be years of fat living. Fat of the land. Fat'll do it to you every time.'

He'd brought a map, and the map showed them how they could leave the car on one side of the hill, hike up towards the trees, go through the wood, and come out above Penarven at the point where Kate and the jeep had taken out the fence. He'd timed the drive so they would arrive at dusk, heavy light settling above the treetops, an inshore wind stirring noise from the landscape. Rooks were twisting and turning above the tallest of the trees, black against near-black, their raw, barking cries echoing into the valley.

Corso said, 'Can we get a good view from cover?'

Kate pointed to some trees below the brow of the hill. 'That spinney; then there's nothing before you get to the outhouses.'

'Okay. Let's go down.' He started to move before she'd finished speaking.

She felt that he was letting her take the lead: wanting her to, but really making the choices himself, as if he'd already sized things up, and seen the spinney, and knew it was the best cover. He led and she followed – a stranger on home ground. When they had found a vantage point, and had the cottage in plain view, Corso took out his night glasses. He kept them on the cottage for a minute or so, then passed them to Kate. The building sprang up, almost luminous and sharply focused.

'Where did you get these?' she asked.

'When I knew we were going to do this, going to come here, I went shopping.'

They were talking in whispers, their voices lower than the wind among the trees.

'Shopping? Where?'

'There are places. What can you see?'

'Nothing. I mean, nothing that worries me.'

'Good.' He took the glasses back. 'You know, I could just as easily have come here alone and brought the disk back to you,' he said.

'I know.'

'But you don't trust me.'

Where did you get those glasses? How did you know where to get those glasses? How did you know we'd need those glasses?

'I think you might want a story. You're a journalist. If you were St Hideout, the patron saint of fugitives, I might feel better about you.'

'This is a man who sponged your naked body without ever letting his fingers slip under the sponge.' He was still looking down at the cottage, his face half obscured by the night glasses and his own hands. Kate couldn't tell whether he was smiling or not.

'I know journalists. A story's better than sex any day of the week.'

'What do you want to do?'

'Sorry?'

'Tell me where the disk is, and let me go down and fetch it, or go yourself?'

'I'll go.'

'Okay,' he agreed, 'you go. I'll watch from here.'

There was a weariness in his voice, a touch of hurt pride, that almost made her change her mind. Then she had moved clear of the tree cover and was going downhill at a loose run. Her legs felt light, as if she were barely making contact with the ground, and she caught a stale whiff of her own illness, the last of the fever sweat, like body odour.

The cottage was ringed by a narrow brick patio that broadened at the back. Kate made a complete circle of the place, glancing into windows, and seeing only lifeless rooms, cold fireplaces, empty furniture. There was a leadenness about the place that all unoccupied houses seem to possess. She tried the back door and it opened to her touch. She walked through to the living room and reached up to the chimney shelf. Her fingers touched the polythene food bag. She put the disk in her pocket and went out the way she had gone in.

There was cloud cover across the moon and a wind off the sea, just as there had been that night when she had first decided it was to be 'flight' not 'fight'. She was looking up towards the spinney and stepping away from the shelter of the cottage wall, when she saw a light up the hill, and people moving against the darkening sky. She went back to the wall and stood still.

Of course they would be here. Of course. But have they seen me?

Her answer was a low mutter of conversation and the side-to-side sweep of the torch as the men came downhill. Two of them, she thought, or maybe three. They paused and one held a light for the other's cigarette, then lit his own. Two; two men. Two men and – she suddenly saw – two dogs. From the glow of their cigarettes, it was clear the men had stopped. Then they seemed to sink into the shoulder of the hill, suddenly invisible. Kate stiffened and prepared to run. Then she saw the bright coal as one of them drew on his cigarette. They had sat down. Sat down to wait. And they were between her and the spinney.

She went back into the house and walked through to the front: safer than walking the perimeter. How many at the front? she wondered. How many altogether? A cloud bank pushed across the face of the moon, and the landscape sprang into focus. Looking out of the window, she saw nothing but the white strip that was the lane under moonlight, and beyond that, dark fields, and then the sea, crumpled, showing light in ragged lines. She could step outside into that pale spotlight, or stay in the house, where they might expect to find her.

The front door opened with a little tic-tic-tic where the wooden sill met the step. Kate stepped through, leaving the door open, and moved quickly to the angle of the wall where she could find some shadow. She felt that whichever way she turned they would be at her back. Her eyes hurt from staring at the lane and the hedgerow and the far fields. Finally, she turned and went along the side of the cottage until she had the hillside in sight again, though this time from cover.

The men were almost on her: not more than fifty feet away and moving confidently. Run, she thought.

Instinct worked her feet. In the same moment that she broke cover, they moved away from her, heading off past the far side of the cottage, still going downhill, but at an angle, now, so that their profiles were presented to her. Walking so that they stayed downwind.

The rush of adrenalin when she first saw them had almost wiped her out, almost put her on the ground. Now she wanted to laugh. The profiles showed her men wearing gumboots and big coats and caps. The dogs on the slip-leashes were lurchers, moving with that nimble, springy walk that no other dog can imitate. They were lamping: looking for rabbits. As she watched, one of them nipped out his cigarette and spoke a word of command. The whole group stopped, and the dogs lifted their heads, expecting to be slipped, but they were too far from the hedgerow. In a second or two, the pose broke and they continued down, going with the borrow of the hill.

Kate waited until they had gone all the way across and into the far field. Up in the spinney, Corso heard her laugh. She was climbing back towards him, leaning against the slope, her hands shoved into the side pockets of her leather jacket, looking easy.

Poachers, she thought, and laughed again. When she was twenty feet from the trees, when she saw his silhouette as he stepped clear, she said, 'It was there. I've got it.'

He said, 'Good. Let's go.'

In the same moment, they heard the helicopter.

Eighteen

He'd been prepared for a police presence; expected it even. The alarm system was a surprise, and he cursed himself as he ran back from the spinney to the hilltop wood. He was clutching Kate's arm and pushing her ahead of him, making her take his pace whether she liked it or not. Whether she could hold it or not.

They must have alarmed the doors and windows. Simple. It's called hedging your bets. He said, 'There's a good chance we're going the wrong way.'

'What?' She could barely speak.

'If they've seen the car, they'll be coming at us from the road.'

'No time,' she said.

'You were down there waiting for those guys with the dogs to clear for fifteen minutes or more. They've had time.'

'Stop,' Kate said, 'stop,' but he pushed her on until she simply fell, leaving him with a dead weight. 'I can't,' she told him, and got to her hands and knees, shaking her head. 'I can't.'

'Okay,' he said, 'you can't.'

When she looked up, he had gone.

The slope seemed empty, so Corso assumed it wasn't. He went down towards the car by making a semicircle that would keep him in among trees, or alongside a hedge, for most of the way. Every fifty yards he stopped to look and listen, but even though the helicopter had gone over the hill, it was loud enough to blanket other noises. His only real defence was to look. He ran in a crouch and, each time he stopped, got down on his belly so as not to present a profile; then he quartered the view – three hundred and sixty degrees – and quartered it again. In each section, he looked for movement or light. If he found nothing, he went the next fifty yards.

He hit the road a hundred yards shy of the car and sat with his back to the roadside hedge. No vehicles; nothing moving. He went to within fifty feet, then took the car keys from his pocket and activated the electronic door lock. All four indicators flashed and the alarm gave a single whoop, like a hunting owl. The road stayed empty.

Finally, he walked to the car, got in, and backed up to the point where he'd emerged from the field. There was no one to stop him, or ask him the questions to which he had prepared impromptu answers.

To take a leak. No I didn't know that. I'm a visitor to your country as you can probably tell. Ever heard of Utah?

'I'm sorry,' he said, 'I hadn't thought of alarms.'

Even though she wanted either to faint or throw up or just die quietly, Kate registered that he'd said it as if he should have thought of them. As if he might be talking about bad preparation. As if that were his job.

'The road's clear,' he told her. 'Take it easy.'

Together, they went back down the slope. This time, Corso was even more careful. Being picked up on his own would have been irritating but probably safe enough. With Kate in tow, he was dead. He repeated the watch and wait technique, keeping a hand flat on Kate's back when they paused to scan the land under moonlight. The flat hand oppressed her, controlled her. It made her want to lash out at him.

When they got to the car, he opened the boot. She shook her head and gave a sour laugh. 'Don't think it.'

'Get in,' he said, 'or I'll put you in.'

Kate folded her hands across her abdomen; she could feel the bile rising in her throat.

'I can't get in there,' she told him. 'Don't ask me.'

'Get in or I'll drive off and leave you. I'll do it because it's the only safe way for me. Either you're out of sight, or you're not in the car. I'm giving you a count of five.'

* * *

He drove cleverly, taking bends tight and fast, and really opening up on the narrow straights. After a mile or so, Kate turned onto her stomach and got her elbows beneath her for support.

Crouched like that, like a dog, she retched and retched until she was dry, then lay in her own puke and waited for the ride to end.

Corso had hoped to make the A-road, but he was still five miles short when he pulled over and went round to let Kate out. She looked like hell and smelled worse. There was puke in her hair.

She looked up at him and said, 'Who are you, and why are you doing this to me?'

Corso pointed through trees to a bend in the road some half-mile away. Spangles of blue and red lights were dancing in the dark. She stared at them as if not sure what they might mean. The lights weren't coming any closer, nor were they moving away. They glittered and flashed in silence.

Kate said, 'Clap if you believe in fairies.'

Corso thought she might have slipped back into the fever, then she started to laugh. 'Oh, Jesus,' she said. 'Oh, Jesus, I don't care what happens next.'

They were parked at the entrance to a broad driveway, but there were no other houses around. He opened the gate that spanned the drive and jogged up to the house. There was a garage with a drop-down door. He swung it up, and it juddered against the frame. No one came; no lights went on in the house. The garage was empty.

The house had shutters upstairs and down; they were fastened across – blind eyes – but the glass-walled porch was littered with junk mail. He found a fist-sized rock and put it through the door pane, then slid the bolts and stepped inside. No lights, no startled voices. The main door was locked, so he went back outside and walked round to half an acre of garden.

There were no shutters at the back. The kitchen window was fake-leaded, a little trellis of diamond shapes. He nudged the pane with the rock, barely a tap, and it fell in. He climbed over the sill and went through the house room by room. No one had

182

been there for weeks; months, maybe. It was cold, and a clinging dampness hung in the air.

Kate was sitting on the ground, her back against one of the rear wheels. He helped her into the driver's seat.

'I'm going to push, you're going to steer. There's an open garage left of the house. That's where we're going.'

She shook her head. 'Jesus . . .'

'What's wrong?'

'I'm for giving up.'

'For what?'

'I could just . . . Why don't I walk over there, walk over to those lights? You can drive through.' She laughed. 'Just hope they don't ask you what you've got in the boot.'

'The garage,' he said. 'It's left of the house,' and slammed the driver's door.

Corso wished he hadn't broken the door pane in the porch, and he hoped that there wouldn't be any junk mail that morning.

He watched the dawn come up while Kate slept. They had switched on the heating and the hot water, but kept the lights out. Corso had ransacked the kitchen and found a torch. He'd masked it with a piece of cloth and they'd found their way round the house by that blinkered light. Kate had washed her hair and her face, then had lain down on a bare mattress and fallen asleep. Corso had covered her with a couple of towelling robes he'd found hanging on the bathroom door.

From an upper window, he had been able to see the lights of the roadblock. Several hours later, just after three a.m., they had moved off, presumably to reposition. Corso knew there was no question of taking to the road again. He'd slept fitfully for a couple of hours, lying beside Kate, then had woken and gone back to the window. The road seemed empty, but he knew it wasn't. For a mile or so, perhaps, but not beyond that. He'd wondered how long it would be before they decided to make house calls. It occurred to him that they might not be trying too hard: might not even be taking the alert too seriously. They had to assume it was Kate Randall who tripped the alarm, but must have known it could have been anyone. Some chancers with dogs, for instance, trying their luck.

He woke Kate an hour after dawn and said, 'We have to move.'

She swung her legs off the bed, and said, 'Okay,' and looked round the room as if she were seeing it for the first time. Sleep had restored her. She seemed to be in possession of new energy. She washed her face with her hands, wiping away the shreds of a dream, perhaps, or the last of her fever.

He didn't take them far. Beyond the garden lay a field that was down to grass, and beyond that some pasture, and in the far, high corner of the pasture a Nissen hut, open at either end, that might once have been a shelter for horses wintering out. They had taken a duvet from the house, cans of food and a can opener, bottles of water.

Kate pulled the duvet to her chin and leaned against the corrugated ribs of the hut. She said, 'We got the fucking disk, though,' and started to laugh. She removed it from her pocket and stared at it: little black icon.

Corso laughed too. 'We did. We got the disk. Now we have to find a way . . .' He left the rest unsaid.

The way was to walk. He waited for darkness, then led her back across the pasture, back across the meadow, past the house and down to the road.

'This is best. We can get off the road if we need to, but we know it's going to take us where we want to go. It's easier walking than fields and woods.'

'Where's that?' Kate asked.

'Where's what?'

'Where's where we want to go to?'

'The main road, then the M-way,' he told her. 'Ever see a roadblock across three lanes making better than seventy miles an hour?'

'We're going to walk up the motorway?'

'Someone's going to lend us a car.'

'Why not take yours?'

'Someone might have seen it when I parked on the road. They'll have appeals out: TV and radio, local house-to-house. It's unlikely, but who knows? Someone takes the licence plate number and type because ... it's a London plate number, or maybe we're poachers, or simply what's it doing there? Maybe a cop car passed it on the way to setting up a roadblock: it becomes "a vehicle seen in the area". It's a long ride back to London. I don't want to make it in that car. It stays where it is.'

'Someone will find it sometime.'

'Not for a long while is my guess. That's a holiday home. Apart from which the car's a rental, and it's not down to me.'

'No? Who then?'

'Ever heard of a guy called John Doe?'

Kate looked at him. 'You're full of surprises,' she said.

They made four miles in less than an hour and only had to look for cover half a dozen times. They could see headlights from way off. It was simple to drop down, facing away from the light, and stay flat. The beam would sweep over them and the engine noise fade into the wind. A moment of brightness and noise, then the country silence settling again.

Corso led them clear through a village and almost out the other side. They were less than half a mile from a motorway intersection. It was a village that had once stood in the heart of nowhere; now you could hear the drone and rush of traffic, day-long, night-long, year-long: an endless ribbon of noise, lights, exhaust fumes, garbage. He was looking for the right house, the right people, the right car.

The right moment.

Kate said, 'I need a pee.' They were walking past houses that stood on the fringe of the village. The people who lived in them were prosperous. In the heart of the village, the houses were small. Nothing lay opposite the houses but fields: the view that the house owners had purchased. The view they'd been promised.

Kate clambered over a gate and squatted on the other side, her jeans round her thighs. Corso watched as a car slowed and pulled into the driveway of a house thirty yards down the road. Before

Kate had returned, another car had followed: just able to tuck onto the drive. She followed his gaze and said, 'What?'

'Dinner party,' he said. 'The guests are arriving.'

'Will this help us?'

'It might.'

She looked at him, his face turned towards the house as the new guests rang the bell, and presented their bottle of wine, and were ushered in. 'Do you know how to . . . what is it?'

'What's what?'

'Start a car without –'

'Hot wire.'

'Hot wire a car. Do you?'

'I'm an American male,' he said. 'Automobile skills are part of our constitutional right.'

The joke wasn't enough to reassure her. She said: 'You can?'

'Yes.'

'Good,' she said. 'Get us out of here.' But she was thinking, *How? How do you know?*

Two more cars; eight guests. Thinking of all that food made the saliva rise in Kate's mouth. The last people to arrive were driving a BMW. They parked it on the grass verge some sixty feet from the house and carried their bottle to the door. Corso said, 'We'll give them half an hour.'

'Okay,' Kate said, 'terrific.' Her voice carried a sour tone. They'd been waiting for twenty minutes and a light rain was falling. She pulled her jacket up over her head and crouched by the hedge.

'I ought to make you ride in the trunk again,' Corso said, 'until we reach the main road. That okay?'

'I'll drive,' Kate told him, 'you ride in the fucking boot,' and she got up to take a swing at him, punching as hard as she could and catching him high on the shoulder.

In the house, someone drew the curtains: a woman. She was laughing. The party was warming up.

Corso ripped out the dash and made the connection, wiping the frayed ends one on the other until the engine fired. He checked the fuel gauge and found it was almost full.

The A-road lights came at her like a Bofors attack, then stopped as the road ran on into darkness. She closed her eyes, but thought she wouldn't sleep. She said, 'You're pretty good for a journo,' sensing it might be a risky thing to say, but not knowing why.

'I had a lively time in my twenties.'

'Don't tell me: the Sharks and the Jets.' Her head nodded down onto her chest. A little dream came and faded. The lights brushed her eyelids.

'No. The army.'

'You're joking.' She laughed but she didn't smile.

'Think so?'

'Serious army?'

'I don't know what it's called over here – SAS, isn't it?'

'The Paras? I don't know ...' She reached for a response. 'Why?'

'That's a long story.'

'It's a long drive.'

'It's a long story for another time,' he said. 'Why not try to get some sleep?'

But she was already sleeping.

Nineteen

They looked at the on-screen text together, Corso peering over Kate's shoulder like an attentive schoolmaster.

He said, 'What's Neophos?'

She shrugged. The document cover page was followed by a FYEO restriction addressed to the recipient: Timothy Farnol (Board). Appended was a list of WWI 'cleared personnel': people who had also had the document circulated to them. There were four: Beverley Ho (NYC), Laurence Packer, Leonard Naylor, and Ralph Farseon (Board). It included telephone numbers for these people. At the foot of each page was a logo of a globe with wings and the legend 'Wideworld Industries' circling it.

The document was short and to the point. Its first topic heading was *Neophos X-9: A Marketing Plan.*

The early release of this most recently developed version of the product has now been agreed between WWI and the ministry. Timothy Farnol (Board) informed the meeting (which had been called to address the issue of deregulation) that the most likely release date is September of this year (1996) in the UK, with a global release staggered throughout 1997. The certificates of suitability issued by the relevant departments in the UK will, we believe, assure us of acceptance in the USA. The rest of the world does not present a problem in terms of marketing licences so far as can be discerned. France and other European countries have already suggested that licences will be issued on the basis of early representations by WWI overseas sales offices and thanks to direct contact made by Beverley Ho during a recent Europe-wide goodwill trip. Mr Farnol has also been instrumental in forging alliances in the relevant departments of foreign (i.e. other than UK) governments. A number of government officials have already visited WWI as guests, and have been recipients of extensive WWI hospitality. Our initial sales assessment for Neophos X-9 is 1.3m throughout the targeted countries where markets are already established. For a forward projection graph based on a planned annual growth of 8%–10% p.a., see page 12 of this document. This projection takes into account the continued sales of Neophos A-9 until deregulation, after which A-9 will no longer be sold. This wastage is allowed for in the sales arc of X-9. In effect, A-9 is already defunct and does not report on WWI computer systems. New orders are being supplied with Neophos X-9 as part of a familiarisation process. The board expressed its thanks to Mr Farnol.

The rest was figures and sales talk. Buried on page fourteen under the general heading of *Marketing Strategies* was this:

The genetic enhancement techniques used in the production of Neophos X-9 are described in the addendum: footnote 27. It is likely that some opposition to the development and marketing of X-9 will be encountered from Green groups, environmentalists, radical scientists and the like. We think that genetically modified products in general will be called into question (especially food, and more especially food sold in supermarkets), and X-9 will merely be one such product. However, WWI publicity offices will be preparing a campaign to counter any such opposition. In short, we have to ensure that our propaganda is more effective than their propaganda. Publicity officers in all locations will report at first to UK PR & Security in the person of Larry Packer.

Kate printed out two copies of the document and gave one to Corso.

It was three a.m. The drive had taken four and a half hours, which had put them at the end of Corso's mews soon after midnight. Corso had given Kate his keys, then driven the car to a patch of waste ground by the river, close to one of the worst of the south-east London estates. The barracks of walkways and sky-high windows was called Linden. Linden House estate. It had put him in mind of the pub where he'd waited; where Kate had gone past him, eyes front, like someone who knew more than the first rule of surveillance.

She's not stupid, he'd reminded himself. He wondered how far her trust extended now. He'd got them clear of Penarven and the roadblocks, but he'd acted like a pro.

I hadn't thought of alarms. He'd heard his own voice saying it, and recalled the sudden wary look on her face, as if she were thinking, *Neither had I – so why should you?*

He'd remembered the exchange they'd had as they were walking away from the holiday home: *The car's a rental, and it's not down to me.*

No? Who then?

Ever heard of a guy called John Doe?

You're full of surprises.

Careful, he'd thought. Be careful. Suddenly the ice gets thinner.

He had used the BMW's tool kit to force the gas cap, then to tear up the fabric of the back seats, which he'd stuffed into the tank. When it had soaked, he'd repeated the process, then a third time, finally throwing the sodden material back inside the car, front and back, and setting it alight.

The waste lot backed on to a hospital that was being demolished. Wards, corridors, staircases and lift shafts stood exposed. Where sick people had lain, where children had been born, where the terminally ill had stared at one another in silence, where anxious relatives had walked the corridors and ridden up in the lifts clutching flowers and fruit. It all hung in tatters, torn brick and smashed windows. Behind Corso, the car had given a sudden *puff*, and flame had billowed backwards, touched at the edges with dirty smoke. He'd rounded the hospital and come to a link fence that cordoned a lorry park. He'd taken the direct route, over the fence, through the park, and onto a main road. Even at that time of night, the traffic had been thick. Corso had walked a mile, maybe a mile and a half, along the verge as vehicles slammed past at his shoulder. There were grimy houses set back from the road, sullen, blinkered by heavy curtains, as if they were still recovering from the first shock appearance of the tarmac, the JCBs, the road gangs, the trees falling, the first high-sided container trucks barrelling through after midnight.

Finally, he'd walked into lights and broad pavements, and then a high street crammed with stores, neon signs making a seamless, lurid line of names and products. He'd found a bus stop and caught the night bus across the river, then taken a cab to within a mile of his house, and walked the rest of the way.

He'd returned to the house to find Kate asleep in a chair, but when he'd gone to his computer and nudged the mouse, the disk text had clarified on the screen.

'Do you understand this?' Kate asked. She was reading footnote 27 in the addenda.

'More or less,' Corso said. 'Neophos is an organophosphate. What they've got is something a bit more. Organo-plus.'

'Meaning?'

'It's enhanced. Don't ask me how.'

'There's something in this footnote – 27; they mention it in –'

'Yeah. Enhanced.'

'Go on . . .'

'Does the job better, I guess.' He flipped back through the pages as if, for all the world, he had never seen the document before. 'The key word here is "deregulation". It means they've removed some or all of the controls that govern manufacture.'

'Been allowed to,' Kate said.

'Yes. Been allowed to. This guy Farnol's the connection, obviously. You mentioned him to me when we were driving down. A politician, right?'

'Used to be a minister.'

'In the right place?'

'Oh, yes.'

'And he's on the board of Wideworld Industries.'

'So he helped it through, don't you think – deregulating Neophos? All this talk of foreign politicians receiving "extensive hospitality" – what does that mean to you? Bribes . . . am I right?'

Corso raised his hands as if in surrender. 'Look out of the

window in a couple of hours. If the sun rises in the west, let me know.'

'These other people . . .'

Corso said, 'Beverley Ho used to be WWI USA. Now WWI UK. I love all the initials. Makes everything sound so official, but at the same time so innocuous.'

This is better, he thought. This is me being an investigative journalist, green issues a speciality; this is stuff I'm supposed to know.

'What does she do?'

'She's the MD . . . just to keep the initials flowing. Farnol – well, we know about him. This guy Packer is obviously security – an outfit which, significantly, subsumes the public relations department. Ralph Farseon: don't know. A member of the UK board. Michael would probably have had a line on him. Another politician, maybe? Leonard Naylor – that's another blank.' He gestured towards the screen. 'This was it? This is the disk?'

'That's it.'

'Nothing on the disk from Michael?'

'I suppose he didn't have time.'

Corso stared at the screen. 'Yeah . . . I'd've thought – you know – some sort of message, instructions, a hello/goodbye?'

Kate closed the file and showed him the files and folders list on the A drive. Just one: Wideworld Industries: Neophos X-9/ 1996.doc. 'Maybe he was in a hurry.'

'He must have talked to you about this stuff,' Corso said. 'You must have more information.'

'Did he talk to you about it?'

'Yes,' Corso said, 'a little. Which is why I assume he talked to you a lot.'

'I think he talked to you because you're already in the know. A colleague. Someone who understands the language. Someone who might have an opinion or be able to help. Michael didn't expect to get any of that from me. We didn't discuss his work very often. He was pretty secretive about it, as a matter of fact.'

'You weren't interested.'

'Who said that? Did I say that? I was. I am.'

'You care about environmental matters?'

'Yes. I do. I'm just not a fanatic.' Her voice was hostile. 'Don't be so fucking pompous.'

'No, I . . . You know. It didn't have to be the case. I mean, did Michael care about music?'

'Not much.' She softened. 'Sorry, you're right. Why should I care, just because I was going with a green journo? But I do.'

Corso tried again, a different way. 'I just thought . . . If Michael had talked to you about this – about Neophos, about WWI – there might be something we could latch on to. Something you remember that might provide a clue. It's tough to know where to go from here.'

'The other names on the circulation list: Farseon, Naylor.'

'Sure . . . Listen' – a last try; a last little push; after this, let it lie – 'if Michael did say anything . . . give you any other information . . . and you remember it, not now, perhaps, but remember it another time, it could be important –'

'Sure. Okay.'

'– I need to know. There's not much to go on.'

'There was nothing. We didn't talk about it.'

So she says. But she doesn't trust me. Does she?

It was too late and too early to sleep. Kate dozed on the sofa, a glass of whisky in her hand. When she woke it was to someone playing the Elgar cello concerto. Kate Randall.

'Why did you get this?'

'Curiosity.'

'Do you like music?'

'Yes.'

She remembered the obvious Brahms, Mozart and Beethoven; the much-less-than-obvious Sibelius.

'What do you like?'

'Lots.'

'Tells me nothing.'

'Everything you would expect. Mozart.' He smiled. 'Mozart and more Mozart and after that, Mozart.'

'And Sibelius.'

'I wanted the violin concerto. The store I went to didn't have it.'

'Turn this off,' she said, 'would you?'

'Sure.' He went to the hi-fi. 'You don't like listening to yourself?'

'I remember the errors.'

'There are things wrong with this?'

'Not enough passion. Me, not Elgar. What's next?'

'Tomorrow? I thought I'd go to a press library: use one of the on-line cuttings banks. I've got a few friends in media jobs.'

'Looking for?'

'References to Neophos. General information on organophosphates. Track down this guy Farseon. Stuff like that.'

'While I do what?'

'Stay here would be best.'

'And prepare something tasty for your return. Hunter-gatherer casserole, maybe. I bake my own bread and skin my own rabbits, too.'

'Kate – what else? What else should you do? Take more risks?'

She sighed and drank her whisky. 'I can't stay here.'

'Why not?'

'I'm in your bed.'

'The sofa's fine. Don't be crazy. You have to walk the streets, get spotted, get picked up by the cops – why? Because I need my bed back?'

Kate shook her head, but it was a gesture of consent. She asked, 'What did you do with the car?'

'Drove it to the badlands and torched it.'

'Jesus.' She looked at him in a new way. 'Torched it? You mean you set fire –'

'That's what they do.'

'Who?'

'Kids. Joyriders. Drive the shit out of it for a night, then burn it and look for another. Stay behind the wheel longer than a few hours, someone's likely to find you.'

'Twoccers,' she said.

'How's that again?'

She'd read it somewhere, or heard it on a newscast. 'Twoccers.

It's what they call themselves. An acronym: taking without the owner's consent; it's the official term for the offence.'

'No kidding.' He laughed. 'Twoccers?' His accent made it *twaccers*. 'Well that's where it is.'

'In the badlands.'

'Way south. Camouflaged by all the other stuff going on. They'll get round to it, eventually, and put it down to kids. They'll have a few dozen rapes, muggings, armed robberies and break-ins to think about first.'

'Where is it,' she asked, 'the badlands?' As if it might be a metaphor, a place of the mind.

'Any place the money has left,' he told her, 'or a place where it never arrived.' And Kate remembered bedding down in rain, feeling the first cramps of her period, lying in the stolen bag, thinking, *One more day is all I can do of this*.

But she thought now that she could last for longer than a day. A lot longer. Remembering how anonymous she had been, how faceless, how *lost*, she thought that she could go back any time, and the thought made her oddly happy. Any time she needed to. A place to be – no place. Someone to be – no one.

She went into the bedroom and lay down on top of the bed. Fragments of the computer text ran through her mind. She thought: *I bet Tim Farnol knew all sorts of things; it's a pity he died*. Then: *Although perhaps some people weren't so sorry*.

WWI. Farnol, Farseon, Packer, Naylor, Ho. It was the first time she had been able to come up with a list of suspects.

I didn't kill Michael.

Perhaps there was a reason to suppose that someone might believe her now that there was something to show, something to point to. He certainly seemed to believe her – Robert Corso. Did she believe him, though?

She got up and undressed apart from her underwear. Climbing into bed again, she remembered her fever, her bruised and broken dreams, as if those terrible images were lying shattered in corners of the room.

She pulled the duvet to her chin. Then she reached between her breasts and took from the cup of her bra a floppy disk. The original, the one Michael had given her, was still in the A drive of Corso's computer. The disk that had lain close to her heart while she'd been speaking to Corso was one of those she had bought to download information from Michael's computer. While Corso had been getting rid of the car, she had copied Michael's A disk, then gone back to the original and deleted an item.

She had left the WWI document: there had to be something there for Corso to look at, and the document was the meat. But she had wiped a little item called *Memos.doc* that related to the principal file. There had been three memos, all of them concerning Leonard Naylor. The first was from Ralph Farseon to Lawrence Packer, the second from Packer to Farseon.

WideWorld Industries International, plc
Memo

To: Lawrence Packer
From: Ralph Farseon
Subject: Neophos X-9
Date: June 10th 1996
cc: Beverley Ho, NYC

Confidential: FYEO

1. You will know that our principal research scientist, Leonard Naylor, has suggested that the enhanced properties of X-9 require additional investigation before we seek deregulation. (His report of last month, copied to you and Beverley Ho.) At present, it is the understanding of the board that X-9 is a trouble-free product, despite the expected opposition from Green pressure groups.

2. Naylor's reservations are based principally on what he claims to be the effect on himself of developing and handling X-9, despite the obvious point that concentrated quantities of the product are a different issue from what will be the properly distributed, controlled and applied quantities of X-9 when it is in normal, commercial use.

3. In the light of Naylor's persistence in the matter, and his requests for independent tests made outside his supervision, we have suggested he take a leave of absence. It is his belief that tests will be put in hand during that time. As you know, there are no reasons to suppose that tests are a necessity, and we fully expect X-9 to be endorsed by ministry-approved deregulation applying to all chemical pesticides later in the summer. This will not require legislation, and our production schedule is already in place.

4. All this being so, we do not propose to instigate any such tests. Our reasons for placating Naylor have to do, as you might expect, with security issues. Our intention is to extend the period of Naylor's (paid) leave until we can, finally, remove him from the company. Interviews for a new research chemist will commence in a week's time. Naylor will, of course, be given full pension facilities. Once he is no longer on the WWI payroll, the 'tests' supposedly conducted in his absence will lie outside his remit. Theoretically, he will not be free to question their validity or, indeed, whether they ever actually took place.

5. Clearly there are security and publicity issues here of which you should be aware. It might be necessary, for instance, to at some point remind Naylor of the confidentiality clause in his contract of employment. Other precautions will — as you will no doubt realise from the tone of this memo — centre on the possibility of press leaks and other unauthorised contacts in the media, against which we must be persistently vigilant.

Why don't I trust him? Kate thought. Why did I squirrel these memos away from Corso? Why do I need an angle?

He set fire to the car. Drove it to — the badlands, he called them. And torched it.

Sure, but he's a journalist after a story. Remember that time Michael hacked into the Central Office computer? Remember when he faked his way into the records room at Dounreay? Lethal cocktails of radioactive waste being dumped in a shaft that was leaching into the sea. Hot plutonium exploding under reaction and showering the locality. Radioactive hot spots on the beach and kids allowed to play there for years while project managers past and present lied in their teeth. Michael was so *angry*. And he faked his way in. Remember?

That was journo stuff. This guy . . . it's different.

Michael would have done what he's done.

Yes. But Michael would have been doing it for *me*. And Corso seems to . . . seems to *know* so much. How to do things. He said, 'I hadn't thought of alarms.' At Penarven. And he knew what to do with the car.

Different folks, different strokes. Tell him about the memos.

Later. I mean, I will tell him. I just . . . I need something. I need ammunition. Something I know that no one else knows.

Why?

Insurance.

What? – to bargain with?

Maybe.

Under what circumstances?

I'll tell you when it happens.

Robert's good for you. I mean, he's been good for you. Christ, you trusted him enough to come here in the first place.

I was ill. I needed help. He was it. Anyway, that's not the problem. I trust him; then I don't trust him. He hasn't turned me in . . . But I sort of think he might if he had to. Or if it suited him.

He helped you get the disk. And here you still are.

Yes, the disk . . . But he thinks I know more than I'm telling. He thinks there's something else.

Well, he's right. There is.

WideWorld Industries International, plc
Memo

From: Lawrence Packer
To: Ralph Farseon
Subject: Leonard Naylor (Ref: Neophos X-9)
Date: November 23rd 1996
cc: Beverly Ho, NYC

You will have received information concerning the death of Leonard Naylor in an automobile accident. No one else was involved. His car drove off the highway on a bend.

A press release has been authorised confirming that Naylor was suffering a bad influenza. Initial reports indicate that his illness was a major contributing factor in the accident. It seems likely his ability to control the vehicle was affected.

The press statement indicates that WWI will continue to pay his widow the pension that Naylor had been entitled to on leaving the company. A floral tribute was sent to the funeral on behalf of the WWI board.

We have requested that Mrs Naylor return to WWI any documentation relating to company business, especially research activities, that might have remained in her husband's possession. She has confirmed that there appears to have been no such documentation among his effects.

That was the packaging, the gift-wrapping, the ribbon on the candy. That was for the filing cabinet. The next document came with a preface that read: *Memo* (unheaded), signed Lawrence Packer.

Ralph: The attached FYEO memo can go on record. Press releases are being prepared. Naylor had some kind of unspecified complaint that seems to replicate OP poisoning.

Company medical records state that he reported with symptoms that included temporarily restricted vision (actual loss of vision on several occasions), lassitude, fluctuating temperatures, nausea, intermittent severe abdominal pain, hair loss, palpitations (anterior fibrillation), and aberrant pigmentation. It's a fair bet that one or some of these caused him to crash. (Most likely, affected vision, since the road took a bend at the crash site, but Naylor didn't.)

The medical records referred to have been destroyed. Medical staff involved have been spoken with and several ex-officio remunerations made. Naylor's widow was approached on the day of the funeral (yesterday). She has been aware of Naylor's symptoms, though I believe she has been persuaded that he reported with influenza while at work yesterday afternoon and was released from duty. His accident occurred en route home.

Mrs Naylor has been notified that her husband's pensionable status has been enhanced fourfold due to a pipeline promotion that will be awarded posthumously.

We have made contact with junior officials at the DOH (via Tim Farnol) and are confident that a post-mortem can be avoided, especially in the light of the widow's compliance.

I hate to speak ill of the dead, Ralph, but I can't help feeling glad that this son of a bitch is safely out of the way.

Larry.

Which is why, Kate said to herself, Robert should have this information: he can go looking, and you can't.

Later. I'll give it to him later.

In the morning.

That's right. In the morning.

No you won't. Why? You believe that as soon as he's got his story, he'll throw you to the wolves?

Maybe.

Why would he do that?

Because to turn me in to the police – that's a hell of a good story, too. Isn't it?

*　*　*

Larry Packer was looking at the same information that Kate and Corso had looked at the night before: the contents of the disk, but without the final memo.

'Yeah,' he said, 'well . . . it's bad enough. Jesus. Lester must have known what this means. Naylor was bad-mouthing X-9. We pushed Farnol on the dereg issue, then –'

'Pushed?' Corso said.

'Money, etcetera. Megabucks. Push fuckin' push. But listen, it was no big deal, you know what I'm saying? They were all set for it. Jesus, you shoulda seen the stash going to good causes from this office. Good political causes, mostly. As big business goes, WWI is one of the biggest; everyone likes that. All governments like that. Even the fucking Chinese like that. We can do business with world leaders the way Joe Normal buys a pack of gum.'

'How much of a problem was Naylor?'

'Problem. Big mouth, no company loyalty, which is a mistake. Take the dollar, you take the oath, you understand my meaning? He had a troublesome conscience.'

'Was he right?'

'About X-9? No evidence.'

'Okay, I don't care one way or the other,' Corso said. 'You whack him?'

Packer laughed without smiling. 'No. We don't do that sort of . . . I told you, Lester was a mistake. The idea was harass him, discredit him, steal his notes, fuck his computer, etcetera. Things screwed up. But with Naylor . . . he simply drove his car off the road. Who knows why?'

'He didn't have the 'flu though, did he?'

'Had something.'

'X-9?' Corso wondered.

Packer said, 'I don't even want to hear that kind of talk from you, Corso, it makes me edgy, you follow? I don't like to hear it.' A secretary buzzed him and Packer stabbed a button on the phone and picked up. 'No,' he said, 'I'm at lunch,' then hung up. 'So I'd better be at lunch,' he said. 'You want lunch?'

They used Packer's company car to drive from the southern

suburbs into the centre: a black Lexus that still had the smell of leather on it. Packer confirmed a reservation using his mobile phone: a restaurant fashionable for its ill-tempered and moody chef. He found it funny.

'This guy – people come to his place, pay, like, a hundred and fifty dollars a head, he insults them. Turn up a few minutes late, your table's gone. Jesus! He wants to know your dad's dick size before you can make a reservation. He's the fuckin' *cook*, for Chrissake.'

'So why go there?' Corso asked.

Packer looked at him, puzzled. 'Everyone goes there.'

'Does he insult you?'

'Motherfucker says a word to me, I'll sit him on his own goddam stove.'

The food was okay-to-good. Packer ate it as if it were cheeseburger and fries. He said, 'What else does she know? Does she know anything?'

'I think so.'

'What is it?'

'I don't know that.'

'But you will.'

'Oh, yes, I will.'

Something in Corso's tone made Packer cock his head. 'You fuck her yet?'

'No.'

'You plan to?'

'Is it in the job description?'

Packer guffawed. 'How soon to know her secrets? To know if she *has* secrets? I've got a meeting with Ho pretty soon. She'll want a report.'

'On the business of Lester's death, you mean?'

'Jesus Christ, she doesn't know about that. Are you crazy? No – a report of Neophos X-9, etcetera. *Lester?* Listen – I know. You know.'

'Did Farnol know?'

Packer shook his head. 'Guessed, maybe.'

'Farseon?' Corso remembered the name from the memo. 'Who is he?'

'Farseon used to have Ho's job. He's in Tokyo. All he knows is sushi.'

'So what will you tell Ho?'

'That there's a possible leak. Danger of X-9 coming under fire.'

'Yes . . .' Corso spread some pâté onto a tiny triangle of Melba toast. 'What does it do?'

'X-9? Kills bugs. Pests, worms, little critturs of all persuasions.'

'Gulf War vets?' Corso wondered.

'A week,' Packer said.

'A week's fine,' Corso told him. 'A week's longer than I need.'

Kate restored the full A disk information to Michael's hard disk and copied it onto five other floppy disks. She thought five ought to be enough. Then she printed out the text the same number of times and made five separate packages: text and disk in each. After that she wiped the memos, leaving just the original document text in place.

She went out, slamming the door behind her, and bought five mail-miser envelopes. The first package she addressed to Stuart Donnelly at his law firm. The other three envelopes she left blank. She put a note in with Donnelly's copy.

Dear Stuart,

This tells you a good many things, but not everything. If the time comes when I have to face a court of law, this information might be useful – don't you think? If nothing else, it proves that Michael was working on something very controversial when he was killed.

2+2=4?

And Farnol's death: what about that?

I'll try to talk to you by phone over the next few days. I know you have to tell the police that you've heard from me, but I'm assuming what's in this package is privileged information. I hope so. I can't come in yet, so don't expect it. Maybe I can never come in.

Yours,

Kate Randall

She mailed that package, then took the tube to a mainline station and put the four unaddressed envelopes into a security locker. She assumed that Joanna's phone was being tapped: there had been no calls to the mobile, and she had made none, apart from talking to Farnol. Now, as she sat in a small, grimy café close to the station, she felt lonelier than she had ever felt in her life before. People moved round her and past her, following the patterns of their lives, and she thought they were like shadows, unsubstantial, speechless. She sat, a woman with no life that she wanted to own, and nowhere to go but back to him; back to Robert Corso. Or back to the streets. And because she felt as if no one had ever held her, as if no one had ever offered her comfort, as if no one had ever welcomed her in, or known her, or claimed her as a friend, she left the café and found a piss-stained corner in a cold alleyway and dialled Joanna's number on the mobile phone.

All she said was, 'It's me. I'm fine.'

As she walked back into the street, she dialled time-check, so that would be on last number recall.

Corso walked through the empty house as if he half expected Kate to be in a room he'd forgotten about; as if he expected to hear her voice or find the note that read: I'm in the . . . *Where?*

Where are you?

He booted-up the computer and ran Michael Lester's disk. He read through the information there, then read it through again. Bad enough, that's what Larry Packer had said. What she knows is bad enough . . . But Corso had a feeling that this wasn't all. This wasn't it. If he'd had a chance to read the disk before Kate, he would have felt happier. But he'd gone to dump the car: man's work, field work, the kind of thing he understood best. He'd gone to dump the car and left her with the disk. Mistake, he thought. Another mistake. How many mistakes can I afford?

Where are you now?

He poured himself a drink in order to top up the lunchtime booze; already he was beginning to feel grey round the edges. Without her, there was nothing to do. Nothing to be done. He thought, When the job's done, then I'll feel differently. Then I'll feel positive. End of one job, start of another. A new commission.

He disliked Larry Packer. He disliked suits like that with jobs like that. Corso's own progression had been straightforward: cop, self-employed investigator, then a specialisation in business and industrial work. He'd been a cop for two years exactly: long enough to learn his trade; long enough to do the groundwork. It paid crap, and the sweaty cameraderie made him sick. He had killed four people, one while he was a cop, the other three all within the past two years. It seemed that the climate was growing hotter in his trade: a kind of professional *el niño*. Of the three, only one had been a genuine mark. Kate was the second. It was as if an 'option to terminate' clause had suddenly cropped up in all the contracts. All those *unwritten* contracts. Corso had taken the job hoping that he wouldn't have to honour the clause. But hell . . .

His first man down had been a punk with a gun in a liquor-to-go store, and Corso's badge had made things okay. The second and third had been men like himself; they'd been working for the wrong side; that was any side that Corso wasn't on.

The fourth had been a little grey man with an attaché case full of secrets. Well, a medium-sized man with light brown hair, in point of fact, but Corso thought of him as grey because grey was what he wore and, in Corso's version of him, his thoughts were grey and his view of the world was uniformly grey. It's a useful attitude to have; if your feelings towards the mark are all negative, you can reduce him to a cipher if you want to: easier to kill. No, not easier; easy. The power of positive thinking.

The problem that the grey man presented was that, even when the contents of the attaché case had been destroyed, the secrets were still inside his head. Corso had said, 'I'll take care of him,' and that's just what he'd done. Good care. The grey man was mugged to death one snowy night and fell into the NYPD stats file like a number finding its place in a logical progression. Soon buried. Corso thought about him, afterwards, as you might think of a man you met on a train journey: that brief intimacy, that guaranteed estrangement.

He thought about Kate. His thought was: Everything's different, as in life. *As in life.* As if life were going on elsewhere. He went to the CD player and put on her Elgar. He was anxious for her return. Her absence made him edgy. It put him out of control.

You know something I don't know. I'm sure of it.

A week, Packer had said.

Corso liked to see his jobs, his tasks, as little playlets; little psychodramas. You go to the movies; each time a different plot, different actors, a different way of doing things. It helped him. It was his way of separating them from the other things he did: the gym, bowling, drinks with the guys, dating a girl. This little play, the one where Kate was his leading lady . . . well . . . it was odd. Things going wrong; mistakes being made. A strange smell was coming off it, a strange feeling, like when you know you're going to be ill, but you don't yet know what's wrong, or how bad it'll be.

Maybe she won't come back. Maybe I'll never see her again. How would that be?

He didn't like the idea, but he wasn't sure why.

Kate was a street or two from Corso's door when she had an idea. She looked round for a quiet place and found a sidestreet that led to a tree-lined square. There were leaves on the pavement, just as there always were. The city's climate didn't allow for clear-cut seasons, just as its weather wasn't the weather of open spaces. She walked widdershins, circling the railings, and put in a call to Wideworld Industries. The switchboard operator answered, and Kate asked for Beverley Ho. What she got was Beverley Ho telling her that she had got through to Beverley Ho's voice mail, and she could leave a message or press zero to be returned to the operator.

Kate said, 'There's a product called Neophos X-9. You know all about it, I'm sure. Tim Farnol knew all about it, too. Now I know all about it.' She paused, then added, 'I just wanted you to have that information.'

She got to his door and paused.

You sure you want to go in?

Why not?

You don't trust him.

I don't trust anyone.

You think he's being tricky, but you don't know why.

Not really; anyway, it's best to be cautious.

What if he's —

I was sick: he looked after me. He came to Penarven with me. We got the disk. He hasn't made a wrong move, not really.

Things . . . things he says.

Drop it. Forget it. Anyway, there's —

Things you think.

— nowhere else to go.

She rang the doorbell, then took a step back like a cold-calling salesman. He said, 'Do I have to give you a set of keys?'

'Or lock me in the tower,' she said. 'Except I've cut my hair and, besides, genuine princes are few and far between.'

'Genuine?'

'Chain-mail, white horse, blond curls, cleft chin.'

He stood aside to let her in, then went through to the kitchen to make coffee. She followed him and lodged on a stool by the counter.

'You don't think it's risky?' he asked. 'Where did you go?'

'I wanted some fresh air. Except this is London: so I went for a walk instead.'

'I was worried.'

She laughed. 'I can't stay indoors all day. I get restless. I have to do something. Think of something for me to do. Think of something for *us* to do. I mean, I'm trying to save my own life. Sitting still isn't the answer, is it?'

'I'm not sitting still. I'm looking at Neophos and Wideworld Industries.'

'Looking . . . for what?'

'Who knows? Something that makes sense. Something that fits the pattern, but isn't obvious.'

'The sky,' she said.

'What?'

'The sky when you're doing a jigsaw. All the other bits have got something on them somewhere, to show you what they are: trees or a toadstool or little wings. But the sky's just blue. Clear blue.'

'What in hell jigsaw is that?' he laughed. 'Trees and toadstools and little wings.' He liked that part of the relationship: liked the acting, the light touches.

'I had it when I was a kid.'

'The little wings were Disney wings.'

'No, not Disney. Never Disney. Fairy wings. So what is it, Robert? Just a news story? Just Michael's story you're after?'

The question came out of a clear blue sky and it startled him; she had also used his name for the first time, which unsettled him.

'Here's another question,' she said. 'What happens when you think you've got all you can get? You won't be worrying about me then, will you?'

'Of course.' Then, as if he'd fallen into a trap, added quickly, 'I hope I won't have to worry. I hope you'll be safe.'

'Safe . . . yes . . .' She spoke like someone remembering a favourite place; a place of childhood. 'There are three possibilities, Robert, that you have to deal with. Michael was killed by a nameless intruder who was after the video. Michael was killed by me in a fit of passion, fear and anger. Michael was killed by a person or persons unknown for reasons that had nothing to do with robbery or sex.'

'But had a lot to do with the story he was compiling . . .'

'Is that a ludicrous idea?'

'No. People have been killed for much less.'

'Does it happen, though? Killing to protect —' She shrugged, as if not knowing quite how to describe 'profit' and 'motive'.

'For secrets?' he asked. 'To protect megabuck contracts? To wipe the company slate? Are you serious? All the time.'

'And is that what happened to Michael?'

'I don't know,' he said. 'I've no idea. Maybe it *was* some jerk after the video. But it wasn't you.'

'No?'

'No.'

'I'm glad you're sure,' Kate told him, 'because sometimes I

dream it was me. I dream I killed him. Then I wake up and wonder if I did — if it's not a dream, but a memory.'

Corso put two fingers of Colombian coffee into a cafetière and poured on boiling water. He smiled. 'Dream all you like,' he said. 'I know you didn't kill him. And the thing to do . . . is prove it.'

'You're right. Just tell me how.'

Corso held up a fistful of photostats trawled from a cuttings library. They were all about Wideworld Industries and organophosphates. All about nothing.

'One thing at a time,' he said.

Twenty

'What's the Polish Café?' George Webb asked.

Webb was heading up a meagre team of five, which made him a lot less than happy. In addition to John Adams and Carol Tanner, he had a DC called Philip Nairn and a civilian cataloguer. And himself. Nairn was spending ninety per cent of his time plodding around after Joanna Randall and writing reports that were indistinguishable one from another.

'She goes there for coffee sometimes.'

'Does she speak to anyone?'

Nairn tried to keep the weariness out of his voice. 'I'd mention it if she did, boss.'

Webb looked up sharply. 'Don't get lippy.'

'Sorry, boss. But –'

'I didn't say, "Does she meet anyone?" I said, "speak to anyone". Someone she sees every day, perhaps. Good morning, hello, how are you today.'

'She orders coffee, then she drinks it.'

'Do you go in?'

'Walk past and wait for her. I've got a little arrangement with a newsagent. He thinks I'm better than off the TV.'

'Nothing else?'

'The kid's school, then college, sometimes the supermarket, sometimes not, then the woman's house who has the kid if she's late back – this is another mother from the school – then home, then kid's supper, then kid's bath –'

'Yes,' Webb said, 'all right. Shut up.' He was looking down an annotated list of phone numbers. 'She called her sister. The answer machine was on.'

John Adams was in the room. He was checking the sightings

reported during the last poster appeal: *Have you seen . . .* He said, 'She did? That's new.'

'I just got it,' Webb said. 'As I came in.'

'With a transcript,' Adams supposed.

' "It's me. I'm fine".'

'Just that?'

'From a mobile phone,' Webb said. 'Where the fuck did she get a mobile phone?'

'Nicked it,' Nairn said. 'Easiest thing in the world. One goes every minute. It's easier than looking for a pay phone. You can get up to an hour before the phone company puts the bar on.'

'More than that –' Webb went on as if Nairn hadn't spoken, '– more than that, how in hell can she be fine? How can she be *fine*? What in fuck's name does she mean when she says she's *fine*?' He wiped a jot of spittle off his chin. After a moment, he said, 'I'm not fine. I'm not fine at all.'

'There's a product called Neophos X-9. You know all about it, I'm sure. Tim Farnol knew all about it, too. Now I know all about it.' A pause. *'I just wanted you to have that information.'*

Beverley Ho hadn't taken her eyes off Larry Packer while the tape was playing. She asked, 'Do you know the voice?'

'No. I know who it is.'

'Don't tell me.'

'I wasn't going to.'

'How much of a problem is this?'

'It's a problem. I won't lie.'

'No.' Beverley Ho shook her head, eyes steady. 'No, don't do that. Will I have to hear more of it?'

'I shouldn't think so.'

'I'd prefer not to.'

'Sure.'

'How did Tim Farnol die?'

'The papers said heart attack.'

'I read the papers.'

'He put a noose round his own neck and tied it off to a light fitting, then he broke an amyl nitrate ampoule under his nose,

211

shoved a dummy dick up his ass and bent his knees till the black clouds arrived. At some point, he slipped up. Literally.'

Ho looked at him for a beat or two. 'You're kidding me.'

'That's what he did.'

'I've just come into this job, Larry, and I've been waiting for it for some time. I'm not planning on wearing any dead men's shoes. You understand my meaning?'

'Absolutely.'

'Everyone does stuff, I know that. Everyone does deals.'

She was sitting in a high-backed leather chair which she had shoved back from her desk. When she tilted it on its rocker, her shoulders rested against a plate glass window that gave a view of distant fields and a motorway and acres of blue sky above. She crossed her legs and half turned to watch a cloud of starlings twisting like smoke.

Packer watched her thighs move, watched her skirt lift. Beverley Ho was a little too short, a little too stocky, and not quite pretty enough to win Larry Packer's cash prize. Two generations of mixed blood hadn't been enough to breed out the peasant strain. She was powerful, though: she had power and she knew how to hold on to it. She was also intelligent and ambitous and, better than all those things, knew how to deliver a low punch. You couldn't say that she had come up the hard way because, to her, no way was hard. Beverley Ho was a born winner, and it came off her in a smell stronger than pheromones, a smell more than enough to heat the blood of someone like Larry Packer. He worked at constructing a little fantasy: Beverley Ho ass-up across her own desk, looking at him over her shoulder as she now looked at the starlings. She was saying, 'Sure Larry, come on Larry, give it to me Larry,' but somehow the image kept slipping.

'Have you ever worked for an oil company, Larry?' Her eyes were on him again, dead level.

'Never have.'

'Ever work for the government?'

'No.'

'People do deals ... I know that. I'll be doing some deals

myself. That's fine. My deals are fine. Do you understand what I'm saying?'

'Sure. You don't –'

'I don't want to hear about anyone else's deals.'

'Okay, Beverley.'

'I don't want to hear a word about any deal anyone did before I sat in this office. Any *deal*, you understand? *That* kind of deal.'

'Sure. Got it.'

'What I'm saying is, I don't want to hear a single goddam word about any *deal* that any sonofabitch made before I stepped off the plane. I just want it disappeared. Come back to me and tell me the problem's been disappeared.' She tossed the answerphone tape across the desk. 'Whoever the fuck she is, whatever the fuck she wants.'

Packer took the tape and went to the door.

'What do you think that did for him?' Beverley Ho asked. 'Strangling. Strangling himself with a plastic prick up his ass?'

Packer had his hand on the door. 'I guess you don't know till you try,' he said.

Kate took her mobile phone and the phone book into a nearby park and tried every Naylor there was; she drew a series of blanks. She called Human Resources at Wideworld Industries and was told he didn't work there any more. The voice from the HR office was young and friendly. Kate said, 'Can you give me a number where I can reach him?'

You will have received information concerning the death . . .

'I can't give out that information.'

'Okay, I understand.' She paused as if puzzled. 'But if he doesn't work for you any more . . .'

'It isn't company policy.'

'Can I ask you to call him on my behalf?'

This time the friendly voice paused. 'I can't do that.'

. . . car drove off the highway . . .

'Right. Okay. It's – They've moved, that's the problem. I've got –' Kate read out a number and an address, hesitating here and there as if reading it from a book: an address book, perhaps.

'But they don't live there any more. I'm a friend of theirs. I only come through London now and then. I was hoping . . . I bought some presents and so forth. I've been working abroad.'

'Yes. I can't —'

'Look,' Kate said, 'don't worry. I understand. I'll have to catch them another time. Maybe Len will write.'

. . . a press release has been authorised . . .

'Look,' said the friendly voice, 'it's not just that I can't tell you where —'

Kate interrupted, letting a note of concern into her voice. 'What? Not just what? I don't understand.'

The friendly voice gave her a number. 'I'm so sorry.'

'Sorry?' Kate echoed. She tried to let worry and puzzlement leak from her voice.

'Don't say I gave you the number.'

'Of course. Right.'

'I'm really sorry.'

Kate tried the number and a man told her that Amy Naylor and the kids had moved. 'We live here now,' he said, as if Kate would know who he meant. He gave Kate Amy Naylor's new phone number and address. Why wouldn't he?

Corso came home bringing Indian food, Californian wine, and a few more red herrings in the shape of news cuttings and research articles on OPs. He busied himself in the kitchen and answered Kate's remarks with Yes and No. When she asked him what his problem was, he said he had a migraine. In truth, his headache was Larry Packer, just as Larry's was Beverley Ho. Twenty minutes earlier, Corso had ended a meeting with Packer. They had sat wedged into the corner of a cocktail bar in Mayfair, while suits shoved and elbowed and bellowed round them: the perfect shield for their conversation.

'Now it's serious,' Packer said.

'Serious for you.'

'Who fucking else would it be serious for? You think I'd be talking to you if it was serious for Mickey fucking Mouse?' Packer downed his drink and wagged a finger at a waiter, who looked the other way. 'I gave you a week.'

'That's right. Five days left.'

'Jesus! She's getting dangerous. What she knows . . . the stuff on the disk alone . . . Now she's making calls.'

'Calls?'

'Ho got a call.'

'From Kate Randall?'

'No, from Santa fucking Claus.'

'So what do you want me to do?'

'*Jesus* . . .' Packer wagged at the waiter again; the guy turned his head. 'I don't want any time bombs, you know? I don't want Beverley Ho stepping on any fucking landmine long after the war's over.'

'You need to be sure.'

'I need to be sure. I need Randall in a body bag. You having some sort of a problem with that?'

'One thing at a time,' Corso told him.

'What's your method here? How are you working on her?'

'It's a matter of trust. And boredom. And fear.'

'No . . . What?' Packer meant he didn't understand. He also didn't understand why the waiter hated him.

'She needs action,' Corso said, 'just like you. She needs something to happen. She's in limbo. Nothing's moving. As things stand, I'm her only hope. Pretty soon, she'll have to trust me with everything. I'm not just her best bet, I'm her only bet.'

'If she doesn't give you more . . .?'

'Means there's nothing more to give.'

'And your time limit on that's a week?'

'No . . . that's your time limit. I'm going along with it because you're calling the shots.'

The waiter floated by, looking over everyone's head. Packer stood up and stepped out in front of the guy. He said, 'Bring me a Dewar's on the rocks. Bring it straight back. Just pour one drink – my Dewar's. Then bring it over here. It's a simple request. Don't let me down.'

The waiter caught something reckless in Packer's eye. He nodded and went off on his errand.

'You're saying . . . what? Things are getting edgy for you?'

'There's nothing else you can do?' Packer asked.

'What?'

'Sweat her?'

'Do what?'

Packer wished that bastard would hurry with his drink. He wanted his drink. He said, 'Hurt her.'

Corso sighed. 'I could do that,' he said, 'but it wouldn't help. Do you want me to do that?'

'Would you do it?'

'I don't think so,' Corso said. 'Not the way you mean.'

The waiter put Packer's drink down on the table. 'Okay,' Packer said. Then: 'They said you were good.'

'You're unhappy?' Corso asked. There was something in his voice; something arctic.

'Jesus,' Packer said, 'don't sound like that. I didn't mean that.'

They stood outside the bar, each looking for a taxi. They might have been strangers.

'When we're on tour,' Kate said, 'we eat curry all the time.'

'It's hot,' Corso said. 'We don't have this in the States. Except Mexican food is hot. They make chilli that can clear a blocked waste disposal unit. That was touring with the quartet you're talking about.'

'Yes. In Great Britain. In France, we ate McDonald's.'

'You're kidding me.'

'Yes, of course.'

'That was good – you enjoyed it?'

'Being on the road?' She shrugged. 'Not the travelling. Sometimes the performances. I liked the hotels. I'm good at hotels.' She drank some beer. 'You play well or you play not so well. Whatever happens, the audiences seem to like it enough to clap their hands off. I don't know why they do that. Play brilliantly, vast applause, you're pleased. Play indifferently, vast applause, you wish they'd all drop dead.'

He liked this. He liked the unforced intimacy of it. She ate slowly, but without pausing for long between mouthfuls, her head slightly bent to the plate, lamplight making her cropped hair seem like a shadow against her cheeks.

Yes, he thought, this is useful. This is really useful.

'We go well together. Nuala Phillips, Annie Forrester, Victoria Pedrales, Kate Randall.' She spoke the names as if she were reading from a playbill. 'We had some times. Viola players can really drink, you know? It's what they're best at.' She raised her head suddenly, and smiled at him, as if a good memory had returned. Corso thought it might have been the first time he'd seen her true smile, unaffected and unreserved. He took it for an omen.

She carried her wine to bed. She was feeling too mellow to read, too wakeful to sleep. He came and stood by the door with his own glass and the nearly empty bottle.

'Will you go out tomorrow?'

'You worry for me.'

'It seems an unnecessary risk.'

'I look different now. I saw a picture of myself on a poster. It was the old me. Anyway, who cares? I'm yesterday's papers. The day before yesterday's.'

'But why take the risk?'

She was on the very verge of telling him about the memos; about Leonard Naylor, about his sickness, about the car crash. About the fact that she had posted the information to Stuart Donnelly and stashed copies in a luggage locker. Now that she had some real leads, she needed to chase them down, and that wasn't easy for someone on her own. She needed a friend. Except that she couldn't make 'friend' and 'Robert Corso' mean the same thing. Not quite; not yet.

'Okay,' she said. 'You're right. But something has to happen.'

'Bear with me,' he said. 'Trust me.' He could see that she didn't: not quite; not yet. But there was something just behind her lips waiting to be said, something at the tip of her tongue. He smiled and walked over to her and poured the last of the wine into her glass.

'Nightcap.'

She grinned, as if drinking wine in bed were a forbidden pleasure. 'Something has to happen,' she agreed. 'What will you do?'

'Wideworld. I'm looking for cracks in the armour.'

'Perhaps it would be best to cut my losses.'

'You mean . . . what . . . go away?'

'Try to.'

'Where would you go?'

'Yes . . .' Her face clouded, and she put the glass down on the bedside table. 'Where would I go? And who would I be when I got there?'

Corso dipped his head and kissed her full on the mouth. She made a slight move backwards, but when he put a hand to her cheek, she stopped, as if the gesture had calmed her, and she allowed the kiss. Allowed it, and offered something back: just a hint, just a touch of need.

Corso thought of the 'something' just behind her lips, waiting to be said; the 'something' on the tip of her tongue. Something he tasted, fleetingly; something dark, like a secret.

He left the room, and she watched him all the way to the door, her eyes big and solemn.

Next day, he didn't go out until early afternoon; as if he were keeping her company, or watching her to see what she might do. She might have been a housewife, with her cups of coffee, her omelette and salad for two. After he'd left, she gave him an hour's grace. It was impossible to say, of course, when he might come back. She took a tube as far as she could, then caught a bus.

Amy Naylor lived in one of those neighbourhoods where clean cars stand at the kerbside in broad roads, and houses are quiet without being empty. She came to the door carrying a three-year-old girl on her hip.

'I just need answers to a couple of questions,' Kate said, 'about Wideworld Industries.'

Amy let her in. They sat drinking coffee in a room cluttered with toys. Amy Naylor was a once pretty woman whose features had blurred with the weight she'd put on. She was broad hipped and big breasted, and didn't look comfortable that way; there was a turn-down to her mouth that would have made laughing that much more of an effort.

She said, 'I don't know anything about organophosphates except that Len was working on them.'

'There's been some stuff in the press.'

'In your paper?'

'I don't have a paper. I'm freelance. I specialise in environmental stories.' Kate was becoming Michael for a while. She had been around him long enough to have picked up more than the basics. 'In any case, I don't need to know about OPs; they're no secret. I need to know about WWI.'

'Do you? Why?'

'They manufacture and market an OP called Neophos. Your husband helped develop it.'

'He was a chemist. That was his job.'

'I'm not criticising; there are some things I don't know, that's all.'

'I can't imagine that I'll be able to help.'

'Was your husband in dispute with WWI?'

'Dispute?'

'Did he argue with them?'

'Why would he?'

'I spoke to someone . . . an ex-employee. This person told me that Leonard was at loggerheads with WWI management. And that the row was about Neophos.'

'I don't think so. I never heard him mention that.'

'I think it's true.'

'He never told me.'

'When he died . . .' Kate began, and Amy was suddenly alert, tense, as if she had smelt gas. 'You don't like to talk about it. I'm sorry.'

'Not really. Which paper are you working for at the moment?'

'No . . . I'm researching a story about chemical manufacturers. When I've got all my notes together, I'll approach a paper.'

'You're not on TV at all, are you?'

Kate heard warning bells. 'Sometimes,' she offered.

'It seemed to me that I knew your face.'

'That might be it.'

'Yes . . .' There was something in Amy's glance-and-look-away that made Kate very edgy. Her spine prickled, and she felt a tiny surge in her limbs that was the ghost of a flat-out run.

The little girl tottered over to Amy and put her face in her mother's lap, like the beginning of hide-and-seek. Amy stroked the child's hair for a moment and she fell asleep standing up. Amy lifted her and carried her from the room.

Kate wondered whether it would be better to leave while Amy Naylor was putting her daughter to bed, thereby possibly confirming any suspicions the woman might have, or run the risk of waiting till she returned. She decided to wait; and walked over to a bookcase to read the titles. She hoped the pose would seem casual and unworried.

The step behind her was all but inaudible. She turned in time to see Amy, arm raised, still advancing. The forward motion lent impetus to the blow. She was carrying a pottery vase, holding it by the neck as a bar room fighter holds a bottle. Kate heard a crack, which was the vase breaking against her head, then a sound like a low, sustained drumbeat, which wasn't real at all, but was happening somewhere back in the far reaches of her skull. The room receded as if some vast centrifugal force had squeezed it to a letterbox shape, all its objects and colours crushed to kaleido-scope.

Kate fell against her attacker, hands clutching the other woman's arms, then her waist, then her thighs, as she hung on, trying to stay upright. Amy stepped back and Kate slid to the floor. She shook her head, frosting Amy's skirt with red pinpricks. Amy spoke, but her words were lost in that relentless back-brain drumming.

Kate went down on her face, then got immediately to her hands and knees without knowing she'd done it. She lifted her head and looked round, but could see nothing clearly. A few seconds went by; a few years. Her head cleared a little, as your ears clear when you emerge after a dive into deep water, and she heard Amy's voice from another room. She was talking in broken sentences: one side of a conversation; then came a clatter of footsteps as she ran upstairs. From far off, a door slammed and locked.

The room went by, then settled. Kate got from her knees into a squat, then straightened up, putting out a hand for support and pushing half a row of books to the back of the shelf. She walked a mazy line to the hall then, seeming to get the hang of it, a straighter route to the next room, where she lifted the phone and pressed last number redial. The triple nine call connected after two rings, and she hung up.

The house was silent: an indrawn breath. Kate looked for her own face in the hall mirror and finally found it, out of focus and pearled with blood. There was blood in her hair. She took a scarf that was hanging over the banister and wiped her cheek; then she folded it into a double triangle, placed it over her hair and knotted it under her chin. She could see the front door reflected in the mirror but, for a moment, couldn't work out how to turn to face it. Then she was outside. Then walking along the road. Then sitting on the upper deck of a bus, empty save for herself and a sleeping man. She closed her eyes and wondered how in hell she'd got there and where she was going. She felt sick and faint.

She slept, but didn't know for how long. The bus had filled up. She woke with her face pressed against the window, and the scarf stuck to her cheek. She pulled it free, wincing, and several people glanced across at her. When a man came along the aisle intending to sit next to her, she got up and went down to the platform, placing each foot carefully. When she got off the bus, she had no idea where she was. She walked along a bright, busy high street, stopping from time to time to look into shop windows whenever she felt nausea overtake her, or when her legs grew heavy and threatened to buckle. She studied diamond rings and bathroom suites and food mixers like a bride-to-be with money to burn, while her head scalded and throbbed.

After ten minutes, it started to rain: a sudden *swish* travelling down the pavements like a new broom. Kate felt the wet on her face. When she raised her fingers to her cheek, they came away watery red. Someone said, 'Are you all right?' and Kate nodded, smiling brightly because she couldn't trust herself to speak. When two other people had approached her to ask if she needed help, Kate found a pub and walked directly through to the women's room.

The rain had cleared her head a little, though she now felt chilled. She was wearing a jacket and T-shirt with blue jeans; the shoulders of the jacket were sodden and the jeans dark below the knee. She peered into the mirror and saw how ludicrous the scarf looked. She took it off, freeing two lines of blood that ran to her chin. She mopped at her face with the scarf to clean it, then held the wadded material to the crown of her head until the bleeding seemed to stop.

A woman came in, glanced at Kate, and went into one of the stalls. She offered no comment. Maybe it was that kind of neighbourhood, Kate thought. She removed the scarf and waited for a couple of minutes; her head felt damp and sore, but the flow had ceased. She went into a stall and sat down, but the very business of relaxing clouded her eye and made the room turn turtle. She pinched the inside of her upper arms, her breasts, her thighs, the back of each hand in turn: little thin pains that made her gasp. Her clearest thought was: 'I feel worse than I've ever felt in my life.' Her clearest need was the need to sleep.

She went back into the rain and knew she couldn't do that for long. Ten minutes later – already eight minutes too long – she found a movie house and bought a ticket. She thought it must be about six o'clock and knew there was little chance of getting back before Corso; and little chance, too, of concealing the state she was in.

Amy Naylor knew she had done a stupid thing. She had done it out of fear. Now she sat on the sofa where Kate had recently sat, and lied to a detective sergeant named Nick Willis.

'An intruder,' she said, 'I found her in the house.'

'You say you hit her?'

'I was frightened – for my daughter. My little girl. She's three. She was asleep upstairs.'

'You hit her . . .' Willis shook his head. There was blood on the carpet by the bookshelf.

'She was in my house. Anyway, she's gone. I couldn't have hurt her. She's gone.'

Amy had changed the skirt with its jots and dashes of Kate's blood. 'But I'm sorry. I'm sorry I did that.'

Willis took out his notebook and asked for a description. Amy gave details of a woman older, shorter, stockier. She provided light brown hair and bright lipstick and a broken tooth. She thought the broken tooth was a good touch.

Willis said he might need to talk to her again. After he'd left, Amy went upstairs and sat by her daughter as she slept. She thought about the questions Kate had asked her. Dangerous questions. Questions that had scared her and made her lash out.

She stroked her daughter's hair. All she cared about – all she knew – was to keep the child from harm.

Symbols chased each other across the screen and the light hurt Kate's eyes. There seemed to be a dozen or so people watching the movie. Kate sat in the back row, hunched down, her head lolling against the plush of the seat. Sleep came at her like a soundless wave. For some reason, out of fear perhaps, she pushed against it for a brief while, then allowed herself to submerge. When she woke, someone was in a room killing someone else, a ballet with a knife, as if the story of Michael's death were being acted out for the screen. The true story of Michael's death.

Kate put her hand over her eyes, but the images persisted. A man, and a man with a knife. She struggled to get the picture clear, but it kept dissolving at the edges. Maybe this would tell her what . . . Tell her who . . . Maybe it would even tell her why. A man, and a man with a knife; that was all she could be sure of. An arm rose and fell and immediately she recognised the gesture. Not Michael and Michael's killer, but herself and Jeff, as she beat him off and watched him slip down into the mud. As if his pain had become her pain, she put a hand to her broken head, finding the damp pulp of an open wound.

*   *   *

Now the screen was black and white: snow and ice and a dark sky. She must have slept for an hour or more, and the murder in the room was old news. If she squinted, she could make out someone travelling across the polar wastes, seeming to come straight towards her. A cold sun burned in a hard, clear sky and all Kate could see of him was a silhouette blurred by snowfall, or lines of static.

She realised that she was talking, but wasn't aware of what she'd said. Sleep leaked in: a narcoleptic's drip-feed. Ten minutes later the soundtrack brought her back. The snowscape was still there, but people were moving across it, back and forth, like figures in a game of chess. And then, suddenly, she herself was moving, as if she intended to climb up onto the screen and join them, purposeless but in motion, like herself, like her new life.

She weaved through the streets, which were now dark, and noisier than before. No one seemed to notice her; she was another of the city's casualties: one of the walking wounded.

All her instincts told her that she was in danger. Collapse and someone will call an ambulance. The hospital will see the head wound and call the cops. Very soon, George Webb will arrive on the scene. These thoughts were in her head, but she couldn't hold them for long enough to take their meaning. The street lights and the lights from windows put a slick on the pavements that shone like the ice field in the movie. She saw herself as if in her own mind's eye, pushing in from the horizon, one step after the other, moving towards the very lip of the screen and the next expanse of snow.

She stopped and sat on a bench by the river, with no idea how she had got there. The water lights danced behind her eyes; each bright point was a point of pain. She slept and no one wondered why. Like the characters in the film, passers-by went to and fro, moving to some pattern of urgency and need. A woman walking unsteadily; a woman dozing on a bench in the rain . . . she was invisible.

*   *   *

224

Maybe she could make another mile. The rain was heavier, now, and she walked into it with her back bent. It seemed to her that her head was cloven: red-raw and open to the weather.

There were people on all sides, umbrellas up, coat collars turned, who moved silently. A mile she thought, no more. And then there was someone who seemed to stand out from the rest: a figure moving directly towards her as if he were the only other person there, and had seen her from a very long way off, moving to intercept her from the far side of the snowfield, their tracks heading for a point of intersection that would cause them to coincide just . . .

. . . *here*, where she reached the very edge, the furthest lip of ice, and fell towards the blue-black chasm where it ended, lost for sure if his hand hadn't moved to pull her back, if his arms hadn't held her, if he hadn't called her name like a summons.

Twenty-one

'You were home,' Corso told her, 'pretty much.'
  'Where?'
'In the mews. I saw you from the window.'
'How did I get back?'
'You tell me.'
'I thought I was miles away.'
'In a manner of speaking, you were. All I could see was the whites of your eyes.'

He waited, but she had nothing to say for herself except, 'I need to be sick.'

He held her shoulders, kneeling beside her as she knelt: a couple of penitents. She dry-retched until she was too weak to continue, then let him half carry her back to bed. She sat to attention while he cleaned and dressed her head wound: a long but shallow cut. Corso was more worried about the soft bruising on the skull.

He watched her all night, worried that she might slip into a sleep too deep for waking, then throw up again. Her sleep-talk was like morse: rhythmic, but coded.

Where were you? he wanted to ask. The same question; the same puzzle. *What do you know?*

Her eyes swivelled beneath her eyelids and her hands fluttered. On the snowfield, she was one of many, but no one saw her, no one heard her, no one called her name.

All the next day and most of the day after that, she rolled in and out of sleep, dreaming the same dreams, making the same journey. He watched every night, sleeping when he felt it was safe to do so: when her sleep seemed almost peaceful.

226

On the third morning, however, it was Corso who woke to clear skies and the distant city-racket. Kate was looking directly at him, a smile on her lips. She said, 'I'm starving. I want some soup.'

He went out once, for an hour, to pick up some things they needed, and to phone Larry Packer, who said, *'Shit!'*

'Maybe,' Corso said, 'but I'm close.'

'How close?'

'Very.'

'You're out of deadline.'

'I think I know that. I'm suggesting an extension.'

'What're you asking for?'

'No,' Corso said, 'you're getting it wrong. I'm *asking* for diddly-squat. I'm *suggesting* an extension. I don't care whether you give it to me or not, because it's your problem.'

But he did care. He cared because he wasn't ready, and because he wanted to do the job his way. That was what he told himself.

'What's her story?'

'She went to a movie because she was bored, came out, got mugged.'

'And what's the *real* story?'

'Who knows? Maybe she went to a movie because –'

'Yeah?' Packer laughed.

'People get mugged. Hadn't you heard?'

'People get hit by meteors, but they're not usually people who have recently been struck by lightning.'

'The answer is, I don't know. What I do know is that she's almost ready to give me everything. How she got crocked will be part of it. But not the most important part, I think.'

'I promised Ho I'd close this off.'

'Sure. That's what's going to happen. But listen . . . it's your call. I'm making no decisions here.'

'Making no promises either, have I got that right?'

'Who can promise anything? Tomorrow you wake up with cancer.'

'You need . . .?'

'Just a few days.'

'Tells me nothing.'

'I can't give it to you as precisely as that. A few days. As opposed to many days.'

'Listen to me,' Packer said, 'I'm trusting you on this. I'm putting my trust in you. I don't expect to be let down.'

'I understand,' Corso said. He thought, I don't like you, Packer. I never did, much, but suddenly I don't like you at all. You are a son of a bitch, and that's an official statement. You can take that to the bank.

All that was left of Kate's concussion was its dreamworld. Some of the dreams were real fears: Michael dying; Jeff going down in the mud. Some took her back to the snowscape and the moving shadows. Others were the kaleidoscope of image and event that shows what the mind is hiding.

In her current dream, she was swimming with dolphins. She had borrowed the image from a television programme she and Corso had watched the previous evening. He'd made some food and sat on the bed to keep her company while they ate. At one point, he'd hoisted his legs onto the bed and they had slouched there, side by side.

As she swam, the lithe, powerful creatures slipped by, nudging her, then circled and came back, making an underwater tide that tugged her along. The water was green and deep, but it held no terrors for her. When she emerged, Corso was waiting on the shore. He held her, and she felt that he was muscled like a dolphin, sinewy and firm. He made love to her, and when she woke to find him standing by the bed watching her, a blush sprang to her throat, though it wasn't from modesty.

He said, 'We've gone as far as we can go, I think. There's nothing else to know.'

'What do you want to do?'

'We could let the authorities have the disk. It makes the link between Farnol and WWI's early release of Neophos X-9. It shows that Michael was working on a controversial story when he was killed. It isn't much.'

'Not enough for me.'

'No. Maybe you were right – your best option really *is* to go away.'

'Where?'

'The States? I don't know.'

'And take up a career as a cellist who happens to look just like me.'

'Or you could fight your case.'

'What case is that? I ran.'

'They still have to convict. You ran because you're innocent.'

Kate paused. 'Michael isn't the only . . . The only *thing*.'

Corso waited but she offered nothing more. After a moment, he switched on a lamp, drew the curtains, and went out of the bedroom. He returned with a couple of glasses of wine.

'I guess you could risk a drink now,' he said.

'There was Jeff. This guy Jeff . . .' Her voice seemed to tangle with his.

He sat on the bed while she told him the story. She didn't once look at him while she was speaking, but his eyes rarely left her face.

Finally, he asked, 'Do they know?'

'I don't think so.'

'But you're not sure?'

'No.'

'Did he die?'

Kate shrugged and turned away, her mouth puckering. She wanted to know about Jeff: as much for her own sake as his; but knowing might be the worst thing.

Corso sat closer and put an arm round her. He said, 'It's a lot to carry,' and it was too much for her to hear; she started to cry, steadily, as if pacing herself.

They sat side by side while Kate cried herself out, then rested her cheek against his arm. She said, 'Where would I be –' lifting her head to look at him, and he kissed her, and put a hand to her cheek, then down onto her breast. The taste her tongue left on his was more of secrets.

She was wearing a T-shirt as a nightdress; he reached down and raised it, drawing it slowly over her head so that he could look at her for a moment without having her look back. She had never felt so naked.

He undressed and lay down with her; they faced one another, touching slowly. She was trembling, her skin hot, that tell-tale blush on her throat. She thought it was like being very thirsty, this fingertip touching, like being thirsty and keeping a full glass of cold water just at your lip, but holding off from the moment of drinking.

Her eyes were bright and wide. Finally, she said, 'Come on. Come on . . .'

Where would I be if not for you?

George Webb had driven six hours to sit by the raised bed and watch the slow smile of a man who had recently emerged from the chrysalis of coma. He had begun the journey that morning in sunlight, but had driven over Bodmin Moor in rain so heavy that it seemed to have washed out all the horizons. Rain was still falling when he took his chair at the bedside and looked into the unfocused eyes and eager smile of a man whose first words on waking had been, 'Kate, that was.'

And now it was still raining, though since the blinds had been pulled you could only tell from the tattoo on the window. The doctors had gone, but a nurse called in every fifteen minutes. Webb was the guest of a detective sergeant called Alan Boyd, who had given him the basic information when he'd arrived late that morning.

'This is Jeff Cotter. Unsolved GBH. Car theft, it looked like. He had this crappy old flatbed truck someone took. Turned up in a ploughed field next to a lay-by. We thought kids.'

'Yes? Why?'

'Bit of a local joke. Simple-minded, really. Lots of big talk about being in the Gulf.'

'Was he?'

'And the Falklands, and Vietnam, and the Western Desert.'

Webb didn't like the sound of that. 'He's crazy.'

'Not really. Harmless, except he got bound over for showing his cock to a couple of women on a walking holiday.' Boyd laughed.

'They didn't seem to want it, though. Not crazy, no. Bit short-handed between the ears, that's all.'

'What did he say exactly?'

' "Kate, that was".'

'Meaning?'

'Meaning, "Someone called Kate did this". Did this to me. Local lingo. I say, "Nice sweater", you say . . . what's your wife's name?'

'Janice.'

'You say "Janice, that was", meaning she knitted it.'

'Then he said more.'

'Before you arrived he'd given us most of it, including a description. No one got it at first. "Kate" didn't mean anything, but it seemed strange to think he'd been attacked by a woman. Then someone remembered the Kate Randall thing over at Penarven. We showed him a picture. His eyes lit up. You'd have thought she was a long lost love rather than someone who all but killed him.'

'You say he gave you most of it . . .'

'Most of what had happened to him – the way he tells it; and he tells it in a pretty odd way.'

'Odd?'

'Jeffish. Jeff's way.'

'What did happen?'

'Well, she did him once in the house, then again in the yard – where he was found. We knew that much already.'

'Did he say why?'

'She was angry with him.'

'Go on.'

'He says he cooked something for her and she didn't like the taste, so she got angry with him.'

'What do you think?'

'Okay, well, looking at the scene of crime details in the light of what we now know, I should think he tried it on.'

'So it was self-defence?' Webb asked.

Boyd shrugged and gave a little laugh. 'A brief might say so, if that's what happened: if he had a go at her. He's got a couple of dents in his head that he'll carry to the grave. Depends what you mean by self-defence.'

'I'd like it kept quiet,' Webb said. 'Nothing to the press.'

'Sure. They're not interested. They had their blood and guts when it happened.'

Webb looked at Jeff's willing smile. He said, 'Hello there, Jeff . . .'

London is never dark. Each night, there's a red glow in the sky, like a bushfire gaining ground, and the undersides of clouds are pallid with sodium.

Kate lay in the half-dark, curtains open, looking out towards the lights of windows. Ships at anchor. Corso's arm lay between her breasts, his fingers brushing her throat, little circles, as if he were trying to stroke away some soreness. She wanted to make love again, but wanted to talk, too. Waiting was a teasing hunger and she liked it because she could satisfy it at any time.

He lay still, apart from his doodling fingers, while she told him everything there was to tell. He thought it must be everything, because she didn't pause, or look for words, or elaborate. Simple stories, simple truths.

'Wasn't there anyone to help?' he asked her.

'No one.'

'Your sister . . .'

She had told him about Joanna, how she'd suggested Penarven, about her divorce, about Nathan; not about the money and the mobile phone; not yet. 'There's nothing she can do,' Kate said. 'She's got a kid. Whatever she does to help is breaking the law. If we speak on the phone, she's compromised.'

He said, 'One duplicate disk and one hard copy to Stuart – what? –'

'Donnelly.'

'– Donnelly, and where are the others?'

She had given him the broad story, and now they were down to details. There was no reason not to tell him about the security locker, except that the phone rang and took him away from her.

She wanted him back because, now he was out of bed, her appetite for him had sharpened.

She heard him say, 'No, don't come here,' then repeat it with an edge to his voice. He came back into the bedroom and looked round for his clothes.

'What?' she asked.

'A journalist. A friend. He's got some stuff for me. Neophos A-9 was used in the Gulf, we know that. No one's denying it. Except this guy thinks it was actually X-9.' He was pulling on clothes, finger-combing his hair.

'Tell him to e-mail it.' She felt like a teenager with an itch.

'He's just around the corner. Not unreasonably, he thought I might invite him here. So I'll have to head him off. He's at a pub. I won't be long.'

'Okay.' She stretched in the bed, and pulled the coverlet towards her chin. 'Wake me up.'

'Count on it.' Stamping into his shoes, buttoning his shirt.

What's the hurry? she thought. Then asked the question out loud.

'He rings the bell, what am I going to do? Tell him we'd be disturbing my sick mother?'

'You said he's waiting at the pub.'

'He's not a patient man.' He bent and kissed her, then left with his shoe laces flopping.

He drove for twenty minutes, then parked next to a flight of steps that led down to the river. It was close to where Kate had slept out that night she'd stolen the sleeping bag. The laws of coincidence operate better when emotions run high.

He leaned against the parapet and watched the gaudy helix of the South Bank Centre climb and twist as the neon tubes fired in rotation. Packer joined him almost at once, as if he might have seen Corso arrive. When Corso looked round for Packer's car, it wasn't in evidence. The man was wearing an off-duty leather blouson and Wranglers.

'Why here?' Corso asked.

'I know a girl lives close by,' Packer said. 'I would have come to you.'

'And what? Louse things up. She's telling me stuff.'

'What stuff?'

'Stuff we know, but there's more to come. Keep cool. A day . . . maybe two.'

More to come, that much was true. But why not tell him what you know? Donnelly, the Naylor memos, all that dynamite. *Why not give her up?*

'I'm here to tell you that we've gone as far as we can go with this.'

'A day. Tomorrow.'

'How sure are you?'

'Absolutely sure. If you hadn't called, I'd probably have been calling you in a couple of hours. As it is you set things back. Thanks.'

'Don't blame me,' Packer warned. 'This sweet'n'low technique of yours has been making me jumpy.'

'I'd noticed.'

You're an asshole, Packer thought, I'd like to whack the fuckin' pair of you, and he felt an itch in his hand that a gun butt would have scratched. He turned away to hide his anger, but he was working the muscles in his jaw. When he spoke, his voice was flat and hard.

'When will you call?'

'By midday.'

'Midday is it. What will you be able to tell me?'

'All there is to tell.'

'Then you tie it off, right?'

'Sure,' Corso said. 'She has a bad accident. We'll take in the view from a high cliff.'

'I don't want to know how –'

'It was a joke,' Corso told him. 'You just won't hear of her again.'

'Or you.'

'That's right,' Corso said, 'unless your cheque's no good.'

London's never dark, and it's never silent. Sometimes there's a night-long hum, as if from vast flywheels or underground machines. There are planes and cars and trucks. You can hear the cops and the bad guys shooting it out on a neighbour's TV. You can hear a husband and wife working up to a hot divorce. And even when you lie in bed in a quiet room in a quiet house in a quiet street, you can hear those little domestic tics and taps, those clicks and creaks, that almost inaudible whirring that nags at you when your lover's had to leave and you want to sleep.

Kate toured the room, but she couldn't find the whatever-it-was.

Whirrr . . .

She walked into other rooms, expecting to find it there, loud and obvious, but when she left the bedroom, the sound disappeared. She went back and climbed into bed and closed her eyes, but the noise was in the bones of her head.

Maybe it's me, she thought. Maybe I'm the whirr.

She got up again and listened at the walls, as if she might find clockwork mice. The idea made her laugh.

On the other side of the room was a chest of drawers, the empty bookshelves that came with all rentals, a closet with slatted doors, a cheval mirror. She looked at her reflection in the glass – dim and clouded by lamplight. She put an arm loosely across her breasts and dropped a hand to the fork of her legs, then smiled knowingly at herself; the pose of the coquette.

The whirr was closer, or seemed to be; still faint though. Corso's clothes, in the closet, were dark replicas of himself. She stood still to listen, and it was there, directly in front of her, *whirrrr-whirrrr-whirrrr*, and might have been a water tank, or the transformer on an interior light, or even that clockwork mouse, but was, in fact, when she parted the jackets and shirts, a videotape that had reached the end of its record length and was racing back on rewind. As she watched, it came to the end of the spool and stopped.

Whirr-clunk.

The bright eye of the lens stared back at her.

She fed the cassette into the VCR and hit 'play'.

Her body was a pale blur against a dim grey light as he sponged her limbs, methodically, dipping the sponge into a bowl of tepid water, turning her, lifting her arms, coming in a long sweep from her throat across her breasts and down over her belly, turning her again, delving the small of her back, up over the swell of her buttocks, parting her legs slightly to reach the insides of her thighs, working on her flanks, behind her knees, her calves, then returning to her face, dampening the hair over her brow, wiping her cheeks, her throat, her shoulders, and again her breasts, budding as the cool water touched them, and again her belly, and again down to the dark smudge where her legs forked.

Corso slaking her fever.

She sat up in bed and took the scrambled eggs from him, eating mechanically, eating from hunger not pleasure. She watched her own face cloud; watched the fork stall in air. She remembered the feeling of that depression: a pit with no echo and no light.

She sat in a chair, listening to Sibelius 4, her face blank. Suddenly, he was there beside her.

'*What was this?*' she heard herself ask. '*Kill or cure?*'

Her voice came back to her from a country called illness; it sounded ragged at the edges.

She saw herself getting ready to go out. There was no recording of him, edgy, drinking, anxious for her return, but she could picture it well enough.

She wondered how he had made his decisions about where to place the recorder. In one sequence she did a slow strip, eyes vacant with fatigue, still feeling shaky and dull from her injury, crossing her arms behind her back and unfastening her bra clip, her breasts coming free with a slight sag, her shoulders dropping, then she thumbed her briefs down before rolling into bed, her back to the camera, the soft cleft of her ass like a lover's brush-off.

In another, she ate a sandwich and looked out of the window, the sheer tedium of the shot seeming to make the tape stand still.

236

Together, they brought the contents of Michael's disk up onto the screen. He was standing behind her and looking over her shoulder. It was the night of their return from Penarven.

'*Jesus,*' she heard herself say. '*Torched it? You mean you set fire –?*'

'*That's what they do.*'

'*Who?*'

'*Kids. Joyriders . . .*'

Their voices seemed not to belong to them: saw-edged, abrupt, unrehearsed.

She was in bed, the duvet pulled to her chin. Look, there was that sleight of hand beneath the cover as she removed Michael's A-disk – the unedited version – from its hiding place in her bra.

Who else could have told what that furtive movement meant?

And this was what she least wanted to see: her body a pale blur, his also, as he covered her limbs, stealthily, Kate lifting her arms, his hand coming in a long sweep from her throat across her breasts and down over her belly, turning her, delving the small of her back, his own back dipping, hands moving up over the swell of her buttocks, parting her thighs, working on her, turning her again, returning to her face, the damp hair over her brow, his mouth on her cheeks, her throat, her shoulders, Kate lifting her arms, lifting her face, her legs forked around him.

Corso slaking her fever.

She took what she could carry and left. It was a little before midnight, but the streets were still noisy and full. People walked past in units of two, units of three, units of five, looking at each other, laughing between themselves, caught up in their own warmth. They might as well have been in glassine capsules. Everyone insulated from everyone else; it was the way the city operated; the way it stayed sane.

By the time Kate had turned the corner, she was anonymous.

237

Corso knew as soon as he walked in through the front door. There was a stillness in the air like a dead echo. He was cursing even as he went to the bedroom, finding the bedclothes thrown back and her few clothes gone, her hairbrush gone, her bits and pieces of make-up gone, her Tampax gone, the Canadian coat gone, the notebook computer gone, her smell gone from the sheets, her reflection gone from the mirrors.

The only thing he didn't look for was the small jet-and-silk evening bag with its mobile phone, Joanna's credit card, and close to three thousand pounds in cash, because that had always been safely hidden from him in the lining of the Canadian coat.

She had taken a small backpack that he'd stored on a shelf in the closet. He pictured her walking the streets with her belongings stowed, the pack swinging from her shoulder. Of course he would check the hotel he'd first tracked her to, and the hotel she'd last stayed in, but he knew he wouldn't find her in either place.

Kate on the street with the backpack, wearing her Canadian coat, striding out, going . . . where? He could picture her, sure, but it was a picture without a frame.

He poured himself a drink and sat down to calculate the damage.

Twenty-two

Corso had a list of two: Stuart Donnelly and Joanna Randall. That was all he had, apart from some straightforward instructions from Larry Packer.

Packer sat in the living room of the house Corso had rented, drinking a fist-sized whisky. Corso was sitting by the window and looking out, as if Kate might suddenly appear, the prodigal returned, hoping for forgiveness and a new start. Packer had stopped ranting and started thinking. He said, 'Just this – if you find her, keep her; call me; don't be clever. Enough of clever.' He paused and drank. Corso reflected that the man had already taken a third of a bottle of Scotch on board and seemed steady enough. Too steady.

'Listen,' Corso said, 'there's something I want to get straight. When your man – your operative – killed Michael Lester, he wiped the computer, right?'

'Wiped it clean,' Packer agreed.

'The A-disk that Kate Randall has: that's the only evidence that Lester was working on this Neophos story – that Lester was getting set to badmouth Wideworld.'

'There's nothing else I know of. Maybe Farnol had something: but it would be the same stuff.'

'Okay, well, Farnol's dead, we took Farnol out. He stopped being a problem when they found him looking like a centrefold for *S-M Weekly*.'

Packer said, 'No, it's just the girl.'

Corso nodded. 'What did you really hire me to do, Packer? Why are Wideworld paying me?'

'If you're asking what I think you're asking – has it come to hardball, etcetera – then the answer is definitely yes. I don't see any alternative now that she's got to Beverley Ho, etcetera.'

'You want her dead?'

'Has to be.'

'Forget what she might know that you don't know, forget any time bombs she might have –?'

Packer interrupted him. 'Too late for that.'

'How bad is it?' Corso asked.

'Bad is what?'

'Neophos X-9. That's what this is all about. Two people have died. At least one more to go.'

'Who cares?' Packer asked. 'Do you care? It's a formula. A formula for money. You put it on crops, it kills bugs, etcetera. Think of it as cash.' Packer smiled. 'You can think of anything as cash, whatever it is, whatever you do with it – mainline it, fuck it, put it in your tank . . . however much it looks like smack or snatch or gas, it's money, if you look close enough.'

'It's a pity that man of yours ever killed Michael Lester,' Corso said.

'It's a pity shit ain't gold,' Packer told him. He drank some more in silence, then topped up his own drink. Corso didn't have a glass. After a while, Packer asked, 'Make it look like she offed herself, a bad accident, like we said. Suicide, plain and simple.'

'Plain and simple,' Corso told him. 'Is that what you want?'

'Sure. She killed her boyfriend, now she's sorry. Can't live with it any more. Whacked herself, etcetera. Best scenario.' After a while he added, 'Got to find the bitch first.'

'I'll find her.'

'You fucked up, Corso. You really fucked up.' Packer wagged his head, a zany wobble; the booze had suddenly slammed home. 'I wish I'd hired some other sonofabitch.'

'You wanted information. I tried to get it.'

'You fucked up, you're an asshole, you fucked up. And etcetera. You lost her. Who the fuck knows where she is, could be anywhere, who knows . . .'

Packer's head slipped sideways, came back upright, slipped again. He dropped his drink onto the carpet, levered himself out of his chair and took a couple of steps into the middle of the room.

'Where's the john?'

'Straight through,' Corso told him, 'on the right.'

When Packer still looked confused, Corso showed him the way. Packer put a hand on the wall to brace himself; the other delved in his pants. Corso shut the door.

Then he went back to the living room and turned off the video recorder.

I could write a book on small hotels, Kate thought. A short book. Just one chapter. In fact, just one sentence. *There is only one hotel.* You think it's a different one each time, different location, different name. No. That's just to fool you. Maybe you are fooled, to begin with. But then you come to see that the room has the same bed, the same wallpaper, the same furnishings. There's that same stain in the washbasin. The window has the same view of the same street. The same guy takes your money and hands over your key. The same key.

Kate sat on the bed and wept. Then she slept.

You dream the same dreams.

Joanna queued for her coffee in the Polish Café and asked if there might be a message for Cybulski. There wasn't. She hadn't expected one. Her long-term fears for her sister had increased, though her short-term anxiety had lessened. It was a bizarre equation that depended on ignorance – on knowing nothing of Kate's immediate circumstances; what had happened yesterday, what might happen tomorrow. That solitary phone call, 'I'm fine', had been enough to keep her from despair, despite the despairing note in Kate's voice.

Corso sat at Joanna's table with his black coffee and Danish. He took a bite and a sip, smiled at her, and said, 'I'm not a cop.'

Joanna felt a rush of adrenalin along her veins like foam in a sluice. The legs of her chair rattled and she looked at Corso with her mouth open: a foolish look, a look that stayed rigid a moment, then fell into a slow dissolve. She was breathing rapidly. Her cup was halfway to her mouth. Corso put out a gentle hand and took the cup from her, setting it back onto the saucer.

He said, 'I'm not. But there is a cop, sure enough – he's reading a tabloid in a little neighbourhood store just along the block. I bet he does that whenever you come in here. I'd give long odds.'

Joanna put her hands into her lap and bowed her head. Little dark patches were dancing at the edge of her vision. Corso said, 'I've been with Kate. She's fine. She's fine now. However, there's a problem and I need your help. How long do you normally stay in here?'

'Long enough for a coffee.'

'Another ten minutes?'

'Five or ten. What do you mean, she is *now*. She's fine *now*?'

Corso's story took six minutes; he was timing himself. He played down the concussion; he played his own role up. He mentioned new evidence, but wasn't too specific. He said nothing about he and Kate having become lovers. He was the journalist friend of Michael's, the crusader with an e-mail address. Then he said, 'I did a stupid thing. I taped her without her knowing it. Now she doesn't trust me, and I don't know where she is.' He added, 'I'm sorry,' as if his contrition might buy goodwill.

Joanna said, 'How do I know? How do I know you're not police?'

Corso shrugged. 'Are you in touch with her? Ask her next time you speak. Ask her who I am. And give her a message. That's all I ask. Tell her I was stupid and I'm sorry. Tell her I'll be sending her e-mails.' Eight minutes had passed. He said, 'You'd better go.'

'Why did you tape her?' Joanna asked.

'I want to help her – really – but I want the story, too. I thought . . . maybe she was holding stuff back. Maybe she didn't really trust me to know everything.' He was staying close to the truth – the cleverest form of lie. 'I'm her only hope, Joanna. Tell her.'

'I don't call her,' Joanna said, 'I wait for her to call me. It's our agreement.'

'How does she do that?'

'She's got a mobile,' Joanna said, and immediately put a hand to her mouth.

Corso nodded, as if he'd barely heard. He was thinking: She's got a mobile phone. Now where was she keeping *that*? He said, 'Take a risk. Call her. But don't phone from home.'

Joanna gave a shaky laugh. 'I'm not stupid.'

'Tell her I'm sorry.'

'You said that.'

Corso looked away, as if his mind were on other things. 'I'm worried about her,' he said, and passed Joanna a slip of paper. 'My number, okay? Whenever you talk to her: tell her –' He shrugged. 'You don't have to give my name. Say "The Trapper". It's a joke between us.' He looked at his watch. 'Eleven minutes.'

Joanna left the café and walked towards the newsagent's. Her legs felt as if they would cave at the knees. It took every ounce of nerve she possessed to avoid glancing into the shop.

As she passed, DC Philip Nairn folded his paper and shoved the glass door. Joanna's reflection flashed twice as it opened and closed. She was walking with her eyes on the ground, as she always did. Nairn yawned. He hadn't noticed whether she'd taken eight minutes or twelve. He yawned and crossed the road without bothering to check that Joanna had also crossed. He knew the route.

The mid-morning sky was dark with clouds that had rolled in off the horizon and lodged like a canopy. They were bruise-purple, tinged with a sick yellow at the edges. The loud, false daylight of halogen was spreading from room to room in the Wideworld offices. If you stood back by the chain link fence that encircled the WWI acres – car park, lawn, car park, flower beds, car park – you would see the random pattern of offices lighting up like cells in a hive.

Packer closed the venetian blinds in Beverley Ho's office while Beverley finished up a call. She hung up, but immediately raised a hand to stop him from talking while she made some notes, then leaned back in her chair and looked at him. She was wearing a dark green silk blouse, and the tips of her little breasts were sharp inside the material, steepling it, so that shimmies of reflected light ran along the creases.

'I'm taking some time out,' he said. 'Jimmy Rose will have my office for a few days. He's a good man.'

'A few days to do what?'

'It's a little . . .' He had been going to say 'clean-up'. '. . . a little business needs taking care of.'

'Am I running any risks here, Larry?'

'No, Beverley. I'd tell you if there was any kind of problem.'

'So why do you need to fix this yourself?'

'Sometimes you have to. You know that. Sometimes it's the only thing that works.'

'Will it cost?'

'Nah . . . Just my time.'

'I don't mind spending money. There's no problem over money.'

'Beverley,' he laughed, 'use the money wisely; give me a raise.'

Beverley Ho laughed with him, but she didn't seem amused. When the laughter had died, she held his eyes. Packer half rose to leave, then saw that she hadn't said all she had to say.

'We call the tune, Larry, you know that. Businesses. Multinationals. Organisations. We fix economies and we fix elections and we fix politicians and we fix ongoing policy and we fix the way money works round the world. Governments come to us and they say, "Help". They say, "Please help us out. Won't you help us out?" And we do. We fix things the way we want them. Most of the time, anyway. This is because we have so much money. It's mythical, Larry. The amount of money we have? – it's a modern legend; it's a force in the world, like nuclear weapons used to be. It dictates history. It prefigures the future. I can tell you what the future is, but I don't look in any crystal ball, Larry, I look at markets. Not the future, Larry; *futures*.

'There's only one thing up there with us. Know what that is? Religion. God and Jesus Christ and Muhammad and Buddha and whoever the fuck and us. Just knowing all that helps me sleep at night, Larry.' She hadn't taken her eyes from his; so far as Packer remembered, she hadn't even blinked. 'Tell you what keeps me awake?' He nodded. 'The fact that the *faces* don't matter. You follow me? The *people* don't matter. The people who think they hold the power.

'Fact is, the organisation runs on people the way a car runs on gas; but it doesn't matter a rat's ass who they are. You, Larry, me, the guys who work for us, the guys who work for them, the guys who work for the guys who work for those guys . . . We're fuel, you see. Get it? We keep the donkeys nodding, keep the armies marching, keep the dollars moving. But it doesn't have to be us. Doesn't have to be you, Larry, doesn't have to be me.

'So why am I telling you this? Here's why: I'm not through with WWI yet, because I'm not through earning. I've got a couple of steps upward I haven't taken yet. Don't pull me down, Larry. I'll say it again so you understand. I'm not through *earning*.'

Beverley smiled at him, seeming to offer encouragement, but she didn't say any more. After a moment or two, she got up and moved to open the door for him, her tiny tits bouncing and jouncing underneath the slub green.

'See this weather coming in? It's a little early for snow, wouldn't you say?'

'Freaky. It's *el niño*.'

She smiled and held the door. 'How's Beth, Larry? How're the kids?'

'Fine,' he told her. 'Yours are, what –?'

'Eight and ten,' she said. 'Having a good time in England. Can't figure out why everyone says please all the time and only five TV channels.'

They laughed together, then she shut the door on him.

Kate: I did a stupid thing. You're right, of course. I want the story – the full story – but that doesn't mean I'm a betrayer. I want to help. Part of the story, if you like, is a headline that reads KATE RANDALL INNOCENT. Who nursed you through pneumonia? Who was with you at Penarven when you got the disk back? Have I let you down? Come back. You can't do this on your own. Come back. I want to help. Call Joanna.

And you know my mobile number.

Robert

Kate read the message through several times, as if it was in code and she'd half forgotten the key. She went to the window and looked out. She could see rooftops under a lowering sky. The clouds seemed almost to have bellied down on the tallest buildings; they were yellow and purple, like a bad wound. Most often, the city's effluents and thermal wastage kept it several degrees warmer than other places, but that morning there had been a rime of frost on grass verges and street signs and parked cars. The promise of snow was in the air, a smell like linen or cut tubers.

Kate remembered Corso's professionalism at Penarven: the way he seemed to know what to do next. She remembered, too, his explanation for that: I was in the army. What do you call it? SAS?

Then that last instruction, mysterious and threatening: *Call Joanna.*

The LCD display on the mobile was blank. She had forgotten to recharge it. She reasoned that she ought to stay in the room and wait for it to charge up, but she badly wanted to be out, out there, out on the streets where she could move and hide and have no face. Already she was feeling stir-crazy: four walls, bed, TV, footsteps passing her door, the air in the room too thick to breathe, the room seeming smaller each time she turned to find a new angle. She tossed the mobile down and went out, walking half a mile or so before pausing at a pay phone.

Joanna said, 'They've asked me to ask you to come in. I'm asking you to come in.' It was what Webb had instructed; saying it let her off the hook.

Kate heard Webb's ghostly voice behind that of her sister. She said, 'I know,' then: 'It's lonely. I miss you. I miss my friends.' *Friends.* She left a name, unsaid, fizzing on the line, an electronic itch.

Joanna said, 'I've spoken to Inspector Webb. We've spoken a number of times. He thinks you should come in.'

'Can I trust him?' Kate asked.

Joanna knew that 'trust' and 'him' referred to the unspoken name, *The Trapper*, that barely audible buzz in the earpiece. 'I think so,' she said. 'He seemed sincere enough when I spoke to him.'

'You trusted him?'

'So far as I could tell.'

'How far was that?'

'Kate, I can't make that judgement. What can I say? You're on the run.'

Listening, Webb tried to gauge how well things were going. *You're on the run.* What did she mean by that? *It can't go on? Your judgement's clouded? Only you can decide whether to trade freedom for justice?*

Kate knew what it meant: *You're still out there. Robert could have turned you in at any time. Whoever he is, he's not the police. So? So, he's probably who he says he is.*

Webb turned to John Adams. 'Have we had the trace on this?'

Adams handed him a BT fax. It gave a location in the north of the city. 'Two units on their way,' he said. 'Let's hope she stays on.'

Webb nodded. A few minutes, he thought. Just a few. Tell her it's folly. Tell her she can't stay on the run for life. Tell her to come in.

'I'm not sure,' Kate said. 'I'll have to think about it.'

'I love you,' Joanna said. She was fighting a losing battle against her tears. 'Are you okay?'

'Tell Webb I didn't do it,' Kate said. The convention of the call was: *Webb isn't hearing this. Pass a message along to Webb.* 'Tell him I didn't kill Michael. Tell him I've got new evidence. Tell him I'll come in when I've got everything I need. When I've got proof positive.'

'I love you,' Joanna said. 'Please take care of yourself.'

A minute or two, Webb thought. He almost wanted to say it aloud, to cut into the call and plead: Just stay where you are a minute longer. A minute or two. Do this as a favour to me.

'I'm fine,' Kate said. Like Joanna's, her face was wet with tears. 'I'm great. I'm okay. I'm absolutely fine.'

She hung up the phone and walked away. She'd gone a street's length and turned the corner when she heard the whoop-whine of a siren. The sound brought a sick lurch to her stomach. She walked into a department store, took the lift to the top floor, and went into the women's room, where she sat in a cubicle and cried silently for ten minutes. Her heartbeat crashed in her skull. The tears were partly shed for Joanna, partly in fear.

How could you have been so stupid? To stay on that long!
   Because I wanted to hear Joanna's voice. To talk about Robert. To ask advice. To hear Joanna's opinion.
   You're crazy. You can't afford those luxuries. They're luxuries!
   I just wanted to –
   You're on your own. Don't you get it? Now they know where you are.
   No they don't.
   The area. The district. You'll have to move on.
   What about him? Do I trust him?
   What – despite the videotape?
   He explained that.
   Yes? That's okay, then.
   So I don't trust him.
   Not yet.
   Means eventually . . .?
   Means not yet. Possibly not ever.
   Joanna's right: he didn't turn me in. You thought the same yourself.
   He didn't, no. But maybe I should.
   Turn yourself in?
   I've got Michael's tape. I've got Naylor's widow. I've got Wideworld belly-up.
   Not enough.
   It's more than I once had.
   Is that why you stayed on the phone so long? So dangerously long? Subconscious desire to see Webb arriving in a squad car?
   Kate didn't answer herself. She left the cubicle and washed her face and hands. She reasoned that the police might have men on the street, so she went to the designer floor, where she carried

fistfuls of dresses into the changing room and spent three-quarters of an hour failing to like any of them enough to make a purchase.

After that, she went to a different part of the store and bought a goose-down sleeping bag, some cleated ankle boots, a fake-fur hat, gloves, and six pairs of long woollen socks.

George Webb asked, 'What the fuck is going on?'

'Triangulating the area,' John Adams told him.

'Bloody wonderful. How much did they miss her by?'

'The earpiece was still warm.' It was a metaphor, but it provided Webb with an agonising picture.

'Every B&B,' Webb said, 'every hotel, posters, local radio, you can do that, regional TV, possibly a reconstruction based on the phone box, we'll need co-operation from the local guys –'

'We're working off limited resources,' Adams reminded him.

Webb's face darkened. 'I think I know that,' he said. 'I think I've been fucking told that. Use Carol Tanner for the recon.'

Adams shrugged. 'She doesn't look a bit like Randall. Shorter, wider, different type altogether.'

Webb turned slowly. 'Then you do it,' he said. 'Put on a frock and hold your dick between your legs and parade up and down carrying a cello. Someone's sure to recognise you.'

Adams turned away. Ten minutes later, Webb picked up his papers and notes and left the room. Adams punched the desk, a solid sound; the wood rang. He waited a minute, then punched again. Webb's face was there in the grain, and the pain in his hand didn't matter.

Kate went back to her hotel and packed her things into Corso's rucksack. She laid the goose-down bag under the flap and buckled the strap to hold it in place. There was an e-mail message for her. It just said, *Still here.* She wrapped the notebook computer in a couple of plastic store bags and put it into one of the rucksack's outer pockets, then paid her bill and walked out into a surprising flurry of snow, soft and dancing in the half-light. She had taken a dozen steps down the street when she passed two cops, a man and a woman, going towards the hotel. They saw her, but hadn't *seen* her. Not yet.

Kate watched them into the hotel entrance, then walked quickly on. The street was busy. Kate threaded between people, head down, repeating a little mantra: *Away-safe, away-safe, away-safe.*

When she came to a sidestreet, she took it, looking over her shoulder. Snow was sifting down, blurring everything: the street lights that had come on with the premature dusk, vehicles in the main thoroughfare, passers-by, the dark shapes that appeared at the far end of the street, looking towards her, one with head bent as she talked into her lapel-radio. The man started to run, coming through the fall like a figure in an old movie, overscored by a thick white morse of dots and dashes. Kate ran backwards a couple of steps, looking at him as if she hoped he might dissolve in the blur, then turned and sprinted flat out for the end of the street.

She turned the corner to an identical street, then another, then another. She was running through a warren of small terraced houses, curtains drawn against the oncoming night. The wind was strengthening, and the few people walking had their heads bent against the fall. She heard a shout behind her, but no one looked up. As she ran, Kate was glancing left and right. She saw a corner pub, a Catholic church that looked like a car-workshop, an alley alongside the church. She ran into the alley and saw at once that it ended in a high wall. She reached it and turned. It was like being the only target in a shooting gallery.

Kate didn't know how much time she had. Maybe a minute, maybe less. She looked to either side. A house wall on her left, the wall of the church on her right. There was a small, plain window at shoulder height in the church wall. Kate unlaced her boot and used it to smash the glass alongside the catch. The window opened. She pushed her rucksack through, then hoisted herself up and went head first.

Inside was dark and cold. A dim light was burning up under the corrugated iron roof; the walls were whitewashed brick; a smell permeated the place – rot, and the thin, dank odour of mice. The

Church of Rome, decaying and out in the cold. She walked between pews of raw wood and up to the altar. A tortured and twisted Christ hung from his wrists, eyes upturned, blood-beads falling from a big, brutal crown of thorns. Kate eased aside the velvet curtain and went through into the musky blackness of the robing room, where she put down her rucksack and sat on it, knees to chin, her breath ragged in her throat. She felt sick and there was a pain in her arm that she couldn't account for.

Close. My God, that was close.
   Close enough?
   Meaning what?
   You almost got caught again. You're looking for it.
   No.
   You've decided to cave in. Subconsciously, that's what you want. To have it over with.
   No.
   Be a relief, wouldn't it? Take a chance on Webb; on justice; on Michael's disk.
   No. But, Christ, it's snowing out there. It's cold out there.
   Best bet, isn't it? Hands up, here I come . . .
   No. But where do I turn for help, now?
   Not to Mr Robert Corso, you've decided. So – obvious choice, isn't it? I swear to tell the truth, the whole truth, and –'
   No. But, oh, it's going to be so *cold* out there.

Kate folded her arms on her knees and rested her head. Her right arm it was – a stinging pain where she'd cut it on the shards of window glass; she shifted it to ease the discomfort. Almost immediately, she fell asleep, because asleep was the safest place to be. When she woke, there was a stillness about things that told her it was late. She came out from behind the curtain and into the body of the church. The light in the roof seemed duller, now; yellower. Kate circled the room, passing, one by one, garish stations of the cross. The smashed widow stood just after Ecce Homo, its ragged shards letting in a needle-sharp wind from the world outside, as if the chastised Christ had decided to forgo glory and make a run for it.

Her watch said nine-fifteen. She had been asleep for three hours. Leaving the window, she walked to the front door and saw that it was bolted on the inside, but otherwise held only on a latch-key lock. She threw the bolts and opened the door an inch. The street was empty and the snow had almost stopped; just a thin, powdery drift in the lamplight, occasionally lifted and turned by a breath of wind. Kate walked away, leaving a trail of footprints from the church steps to the main street where the fall on the pavements was already black and mushy.

She walked past an arcade of shops and hopped on a bus that would take her down towards the river, down towards the communities of rough sleepers.

I knew I could come back, she thought. A face no one wants to look at; a blank face; a face that makes others want to turn their faces away.

George Webb sat alone in the team office. Words he had spoken earlier seemed still to hang in the air: words to do with ill-luck; sour words, angry words. He could see Adams and Nairn and Carol Tanner looking down at their hands, moving their hands to their knees, shifting their feet.

He walked out to the car park slush, feeling the cut of cold through the soles of his feet, and got into his car without starting the engine. The only place to go was home.

Home. Where he sat opposite to Janice at their dining table and ate a freezer meal and spoke of nothing in particular, nothing that mattered, and heard about her day: nothing in particular, nothing that mattered.

Where he read the paper and watched TV at the same time: a programme previewing a movie about a plane crash investigation team. Janice had seen the movie and told him it was a washout.

Where he stretched out in bed, wanting to offset the discomfort of a late meal, a heaviness in his gut, and watched Janice strip, letting her clothes stay where they fell, and thought how lithe her body was, how sleek, its faint odour of scent, its underlay of sweat.

Where he lay in the dark wondering how Kate Randall was managing to stay alive, stay out of his hands. Wondering where she would go next; what he would do in her place; wondering how long she could possibly hold out; wondering – though he only ever allowed the thought in silence, in silence and in darkness – whether she really *had* killed Michael Lester, since the more he thought about it, the less reason there seemed to be for her to have done that.

Where he closed his eyes and ran through the scenario he'd rehearsed so many times before: Kate the murderer. All the evidence said she was. Logic said she was. Experience said she was. Then the other scenario that was like a filthy thought in a world of pure certainty: Kate the innocent. Because despite evidence and logic and experience, Webb had begun to feel like a man in pursuit of a bad idea.

Where he fell into a sleep of fitful dreaming: Kate approaching through the dark and speaking the truth, though he heard her as a man underwater hears – her voice distorted, her words running into one another like snow-melt.

Where he woke, at three a.m., and wondered when Janice had seen the air crash film to know that it was a washout, and why, when they made love, he sometimes looked at her and surprised a little frown on her face and a vacancy in her eye.

Twenty-three

Stuart Donnelly's office was in a small Victorian house in an area of the city that was neither centre nor suburb. There was a park opposite and a bookshop next door. People who lived there thought of it as a place to stay a while before going somewhere else. Corso looked into the bookshop window until the street cleared a little, then took a quick look at the lock arrangement on the outer door of the office. There was a latch and two mortises. He went past to the pub on the corner and bought a drink. Ten minutes later, he walked alongside the pub and round to the backs of the buildings. Donnelly's office had a walled yard. Built into the wall was a blank back door that carried a latch only, but was, Corso thought, probably bolted too. The wall wore a roll of barbed wire.

Corso took off his coat and threw it across the wire, then took a run at the wall. His heel skidded in the snow and he fell back, going full-length. A snow angel stayed behind when he rose.

His next jump took him up onto the wire, then over and down into the yard. He hauled his coat after him. The office had a fortified back door, but a couple of stupidly obedient sash windows. Corso took a heavy, saw-toothed hunting knife from a sheath under his jacket and rammed it into the jamb. When he knocked the haft sideways, the frame eased out an inch or two. He did the same on the other side and got leverage, so that now the sash was exposed on both sides. He cut the cord, got the blade in again and eased the frame until he could get a grip left and right; then he yanked the frame hard, and it fell outwards. He peered in and saw the wires leading to the jamb of the sash. Bells and lights if you open the window; nothing if you remove it wholesale. He took out a torch and sent the beam round the room until he found the control box. He smiled: *installed for you by Mickey Mouse*. He used the knife to cut the window wires, then climbed in and dismantled the two remaining circuits.

Why not put your valuables out in the street? he thought. Less chance of their going missing.

The whole place was a cinch, filing cabinets unlocked, in-trays full, security non-existent – Corso was shaking his head in wonder, until he saw the safe in Donnelly's office, which would have taken gelignite or the word of God to open. If Stuart Donnelly had any confidential material in his office, Corso knew that's where it would be. Even so, he went through every cabinet, every tray, every pile on every desk – not knowing what he was looking for, but scanning each document for *Lester*, or *Randall*, or even *Wideworld*. There was nothing; he was fishing in an empty lake.

He went to the desk outside Donnelly's door and flicked through the Electrodex until he found the man's home address, then used the phone to call all three numbers listed there: two answerphones and a fax. The first answerphone gave the office number, the second simply asked the caller to leave a message; on that one, you could hear music playing in the background. So, Donnelly had an office at home with a direct line, but he wasn't there, and he wasn't having a quiet evening in front of the TV either. Corso wondered whether the security system at Donnelly's apartment was as basic as the one at his office.

It was. A straightforward infra-red eye, coupled to a serial switch that turned lights on and off in various rooms on a rota system. If you'd videoed the place from eight till eight, then played a telescoped version of the tape, you'd have seen the lights revolving in a ludicrously predictable pattern: back, front; this room, that room. It was a garden flat in a well-lit street; people went to and fro with their heads down. Corso waited for the passers-by to pass by, then popped a window lock, climbed in, and broke the alarm circuit like someone snapping cotton.

He walked into every room, glancing first down then up. There were two safes, both socket outlet dummies. The one in the living room contained a Rolex Oyster, an antique diamond tie-clip, some women's jewellery from the twenties, and a thousand in cash. The one in the bedroom contained Donnelly's will; also Michael's disk, together with the hard copy printed from it. Corso hadn't known what he was looking for; now he knew.

He sat on the bed and read the hard copy. He didn't need to read it all: it was easy to see where it differed from the version Kate had shown him. He didn't even need to take it with him. It was enough to memorise the salient details from Packer's postscript to Ralph Farseon. Naylor had died as a result of Neophos X-9 poisoning. The manner of his death had been concealed and his widow paid off.

'Well, Kate . . .' He imagined her there, listening to reason. 'Now I know everything you know. The question is: who else have you told apart from this guy Donnelly?' He answered his question with more questions, a small smile of regret on his face. 'One other person? Two? A dozen? A small library of disks and print-outs stashed in various locations, waiting there to be opened "in the event of my –"?

'You think that makes you bomb-proof? Nah . . . All this is going to come out sooner or later. Bound to. If you die – what? – it finds its way to the press; if you don't, well, you'll need to use it sooner or later. Question is, which is better for Wideworld? Easy. Better for them if you're dead. Bad news with no one to back it up is easier to handle than bad news brought by you and your big mouth. That's the way Larry Packer's going to read it. He's already told me to whack you, Kate. What now? I can't kill you twice, but I bet you old Larry would like it if I could. He's really taken against you, Kate. I think it might have something to do with his salary; something to do with his position in the company, which is rapidly threatening to become ass-up.'

While thinking this, Corso restored the material to the socket outlet safe and shoved the cover back. He smiled. The safes were advertised in every insert magazine. If you looked round a room for a hiding place, you'd have to be half blind or half stupid to miss them.

He opened a few drawers and threw things round the bedroom,

then went back to the living room and did the same. He opened the wall safe and took the money, but left the tie clip and the other jewellery. It would look like the work of a shit-head lucking in to more than enough to keep the crack pipe smoking. On his way out, he restored the alarm circuit, then looked out into the street. When it was clear, he tripped the bell, then hopped out into the garden, and broke a pane in the window. No one came. No one ran out into the street. After he'd gone, no one passing looked up or paused.

City dwellers, shrouded in themselves.

He poured a drink and took it to the phone. His first call raised Packer's answerphone, as he had known it would. However, the message was unexpected.

'This is Larry Packer. I'll be away from my desk for a few days. During that time, James Rose will be managing the office. Please leave your number and state the nature of your business. Your call will be dealt with as soon as possible.'

Corso glanced at his watch – it was ten-thirty p.m. – then called Packer's home number. Beth Packer picked up after half a dozen rings. She said, 'Well, he's not here . . .'

Corso could hear the booze behind the voice. She sounded amused. He asked, 'Did he leave a number?'

'No, he's on some assignment. He'll be calling in. I could give him a message.'

'Ask him to call Robert Corso?'

'Sure.'

'When does he get back?'

'He said a couple of days. Maybe three.'

'Is he in the States?'

'Gee, no, I don't think so.'

'Okay. Ask him to call Robert Corso, would you?'

'Sure.'

'Ask him to call my mobile.'

'Sure.'

'Tell him it's important.'

'Sure.' She was barely listening.

Corso hung up. In addition to the husky-whisky tone of Beth Packer's voice, he'd been able to hear music, and he wondered what had contributed to her good humour. Packer away, he decided, and the kids sleeping over with friends, and someone there, waiting for Beth to get off the phone, stroking her hair while she spoke, perhaps, and bringing a smile to her lips, or letting a hand stray to her breasts, a promise of what was to come.

He was half right. Beth had prepared a late supper and put on a black silk wrap, a black shift underneath, its lace neckline soft on her pale skin. A single candle burned on a table set with a white linen cloth, white linen napkin, white plates. The supper was simple: oysters, then a lobster salad. It was her favourite. A bottle of Veuve Clicquot was cooling in an ice-sleeve.

The wrap, the shift, the feel and cling of them, was for her. The candle was for her. The white napkin was for her. The food was for her, and so was the champagne. Just for her. She poured a glass and raised it in a toast.

Absent husbands.

Kate's boots still looked new, but the goose-down bag was already stained and dog-eared. She had wedged herself into a doorway and turned her face from the wind. Her new friend, Stacey, sat at the opposite angle, her legs shoved against Kate's for warmth. Stacey's bag was torn in several places, the stuffing thin and soiled. Whatever she owned was in a canvas sling-bag that she'd carried over one shoulder as they'd walked through Soho, earlier, looking for what Stacey had called 'the right place'. Kate wasn't sure how she'd known it when she'd seen it, but Stacey had settled on *this* doorway, close to *that* pub, and just around the corner from a certain alleyway.

She said, 'It would be good to get off the streets tonight. I might try to get off the streets.' The wind was thin as a blade; there was no avoiding it.

Kate had been sitting on a bench in the middle of a tiny, polluted patch of grass when Stacey had joined her. Late afternoon, the light just beginning to fade. Stacey had offered a can of beer and

Kate had taken a slug. It had jolted her; the beer was laced with something fierce. When they'd left, they'd left together. Stacey had talked about the snow, and how she'd once hitch-hiked down to southern France where she'd begged from the English tourists; the idea had made her laugh. She'd talked about swallows circling and screaming in town squares at dusk, and living off rough wine and bread and olives, and sleeping in fields of sunflowers. She'd said she was going back as soon as she got the chance. She'd wondered aloud why she wasn't there now. 'I want to get off the streets tonight. It's a bad night to be out.'

So far as Kate could understand, Stacey's ambitions seemed to depend on the right sort of luck. Stacey had been having bad luck lately. English luck. Soho luck. It had brought her to this doorway in several degrees of frost.

She said, 'I'm hungry. You fancy a pizza?'

'Yes,' Kate said.

'Got any money?'

Kate had plenty in the silk-and-jet bag in the lining of the Canadian coat, but she didn't know Stacey well enough for that. She shook her head. Stacey nodded in return, and started to watch the people going by. The snow had started up again, drawing swift curtains across the breadth of the road. Their sleeping bags were crusty with it, and their sleeves, on the side turned to the wind.

Stacey said, 'I'm really hungry. I wouldn't mind getting off the street for a night. Just tonight.' She shuffled out of her sleeping bag and stood up. Kate could see that she was pretty in a sharp-featured way: little pointed chin, bee-stung lips, dark brown hair, her eyes and cheeks shadowy with fatigue. She was wearing a long skirt that might once have been a curtain, and a torn flying jacket over a man's roll-neck sweater.

'You're going?' Kate asked.

Stacey shook her head. 'Look after my things,' she said, 'okay?'

Kate nodded, and Stacey turned the corner into the alley. After she'd been gone fifteen minutes, Kate kicked off her own bag and walked the few steps to the mouth of the alley. The path sloped up and away into the dark. She couldn't see anything, but she could hear someone dancing: a soft-shoe shuffle in the sludge. She walked a few paces in, and waited. The sound was nearer: someone dancing, the steps putting whoever it was out of breath, because Kate could hear the *hah-hah-hah-hah-hah* as the dance grew faster.

Then she saw, on the far side of a little buttress in the wall, Stacey with her long skirt dragged up, her back to the wall, her legs spread, and the man between them, his *hah-hah-hah-hah-hah* as he shoved at her, his bootsoles and hers making that shuffle, that slippy dance step. Kate watched, unable to turn away or back off. She stood in the thick twilight of the alley as if a wall rose between her and them, as if she were watching from cover, stooping to a peephole, as his hands moved under Stacey's thighs, the only flesh visible, stark white in the half-dark and trembling slightly under their load.

The man's head was hidden in Stacey's shoulder; he was bent with effort; but as Stacey turned her face from him, her eyes met Kate's. She was blank, eyes blank, features blank, as if they had been wiped. The man quickened, and Stacey's shoulders rocked against the brickwork, making her head nod back and forth, but still there was nothing on her face. She stared at Kate, unblinking, head wagging, the man's *hah-hah-hah-hah-hah* rising in pitch as he punched with his body, rocking her, until he stalled and grew still.

Kate moved back a step or two, then turned and went back to the doorway. Stacey joined her a couple of minutes later and started to roll her sleeping bag. She said, 'We can get a room. Get off the street. It would be good to get off the street tonight. Cold as fuck tonight.'

The room was a little warmer than the street, but the bed had been slept in before. They unzipped their bags and put them on top of the counterpane, then got undressed. There was a sink in one corner. Stacey washed the underclothes she was wearing, then washed the spares she kept in the canvas bag. She lay naked on the unzipped bags and pulled the top across. Kate got in alongside her.

Stacey slept at once, the rhythm of her breathing settling to a slow rise and dip. She pushed her backside into Kate's lap and gave a little shudder, as if a dream had suddenly come at her. Kate felt the flow of warmth from Stacey, and didn't draw back. She put her arm over the naked girl, her wrist brushing the small breast, and brought her knees up. They lay like forks in a fork drawer.

Kate slept, lulled by Stacey's breathing. Her dreams were of almost nothing: of snow and snow clouds, of distant music.

Next morning, Stacey turned to her like a lover, arms reaching into warmth, and kissed her briefly, then got up and stood at the sink to wash.

'It's only just warm,' she said of the water, and stood with legs akimbo, splashing water up between her thighs and over her belly, then using a threadbare towel to dry off. Kate looked out of the window. Snow was sifting down through the freezing air, and the glass was frosted at the edges.

Stacey said, 'Do you want to get out, back out, or stay a bit – we can stay here till ten, I think it is, do you want to eat downstairs, they do some sort of breakfast, or get something outside, are you in trouble, what is it?' As if all her questions added up to the same thing. 'Some sort of trouble?' she asked again.

'Yes,' Kate said.

'With the police?'

'Yes.'

'Bad?'

'They think I hurt someone.'

'Did you?'

'No.'

'Is that why you're sleeping out?'

'That's why.'

'What are you going to do?'

'No idea,' Kate said. 'Absolutely none.'

Stacey weighed this up for a moment. She was getting into her clothes. After a moment, she seemed to think of something important. 'Are you famous?' she asked.

Kate laughed. 'No.'

'Famous for what they think you did?'

'No.'

'Is it – killed someone? Do they think you killed someone?'

'Yes.'

'Jesus Christ.' Stacey paused, about to pull on a sock. 'What do they say?'

'I stabbed him.'

'But you didn't?' On a held breath, her eyes wide.

'No, Stacey. I didn't.'

Stacey dressed in silence. She said, 'Let's not stay here.'

She's frightened, Kate thought. She'll be gone in a moment. Gone as soon as we hit the streets.

'So . . . *have* you got any money?' Stacey asked.

Kate rummaged in the lining of the Canadian coat and brought out the little bag. She showed Stacey the roll – better than two thousand – then immediately thought: *Could be a mistake.* But Stacey just stared at it for a moment, then gave a sour laugh. 'I turned a trick to get this room. This room and a Neapolitana with extra ham.'

'I'm sorry.'

'You didn't trust me.'

'I didn't know you were going to give sex in an alley.' Kate peeled off a banknote and held it out.

'No thanks,' Stacey told her, 'I left your share in the alley.'

'Take it.'

Stacey salted the money away and moved towards the door. Kate watched her. She almost lifted a hand to wave goodbye.

'Come on,' Stacey said. 'I'll show you a place where you can spend your cash.'

Corso and Packer met at the restaurant where the man on the door really wanted to hit you, and the chef resented having to cook for you. It was packed. People stood outside in the snow, in the hope that someone with a one-thirty table had died that morning.

Corso said, 'There's a memo you wrote to Ralph Farseon. Not the memo for filing, but the memo –'

Packer held up a hand. 'She's seen that?'

'She's *got* that.'

Packer picked up his menu and stared at it, as if he might find something to his taste. Revenge, perhaps: a dish best eaten cold. 'Who else has got it?' he asked.

'Stuart Donnelly.'

'Just Donnelly?'

Corso laughed. 'How the fuck would I know? No, I shouldn't think so. Or, at least, I'm prepared to bet his isn't the only copy.'

'Jesus!' Packer sipped some iced water. 'Where is it?'

'In a wall-socket safe at his apartment.'

'You brought it away with you?'

'No point. He's read it. You wrote it. Disks can be infinitely reproduced. She could post it on the internet if she felt like it.'

'You should have removed the evidence.'

'You don't think he'd have noticed? As things are, he thinks he had a visit from some crack-head.'

'Would he take money?'

'Donnelly? Who knows? Somehow I doubt it.'

'He's a lawyer, right?'

'This isn't like the States.'

'Yes it is. It just isn't dollars.'

'It's something you could have in reserve.'

'Give me his address.'

'You're probably wrong. Almost certainly wrong.'

'Okay, I'm wrong, he's Prince Perfect, now what's his fucking address?' Corso told him. 'What about Randall?' Packer asked.

'I'm talking to her.'

'She called you?'

'I'm talking to her through e-mails.'

'What does she say?'

'She says she's coming back.'

Packer nodded. A waiter arrived at their table and took their orders in silence, an expression of faint disdain on his face, as if their choices were obvious and timid. After he drifted away, Corso said, 'You're taking some time off.'

'Things to do,' Packer told him.

'Am I involved?'

Packer laughed. 'You think this Randall shit is the only shit I have to eat?'

Corso looked away as if he were mildly disappointed. Packer's lie worried him. He wanted to know more, but would have to settle for guesses.

'What does "coming back" tell us?' Packer wanted to know. 'Because I've heard it before, and etcetera.'

'There's nowhere else for her to go,' Corso said.

'No? Then where is she now?'

'In limbo. She won't be there long.'

Packer thought: This guy isn't going to give me Randall. He wants Randall. There's something between him and Randall. Something that keeps me out. I need a line on this guy. I need to hook up to this guy and fucking stay hooked.

He said, 'I have to leave town for a couple of days. Here's a number. Mobile phone.' It was a number that would never answer.

'Okay.' Corso took the slip of card Packer held out to him.

The waiter showed the label of a bottle to Packer, then uncorked it and poured a little into Packer's glass. 'Just fill the glass,' Packer told him. 'If the wine's bad, I'll spit it at you.'

A little shopping expedition. A little spree. Stacey took Kate through a couple of stores, amassing packages. They didn't spend much. If Stacey had ever had expensive tastes, she'd lost them somewhere on the streets. She wanted to be extravagant, but didn't know how. They went to an indoor market where she bought an embroidered jacket and a glass sphere on a little enamelled stand. She held it up to the light to get a reflection of them both. Kate saw her own face, and Stacey's, sliding round the surface of the glass, first wide, then narrow, disappearing into the stem as the globe was tilted.

Stacey grinned. 'Tell your future,' she said.

'Go ahead.'

'It's in the crystal ball.'

'Yes? What?'

'A place to be. Until you decide what to do.'

It was a squat and the deal was simple. You had to buy in, and pay rent to the guy who ran the place. His name was Mario, and he knew that private enterprise worked. He controlled the cash pool, he allocated rooms, he figured out the work rota. Kate could see that Mario had a foot on the bottom rung of the ladder, and he was looking up. She and Stacey sat in one of the bedrooms and conferred.

'Mario's a creep.'

Stacey shrugged. 'It's a place to be,' she said. 'You need a place to be. So do I. It's snowing.'

'I know.'

'It's too early for snow. It's the wrong time of year – wrong side of Christmas.'

'I know. How many people here?'

'Six. Eight with us. People come and go. You need money to stay here.'

'How do they get it?'

'Beg and steal, mostly. It's a place to be, Kate. It's off the street.'

'He's like a landlord.'

'That's the way it works. Does it matter? You've got money. It's a place to be.'

Mario came in. He was slight, about thirty, and wore stubble that was almost a beard. His jeans and leather jacket were almost new. His hair was pulled back and fastened in a ponytail. A snag-tooth showed when he smiled, and he was smiling, now, as he held his hand out for Kate's money. She had switched a small amount from the little bag to her pocket. Some she gave to Mario, some she held back.

'Welcome,' he said, 'and thanks.' His eyes were on the store bags that held Stacey's purchases.

'Is this our room?' Kate asked.

'There are six apart from you. People move around.'

'But can we have this room?'

'We share things here. Sharing's the way it works here.' Kate gave him the little she'd held back. 'Okay.' He folded the money into his pocket. 'You get the room.'

After he'd gone, Stacey started to rearrange the furniture. There was an old sofa, a chair, a low table, a mattress. A paraffin stove was burning and the room bore the taint of fuel, gassy and sharp. A cold snow-light shone in at the window, and objects in the room bore a stark, luminous quality; unreal. The fall had picked up, now: big, feathery flakes falling thickly, muffling the city's sounds.

Stacey put the globe on the low table and peered into it, hands cupped round the glass.

'What do you see?' Kate asked.

'Snow,' Stacey told her. 'The future's white.'

When Packer and Corso left the restaurant, Packer was drunk, though his speech was level and his step steady. A couple more drinks would have made him slurred and shaky, but this time he had stayed on the right side of that. He asked Corso for a lift.

'Sure. Where to?'

Packer named a main line station. 'Going out of town,' he confirmed. 'Stuff to do. Etcetera.' He liked it; he liked this drunk-but-not-too-drunk. He felt powerful and tricky. He slipped a strip of gum into his mouth and threw the wrapper over his shoulder. 'Cinnamon gum,' he informed Corso, 'you like that?'

'No.'

'Can't get it here.'

'Is that right?' Corso blipped the electronic lock and Packer piled in to the passenger seat, half sitting, half falling.

'Is it company business?' Corso asked.

'Oh, sure,' Packer said. 'What else is there? Company business, etcetera and so forth.'

Corso drove through the snow. His new hire car was a basic Ford, one of a million and comfortably anonymous. There was a lot of slip-sliding going on round him, and the wipers were stacking snow into his peripheral vision. Packer opened the window and threw his gum out. At least, he seemed to.

At the station, Packer lifted a hand in farewell. Corso pulled out into the traffic, spinning a wheel. The tracker bug under the passenger seat was glued to a small wad of cinnamon gum.

Mario was taking his electricity straight from the grid. Now and then, someone from the power company would sabotage his system by disconnecting the street supply, then Mario would go out and re-rig it. It was a game they only played in good weather. No one from the company was going to start by wiping three inches of snow off the manhole cover.

Kate plugged the notebook into the hijacked current and typed an e-mail.

I can't think why I should trust you.
You spoke to Joanna? Stay away from her.
Give me one good reason.

One good reason? Okay – because *you* deceived *him*. It wasn't one-way traffic, was it?

I didn't trust him then. I trust him even less now.

Why didn't you tell him about the memo?

I didn't trust him.

Why didn't you tell him you'd seen Naylor's widow? That she slugged you? That she clearly has things to hide?

I didn't trust him.

And you were right not to trust him, because he taped you in the hope of finding things out, right?

Right.

In case you were deceiving him. Which you were.

Listen, I don't know who he is. He could be anyone.

No. He's a journo, a friend of Michael's, he nursed you when you had 'flu, he nursed you when you had a broken head, he got you back from Penarven, he could have handed you over to Webb any time, *any* time, and he's a pretty good fuck.

Sorry?

I said he's –

What would you do?

Tell him about the memo. Get his opinion. Is it enough to go to

Webb with? Tell him about, what's-her-name-Naylor – Amy. Tell him about Amy Naylor. Go back there, go back there with him. There are things you haven't tried yet.

I'm okay here.

You sure?

I feel safe here.

And you think perhaps you'll stay here forever, is that right? With Stacey and Mario, your new home-from-home, your new life. Sounds good.

I could go abroad.

He suggested that: Robert. Remember what you said?

Okay.

Okay what?

Okay, give me space to think.

How much space do you need?

Shut up, Kate told herself. Shut up, shut up, shut up.

She sent the e-mail unchanged.

Packer drank a cup of coffee at the station, then took a cab back to the apartment where he'd spent the previous night. It was the place near the embankment where he and Corso had looked out over the river while Kate had stared into the cold, unblinking eye of the video camera. The girl who lived in the apartment was called Susan, and she liked Packer because he knew how to spend money.

It was a little after four when he got there. He dropped his clothes on the bedroom floor, climbed into bed and went to sleep immediately.

Corso picked up the e-mail and sent a reply.

It said: *No reason. Just – I'm all you've got. You know my number.*

Stacey went out and got something to eat. She came back in through the barred window that everyone in the squat used at night. The door was vulnerable and darkness made it more so.

Kate picked at the food. Stacey had found a Chinese place:

chicken noodles, rice, sweet and sour pork, vegetables in oyster sauce. They ate in silence until Kate said, 'Do you often do that?'

Stacey had a fork loaded with food halfway to her mouth. She smiled a sweet smile and ate the mouthful. 'Do what?' she asked, then, before Kate could reply, said, 'Well . . . I've done it before. Haven't you?'

'Not in an alley for money.'

'No. Well, the alley was fucking cold. I wasn't too keen on the alley.'

'But you didn't mind –?'

'Screwing for money?' Stacey asked. 'Why? What do you do it for?'

'Because I want to.'

'Yeah . . . And I wanted to. I wanted the money.'

'I didn't mean that sort of want.'

'You mean you do it for love?'

Kate smiled. 'Well, I *have* done it for love.'

'Me too,' Stacey said, 'me too. But all the other times – what were you doing it for then?'

Susan climbed into bed with Packer and put her arms round him. He woke and grinned at her, then got up and started to dress. He felt jumpy and excited, like a driver on the grid, like a jockey in the stall.

Fieldwork, he thought. I haven't done this for a while. *Hey!* Fieldwork.

He said, 'I have to go out.'

'Okay.'

'But I'm coming back.'

'Okay.'

'What time is it?'

'About ten.'

'Yeah . . . I'll be back later. Make some food.'

'Pick some up,' she told him.

'What?'

'Chinese or whatever.' She looked petulant. 'Where are you going?'

'Just some business.' He was smiling, but there was tension in his voice. Just some *fieldwork*.

'Sure about that?'

'Sure I'm sure. Why?'

'You're getting a hard-on.'

Fieldwork. Fear and thrills, thrills and fear.

'It's you, honey. You lying there.' She kicked the covers off to let him see. 'Save it for me. I'll be back.'

Susan turned on her stomach and put her face in the pillow. 'No MSG,' she said. 'It makes me throw up.'

Twenty-four

He stepped out into the night, the air still and cold, the fallen snow bringing a ghostly, shadowless light to the cityscape.

Fieldwork.

He parked two streets away from Stuart Donnelly's address, then walked a slow circle to the apartment and rang the bell. Donnelly answered the door and Packer smiled at him, as if they might have met before, a winning smile, a smile full of confidence and charm.

'Stuart Donnelly?'

'Yes.'

Packer's tone was low and confidential. 'There's a message from Kate Randall.'

Donnelly didn't speak. He stepped back slightly, allowing Packer to take a step forward: a step that brought him over the threshold.

'Is it difficult to speak?' Packer asked. 'Is there anyone else here?'

'No, there's –' Donnelly was still reacting to the smile, the low, warm voice. Into the living room, Packer thought. Just through into the living room and everything will be fine.

'Kate told me where to find you. I didn't want to come to your office.'

'Right.' Donnelly was ordering his thoughts. 'You're in touch with Kate?'

'I'm a journalist,' Packer said. 'Green Globe? She got in touch with me. I used to work with Michael Lester?'

'You've seen her?'

Packer laughed and shook his head. 'She e-mails me.'

'Where from?' Donnelly was back-pedalling into the living room.

'Where from? Cyberspace. Webworld. From the tips of her fingers.' Now Packer had got the deception established he was reluctant to let it go. It was too much fun.

'Can I get you a drink?' Donnelly asked. 'Can I take your coat?'

'Drink would be great. I'm just here to pass the message along. I won't stay.'

There was no sign of Corso's visit apart from a spiderweb crack in a mirror over the mantelpiece. Everything was back in order: books in the bookcase, drawers replaced, objets d'art resited. A bronze figurine of a rearing horse stood on the coffee table; it was rough-edged and rooted in a weighty bronze block.

Donnelly turned towards a sideboard and a tray of bottles. 'Scotch, gin, vodka, wine . . .?'

'Scotch would be nice.'

Donnelly started to pour. He said, 'What did she –'

Packer lifted the bronze and took a long stride forward, swinging as he moved. The block took Donnelly behind the ear, making a noise like wood splitting under an axe blade. Donnelly stepped back, dropping the bottle and the glass. He sat on the edge of an armchair and stared straight ahead. Packer hit him again in the same spot. The man's limbs loosened, as if he had come unstitched, and he fell against the chair, his head overhanging the arm. Packer took a breath and moved to get clearance, then swung a third time, huffing with effort, up on his toes to get maximum impact. This time the connection had a wet sound; spongy.

Packer found the bedroom and removed all his clothes, examining them, item by item, for bloodstains. He could find nothing, apart from smudges and spatters on his gloves. Among the items he took off was a spring-loaded belt holster carrying a snub-nosed .38. It was back-up. Donnelly's death had to look like a crack-head come back for the rest.

He walked naked, but still gloved, to the kitchen and found a good knife. Donnelly hadn't moved. Packer slit the man's throat and stepped back smartly; even so, there was stuff he couldn't avoid. A line of blood had struck his forearm and was pearling in droplets, running down the underside to circle his wristbone like a bracelet. He dropped the knife on the carpet, switched off all the downstairs lights, and went to the bathroom, where he turned on the shower. He waited until it was running hot, then showered with his gloves on. After he had towelled himself, he washed the shower down thoroughly, then dressed and went back to the kitchen, where he found a bin liner for the towel. He folded it flat three times and pushed it beneath his topcoat so that it lodged under his arm.

Fieldwork, he thought. He felt light-headed. The shower had brought a flush to his cheeks.

Back in the bedroom, he pulled the wall-socket safe out and removed the disk and the hard copy, glancing at the sheets, finding the memo he'd sent to Farseon.

Bitch, he thought. *You're trouble; pure trouble. I'm going to have to find you.*

He went downstairs and found the second wall-socket safe. He took the tie-clip and the jewellery. He found Donnelly's wallet in his jacket on the back of a chair in the kitchen, and emptied it of cash and cards. Then he checked the street from the living room window. Empty. Outside, he walked from door to pavement like a cross-country skier, toes down and dragging, to wipe his prints. As he walked the circle back to his car, he noticed the stars were out, shedding a hard and heavy light in the frosty air.

In the stars, he thought. It was in the stars, Donnelly, you poor sonofabitch. Nothing you could do about it. I was just an instrument of fate.

He laughed. Fieldwork. Old times.

Corso sat in a restaurant, the last person in there, his food eaten, his second bottle of wine half gone. It was one of those inescapable patterns, one of the unknowable laws of the universe, that he had eaten Chinese food that evening.

The snow disturbed him, as if he really were a trapper, and a fresh fall had hidden the tracks of his prey and cloaked its spoor in frost. He thought about the grey man, the man he'd killed, the fourth victim. That had been in the snow, one night on the lower west side close to the river. The man had been walking home, his usual route. Corso had put him down, another mugging in NYC, another body in the morgue. He had taken the guy's billfold to make it look good, and he remembered how a smudged, red halo had sprung up as blood from the grey man's head seeped into the snow.

A waiter put chairs up on Corso's table, but patted him on the shoulder as if to say, 'Stay as long as you like. Stay all night.' After a moment, the waiter reappeared and sat with others at a table near the back. They were eating soup and smoking and talking. Corso wanted to go and join them. He wanted to ask, 'How do you live a life where it's possible to smoke and drink soup and talk to your friends, and the same thing will happen tomorrow, and the day after, and each night you walk home through the snow?'

He wanted to ask, 'How do you do that?'

Kate's chicken noodles, Corso's chilli beef, the cartons of wonton soup and Szechuan prawns that Packer took back to the apartment by the river ... The unrepeatable pattern of a snowflake, galaxies shifting, the universe turning like a great wheel.

Susan liked to use chopsticks and keep the bowl close to her chin. She said, 'Good business?'

'Pretty good business,' Packer told her. 'Pretty good, yeah.' He felt wide awake and strung out. He could scarcely believe how easy it had been. Strung out and fizzing with energy; the muscles in his calves and biceps were bunched like cable.

Easy, it had been so damn *easy*.

And those other times – those early days. So *easy*. Packer had been part of a team, then; part of a family. It was all the same, he thought: the Mafia family, the corporate family, the family of politics. In Packer's case, the family out at Langley, Va. The world was tribal. The world had its laws. There was a certain law, he'd realised, of inverse proportion when it came to success. If some people went up, others had to go down. Sometimes, they had to go down and stay down. There were deaths to be accounted for.

In those early days, those heady days, Packer had seen a few go down. He'd been there; in fact, sometimes, he'd been the man. They'd called it fieldwork. All in all, it was odd that his path and Corso's had never crossed before. Not in the stars, he thought. Not in the great scheme of things.

Life had changed a little now, but it was still business. It had always been business. It was a rare thing to hate the guy, to want him dead as you might want a blood enemy dead. No. It was more like – putting someone down, watching him go down – it was more like cutting a terrific deal, or moving in on a company, or beating some sonofabitch to that ten-thousand-dollar promotion. Just business.

Susan knelt astride him and grinned. She leaned forward so that he could get to her breasts.

'Tell me something,' she said, 'what do you do? What business?'

'We run things,' Packer told her.

She lowered herself, slowly, softly. 'What things?'

'Everything.'

George Webb heard about Donnelly's death from John Adams, who'd received a memo from Carol Tanner; she had logged it as relevant material.

'What happened?' Webb asked.

'They turned him over, got lucky, went back for seconds.'

'Who?'

'Take your pick. One of thousands.'

'What do the squad say?'

'Just that – some crack-head with an empty pipe, Donnelly must've come back while the guy was still in there. Or else he'd never gone out. Lousy luck, either way.'

'Nothing in it for us?'

'Nothing.'

'Ask for a look through the house, okay? In case we find . . .' Webb shrugged. 'Find something.'

'I've done that. No objections.'

'Good.'

Webb was reading through the collated material on recent sightings of Kate Randall. Kate Randall was every-fucking-where. Given the number of people who saw her in the street, on buses, on trains, or lived next door to her, it was a miracle that Webb hadn't knocked into her at his local pub.

'Good,' he said again. 'Perhaps we'll find Kate Randall's signed confession and a little map of her whereabouts.'

Corso heard about Donnelly's death on breakfast radio. As soon as he'd listened to the report – brief and unadorned – he sent an e-mail. Then he went into the bedroom and removed a gun and four clips that were taped to the bottom of a chest of drawers.

He checked the gun, firing it empty, slipping the magazine in and out. Then he reached into the inside pocket of his jacket. Passport, wallet, a pen. He particularly wanted to check on the pen. He always carried it.

He put in a call to Packer's office and got Jimmy Rose, who offered to take a message.

He sat in a chair because there was little else he could do.

His phone rang and he guessed Packer, but it was Kate.

'Who killed him?' she asked.

'I don't know. You expect me to know?'

'They said it was a robbery. Someone had broken in the previous night, then gone back. That's the police theory.'

'I heard that too.'

'Why would anyone kill Stuart?'

Well, you know the answer to that, Corso thought. *Don't you? Papers you sent him; papers and a disk.* He said, 'I don't know. But it scares me. Doesn't it scare you?'

'Of course.'

'Listen,' he said, 'I'm sorry about the tape . . .' Then, 'Kate –?'

But she had hung up.

After an hour, she called back.

'I don't want to talk about the tape.'

'Kate, you tell me what to do. I don't know. Whatever you want to do – we'll do that.'

She told him to drive into Soho and wait for her in the pub close to the doorway she and Stacey had shared the previous evening. He'd been there half an hour before she sat alongside him and ordered a drink. He looked at her and laughed: the boots, knots in her hair, the backpack propped against the bar stool. The laugh almost restored her to him.

She said, 'I don't know whether to go or stay.'

'No. Okay. I told you – whatever you want to do.'

The barman gave Kate her drink – brandy and ginger ale. She sipped it and set it down, as if a decision had been reached.

'We were on the tape. You and me . . . together.'

'I know. I'm sorry.'

'Have you done it before?'

'Taped people –?'

'Yes.'

'You think I'm some sort of freak –'

'Not screwing, I don't mean that. Have you taped people in the hope of getting information?'

He shrugged. 'Simple answer – yes.'

'Did it work?'

He could feel her coming round. She was normalising the tape; putting it into context. 'Sometimes it did, yes.'

'You thought I knew things that I wasn't sharing with you.'

It was an admission. It was what he'd been waiting for. 'Yes, that's what I thought. I still think it.'

'What made you feel you had a right to know?'

'The story, Kate. Why did I tape anyone, ever? The story: what else?'

He waited. Behind his smile, a voice said: *Here she is. Don't let her go again. You could finish the job and be on a plane by this evening. Clean and gone.*

Kate sipped her drink. She was listening to a voice, too. *It's this or the police. What have you got to lose?*

Corso could feel the weight of the gun on his ribs.

* * *

'Two things,' Kate said. 'There are two things.'

First, she told him about the memo from Packer to Farseon, then about her visit to Amy Naylor. Corso looked at her in astonishment.

'She hit you?'

'It was a vase, I think. She hit me and ran away – off into the house somewhere. She was scared.'

Corso nodded. 'I can see that.' After a moment, he added: 'We'll talk to her.'

No, the voice said, *you've got it wrong. There's no need to talk to Amy Naylor. You already know what she knows. Do the job, catch the plane.*

In the car, Kate asked: 'What did you do with the tape?'

'The tape?'

'Of you and me.'

'I watch it every night.'

She tried not to smile. 'You're a sick bastard.'

The bug registered as a moving line of dots on a scrolling LCD map. Packer was able to stay back, unworried by being out of sight. There was music on the tape deck, and he sang along with it: feeling fine. Even when some guy in a Range Rover cut him up at an intersection, he felt fine.

You asshole, Corso, he thought. I've had enough of you. I've had enough of her. I've had enough, *etcetera*.

He was grinning and singing and making plans.

Fieldwork.

Amy Naylor half closed the door before Corso grabbed it, his hand over her hand. They all went into the living room together. Kate found herself looking round for the vase and her blood on the carpet as if they were figments of a dream.

Amy sat in a chair, knees together, her arms lying flat, head erect, the sinews in her neck out in cords. She might have been sitting in Old Sparky, and someone's hand about to throw the switch.

278

'Leonard just got worse and worse. Loss of memory, vomiting, weakness. He didn't take any medical advice. I mean, he didn't have to. He knew what it was.' She gave a little start, as if some memory had returned to her; or some fear had arrived at the door. 'What will happen to me for telling you this?'

'Nothing,' Corso said.

'What will happen to me for –?' She was looking at Kate.

'I'm okay,' Kate said.

'I recognised you.'

'I'd worked that out.'

'Your friend phoned me. Michael Lester. He kept on at me. He kept phoning. I changed the number and he still phoned.'

'I didn't kill him,' Kate said, as if it mattered that Amy Naylor should believe her.

'No.' Amy shook her head. 'No, all right.' Then she said, 'She's playing at a friend's house. She'll be home soon.'

Corso looked at Kate, who said, 'A little girl. Amy has a daughter.'

Amy nodded as if Corso might need confirmation. 'You have to be gone by the time she gets back.'

'We'll try to be,' Corso said. 'No guarantees.'

Amy stared at him as if he'd suddenly spoken in Venusian. 'No. Have to be.'

Corso produced a smile utterly devoid of warmth. He said, 'Your husband was poisoned by the OP derivative he was working on. The company that employed him paid various people to make sure that the compound was released for general use without proper testing or safeguards. You knew this. Michael Lester knew this. You said nothing. Michael Lester is dead. Perhaps you can see the connection.'

Amy looked at Kate, as if she might find kinder words. Kate said, 'And they paid you. They're still paying you.'

Amy went away and came back holding a box file. She said, 'Please go now. This is all of it, everything he saved, everything he wrote.'

Corso took the file from her and opened it, leafing through the documents. Kate said, 'What?'

He handed her the file. 'See for yourself.'

Page one, line one: *TEPP was the first. The Germans developed it during the second world war* . . . There was a lot of detail, but the broad story was clear enough. Neophos X-9 killed Leonard Naylor and here was the evidence. Kate read in silence for a while. Amy said, 'You'll have to go now.' When Kate and Corso stood up to leave, she said: 'We'll be all right. No one knows.' They were questions trying to sound like statements.

'You'll be fine,' Corso said. 'You're right. No one knows.'

Packer sat in his car at the far end of the street, deliberately boxed in between two other vehicles, but with a clear view through the windscreens.

Amy Naylor, he thought, would keep for another day.

When Corso pulled away from the kerb, Packer gave him a street's length before following. The traffic pushed him along once he reached the main road, but that was okay, he reasoned: everyone following everyone else. He worried a little about the fact that he was driving his own car: the Lexus he and Corso had taken to the restaurant everyone loved to hate. To be on the safe side, he dropped back by letting a couple of cars in from a side road. When other vehicles turned off or parked, bringing him closer to Corso and Kate, he deliberately slowed for a red light.

Caution was the error, because it wasn't really in Packer's nature. Caution made him clumsy. Drivers hooted at him when he stopped to give leeway to the cars from the side road. At the lights, he pulled up too sharply and the car behind him gave a little swerve, a little squeal. Corso noticed him when he held back for the side-street cars, but picked him up for sure at the light. He recognised the tactics, and then he recognised the car.

To Kate, he said, 'Look straight ahead, okay. Which means: don't turn round.' His saying it produced the impulse and she shifted in her seat. *'Don't!'* He used his free foot to kick her and she winced but settled in her seat, her back tense as if she were expecting a blow from behind.

'Who?'

'I don't know.'

'Not the police.'

'That's right.'

'Are you sure?'

'He's doing things to make it seem less obvious. Which is making it more obvious.'

'What do we do?'

'Okay . . . Where have you been staying?'

'On the streets,' she said, as if it were an address. Then: 'In a squat.'

'You feel safe there?'

'Yes, I think so.'

'Where?'

Kate told him. 'Okay,' he said, 'I'll take you there. Stay inside.'

She asked, 'What do I do then?'

'Wait.'

'For you?'

'Yes, for me.'

'Who?' she wanted to know. 'Who would follow us? Who would know where we were?'

Corso knew the answer to the first question, but he hadn't quite got a handle on the second. He pushed up to a green light, expecting it to change. When it did, he cruised through on amber, no real hurry, as if he were simply playing beat the red. He saw the following car baulked at the intersection. He drove a slow bend behind a delivery truck, and when this took him out of sight of the Lexus, made the first left turn he came to and drove fast to the end of the street, where he turned again, finding a web of side streets that finally took him onto a route for the squat.

He said, 'I could be wrong.' He didn't want to scare her. She might find a new address.

'Could you?' She sounded as if she'd believed him the first time and could hear the false reassurance in his voice.

He reached over and pulled down the sun visor on her side. 'It's a black Lexus,' he said. 'If you see it, let me know.'

Corso could hear Larry Packer's voice, as if he were sitting in the back seat, large as life, but with death on his mind.

'Okay, you've got Naylor's files, etcetera, here's the girl, Donnelly's not going to trouble us at all, job's over. Finish off. There's a flight around six.'

'If the disk is in other hands?'

'Nah . . .' Packer was shaking his head, smiling. 'We know what it is now. We know the worst. Damage limitation's already in hand.'

'You'll need a lot of that.'

'Sure. I know. But listen: forewarned, etcetera. We have friends. We can get some of this stuff stopped. The rest – we'll find a way of living with it.'

'So I could – what – hand her over to the cops?'

The back-seat Packer was laughing. 'I don't think so. Someone decides to talk about X-9? Embarrassing. They say that Kate Randall had sent them a disk? Yeah, well, we know that her boyfriend was a greenfreak. The one she murdered. The one she was so guilty about she killed herself. Okay. He thought he had some dirt to spread about X-9. Maybe we have to make a few payments. Maybe we even have to say sorry. But make it Randall who stands up to shout? – I don't think so. It's different. Why? She's using it as a defence in a murder case. In a trial. It's, like, evidence, etcetera. She's going to be saying a lot more than, "This OP kills people". She's likely to be saying, "The people who make this OP – they kill people". So, listen, earn your pay, and after that take a taxi to the airport. Go home. Aren't you missing the Black Hills?'

'It's Utah,' Corso was saying, 'not Dakota.'

'Whatever. Take her somewhere, do it, forget it; you'll be airborne in a few hours.'

Corso looked sideways at Kate. He pictured her with the gun at her head, a moment, just a moment in time, then the gun hopping in his hand, Kate falling away. He saw himself on the plane with a drink and a steak and the inflight movie. Just a moment in time. Kate falling away for ever.

'Yeah, that's right,' said the back-seat Packer. 'Gone. Out of time.'

282

Corso glanced at Kate again, and she turned to him, feeling his gaze. 'Almost there,' she said. 'Next street.'

'*So . . . what?*' Packer asked. '*What's next?*'

'*Next is you may as well keep quiet,*' Corso said, '*because I've stopped listening.*'

'*You're not going to do it, are you?*'

'*Not for you, you bastard.*'

'*Not for me, not for yourself. Just not. Am I right?*'

'*I don't have to listen to you.*'

'*I knew it. I knew this was coming. You're into her. Listen . . . you fucked her. Good. Who cares? What difference? You were hired to do a job, remember? You know what this is? It's Stockholm syndrome, except you're hooked on her instead of the other way round. What have you got planned here, Corso? Marriage, kids, picket fence, rocker on the porch?*'

'*It's easier than that. I'm just not going to kill her.*'

'*You asshole,*' Packer said.

'Over there,' Kate said, and pointed at the boarded windows of the squat. 'Stop over there.'

'*I'm not going to kill her,*' Corso said, '*because I don't want to. Because you want me to. Because I'd sooner kill you.*'

Kate said, 'What do I do?'

'I'm not sure,' Corso told her. 'Give me your number.'

'What?'

'Mobile phone. There's a pen under the dash.' She wrote it on the back of his hand as he drove. 'Wait for a call,' he told her, 'be sure it's me.' He handed the box file to her. 'Take this.'

She jumped out and ran round the side of the house to the barred window. Corso waited long enough to see her in, then drove off, fishtailing in the slick of snow-mush that still hadn't cleared from the side streets. He'd been gone a good three minutes when Packer's Lexus pulled round the corner. The blip on his screen showed that Corso had returned to the main street and had circled to backtrack.

He's looking for me, Packer thought. He's offering himself. He smiled at the idea. He's coming at me nose to nose. *Mano a mano.*

Packer knew he'd been seen as soon as Corso took avoiding

action. His advantage was the tracker bug. He thought Corso might head for his rented house: which would be fine. Anywhere confined, anywhere private would have suited Packer. However, he couldn't be sure. Maybe Corso and Randall would have more calls to make, more people to see. Maybe he'd find out who else knew things they shouldn't know.

Then he'd seen the blip on the screen stand still for a while, and he knew he'd got lucky. Corso driving solo, now; the girl holed up in . . . he checked the street name. Sure. He leaves her somewhere safe, then he circles around looking for the enemy.

Because that's me, now, isn't it, motherfucker? – the enemy.

The enemy; that's you.

He got to the street, drove through, parked and walked back. A red-brick terrace, steps up to each front door, a basement, neat gardens, modest cars. The boarded-up windows of the squat were blind eyes, the locked door a closed mouth. Packer could hear a bass-line somewhere deep inside the place, like a jazzy heartbeat.

He walked past, looking at the door and deciding immediately that it was too tough. He found the barred window. There was a padlock between the outer bar and a wall-ring. You could get in if you had a key. The system depended on the notion that a full-out assault by bailiffs was unlikely to come via a window. Bailiffs just stood in the street with a task force of cops, a couple of kanga hammers and an earth mover.

Packer knocked off the lock with the butt of his gun, then kicked down the inner board. The house was full. The people who lived there had had enough of streets and snow. The window let into a kitchen. A woman was at the stove, making a meal. The music had been almost enough to cover his entrance. She didn't look up until the window board clattered onto the floor. Packer showed her the gun and she backed off, silent, eyes wide.

'How many here?' Packer asked.

'Eight,' the woman whispered. 'Eight people.'

Packer smiled at her. 'What's your name?' he asked, whispering too, as if it were a game.

'Tina.'

'Tina . . . okay, Tina, I'm going to ask you a question, now. If you tell me the truth, everything's going to be fine, etcetera. If you tell me a lie, I'm going to shoot you with this gun.' He grinned at her and nodded encouragement. 'Okay?'

Tina had started to pant. It wasn't easy for her to speak.

She nodded – yes, it was okay.

'Is there someone called Kate staying here?'

Tina nodded.

'Is she here now?'

Another nod.

'Fine, that's fine. Now, Tina, you're going to have to speak to me for this next one. Where is she?'

'Upstairs.'

'Good. That's good. Now, Tina, here's the difficult one. Exactly where upstairs?'

'You go up . . .' She paused for breath, gulping, her hand pressed between her breasts. 'Go up . . . there's a room ahead of you, not that one . . . not the bathroom . . . bathroom is after that room . . . but the room after that.' There were tears on her cheeks, but she made no sound of crying apart from the little gasps for breath.

'Good,' Packer said. 'Now, here's another question . . . sorry, I'll try to make it the last, okay?' When she didn't respond, he said, 'Will that be okay?' and she nodded, quickly, sensing that every question had to be answered, even the ones he was asking for fun. 'What's the room beyond this room?'

'Living room.'

'Anyone in there?'

'Yes.'

'Who?'

'Mario and Ben and Hel –'

Packer stopped her with a gesture: the gun wagging close to her face. His whisper had a little edge to it; an edge of boredom. 'I don't care what their names are, Tina. How many men and how many women?'

'I don't know.'

'When you last looked.'

'Two men, three women.'

'But Kate wasn't among them?'

'No.'

'Why not?'

'They keep to their room.'

'They?'

'Kate and Stacey.'

'Stacey?'

'Kate's friend.'

'A girl?'

'Yes, a girl.'

'Fine. That's great.' His grin broadened. 'You've been a great help, Tina. I'm very pleased with you. Now, here's the next thing. I want you to walk into that room, very calmly, and sit down with your friends. I want you to tell them I'm here and that I have a gun, etcetera. The music's pretty loud in there, but you should tell them that if they make a noise, I'll have to shoot everyone. Okay? That's any kind of a noise *at all*; and shoot *everyone*. You understand, don't you?'

Tina said yes.

'And will you do that for me?'

Tina said yes.

'And will you remember, all the time, that I'll be just behind the door and that I've done this . . .?' *This* was take the safety off the gun.

Tina said yes, she would remember that, yes. And she went in, the others looking up, smiling, saying, 'Hi, Tina', and 'Food ready?' and she sat down with them and passed on Larry Packer's message, keeping her voice low, under the music, though her eyes were loud. Her eyes were screaming.

Packer came into the room surrounded by the bubble of calm that followed that first seismic moment, the moment of Tina's whispered message, their energy drained, their capacity for surprise used up. They sat like a class of children, looking up at him and waiting to be told what to do.

Packer beckoned Tina to him and held her loosely by the arm, as though it might be she who would demonstrate to them just what it was he required. He said, 'I'm here to take Kate Randall home. There are people who miss her. People who worry about her, etcetera. They sent me to find her and –' he offered a happy grin '– hey! – here I am.'

Mario stood up. Packer moved forward, still holding Tina's arm, and hit him alongside the head with the gun.

Mario said, 'Uhhh,' and sat down. A web of blood crept across his cheek.

'No,' Packer said, 'wrong. I'll tell you when and I'll tell you what.' He waved the gun at Mario. '*Now* stand up.'

Mario got up, backing off at the same time. Packer gave a little chuckle. 'It's easy,' he said. 'Just do it when I say it. Now, there's a little closet somewheres about, am I right?'

'Along the hall,' Mario said.

'We're all going down there. Very quietly. I don't want to use the gun, because it makes a hell of a lot of noise, but if you make a noise – well – what difference?'

There was an understairs space converted to a cupboard. Packer opened the door and motioned with the gun. It was like herding sheep. They sat cross-legged in the half dark of the space amid a jumble of brooms and buckets and ripped underfelt, their eyes wide and unblinking.

Packer said, 'I'm going to close the door. If you come out before I've gone, I'll shoot all of you. If one person comes out, I'll shoot all of you. If you make a noise, I'll shoot all of you. If any *one* of you makes a noise, I'll shoot all of you – etcetera. I bet you can see the pattern, can't you?'

He closed the door. There was a grab handle on the outside, and he fetched a wooden chair from the living room and wedged it there, the tilted feet hard against a gap in the floorboards. But no one was coming out of there for a while; he might as well have dropped a time-locked steel sheet.

In the upstairs room, Kate and Stacey were examining the contents of the box file. Neither of them looked up as Packer sidled in. He laughed.

He said, 'Hey, look who's here.'

Twenty-five

TEPP was the first. The Germans developed it during the second world war: a by-product of nerve gas development. Nerve poisons, that's what OPs really are. Phosphoric acid. Tetraethyl pyrophosphate was the Nazi mix. I'm impotent. There's no doubt about it. Dead meat. Also, I can't remember simple things, simple words, people's names.

OPs are widely used for agricultural purposes, but also against household pests, and pests found in catering establishments. They have also been found efficacious against head lice and a number of ectoparasites in animals. A number of agencies have expressed concern about the health risks involved when OPs are used in sheep dips, as insecticides in military premises, and as parasite preventatives on military personnel during the Gulf War.
   So says 'Science World', thereby radically understating the case.
   No one listens, not really.

I stood in the doorway of her bedroom. I was late back from work. She was asleep. I heard Amy's voice from downstairs asking me if I wanted a drink. She was offering a choice – Chardonnay or something red: Shiraz, I think. I didn't know what I wanted because I couldn't really remember what either of them tasted like. I hadn't tasted anything for a while. But something worse than that was happening. I watched her sleeping, and I went across to the bed, and I kissed her on the forehead. I said, 'Good night' just 'Good night', only that, because I couldn't remember her name. I couldn't remember my daughter's name.

All OPs are EU Black List substances. In order to protect the aquatic environment, they are so identified in EU Directive 76/464/EEC.

I have stopped pretending to Amy. She insists it's overwork. Today I sat in the car for several minutes trying to work out what to do next.

An application for funds to investigate OPs was made to the Medical Research Council by scientists at Liverpool University, led by a professor in medical genetics. This was rejected. No explanation was given.

I take these clippings from scientific journals, broadsheets published by Green organisations, Green websites, the Gulf War Veterans' action campaign sheets, and so on.

What I'd really like to do is make my own contribution. Put in my ten cents' worth. But I have Amy to think of – to protect. Amy and the child.

They wanted an enhanced OP. That was my brief. The lab reports are endless, but the short version is easy:

1. Any chemical manipulation is closely related to nerve gas development.

2. Experiments of that sort have been carried out for the past 30–40 years, so there's plenty to go on.

3. We try variations on a theme, really – make hundreds of compounds, then watch to see how each reacts to stimuli. And how it develops structurally.

An application for funds was also made by Dr Goran Jamal, a consultant neurologist. He had been carrying out neurophysiological tests on members of the farming community and on Gulf War veterans and had discovered specific patterns of neurological damage. His application was rejected without explanation. This is from the Gulf War vets. Their campaign dossiers are full of stuff like this. No one listens. I didn't listen. It might be a toxic multispray to you, but it's bread and butter to me. Ha ha.

Crop duster, flea collar, wasp killer, fly and moth strip, cockroach spray, certain death to ants, beetles and other crawling insects, sheep-dip, scab-dip, ecto-dip, winter-dip, azamethipos, bromophos ethyl, chlorfe-vinphos, coumaphos, demeton-O, demeton-S, diazinon, dimefox, dioxathion, EPN, ESP, etrimfos, fenchlorphos, fensulfothion, heptenophos, isazofos, malathion, methamidophos, oxydemetonmethyl, parathion, phosmet, prothiofos, pyridaphenthion, quinalphos, schradan, temephos, tetrachlorvinphos, vamidothion.

   I spoke to Farseon today. No one listens.

So, it's cookery; basic cookery. First catch your established OP. Mix in whatever takes your fancy. Pyrethrum, perhaps. Add piperonyl butoxide, so that the pyrethrum can be used in smaller doses, even though the resulting compound will be more toxic. Season with a little nutmeg to taste and pop into a warm oven. Kills more for less cash. This cake took three years to bake. My project; and although assistants came and went, I worked on it solo for most of the time.

Excessive sweating. Excessive salivation. Vomiting. Diarrhoea and abdominal cramps. Lassitude. Headaches. Inability to concentrate. Respiratory problems. Depression. Confusion. Anxiety attacks. Mood swings.

In simple terms, this is what we did. Used a natural product as a compound base. We tried this and that: plants, animals, marine life. Squid looked promising for a time. We also experimented with bacteria that can survive extreme conditions. It sounds terrific. It sounds Green, doesn't it? – natural products, blah, blah, blah. Only problem – it seemed likely to have long-term toxic effects on human neurotransmitters, not least the GDNF. Since the glial-cell-line- derived neurotrophic factor is vital to the dopaminergic nerves, it was thought (by me, as it happens) that the compound might well block their development in the foetus. Who knows? Who'll ever know?

290

How to find out for sure? How to screen your engineered molecule, your little mutant? Well, Baron Frankenstein, you simply inject lots of little animals and wait to see how they like it.

In the meantime, what are we getting? We're getting Neophos X-9. An organophosphate for the millennium. Green-based and goody-goody and cheap. Oh, yes, cheap. Don't forget cheap. Much more effective in the control of infestation and fungal damage to crops, and in the eradication of parasites infecting livestock. And in making you throw up and suffer blurred vision and get the shits and have to sit down all the time. Also good at giving you a dead dick.

He said it with a little chuckle in his voice: 'Hey, look who's here.'

Stacey got up and backed off until the wall stopped her. Kate said nothing; the pages she had been reading drifted from her hands. Packer crouched down and pulled Naylor's box file towards him. He said, 'I wondered what you were carrying when you came out.'

The black Lexus, Kate thought. She was surprised that she could think at all.

Packer retrieved the dropped pages. 'Maybe you could put these back into the file, Kate. I think it would be a good idea to take it with us.'

'Who are you?'

'Well . . .' Packer tapped his nose with the barrel of the gun, as if he couldn't quite remember. 'I'm someone who's been sent to find you, Kate. And look – here you are.' He glanced at Stacey. 'Does she know anything at all?'

'No.'

'Nothing about Michael Lester and Wideworld Industries . . . any of that stuff?'

'Nothing.'

'She was looking at these pages, wasn't she?'

'She doesn't know what they mean.'

'Doesn't know who Leonard Naylor is?'

'No.'

'No. Well . . .' He smiled reassuringly at Stacey. 'That's good. That's terrific. Still, I'll have to think it through, because . . . I don't know . . . maybe you're being a little free with the truth.'

'I promise you.'

'Yes . . .' Packer laughed as if he were hearing it from a child, and had heard it before. 'Here's the next move – empty out the bags.' Stacey was still standing by the wall. Packer said, 'Do it now, because I can feel myself getting angry.'

From the litter on the floor, he took only Kate's mobile phone. 'I'm going to ask you a question, now, Kate, that'll show you how well acquainted I am with you. How well I know you. Does Robert Corso know you've got this phone?'

She knew it would be a mistake to ask, 'Who's Robert Corso?' so she said, 'Yes.'

'And does he have the number?'

'Yes.'

He switched the phone off. 'You send him e-mails, don't you?' Packer nodded at the notebook computer, set up on the low table. 'Let's send one now.'

As Kate sat at the keyboard, Packer moved to stand behind her. Stacey had again retreated to the wall after emptying her bag. Packer said, 'It's Stacey, isn't it? Sit down, Stacey. You can sit down just there and wait.' To Kate he said, 'Just type: I'm with Larry Packer. He'll phone later.' Kate typed the message in and sent the e-mail on a bookmarked number. Packer watched closely, then he cocked his head and frowned, as if he'd suddenly thought of something.

'Oops!' he said. 'You must have heard that. You must have heard my name. Hey, that was silly of me.' He was talking to Stacey.

She shook her head. 'I didn't hear anything.'

'Yeah? That's good. But you're still going to have to come along.'

He yanked the lead out of the computer, then smashed the screen and the keyboard with his gun. He seemed to enjoy doing

it: picking his blows, using his heel when the notebook finally fell
to the floor.

'Here we go,' he said.

He led them past the stairs cupboard. The chair was still under
the lock. Kate glanced at it: the chair wedging the door. She said,
'Where's everyone else?'

'Everyone who?' Packer asked.

'The others.'

'No one here when I arrived.'

In the kitchen, he said, 'We're going to do a little cooking, girls.
Okay? So let's see what we've got. Open all the cupboards.'

Kate and Stacey opened the cupboard doors.

'Take out the oil. Olive oil, all that stuff. Empty it onto the
floor.'

'There are people in the house,' Stacey said.

'Yeah? Did you see any?' Packer took a step forward and put the
gun against her temple. 'Just empty the fucking bottles, etcetera.'

He glanced round the room and found a box of kitchen matches
on the worktop. When he and the women were on the outside
looking in, he struck a match and dropped it into the box. When
the box flared, he tossed it into the room.

'You drive,' he told Kate. 'Stacey and I will be in the back.'

'Where are we going?'

'For a spin. A spin in the country.' The expression seemed to
amuse him a lot. 'We're going for a spin.'

As Kate pulled away, she heard a sound like waves striking the
base of a cliff. *Whumph.*

Packer looked back briefly. Things getting out of hand? Nah. *In*
hand. Everything in hand.

'People live in that house,' Kate said.

'I sent them all away. I told them to go.'

'What do you want?'

'I want you to drive carefully, Kate. This is bad weather for
driving.'

'How do you know Robert Corso?'

'Robert? Why, I've known him a while. Old friends, etcetera.'

Kate drove across town, taking directions from Packer. He guided them through the northern suburbs and out towards open country. As if it were an afterthought, he said: 'We'll be seeing him later. We'll be catching up with Robert later.'

Kate flashed her lights at a couple of oncoming cars. Packer said, 'Do that again, Kate, and I'm going to shoot Stacey in the leg. Okay?'

After that they drove in silence.

Corso waited a couple of hours, all the time expecting to open the door to a visitor. He checked his gun again, and realised that it was a sign of boredom allied to anxiety. He set out a couple of safeguards of his own invention: things that had worked well in the past. One was a kitchen knife taped to the back of the sofa. The second was a good measure of bleach in a glass next to the bottles of liquor and ice bucket on the kitchen work surface.

He needed to be doing something but, at present, all he could do was wait for Packer to arrive.

Packer didn't arrive, but Corso figured he would – he must – before long. Then he began to picture the man: *driving round, looking for my car, hoping to find it parked outside some house or another, Kate and me on the inside, looking like easy pickings.* Then he grew puzzled; and, after that, began to get a gripe in the gut that he didn't like at all.

He made a dozen calls to Kate's phone, each ten minutes after the other, and got the pager each time. Finally he went back to the area of the squat, parked three streets away and walked the rest. There was a smell of charring in the air, charring and soot, that made him quicken his pace.

The crowd was still there, but the spectacle was almost over. Corso pushed through. Two fire tenders were parked nose to nose, firefighters still going in and out, three men on a low turntable ladder dousing the roof. The tiles had fallen down into the house, leaving the rafters naked to the world, like ribs on a carcass. The smell of charred timber was strong, crackling in Corso's sinuses, and broken glass crunched underfoot along with the frozen slush.

Ragged streaks of black surrounded each window. Harlequin make-up.

Corso nudged up as close as he could get, standing alongside a woman wearing an eager stare. She started talking to him because others there had heard it before. She was an eyewitness, anxious to share.

'It was waiting to happen,' she said. 'They brought out four, four in black bags. And two that weren't dead. At least, when they left here.'

'How many people?' Corso asked.

'Six. They had the electrics wired up from the street. It was waiting to happen.'

'Where have they gone?'

The eyewitness nominated a hospital. 'You should've seen it when it was really on. Flames, roof falling in, windows exploding. Hell of a fire.' Corso started to move away, pushing between sightseers who were just appearing on the scene, each of them looking up to the burned-out rafters and the lowering sky above. The eyewitness swivelled her head, sad to lose him.

'They had cables running into the house direct from the street. It was waiting to happen.'

As Corso turned and walked away, she looked past him to the new arrivals.

They were driving a side road out in the country, trees and fields on either side, when Packer tapped Kate on the shoulder and told her to pull over. Crows were beating against the wind, just black blurs amid the white, as snow piled in from a yellow-grey sky. Packer had seen a long, curving lay-by behind a screen of trees.

'We can stay here awhile.'

'What for?' Kate asked.

'Well, there are a couple of places your friend Corso might try looking for you. I don't know how smart he is, but I don't want to meet him until the time's right. Yeah . . .' He stretched, both arms out, the gun waggling slightly as he took the tension out of his shoulders. 'Right time, right place.'

'Where's that? The right place?'

Packer said, 'You'll find out. You'll be there.' He was leaning forward, talking to Kate over her shoulder, the gun dangling casually between his knees.

'Who are you?'

'You asked me that. I told you: someone hired to find you. You ever see any of those old Western movies? You'd have bounty hunters, remember? They were either ratty looking guys with a squint and a stain on their chins from chawin' t'baccer, or else they'd be flashy dudes with rhinestone hatbands and a crossover draw.' He laughed and said, 'Chaaaaawin' t'baccer,' again, in a down-home accent that pleased him. 'That's me, Kate. Bounty hunter.'

'Who are you working for?'

'Working for the man with the money. Wouldn't you?' He grinned and leaned over to whisper in her ear. 'Wouldn't you . . .?'

He was still grinning when Stacey yanked the door handle and jumped out into the snow, but Kate couldn't see the grin because it was behind her. She half turned, as Stacey stumbled off through the fall, and saw her form dwindling in white.

Packer said, 'Damn!' He hauled Kate out of the car and opened the boot. 'Get in,' he said. When she seemed reluctant, he tapped her beside the head with the gun barrel; just a tap; it rang in her head like a gong. He produced a pair of handcuffs, as if it had always been the next thing on his mind, and cuffed her to a hinge, then slammed the boot and activated the automatic lock, getting a bleep and a double flash from the indicators. He looked in the direction that Stacey had taken, her tracks leading off into nowhere.

'Damn!' he said again. But he was smiling.

Corso had waited in A&E to be told that the two survivors were men. The nurse who told him this also gave him directions to the morgue, where he lied to a police officer named Mitchell who was eager to match names to faces.

Two men alive, both in ITC. One man dead. Three women dead. The morgue attendant unzipped the body bags, while

296

Mitchell stood at a discreet distance. The faces were still faces, more or less. They had died, all of them, from smoke inhalation. The flames had done some damage – blistering and hair loss mostly – but the features were pretty much intact.

Mitchell said, 'Take your time.' He knew that relatives of the dead often didn't recognise their loved ones.

Loved ones, he thought, and watched as Corso stood by each body in turn.

Blackened faces of the loved ones. Hair of the loved ones burnt back to a charcoal frizz. Skin of the loved ones blistered and peeling and red.

Corso looked last at Tina, the red-black bubble-wrap of her skin, the electric hair, lips gritted over her teeth as if in anger. He said, 'She's not here.'

'Then where might she be?' Mitchell asked.

Corso shook his head. 'That house – it's where she was when I last spoke to her. She could have moved on. Who knows?'

'Your sister . . .?'

'She was sleeping rough, then in another squat, then in the squat that burned. It's a couple of weeks since I saw her.'

Corso was heading for the door. Mitchell looked him up and down: the rough sleeper's brother in his USAF flying jacket. 'Why was she doing it?'

'Breakdown,' Corso said. 'She went to pieces.'

Mitchell held the door open for him. It slapped back, bringing a chill. The morgue attendant followed Corso. He asked, 'Anything you need?'

Mitchell shrugged, meaning *any job but this*, and the attendant laughed as he left. Mitchell made a note about Corso's visit. He thought, I wonder if he'll ever find her: the loved one who went to pieces.

Despite the thickness at his waist, Packer moved fast over Stacey's tracks, making twice her pace even though fear was helping her speed. He came to a place where she had run fifty feet on round a bend, then doubled back and climbed a gate, and read the signs at once, huffing with laughter at their obviousness. He topped the gate and stood there for a moment to give himself height. Stacey was two-thirds of the way across a rising field, heading for a small plantation of conifers that stood on the crest like a ragged crown. Packer dropped down and started after her, getting more than two paces to her one. Even when she looked back and saw him, then increased her pace, going slip-slide on the snow-covered grass, he gained on her with every stride, and when she finally hit the trees, he was thirty yards back, no more.

Stacey ran through the plantation, swerving and switching direction when she could. The light was green-white, and thickened the deeper she went between the neat rows of fir trees. She wanted to find a place to hide, but there was no time for that; wanted to see him go past, lost, as she watched from cover, giving him five minutes – ten – to lumber on through the thickening fall, before she backtracked to the car and Kate. She wanted to turn and find him gone: victim of a wrong turning, a broken ankle, a heart attack. As it was, she could only shout, 'No, no, no, no,' with each pace as he closed on her. Finally, she grabbed at a fallen branch and turned to swing at his head. He stepped back, then forward, and punched her hard on the upper arm, taking the strength from it. She dropped the branch and stood, half doubled, her hand to her arm where he'd struck it, her breath coming in great, sawing gasps.

'We'll have to go back, Stacey,' he told her. 'Okay? Kate's in the trunk of the car and she's going to be cold and uncomfortable.'

Stacey said, 'I don't know anything about anything. Just let me go. I don't care about her and I don't care about you. It's none of my business, okay?'

'Sure, listen, Stacey, hell, I'd love to let you go. *Love* to. And pretty soon, I will. But I have to hang on to you just for the time being. You know that song? *You just keep me hanging on . . .* That's me; that's you.' He lifted his hands in regret. 'What can I say?' He was breathing hard. He could hear a loud, stereophonic tinnitus, like a scream on the wind, and his chest burned.

He motioned back the way they had come, and Stacey started out of the plantation. From the fringe, you could see their double tracks leading across the high field towards the road, and the line of trees that shielded the lay-by. She paused to look, and Packer swung the branch, the one she had swung at him, wielding it two-handed like a broadsword, leaning back slightly from the tight arc it made, bringing it round hard and fast and against the side of her head with a fierce, plosive crack.

Stacey's head went over and back, like a puppet on a stiff spring, and she dropped instantly. Packer pulled her back into the trees and hit her again, standing back to measure the blow, then he lifted her and carried her further in among the trees. After walking with his burden for fifty yards, he found a steep declivity in the ground, a natural dell, where snow had drifted. He dumped Stacey, then turned her over to check her vital signs. Her pulse fluttered under his fingers like a moth's wings when you hold it cupped in your hands. Her breathing was noisy and troubled.

He was still carrying the branch in his free hand. He hit her again with it, four times, five, six, until he knew from the lack of resistance, from the spongy feel of things, that her head had caved in. He flicked through her pockets and took anything that told who she was, then stripped her of her clothes and made a bundle of them, tying the arms of her coat round to make it secure.

Stacey's head was a smashed gourd, blood and brain and matted hair. Her body was pale and perfect, white on white, blue-tinged where the flesh threw shadows: the loll of a breast, the crook of a knee.

Packer tossed the branch down into the dell and rolled Stacey after it. She went into a drift three feet deep, though still just visible – a hip jutting, a hand thrown back – and he used the branch to shovel down onto her the blood-soaked snow where her head had lain. Then he swept in as much clean snow as he could from the lip of the dell and turned on his heel, carrying the bundle of Stacey's clothes.

Before he released Kate from the boot, he shoved the bundle under the rear of the car. Kate looked up at him, her face pinched and blue, her arm raised by the open hinge as if she were applying to ask a question.

The question was: Where's Stacey?

Packer installed her in the car, cuffing her to the seat stanchion, went back and threw the bundle of clothing into the boot, slammed the lid, and got into the driving seat.

'Where's Stacey?' Kate asked.

'Good question.' Packer started the engine, turned the fan full on, and waited for the ice to melt from the windscreen. 'She's gone. So are we.'

'Gone?' There was fear in Kate's voice.

'Yeah, *gone*,' Packer said. 'Gone – as in, I couldn't catch the bitch.' He looked at Kate's face and laughed. 'Thinking bad thoughts, Kate,' he said. Then, 'Did you hear a gunshot?'

'No.'

'No, me neither.' He shrugged. 'She's gone. Which is why we have to get the fuck away from here.'

'She'll tell people. She'll tell the police.'

'You're right, she will.'

'Let me go,' Kate advised. 'Why not just put me out here? Things have gone far enough.'

Packer laughed. He seemed to find the expression funny. 'Far enough,' he said, 'yeah, good, hey, that's English, you know what I mean? Things have gone far enough is really *English*. Americans don't really think that way. We think things can never go far enough. Too far isn't far enough. That's American, yeah? That's the American way of life for you; that sums it up. Too far, *much* too far, further than anyone can ever go – that's just about halfway there if you're an American.'

'What do you want? What are you going to do?'

'With you? Because that's what you mean, isn't it, Kate? What am I going to do with *you*.' The ice had melted; Packer swung the car back onto the road, a funnel of flakes coming at them out of nowhere. 'Well, I'll tell you. You're a trade. You're a means to an end, etcetera. You're bait.'

The light in the plantation was blue; deeper blue where the trees threw snow-light shadows. The sound of snow on the wind only served to make the silence more profound. Big flakes fell between the boles of the trees, filling the wood, filling the dell where

Stacey lay, naked and blue-white, blood from her wound seeping through the frozen fall, dark red underneath, fading to pink as the snow grew thicker, soon to be unblemished white.

She was almost covered, almost gone; the jut of a hip where one leg lay across the other, the curve of a breast, one ear, a lock of hair stained red. Her hand, flung back, was stiff, now, fingers brittle. It was like a marker, pointing out the direction Packer and Kate had taken.

Corso waited for the bad news, since that was all it could be. He sat with his phone and his gun, his taped knife and his booby-trap drink, like a magician whose audience has failed to arrive.

He thought about the plane he could be on: the drink, the inflight movie, the air miles racking up between him and this job he'd screwed up. There was Packer, though. There was Larry Packer. Packer was one factor that kept him off the plane, because you can't spend your life with a chill at your back. The other factor was Kate. He knew it, but he didn't want to think about it.

He was staying for Kate and for the bad news.

Twenty-six

Packer drove through the city towards the river. Not Susan's place. Even if he could have persuaded Susan to take off, spend the night with a friend, this was something that had to be flawless, had to be clean. Kate Randall's suicide. And, if necessary, Robert Corso's disappearance. Killing Corso was on Packer's mind, though he'd sooner avoid it. Better to pay him off and get him out of the country. It's not easy to kill people, and it's not easy to keep death a secret. But Packer knew what Corso knew – that he was staying for Kate. And like Kate, Corso had become a loose end; a loose mouth.

Packer was putting together a plan, ways and means, a method for coming out clean. He had Kate, Stacey was no longer a complication, but Corso was still a problem. There was no way of knowing exactly how good Corso was, but he could guess: he'd hired the sonofabitch.

Kate was going to commit suicide – remorse and guilt were already written into the plan. What he needed were place and time. Place and time. And, in the meantime, somewhere to go; somewhere to think.

Not Susan's place, no. But he could use one of Wideworld's company apartments. When no VIP was in town, the two apartments lay empty. The nearest was in a skinny tower close to Chelsea Harbour, and he headed for that.

Going there was a risk, but he knew he could take it. He felt good about things, he felt *up*. Stacey's death was still close to him, like something he owned. He'd felt it before when someone had gone down, like you were hot, like you knew you could expect a run of luck.

The old days . . .

302

As they drove towards the ramp, Packer said, 'We're going to wait until there's no one else in the car park, then we're going to walk over to the elevator. If other people are walking through, we stay in the car. If you do anything to draw attention to yourself while we're waiting in the car, I'll have to shoot you and make the best of it, okay? Probably have to shoot the other person, too. Same thing if we're on our way to the elevator and someone steps out of it, or drives in to park, etcetera. Don't want to, but I'll have to. You got that?'

Kate nodded. Even so, she was looking – for people, for a chance. The car park was deserted. Packer uncuffed her, then walked her to the lift and pressed the call button. Kate watched the green numerals counting down, and tensed herself for the moment when the doors would part and four men step out, each carrying an automatic weapon, each saying, 'You're safe now, come with us.' When the light hit 'B' and the doors slid back, her nerves were so ragged that she almost screamed. The lift was empty.

Packer nudged her into the lift and pressed for the penthouse. After two storeys, the lift came out into twilight, a glassine bullet travelling up the side of the tower, over the rooftops, over the river, flurries of snow chasing its sides as it pushed through its own slipstream.

Three people got in at seven and out at nine. One person, a woman in a green coat, got in at nine and out at fifteen. The three glanced at Kate and Packer, then picked up their conversation. Packer had an arm round Kate under her coat; the gun was hard in her back, low on the spine and angled up. She could feel the bruise spreading.

The woman smiled at Kate, almost, it seemed, a smile of recognition. *Do I know you from somewhere?*

She thought that Kate might not be well, the way her husband was supporting her, the stretched look on her face. She turned towards the door and saw the green light under the penthouse button. As she stepped from the lift, she heard the woman gasp. It sounded as though she might be about to faint, and the woman in the green coat was glad she didn't have to travel with them further.

In fact, Kate had stepped forward to grasp the woman's hand, her sleeve, her shoulder, anything that would mean 'Help'. There are two kinds of fear: the rational and the instinctive. Kate had heard Packer say he would kill her and anyone she signalled to. Her rational mind believed him; her instinct said, Do something. Do *anything*.

Packer had grabbed her hair with his free hand and yanked her back, hard, choking off any sound but the raw gasp. As the lift doors closed, he said, You're a surprise. Now let me tell you something. She was looking the right way. If she'd turned, you'd both be dead. Okay, face me.'

Packer opened her coat, then yanked her sweater and T-shirt free, shoving the gun up between her breasts.

'Now you're facing me,' he said, 'and we're having a little moment, an intimate moment, in the elevator. Try shit again, and it'll be as intimate as two people can get. I'll be your executioner. That intimate.'

Kate was shivering; her head swam and, for a moment, Packer saw the whites of her eyes. He shook her and, when she seemed about to faint, jacked her up with the gun, scoring her breast with the barrel. 'Stay up,' he said. 'Stay up, you dumb bitch.'

She sat on the penthouse sofa and put her head between her legs. Packer watched until she straightened up and looked at him.

'I hope you die soon,' she said.

He laughed, then locked the outer door, letting Kate see him do it. 'You can try for a window if you feel like it,' he told her, 'but it's twenty storeys and sheer. So stick around, okay?' Even so, he took her with him when he went into the kitchen to make coffee. 'Two things we have to do. One, we make a call to Corso and ask him to meet us. That'll keep; tomorrow will be soon enough for that. Two, you write me something I need.'

'Write what?'

'A confession. You write that you killed Michael Lester, you told him goodbye, he got heavy, raped you, etcetera, a fight, the knife, blah-blah.'

Kate laughed. 'Why would I do that?'

'Oh, easy . . .' He spooned coffee into a cafetière and poured on water. 'Because I'll kill you if you don't. One way, the police get a confession, you go to jail, come out in, like, eight years. This is England, I keep reminding you of that. Kill someone in the US of A, and you fry. Or lethal injection. Whatever. You might spend twenty years on Death Row, but they kill you at the end of it. Most places, anyway. People like it. Eye for an eye, etcetera. Land of the free. Not so here. So, that's one option. The other is I definitely kill you.' He raised a hand like a man taking a vow. 'I'm under instructions.'

'Who gave them to you?'

'Now, I can't tell you that unless I kill you, and we haven't quite decided on that just yet, have we?'

Kate remembered the way he'd looked at Stacey just after he'd walked in on them at the squat.

Does she know anything at all?

No.

Nothing about Michael Lester and Wideworld Industries . . . any of that stuff?

Nothing.

She was looking at these pages, wasn't she?

She doesn't know what they mean.

Doesn't know who Leonard Naylor is?

No.

As if he'd read her mind, Packer said, 'Certain things – try not to know them. Even if you do know, don't tell me you know.' He sounded earnest: concerned, almost. It was a clever way of persuading Kate that she had a chance to live, and it worked.

Someone had stayed in the flat less than a week before, and there was food in the fridge. Packer treated himself to a Scotch and fetched the same for Kate. He said, 'You play the cello.'

'In another life.'

'What's that like?'

'Like?' The question was so odd that Kate laughed.

'Yeah, what's it like? Like to be able to do it, etcetera. I wondered what it would be like to be able to do that.'

'The cello?'

'Jesus, no, anything, to play anything, like piano or, Jesus Christ, who knows? – anything. What's it like?'

'I don't know,' Kate said.

'You gotta know. You do it.'

'It's been so long since I didn't know how to play that I've forgotten what that's like. So I can't really tell what it's like to be able to do it, because I've forgotten the opposite. Suppose I asked you what it's like to be able to walk.'

Packer shook his head. 'Jesus, listen, I wish I hadn't asked. Just write. Write the note.'

Kate had the paper in front of her. She asked, 'What do you want me to say?'

Packer looked at her in amazement. 'You're asking me? Hell, I don't know. You expect me to know? Write whatever they need to hear.'

'Whatever *you* need to hear.'

'That too. You're not stupid. Pretend it's true. What do you want to eat?'

She looked at him, her face blank. 'To eat?'

'Sure,' he shrugged. 'I'm hungry. Aren't you hungry? There's stuff in the fridge – eggs, etcetera. Tell me what you like. I'll fix you something.'

Talking of playing made her want to hear music, though the thought disturbed her; as if she were inventing a last wish.

She turned on the radio and found the Fauré Requiem, Pie Jesu, and the pure note of the treble voice cut like a blade.

Cut to the bone.

He made cheese omelettes and a salad. He constructed the omelettes with a brisk skill, folding them at the right time, and taking them from the pan still moist. Kate felt a skitter of near-hysterical laughter take her. When he turned to the sound, she laughed louder.

'You're making omelettes,' she said.

'Isn't that what you want?'

'Oh, yes,' she said. 'Thank you kindly. Omelettes would be perfectly wonderful.'

He poured her another Scotch and went back to his cooking.

They ate in the kitchen sitting at high stools. Kate wondered whether doing this had in some way altered things. As if this normalcy, this cooking of omelettes, Fauré on the radio, could somehow change the balance of events, as if the extreme and the banal couldn't exist side by side. As if some magic of transformation would push domesticity in, push horror out. Then she thought of the last meal of the condemned. She thought of music in Auschwitz.

Packer pushed his plate aside and found the paper and a pen. 'Just say you killed the sonofabitch.'

Kate handed him the finished note and walked towards the lights of the city, the river, the lights of boats. The southern wall of the penthouse was glass from ceiling to floor. She stretched out her arms and leaned against the wall, a bird in flight, held up by the wind and the flurries of new snow.

Packer was leafing through the box file. He was amused by Naylor's anger, by the way the man had taken notes from Green bulletins, had listed accounts of government cover-ups, as if that brand of mendacity were new-minted, and the way he talked about Wideworld's OP development programmes as if they'd been fronted by two other guys.

You, Naylor. You were the man in the white coat. No one but you. And things were just fine, weren't they, while the salary was coming in, the bonuses, and you felt okay? While you were feeling good, feeling healthy? Things are different when you've sniffed a few ounces of something with a long name and a bad rep. Things are different when you're fucked-up.

307

"Government bodies have consistently denied that inhalation is a potent route of exposure to OP poisoning . . ."

Well, they would. I live inside a fog; I walk round in a fog. It takes me hours to write these notes. I forget everything. There was a piece of music playing, a song I knew but I couldn't remember. I still can't.

"Subtle changes to the nervous system may be associated with OPs. Research reports have suggested that exposure produces depression, a major risk factor in suicide."

Which is why, no doubt, I think about it every day – about killing myself. And would, if it were just me, and no Amy, no Marianne. I think about how – jump from a high place, hose pipe from the exhaust into the car, pills and booze; I invent little scenarios; I see myself being found, with these notes, this journal, whatever it is, lying beside me. And then I realise that I've done it. I've already done it. I'm on the way.

Every year: three million acute cases of pesticide poisoning. Each year, twenty thousand unintentional deaths. And here's another. Just give it time.

I fell over today; just fell over. Didn't trip or faint or suffer a collapse. Just fell over. I stayed down because I couldn't see for ten seconds. Blind for ten seconds.

I'll publish these notes. There's a guy called Michael Lester who's got my name from somewhere. A journalist.

Kate was at the window-wall, arms raised, watching a plane go over. You could see the cabin lights; free souls, all with futures to look forward to.

Gone to the wall, she thought. The weakest goes to the wall.

Packer came up behind her; she saw his reflection tangling with spires and the lights of cranes. He looked over her shoulder. His breath was a soft lick on her cheek. 'What's out there?' he asked.

'The cities of the plain.'

'Say what?'

'It was a joke.'

'I didn't get it.'

'It's not important.'

'Okay, sure, whatever.' He touched her hair and a charge of fear started in her gut and flooded her head, making her stagger slightly. She lifted her hands to steady herself and saw his grin in the glass.

'Suppose you could jump from here,' he said, 'and make it to the ground. Like a bird, etcetera. Like the wind was underneath you, and you put your arms out, and just *did* it.'

'Suppose I did,' Kate asked, 'what would you give me?'

'Give you?' He laughed. '*Give* you? Hell, I'd give you a head start, that's for sure.'

She drank more of the whisky, carrying the glass round the room with her, pacing like a caged cat, always returning to the window-wall and its view of the great leap.

She said, 'You killed Michael.'

'No, that wasn't me.'

'You killed him because of Neophos X-9. Neophos X-9 killed Leonard Naylor.' A sudden thought struck her. 'And you killed Tim Farnol.'

'Not me,' Packer told her.

'You — someone — broke into Michael's cottage and wiped his computer and killed him. Was it you? It was you.'

'No,' Packer said, and he wagged a finger at her. 'You're wrong.'

'I was there,' she said, as if a sense of outrage had suddenly returned to her. 'I was there when he died.'

'I heard that,' Packer said.

'I was there when he died, you *bastard*!'

Packer smiled. 'Sure you were. In fact, there are people who believe you killed him: isn't that right?'

Kate turned from the window and threw her glass all in one motion. Packer had seen it coming: the lines of tension in her body, the little tics in her arms that were energy arrested. He moved sideways slightly in his chair and the glass hit the carpet behind him.

Kate beat on the glass wall like a trapped bird. She was crying and shouting and beating and Packer watched her, his eyes bright.

'*I was there, I held him, he died as I held him, you bastard, I was there when you killed him!*'

Packer said, 'No, you've got the wrong guy.'

But he could picture the scene: the cottage, the kitchen where the knives were kept, the living room, where Lester died, blood all over the place, all over Lester, all over Kate. Blood all over Kate.

He smiled and filled Kate's glass for her and walked to the window-wall. 'Not me,' he said, 'you've got that wrong.' He handed her the glass like a parent handing a sick child its medicine.

Now he knew where it would be. Now he knew where she would die. A place perfectly suited to Kate-the-murderer. A place of guilt; a place of recrimination.

Michael Lester's cottage.

He took her to the bedroom and showed her that the window was locked. The window in the bathroom was locked, too. Then he locked the bedroom door, himself on the outside. His mind was on getting the job done. One day was all it would take. After that, he'd give Susan a call. Then he'd go home: Beth, the kids, that brand of shit.

One day. A day's fieldwork. Clean things up. Make things clean for himself. Make them clean for Beverley Ho.

Corso was asleep, facing the door. His sleep was so light that a change in the wind woke him.

He tried Kate's phone and got the pager.

Kate went into the bathroom. It was stark: chrome and glass, frosted hexagonal shower stall, frosted glass shelving, frosted glass tiles with chrome beading, a wall-length mirror in a chrome surround. She took a shower, hot water in a frosted landscape. As she dried herself, she examined the long, transverse friction burn on her breast where the gun barrel had travelled. She ran water at the washbasin, and cooled the place, then soaked a washcloth and held it there.

She went back to the bed and sat cross-legged to watch the continuing fall of snow, endless, seeming to drop from the lowermost layer of the city's orange-pink sodium glow. It was a little after three a.m.

I've forgotten who I am. Who you are.

Kate Randall.

I feel as if I've been in a war. Displaced person. Displaced personality. I feel as if all the people I'd ever loved are dead. What does he want, this guy?

You to confess. It's what Webb wanted, too. It's what everyone wants.

Fuck them.

Yes, fuck them.

It's Wideworld, am I right?

Sounds right to me.

Can they do this kind of thing? A *company*? A *business*?

Pretend Michael's here. Ask him what he thinks.

I've written him his confession. Why is he waiting? What for?

Robert Corso; that's what he said . . .

But why?

You guess.

The woman in the green coat had wondered whether she knew Kate from somewhere, and when she thought about it, much later, wondered if she might be the woman whose face had been on TV, the woman who had killed her lover, the woman who was famous for that, and for playing the cello. It seemed unlikely; it also seemed possible.

She wasn't sure, and she decided to sleep on it.

Owls were hunting below the fir plantation, flying low over the snowfield, their cries cutting rips in the cold air. Among the trees, there was silence and darkness.

Stacey lay beneath a sheet of snow, pure white, her white flesh hard as iron, iron filigrees of frost etched across the whites of her eyes.

Twenty-seven

When Kate woke, the snow had stopped. The light in the room was like knives. She went into the bathroom and lowered herself onto the seat. Packer spoke from directly behind her, and Kate gasped, then swivelled to find the voice. She was staring at the wall. The voice was loud, but a little blurred. Kate looked round and saw a glass tumbler in a metal hoop above the sink. She put it up against the wall, her ear to the base, and Packer's voice cascaded down from the rim.

'. . . listen, Corso, she's with me. I have her. Now all I want you to do is your job. Understand? Just to do your job. You took on a job of work. I want it finished.' A pause, then: 'Right: that's where we'll be. And I want to see you there. Time to end this. Listen — pack, okay? Pack your things, etcetera. Go straight to the airport. After you've finished the job. After you've tidied up.'

He switched off the phone. He was trying to calculate the odds on Corso believing him — about finishing the job; about packing; about going home. He didn't think they were very high. He had decided it would be best to shoot Corso pretty much on sight.

One night at the penthouse was enough. Maybe Beverley Ho had taken a phone call: visitors on the next plane. Maybe someone would be in soon to get the place ready. Maybe Beverley used the place herself on those late-meeting nights; maybe she arrived some nights with champagne and a stud hung like an ox.

Keep moving. Wait for dark. That was the instruction he'd given Corso. *After dark.*

Kate stood over the washbasin, her hands braced on either side. She spat a string of saliva down and wiped her mouth with her hand.

I was right about him.

Yes, you were.

I was right not to trust him.

Yes, you were.

Finish the job: what do you think that means?

We know what that means.

Why didn't he kill me when he had the chance?

Trying to find out things, remember? You kept some stuff back from the disk. He suspected that.

That's why he taped me. I was right.

Yes, you were.

They needed to know how much I knew. Now they know everything. They've even got Naylor's file.

Just a minute . . . He had Naylor's file when he dropped you at the squat. He knew everything then. But he let you out; and he tried to lose this guy: lose the black Lexus. There's something in that.

Yes? So ask yourself a question. How else did this . . . Packer . . . how did he know where to find me?

Packer unlocked her door and put his head into the room. 'Time to go,' he said.

Kate got off the bed. She tried not to meet his eye, as children will when there's something you shouldn't know. Packer went through to the bathroom. On the mirror, written in soap, was Kate's name.

He smiled the smile of the indulgent parent. 'Take it off,' he said.

She soaked the washcloth and wiped the mirror. Packer nodded, still smiling, and waved her out of the room.

Webb took the shout himself. The woman in the green coat told Webb what she thought she might have seen and when. Webb didn't bother to ask her why she'd delayed, because he already knew the answer; it was a 'maybe'; and since the maybe sightings were listed at just a few short of a thousand, he sighed and told John Adams to make the call.

Adams checked the address and came back to tell Webb that the penthouse was registered to Wideworld Industries.

'Do we know them?' Webb asked.

'Big company: here, the States, all over. They're a chemicals manufacturer among other things.' He gave Webb a phone number. 'Greens don't like them.'

'Sorry?' Webb looked at the phone number, then back at Adams.

'Not popular with Green activists.' Adams waited, then he said, 'People like Michael Lester.'

Webb looked as if it were the last piece of information he wanted to get, apart from 'I'm afraid the tests have returned positive'.

'Go down there,' he said, 'and I'll make the phone call.' Before Adams had left the room, he added: 'It's a coincidence.'

'I know,' Adams said.

'It's nothing.'

'Sure,' Adams said, 'I know that.'

Beverley Ho had removed her earring to take the call: pearl and silver; she nudged it round the desk as she talked.

'It's a company apartment. We often have people staying there.'

'Who stayed there last night?' Webb asked.

'I'd have to check that. I'm sorry.'

'You don't know?'

'Mr Webb, I'm the managing director of this company; I don't handle the catering. I'll check and get back to you. Now, here's a question for you. Why do you want to know these things?'

'We had a report of someone we'd like to interview being seen there.'

'In the apartment?'

'On the way to the apartment.'

'On the way?'

'In the lift.'

'Sorry. Did you say in the lift?'

'The person who saw this person said that the penthouse button had been pressed. The penthouse is registered to Wideworld Ind –'

Beverley's voice was both waspish and weary. 'Someone was seen in an elevator? Someone who could have gotten off anywhere – any floor – and because the penthouse button had been pressed you're asking me for confidential company information about who might have been a guest with us last evening?'

'This is a police investigation. Company information isn't confidential.'

'It is with this company. Who's the person in question? The one you want to interview?'

'I can't tell you that.'

'You'd classify that information as confidential, would you?'

'I'd like to know who, if anyone, was staying in that flat last night.'

'Fine. I'm happy to co-operate. When I find a moment, I'll have my secretary ask whoever it is makes arrangements for company accommodation, and when she has time, she'll give you a call and let you know what, if anything, she managed to discover.'

Beverley hit the cut-off button on her phone, waited a beat or two, then freed it and dialled a number. When Jimmy Rose answered, she asked, 'Do we have anyone in from out of town at present?'

'No, Beverley.'

'The penthouse at Brewer's Wharf wasn't in use last night?'

'Shouldn't have been, no.'

'Who has keys?'

'Here in London – you do, I do, personnel does; from New York –'

'No. Here.'

'Like I say.'

'Larry Packer?'

'Sure, yes, Larry has keys.'

'Where is he?'

'Gone fishin'?'

'Where?' Beverley asked; and Rose heard the ice in her voice. 'There's a problem?'

'I'm not sure, Jimmy. Where is he?'

'I'll call Beth.' Rose paused. 'Beverley, is there something I ought to know?'

'I'll tell you,' she said, 'when I know myself.'

Adams spoke to the woman in the green coat. She looked at pictures of Kate and said, 'Yes, I think so. I'm pretty sure. I only saw her for a moment. It's so difficult, isn't it?'

Along with two other officers, he covered the flats in the block and talked to people where he could find them in. It didn't come to much. All in all, Webb might have been inclined to add it to the list of maybes, but the connection between Michael Lester and Wideworld, though slight, was the only connection he'd had in a long time. In addition to that, Beverley Ho had annoyed him. He called her again, and was told she was taking a meeting.

'Tell her I need to speak to her.'

'I'll tell her as soon as the meeting ends.'

'Tell her now.'

'I can't do that, I'm afraid.'

'Really? Can you get down to my office, or shall I come up there to arrest you?' Webb asked.

Beverley Ho was cautious. She was beginning to think of Webb as a dangerous person. She said, 'I imagine from what you're saying that there's been some sort of development.'

'The development is that I've applied for a judge's warrant to search the premises at Brewer's Wharf. You can either wait until that warrant is issued – about half an hour from now, I'd guess – or you can agree to co-operate. If you co-operate, you can be present when we make the search. Also we won't take the door down with a kanga hammer.'

Beverley Ho made a call of her own. She said, 'I need a lawyer and a press officer standing by in this office until further notice.' Then she asked for her car to be sent round.

A day or so after Michael's death, Kate had talked to George Webb.

Now Webb stood behind a forensic officer – white overalls and white sterile beret – as the man lifted a set of prints from the glass wall-window at the penthouse. It was one of several sets.

'How long for the match?' Webb asked him.

'Difficult to say, boss.'

'How long if I shout?'

'Depends on what's happening at the lab.'

Webb hissed through his teeth. 'Hear that?' He was talking to John Adams, but he turned to Beverley Ho, who was sitting in an area of the apartment designated 'clean' by the men in white. 'How often do people say "maybe" to you?' he asked.

'Never.'

'I thought so.'

A man in white walked through from one of the bedrooms and put his mouth close to Webb's ear. Webb smiled, then he followed the man out of the room. A moment later, he returned and beckoned to Beverley Ho.

The mirror in the bathroom sparkled. The frosted glass tiles and the chrome surround sparkled. Frost and white light; it was like bringing the outside inside. Beverley wondered what it was that had made Webb so pleased. Then she saw that the door of the hexagonal frosted glass shower was open. She took the direction of his gaze and saw, low on the glass, at about ankle height, the merest trace of something: a smudge, an irregular tidemark.

The forensic man was pleased with himself, too. He reached in to the shower and turned on the jet, switching it to hot, then closed the door. George Webb and Beverley Ho and the man in white stood and watched as steam filled the shower cabinet and the smudge grew more defined, sharper-edged, its zigs and zags finally coming clear. A finger-trace spelling a name. Kate Randall.

John Adams was standing in the doorway. Webb said, 'You needn't hurry for that fingerprint match.' Then: 'Why would she do that? Write her name in the steam down low and out of sight?'

'She wasn't here from choice,' Adams said.

'You're right.' He turned to Beverley Ho. 'He was in his forties, tall, heavy, dark hair worn short and off his face. The woman who saw them together said he looked like a boxer, which might mean he had a busted –'

'His name's Larry Packer,' Beverley said. 'Laurence Packer. He's our head of security.' She shook her head like someone emerging from water. 'Who in hell is Kate Randall?'

Beth Packer asked the same question. When she got her answer, she laughed. 'You're telling me that Larry is harbouring a fugitive? Why? What for?'

'Do you know where he might be?' Webb asked.

'On business, he told me. He's often away on business. Who knows? Maybe sometimes it *is* business.'

'And when it's not business?'

'Girl or girls.'

'You have their names?'

'Please . . .'

'He didn't say where?'

'He said out of town.'

'Can we look around?' Webb asked.

'Sure. There isn't anything to find.'

'How can you be sure?'

Beth smiled. 'I check on a regular basis. Not that I care, but I like to have the drop on him.'

Adams started the search, along with Nairn and Carol Tanner and a couple of the forensic team.

Webb said, 'We need to speak to him. It's important.'

'I know the feeling,' Beth said, 'or I used to. But I really don't know where he is.'

'Did he ever talk to you about his work?'

Beth was making coffee. She laughed, sending a little gout of granules over the work surface. 'He didn't talk to me about the weather.' As she poured water onto the coffee, she asked, 'What's he done?'

'We're not sure,' Webb told her. 'We don't know for sure that he's done anything.'

'What's your job?' Beth asked.

'Job?' Webb looked at her, puzzled.

'I don't know what you call it here — felony, grand larceny, homicide, vice.'

'Homicide would be right.'

Beth looked at him, her eyes wide.

Beverley Ho had a call in to a New York number. She was talking to a man called Steve Letterman. Ho worked for Letterman, but Letterman worked for someone else in turn. It was difficult to figure out if there was someone who worked for no one. Someone who received reports, but never wrote any.

Beverley said, 'We have a situation here, Steve, but I'm not sure I know just what it is.'

'Who does know?'

'We believe Larry Packer knows.'

'So let me talk to Packer.'

'That's the problem. He's not here. The police want to talk to him.' She explained as much as she knew about Kate Randall: what George Webb had told her.

'How is the company implicated here, Beverley?'

'It's tough to say. We think it has to be Neophos X-9.'

Letterman said, 'We have a clean bill of health on that.'

'Sure,' Beverley said. 'Is there someone we can talk to?'

'Who?'

'You know what I mean, Steve. People. People who help us out.'

'It's that bad?'

'I don't know. I can't tell you. I know about X-9.'

'We're clean on that, Beverley. We had clearance in the Senate, clearance with the FAA, clearance with the EC – we had clearance, that's all there is to say. Okay, I'll talk to a few people, a few friends, but there's nothing in the closet with this. Whatever Packer did, he did without company authorisation. As of now, he no longer works for Wideworld. Make that known.'

'There's a killing involved somewhere. A man was killed. A journalist.'

'Get us clear of this, Beverley. Clear and free. Packer's a maverick – sell them that. Sell it to anyone who wants to put Packer and Wideworld together. Get to his files –'

'That's done, Steve.'

'Anything there?'

'Not a thing.'

'Talk to the wife?'

'She doesn't know where he is.'

'That right? Good. Eccentric behaviour. Start talking breakdown as well as maverick. Maverick and breakdown, okay? Stress. What do his expenses currently run at?'

'Company expenses? Ball park? Thousand dollars a month?'

'Okay. I'll get some of our people on it. Rack up twice that on the computer, three times. Start talking misappropriation. Maverick, breakdown, misappropriation. We're getting somewhere, now.'

'Okay, Steve. Listen, I'm sorry I had to wake you.'

'Wake me? Jesus, Beverley, it's six a.m. Do you sleep past six a.m.?'

'Is it?' she asked. 'I must've lost track.'

'Don't do that, Beverley,' Letterman said. 'Don't lose track.'

He hung up. Beverley put the phone down. 'Packer,' she said, 'you bastard, you sonofabitch, may you get cancer.'

Packer had driven across the city, heading east until he found the warren of streets around Limehouse. He'd worried a little about Kate being recognised, or deciding to do something to attract attention. He'd told her, carefully, that she shouldn't make that mistake, but he remembered the woman in the green coat, and Kate moving forward, hand outstretched. Because of his worries, Kate was riding in the boot, her wrist cuffed to the hinge, a kitchen towel wadded into her mouth and held with scotch tape. That only left him with the problem of getting her out unseen. Which, he reflected, wouldn't be a problem at all.

He drove down towards the river, turned into a street that was given over to small workshops, then past a pumping station that no longer functioned: its windows long since smashed, its roof timbers rotten. Finally, he took an asphalt track that ran through a wasteland of cinder, and into a warehouse that fronted the river. Thirty years before, barges had landed iron ingots there; now it served as a boathouse. There were two boats up on chocks and three more outside, moored to a short jetty.

He took a big plastic laundry bag from the car: he'd found it in the penthouse utility room, and had loaded it with food and drink from the fridge. He opened the boot and unshackled Kate, then stripped off the tape. Kate unravelled the towel and bent over, hauling breath into her lungs. She said, 'I couldn't breathe, you bastard.'

'Yes you could,' he said. 'You did.'

They walked down the jetty towards the boats. They were tasteless and expensive craft, tricked out in brass and braided cord, and fitted with a high wheelhouse where someone with a full glass and a peaked cap could trade jokes with the girls in bikinis, ass up on the foredeck.

Kate looked round. There were warehouses on the far bank, their sooty brick walls abutting the water, but no one was working them; they looked silent and dead. The sky and the water were the same colour, sulphurous and dull. The tide was low, and gulls patrolled the water's edge, or circled and turned overhead, their cries like ripped tin.

Packer went aboard one of the boats, pulling Kate with him, and knocked the cabin lock off with the butt of his gun. He sent Kate ahead down the stairs. The cabin smelled of bilge and stale smoke.

'A guy called Jimmy Rose owns this. Chugs up and down at weekends.'

'Why are we here?' Kate asked.

Packer stripped the wrapper off a carton of guacamole dip and opened a box of tortilla chips. He uncapped the Scotch and found a couple of glasses. 'Breakfast,' he announced. 'We didn't eat yet.'

Kate looked upriver. The clouds had lifted a little and the light hardened, putting a sheen on the water that made it appear thick and scaly. She took a drink, and the whisky burned. Packer was opening and closing cupboards like a new tenant. He took out some magazines, a torch, distress flares, canned food, and a length of rope. He tossed the magazines to Kate and shrugged. 'Pass the time?' Then threw the flares and the cans back. He kept the torch and the rope. Kate thought he was going to tie her up again, but he didn't do that. He sat down and took a fistful of chips.

'Why?' he asked, as if he'd only just heard her question. 'Well, Kate, we're waiting for the night.'

Joanna was working on student papers at home when Webb rang her door bell. She stood on the step, the door part-open, as if expecting bad news.

Webb said, 'If there's any way of talking to her, you have to try.'

Joanna took him through to the kitchen. She asked, 'What's happened?'

'We don't know, not really. Things have changed a little.' He told her how.

'Which means what?' Joanna asked. She was sitting on a stool, one arm wrapped around her midriff like someone nursing a wound. She was trying not to think good thoughts in case that was a wasteful thing to do.

'I don't know,' Webb told her. 'I can't say anything, except things clearly aren't what they seemed.'

'No. But what are they?'

'It's worth a try, isn't it? Talking to her . . .'

'Is she at risk? This man . . .?'

'It's possible.'

'Likely?'

'Likely.'

'If she answers, what do I say?'

'I don't know,' Webb said, 'whether it's a good idea or not. It's something to try. Wait for her to speak: take your lead from her.'

In order to make the call, Joanna had to admit that she knew the number. She dragged the phone over and dialled. There was a pick-up, but no one spoke. She said, 'Kate? Kate, it's Joanna.'

Webb made a sign that said: Hang up and redial. She did, and the same silence was on the line: not the silence of a missed connection, but of someone listening. Webb held out a hand and took the phone from her. He listened hard for any ambient sound that might give a lead, but there was only pause: the sound of withheld speech.

What happens, he thought, if I say: 'Packer? Packer, is that you? Laurence Packer?' Would he panic, make a mistake, want to talk? Would he see there was no way out now? Would he want to come in, maybe bringing Randall with him? Would he want to cut a deal? Would he tell me things to make everything clear, make everything simple?

It was on the tip of his tongue.

Kate's death was on the tip of his tongue, but he hung up.

Joanna said, 'Was it him? Packer?'

'Must have been.'

'What will you do?'

Webb said, 'Try and get to him via his company, his wife, friends who might have a lead on him, try familiar haunts, maybe hope to get a sighting of them, check airports and so on, or it might be better to let him make the first move.' In truth, Webb didn't know what he would do. 'If he intended to harm your sister,' he said, 'I think he would have already done that.'

He thought: *But Packer doesn't know we know. He thinks he's in the clear. Whatever he's got planned – he thinks he's going back to the office afterwards, back to his day-to-day, back to the wife who's got the drop on him.*

Packer said, 'Who's Joanna?'

'My sister.'

'What does she know?'

Kate was sitting on a banquette by the wrap-round glass of the cabin; Packer sat on the other side, nearer the hatchway. 'She knows I'm in trouble.'

'Yeah ...' Packer took a slug of whisky and a mouthful of guacamole. 'How will she like having a convict in the family?'

'You think I won't deny the confession?' Kate asked. 'You think I won't tell them about you?'

There was a moment's pause. Packer kept up his little double-handed routine: eat, sip; eat, sip. Kate watched a couple of gulls stalling and banking on the breeze. It was like the moment before an accident; the moment when you sense the tyres losing contact, or feel your balance slip.

And then the knowledge bore in on Kate: the sudden under-standing; and she leapt in her seat as if she'd been stung. Of course he would never let that happen. Of course he would never expect the confession to be enough.

Of course he was going to kill her.

She thought about Stacey, disappearing through the snowfall. Disappearing.

Packer saw Kate give that sudden start – escape scaled down to a gesture; he saw the darkness in her eye.

'Have a drink,' he said, 'have something to eat.' He tapped her arm as if in encouragement, and gave a laugh. 'Prison food – not that much to recommend it, so I hear.'

But he knew she was thinking about her own death.

He went out on deck, thumbed buttons on her phone and raised Corso.

'I just want to be sure that you're paying attention.'

'I'll be there,' Corso said, 'and I'll be on time.'

'That's good.'

'Why wait? There's a plane I could catch, leaves at six.'

'Time and place,' Packer said, 'time and place.'

'After dark.'

'That's right.'

'Where are you?'

'We're holed-up, having a little party, a drink, a guacamole dip. All very civilised.'

'She must be thrilled skinny.'

'Sure. Good company; sparkling conversation.'

'I could come to you,' Corso said. 'Why not?'

'I won't be calling you again,' Packer told him, and switched off. Then he tossed the phone overboard.

I'll need to be nimble with this, he thought. Fast on my feet. No one believes anyone.

George Webb sat on the lowlife side of Ian Grant's desk and waited for a response. Sunlight was filtering through the slats of a blind at Grant's back and making dust patterns visible in the air.

Grant was writing on a multicoloured noteblock, his hand steady and slow. Webb felt as if the moment were being played on a held breath. He wanted to slap Grant's pen out of his hand. Instead of which, he said: 'I need manpower. It's all there is: all I can count on. This guy Packer has a life: his office, his home, his friends. Too many places to go, too many people to see. Unless I get help.'

'You think a mistake was made, George, is that it?'

'If I find them, I'll know more.'

Grant ignored the implied criticism. 'You think there might be more to it than a simple crime of passion. But you're not sure. You think this guy's involvement – and you don't know what that is, do you? – but, anyway, his *apparent* involvement provides a link with Lester's reputation as a pain-in-the-ass journo. But you're not sure. You think that Kate Randall must be with him. But you're not sure. And if she is, it's not because she wants to be.'

'I certainly think that things have become less easy to –'

'But you're not sure,' Grant looked up from his writing, 'are you?'

'Yes, I am. I'm sure.'

'Oh . . .' Grant smiled and went back to making notes on the pad. 'I've got a figure in my head, George, for this investigation and it's a high figure. It seems particularly high when you consider that there was no positive result.' He pushed the pad aside. There was nothing on it but doodles, anyway. 'All right, George,' he said. 'Take what you want. Just remember: to you it's manpower; to me it's money.' As Webb was leaving, Grant added, 'And enough rope to –'

He left the rest unsaid, but tore the top page from the block and held up the doodle.

A hanged man.

Kate watched the afternoon sun sink along the river. A couple of times a strange fatigue had hit her, a sort of sick lassitude that weighed her down; but when she'd closed her eyes, dreams had swarmed in on her, dreams that made her shake and cry out.

Packer said, 'Sure. Get some sleep. Plenty of time.'

Kate laughed and looked away. 'Why not kill me now?' she asked. 'Isn't this a good place? It looks like a good place to me.'

'Kill you?' Packer waved the idea away; waved with the gun. 'I wouldn't kill you. Not me.'

Twenty-eight

Corso had staked out a little patch of ground alongside the river. The patch was bordered by trees: five pollarded willows in a line. The river ran down to a bridge and the bridge was a way in to the park. It was where he had sat when he'd first seen Kate through his night glasses. Now he had those same glasses trained on the back of the house, and the dark windows.

It was deep dusk. A new fall of snow had begun, soft and slow and heavy. Packer had given him a time, but Corso had arrived long before that. He knew Packer knew he would do that. It was all bluff and double bluff now. He tried to figure out how Packer would want to play things and reasoned that the game couldn't begin until they were all together because Packer would want to kill him first.

That's one version, he thought. Kate draws me in. I'm his only real opposition. I have to die first. Kate's safe until I get there.

But there were other ways of thinking about it.

Why Michael Lester's cottage? Because Kate has to die there? Why? To prove she killed Lester. How? Suicide. In which case, my dead body on the floor isn't going to help the story. I have to be killed somewhere else. Which means he can kill Kate first.

Except . . . if I think that, if I think she might be dead, why would I walk in there? I'd have to know she's alive before taking that risk. I'd want proof: to talk to her, to see her. So she'll have to *be* alive.

Whatever he's devised depends on my being powerless from the start. Whoever's supposed to die first, he has to have me so I can't defend and I can't attack.

So that's just what'll happen. That's exactly what he'll see. What he'll *seem* to see: me with my pants down.

Bluff and double bluff.

Packer would have expected him to arrive early. He had. And to have staked the place out. He had. And he'd seen nothing, which Packer would also have intended. Next move? Go in first. Be there when they arrive. Was that bluff or counter-bluff? Corso couldn't decide; but he thought it must be what Packer intended, so that's what he did.

The park was empty, a sweep of white from river to road, a clean sheet. The snow bore the tracks of birds and small animals; it bore Corso's tracks as he walked the line of the willows to reach the backs of the cottages, then made a crouching run to Michael Lester's gate. The key was still in place under the patio stone. Corso unlocked the rear door and went in, leaving the door part-open.

The house was more than still: lifeless. It seemed you could smell the blood. He sat down in the dark with his back to the wall.

Kate woke to the knock and slap of wavelets against the hull. For a moment, she thought the boat was on the move, but it was Packer jogging her shoulder.

'Time to go.' He was holding the kitchen towel and the tape.

They emerged into snowfall, slipping a little on the jetty. The tide was at the full, and Kate knew it must be past midnight. Packer opened the boot and shrugged apologetically. Kate lay still while he cuffed her.

She could hear rhythms in the sound of the tyres and the jolt in the suspension. Like strings in the lower register.

That first attack in the Elgar, the bloody Elgar, why think of that for Christ's sake?

But there were tears standing in her eyes, because she knew the answer.

Think of anything. Think of anything but.

It was tough to breathe and the smell of petrol made her nauseous. *If I throw up with this in my mouth, I'm dead.* They hit a rough patch of road, and she put her bound hands under her head to

329

absorb the bounce. Doing that made her think of Michael, of cradling Michael's head, of the way it grew heavy as his eyes closed and his limbs slackened. She tried to dismiss the thought, but it held her. Michael wounded, running through the house; Michael crying out; Michael dying.

It was like a dream that she couldn't wake from. She went back to the moment at the airport and Annie keeling over holding her side. Then sitting in the jeep, deciding . . . deciding the rest of her life. His fury, the sharp pain in her face as he slapped her, their lovemaking, the dreadful loneliness of that . . .

Anything but.

. . . the way he ran from room to room, the sound of the knife as she withdrew it . . .

So that when Packer opened the boot and she stepped out into the deserted street and saw where she was, she almost fainted. As if Packer had read her mind. As if she had dreamed herself there.

They walked to the front door like dinner party guests, and Packer rang the bell. Except it was late to be arriving for dinner: a little after three a.m. He stood slightly behind Kate, one hand under her coat and firmly into the waistband of her jeans, the other holding the gun tight to the back of her head.

Corso opened the door. He looked past Kate to Packer, and said, 'Clever.'

'Back up,' Packer told him. 'Walk backwards until I tell you to stop.'

They went through the hall to the living room. The street lamp glow gave enough light to see by. Packer said, 'Wait,' and Corso stopped. Packer gave Kate a little shove, propelling her towards the sofa. 'Pick up one of those cushions,' he said. Then they continued, Corso backing off, Kate clutching the cushion, Packer steering with the gun, until they reached the kitchen.

When they were in and the door closed, Packer said, 'Bring a chair over here.' He was talking to Kate. She fetched a kitchen chair and placed it in front of him. 'Sit down,' he told her. Corso was on the other side of the room, hands in view. Kate sat. Packer put the gun to the back of her head, then reached into his pocket and removed the torch he'd taken from the boat. He crouched down so that the glow would be at floor level, then said, 'Pull the drapes.' He was talking to Corso.

As Corso cut out the view to the park, Packer crouched again, retrieved the torch and put it on the work surface to his left, angling it so that the beam hit Corso around the level of the belt-buckle, the same level as Kate's head, the same level as Packer's gun. As Packer had taken the torch out, the rope had come with it and fallen to the floor by Kate's foot. Packer gave her a little nudge with his gun hand. 'Pick it up,' he said.

She leaned down to get it, and reached to put it up on the work surface, alongside the torch. 'No,' he said, 'keep it. Hold on to it, Kate. You're going to need it.'

Now she knew what the rope was for.

'Okay,' Packer said, 'let's get organised here.' He pointed at Corso. 'Empty out.' He seemed good humoured, his voice soft and even. Corso reached into his pocket and took out his gun, holding it between finger and thumb. 'By the barrel,' Packer told him, 'and remove the clip.' Corso did that. 'Okay. Toss the gun to the right, the clip to the left.' Corso did that too. 'You're a damn fool,' Packer said. 'What a fool. You could have got clear. Okay, you screwed the job. But you could still have got clear. You could be on a plane now. What's she to you? I don't get it.'

'It's not her,' Corso said, 'it's you.'

'No, it's not.'

'Sure it is,' Corso said. 'I came for you, Larry.'

Packer laughed. 'Yeah? Well, you sure made life tough for yourself. Know what's going to happen here?'

'I can guess.'

'I'll bet you can,' Packer said. 'Kate, give me the rope, then hold the pillow up behind your head.' When she'd done that, he put a hand on her shoulder in order to get her attention. 'Now, I'm not going to shoot you,' he said, 'at least, I don't want to. But if he makes a move on me, I will. That's why you're holding the pillow up there. To deaden the sound.' He laughed. 'It might seem a little unfair to you that you should be holding it, but the fact is – what else can you do but obey me? It's odd, don't you think?'

He made a bowline with the rope, working easily, the gun still pointing at Corso, then he told Kate to lower the pillow and dropped the rope round her neck. To Corso, he said, 'You're good at this stuff, aren't you? Lynching, etcetera. How long does it take? A couple of minutes? Five?' Corso shrugged. 'Well . . .' Packer shrugged back, a comic echo. 'We'll just have to wait it out, won't we? Just have to hang around and see.' He didn't laugh at the joke. He was watching Corso, looking for a sign: anything that might spell sudden movement.

The rope prickled and scratched. Packer held it as a dog owner holds a leash. He said, 'Stand up, Kate.' He was looking round, while keeping Corso in his eyeline. Looking for somewhere to tie off the rope. Already, as his hand tightened, as he pulled, wanting her to stand, Kate felt the noose close: a foretaste of what her body weight would do. She gagged as the rope bit, a sharp pain under her thorax, pains shooting into her head; and the breath caught in her throat like a stone. In the same moment, Corso made a gesture towards his pocket. A half gesture. A hint.

Packer thrust Kate back into the chair and brought the gun up to point at Corso. 'Unload,' he said. 'Whatever it is. Make it slow. Onto the table.'

Corso reached in and removed the spare clips. Which made Packer think another gun was coming. He said, 'Real slow, finger and thumb only, let me see what it is before you put it down.'

The passport came next. Anticlimax. Then the knife Corso had taped to the back of his sofa. Packer watched it onto the table. Then came the pen.

Then came the Finger of God.

Packer was blind. The finger touched him, and he was blind. It was a laser pen that Corso had brought out, the pen he had so carefully checked along with the gun and the clips, the pen he always carried, holding it just as Packer had instructed, finger and thumb, the perfect operating grip, and the line of light had struck into Packer's eyes and scoured them to the whites. A red-white fire blazed in his vision, so close, so hot, that he could see nothing but the heart of light.

He fired on instinct, but Corso had already moved to scoop up the gun and the clip, going first left, then right. Packer turned to the sound, stepping back, trying to find a form in the inferno. He dragged Kate with him. Her hands went to the noose, trying to get her fingers between her throat and the rope, but it had already tightened too much for that. She felt her neck would crack, the cartilage and small bones uprooting as the rope dragged. The sound of the sea was in her ears.

Packer tried to get the gun back to Kate's head, wrenching on the rope, yelling at Corso to stay back. Corso stepped inside the man's reach and hit him hard behind the ear, using the side of his gun. Kate felt the pressure fall away. She dragged at the rope, but couldn't free it. The breath had stopped in her chest, balled there, killing her. Then Corso pulled the knot loose and she fell onto all fours, gagging, breathing so hard that her ribs hurt. It took her a while to realise that the hardness under her hand was Packer's gun. She stayed still for a while, then got to her knees, and turned to find Corso.

He was on his haunches alongside Packer, holding the cushion in one hand, the gun in the other. He said, 'Someone might have heard that. If so, they'll have called the cops. I'm not sure of the response time. Not long.'

Kate held Packer's gun, and looked at him. Then she pointed it. 'I know,' she said. 'I know what your job was.'

Corso's gun hand was low, elbow resting on his knee, the gun dangling. He said, 'Do you?'

She was holding the weapon like an amateur, and it shook slightly in her grip, but no one could have missed from that range. The muzzle was pointing at his chest: the broadest part of the target – she knew that much.

If you kill him, you'll be safe forever. Say Packer did it. Kill him, then just wait for the police to turn up. Kill him and you'll never have to worry about him again.

'Are you worried, Kate?' he asked. It was as if she had spoken aloud. She gave a little start and the gun wavered. 'What have you got to worry about?'

'I trusted you. I trusted you once. You made me trust you. I thought you were who you said you were.'

'You're here,' he said, 'aren't you? You're alive.'

He put the cushion down on the floor along with his weapon, then got up and walked towards her. She tracked him with Packer's gun, lifting it, panning with it, until he reached her and she would have to shoot or let him take it from her.

She decided to shoot, but nothing happened.

He stood close. The barrel was over his heart. She looked straight at him and decided to shoot, but nothing happened.

Her finger was so tight on the trigger that she couldn't release it. Instead, he folded her hand in his, and moved it aside, and carefully unwrapped the gun from her grip. He reached into his pocket and took out a set of keys.

'Go to the house,' he said. 'I left something there for you.' She took the keys, but didn't move.

She said, 'I trusted you.'

'Go,' he said. 'Please go.' He went back to Packer and waited by the man's side.

'What will you do?'

'You must go,' he told her. Then: 'Wipe it,' meaning Packer's gun.

There was a dish-towel hanging by the stove. Kate used it to wipe the grip of Packer's gun, then put the weapon down on the table. She was left holding the dish-towel, and looked at it stupidly. Michael's dish-towel. How could it still be there?

'Good,' Corso said. He picked up the cushion and the gun from the floor. 'Now go. Go through the park.'

Kate felt something rising in her, like a sneeze, and realised it was either tears or a scream. She put out a hand and held the edge of the table.

He said, 'Kate. For God's sake. I don't have much time,' and, for a moment, the gun in his hand seemed to waver between Packer and her.

'Why?' she asked: meaning Packer; Packer's death.

'He knows who I am.'

Kate went to the door that led from the kitchen to the patio, from the patio to the park in darkness. The park at three a.m.

She said, 'And who are you?'

It was white and cold and flawless. The snow still falling, covering the tracks of predators, covering her tracks as she walked away. There was a pain in her throat, hot and rough. She bent down to scoop up some snow, and bit a mouthful, letting the ice water trickle down over her tongue.

A sudden image came to her of Packer getting into the car, Stacey gone, the snow quickening, the landscape a cold blank.

'Did you hear a gunshot?'

'No.'

'Me neither.'

Twenty-nine

Corso said, 'I'll need time to find a plane. Or maybe I'll drive to the coast and cross to France, if the weather continues bad. If the planes aren't flying. I don't know. You'll figure how much time I need.'

He was looking straight at her. His face filled the screen.

Kate reached out. There was a bottle of Scotch on the table. It was a third empty, but she wasn't drunk.

'So what I'm asking is: give me whatever time you think I'll need. Destroy this cassette. Hand the other cassette over to the cops. I know you don't have to do that. It's what I'm asking you to do.' He smiled. 'See you, Kate.'

He had recorded onto the first few minutes of an old tape. Now, his face broke up, and the screen went to blue. Then . . .

. . . *what she least wanted to see: her body a pale blur, his also, as he covered her limbs, stealthily, Kate lifting her arms . . .*

She lifted the phone and called Joanna. She said, 'I'm okay. I'm fine. Don't worry about me. You don't have to worry any more.'

After that, she dialled triple-nine and gave George Webb's name.

Webb watched with her. They sat side by side on the sofa, sharing the whisky, like any married couple settling down to an evening with the stars.

Packer was in close-up. Getting drunk, but not drunk yet. Corso was just a voice.

'Listen, there's something I want to get straight. When your man —

your operative – killed Michael Lester, he wiped the computer, right?'

'*Wiped it clean.'*

'There was a call earlier. A car went to Lester's place: someone had heard noises. Packer was there. He was dead.' Webb had stopped the tape. He looked at Kate as if she might take up the story of Packer's death.

'I got away from him,' she said. 'I came here to look for Robert Corso.'

'And where is he?'

'Gone. Gone, apparently.'

'Is that Corso on the tape – talking to Packer?'

'Yes.'

'*What did you really hire me to do, Packer? Why are Wideworld paying me?'*

'*If you're asking what I think you're asking – has it come to hardball, etcetera – then the answer is definitely yes. I don't see any alternative now that she's got to Beverley Ho, etcetera.'*

'*You want her dead?'*

'*Has to be.'*

'That's him?' Webb asked. 'That's Corso talking?'

'Yes.'

'This is the only tape?'

'It's what I found when I got here.'

'And you think that was his job? That he was hired to kill you?'

'He told me he was a journalist. A journo after a story.'

'And you trusted him?'

'Well,' Kate said, 'I'm here. I'm alive . . .'

Beverley Ho said, 'I'm sorry to wake you, Steve.'

Letterman got up on an elbow and looked at his digital alarm. He said, 'This better be good, Beverley.'

'No, Steve. It's not good.'

'Has Packer been found?'

'Yes.'

'Good. So that's good.'

'No, Steve, it's not.'

Letterman put on his bedside lamp. His wife stirred and said, 'Goddam . . .' and turned from the light.

'How bad is not good?'

Beverley told him.

Letterman said, 'Isolate him. Make it him. Just him. What have we got? Maverick, breakdown, misappropriation? Okay. Now he's dead; that helps us. This was a man acting on his own. No one gave him any instruction in this matter. Are you hearing me, Beverley?'

'As it happens, Steve, that's the truth.'

'Does anyone believe it?'

'I don't think so. That's not what I hear.'

'Keep the media off.'

Beverley laughed. 'Kidding me? Look for the word Neophos in tomorrow's headlines, Steve.'

'On his own,' Letterman said. 'He was acting on his own.'

'I know that,' Beverley said. 'I've said that. I've said it over and over. No one seems to be listening.'

Letterman hung up, then redialled. He had a few dues to call in.

Thirty

. . . Kate lifting her arms, his hand coming in a long sweep from her throat across her breasts and down over her belly, turning her, delving the small of her back, his own back dipping . . .

She stopped the tape and went to the window. It was the hour before dusk, and the high pasture behind the house was darkening, as if a long shadow was falling over the house, out towards the cliff path and the sea. She put on the Canadian coat and went out. There were traces of snow in ridges and furrows, but the western sky showed pale blues and fragile reds.

The field, the lane, the cliff path, the path worn into the cliff face . . . Kate went down as she had before, leaning against the vertical, her feet shuffling sideways. The tide was on the ebb, the long, low roar of sea and shingle mingling with the ragged cries of gulls.

A small place; a dark place.

She found the cave with the leaf-shaped entrance and went in. She could hear the shifting and shuffling in the arch of the roof. The plank bed was still in place. She found a yoghurt pot and a plastic egg carton that must have washed in and out each day with the tide.

Kate lay down on the plank bed and listened to the slow sound of the sea.

Joanna had suggested Penarven. At first Kate had thought she would go to the ends of the earth, wherever they might be. As far as you can go without being on the way back. Then she saw why Penarven was the right place to be, now that her life had changed;

now that she was clear of courts and charges and questions; now that she was free to go where she chose.

She dozed in the cave, and woke to darkness leavened by moonlight. The wind was brisk and cold. She hiked back to the cottage, glad to be alone, glad to have no one to talk to. She put a CD on and made herself a drink. It was the Elgar. She was running a series of tests on herself, and playing the Elgar was one.

. . . his own back dipping, hands moving up over the swell of her buttocks, parting her thighs, working on her, turning her again . . .

His face so often in her mind's eye; now his face filling the screen.
  'See you, Kate.'

. . . returning to her face, the damp hair over her brow, his mouth on her cheeks, her throat, her shoulders, Kate lifting her arms, lifting her face . . .

His smiling face. 'See you, Kate.'
  She watched the tape to the end, then watched again. Then she rewound and switched to 'record', and wiped the tape. Wiped his face. Wiped her face.
  'See you, Kate.'

The tape running on, blackly.
  Hissssssssss . . .